Storm Force from Navarone

Alistair MacLean, who died on 2 February 1987, was the bestselling author of thirty books, including the world-famous adventure novels *The Guns of Navarone* and *Force 10 from Navarone*, both of which have been made into thrilling and internationally renowned films.

Sam Llewellyn is the author of several hugely successful nautical thrillers, including *Hell Bay* and *The Iron Hotel*. An experienced sailor, he has sailed all over the world and now lives in Herefordshire.

SAM LLEWELLYN

STORM FORCE
FROM NAVARONE

The sequel to Alistair MacLean's
Force 10 from Navarone

HarperCollins*Publishers*

HarperCollins*Publishers*
77–85 Fulham Palace Road,
Hammersmith, London W6 8JB

This paperback edition 1996

1 3 5 7 9 8 6 4 2

First published in Great Britain by
HarperCollins*Publishers* 1996

Copyright © Characters and Ideas: Devoran Trustees Ltd 1996
Copyright © Text: Devoran Trustees Ltd and Sam Llewellyn

ISBN 0 00 649625 3

Set in Meridien

Printed and bound in Great Britain by
Caledonian International Book Manufacturing Ltd, Glasgow

To David Burnett

PROLOGUE

March 1944

The radar operator said, 'Contact. Three bloody contacts. Jesus.'

The Liberator dipped a wing, bucking heavily as it carved through one of the squalls of cloud streaming over the Atlantic towards Cabo Ortegal, at the top left-hand corner of Spain. 'Language,' said the pilot mildly. 'Bomb-aimer?'

Down in the nose the bomb-aimer said, 'Ready.' The pilot's leather-gloved hand went to the throttles. The note of the four Pratt and Whitney engines climbed to a tooth-rattling roar. The pilot eased the yoke forward. Girders creaking, the Liberator bounced down into the clouds.

Vapour streamed past the bomb-aimer's Perspex window, thick and grey as coal smoke. At five hundred feet it became patchy. There was sea down there: grey sea, laced with nets of foam.

The bomb-aimer's mouth was dry. Just looking at the heave of that sea made you feel sick. But there was something else: a wide, smooth road across those rough-backed swells, as if they had been ironed –

'See them yet?' said the pilot.

The bomb-aimer could hear his heart beat, even above the crackle of the intercom and the roar of the engines. 'See them,' he said.

At the end of the smooth road three long, low hulls were tearing chevrons of foam from the sea. The hulls were slim and grey, with streamlined conning towers. Slim, grey sitting ducks.

'They're bloody enormous,' said the radar operator, peering over the pilot's shoulder. 'What the hell are they?'

They were submarines, but submarines twice the size of any British or German craft the pilot had seen in four years of long flights over weary seas that had made him an expert on submarines. They were indeed bloody enormous.

1

The pilot frowned at the foam-crested waves of their wakes. Hard to tell, of course, but they looked as if they were making at least thirty-five knots. If they were theirs, thought the pilot, they could really do some damage. Hope they're ours –

Glowing red balls rose lazily from the conning towers and flicked past the cockpit canopy.

'Theirs,' said the pilot, slamming the plane into a tight 180° turn. The tracers had stripped him of his mildness. 'Commencing run.'

There was a lot of tracer now, pouring past the Liberator's cockpit, mixed with the black puffs of heavier flak. The Liberator bucked, its rivets groaning in the heat-wrenched sky. The bomb-aimer tried not to think about his unprotected belly, and closed his mind to the bad-egg fumes of the shell bursts and the yammer of the nose-gunner's Brownings above his head. It was an easy two miles to bombs away: twenty endless seconds, at a hundred and eighty knots.

'Funny,' said the pilot. 'Why aren't they diving?'

The bomb-aimer stared into his sight. 'Bomb doors open,' he said. He felt the new tremor of the airframe as the doors spoilt the streamlining. The sight filled with grey and wrinkled sea. The submarines swam in V-formation down the stepladder markings towards the release point, innocent as three trout in a stream, except for the lazy red bubbles of the tracer.

The bomb-aimer frowned, pressing his face into the eyepiece of the sight. There was something wrong with the submarine in the middle. The deck forward of the conning tower looked twisted and bent. Christ, thought the bomb-aimer, someone's rammed her. Nearly cut her in half. That's why she's not diving. She's damaged –

Something burst with a clang out on the port side. Icy air was suddenly howling at the bomb-aimer's neck. The little submarines in the bomb-sight drifted off to starboard. 'Right a bit,' said the bomb-aimer, calmly, over the hammer of his heart. 'Right a bit.' The three grey fish slid back onto the line. 'Steady.' His leather thumb found the release button. The tracer was horrible now, thick as a blizzard. The bomb-aimer concentrated on hoping that Pearl in the mess wouldn't overcook his bloody egg again, like cement it was yesterday –

'Steady,' he said. The grey triangle was half an inch from the release point. 'Going,' he said. 'Going –'

A giant hammer smashed into the fuselage somewhere behind him. He felt a terrible agony in his left leg. Hit, he thought. Bastard hit us. His hand clenched on the bomb-release button. He felt the upward bound of the aircraft as the depth charges dropped free.

Too early, he thought.

Then there was no more thinking, because his face was full of smoke and his head was full of the agony of a leg broken in four places, and someone was howling like a dog, and as the grey clouds reached down and closed their hands round the Liberator, he realised that the person making all that racket was him.

Ten minutes later the radar operator finished the dressing and threw the morphine syrette out of one of the rents torn in the fuselage by the shell. He thought the bomb-aimer looked bloody awful, but then compound fractures are not guaranteed to bring a smile to the lips. To cheer him up, the radar operator gave him the thumbs up and mouthed, 'Got one!' Through pink clouds of morphine the bomb-aimer saw his lips move, and tried to look interested.

'Hit one,' said the radar operator. 'Saw smoke. One was damaged already, looked like someone rammed it. And we hit at least one.' But of course he might as well have been talking to himself because you couldn't hear anything, what with the engines and a sodding great hole in the fuselage, and anyway, the bomb-aimer was asleep.

Bloody great U-boats, though, thought the radar operator. Never seen anything like them before. Not that big. Nor that fast.

The Liberator droned north and west across the Bay of Biscay, above the corrugated mat of cloud, towards the Coastal Command base at St-Just. There the crew, nervously preoccupied with the hardness of their eggs, were comprehensively debriefed.

ONE

Sunday 1000–1900

Andrea stared at Jensen. The huge Greek's face was horror-stricken. 'Say again?' he said.

'A job,' said Captain Jensen. He was standing in a shaft of Italian sun that gleamed on his sharp white teeth and the gold braid on the brim of his cap. 'Just a tiny little job, really. And I thought, since the three of you were here anyway . . .'

As always, Jensen was dreadfully crisp, his uniform sparkling white, his stance upright and alert, the expression on his bearded face innocent but slightly piratical. The three men in the chairs looked the reverse of crisp. Their faces were hollow with exhaustion. They sat as if they had been dropped into their seats from a height. The visible parts of their bodies were laced with sticking plaster and red with Mercurochrome. They looked one step away from being stone-dead.

But Jensen knew better.

It had cost him considerable effort to assemble this team. There was Mallory, who before the war had been a mountaineer, world-famous for his Himalayan exploits, and conqueror of most of the unclimbed peaks in the Southern Alps of his native New Zealand. Mallory had spent eighteen months behind enemy lines in Crete with the man sitting next to him: Andrea. The gigantic Andrea, strong as a team of bulls, quiet as a shadow, a full colonel in the Greek army, and one of the deadliest irregular soldiers ever to knife a sentry. And then there was Corporal Dusty Miller from Chicago, member of the Long Range Desert Force, sometime deserter, goldminer, and bootlegger. If it existed, Miller could wreck it. Miller had a genius for sabotage equalled only by his genius for insubordination.

But Jensen valued soldiers for their fighting ability, not their standard of turnout. In Jensen's view these men were very useful indeed.

The gleam of those carnivorous teeth hurt Andrea's eyes. It does not take much to hurt your eyes, when you have not slept for the best part of a fortnight.

'A tiny little job,' said Mallory. His face was gaunt and pouchy. Like Andrea, he was by military standards badly in need of a shave. 'Are you going to tell us about it?'

The grin widened. 'I thought maybe you would be feeling a bit unreceptive.'

Corporal Dusty Miller had been almost horizontal in a leather-buttoned chair, staring with more than academic interest at the frescoed nudes on the ceiling of the villa Jensen had commandeered as his HQ. Now he spoke. 'That never stopped you before,' he said.

Jensen's bushy right eyebrow rose a millimetre. This was not the way that captains in the Royal Navy were accustomed to being addressed by ordinary corporals.

But Dusty Miller was not an ordinary corporal, in the same way that Captain Mallory was not an ordinary captain, or for that matter, Andrea was not an ordinary Greek Resistance fighter. Because of their lack of ordinariness, Jensen knew that he would have to treat them with a certain respect: the same sort of respect you would give three deadly weapons with which you wished to do damage to the enemy.

For in that room full of soldiers who were not ordinary soldiers, Jensen was not an ordinary naval captain. As an eighteen-year-old lieutenant, he had run a successful Q-ship, sinking eight U-boats in the final year of the 14–18 war. Between the wars he had been, frankly, a spy. He had led Shiite risings in Iraq; penetrated a scheme to block the Suez Canal; and as a marine surveyor employed by the Imperial Japanese Navy, perpetrated a set of alarmingly but intentionally inaccurate charts of the Sulu Sea. Now, in the fifth year of the war, he was Chief of Operations of the Subversive Operations Executive. Some said that Allied victory at El Alamein had been partly due to SOE's clandestine substitution of a carborundum paste for grease in a fuel dump. And in the last month he had successfully planned the destruction of the

6

impregnable battery of Navarone, and the diversionary raid in Yugoslavia that had led to the fall of the Gustav Line and the breakout from the Anzio beachhead.

But Jensen had only done the planning. These three men – Mallory, the New Zealander, a taciturn mountaineer, tough as a commando knife; the American Dusty Miller, an Einstein among saboteurs; and Andrea, the two-hundred-and-fifty-pound man-mountain with the quietness of a cat and the strength of a bear – were the weapons he had used.

If there were deadlier weapons in the world Jensen's enquiries had failed to reveal them. And Jensen's enquiries were notoriously very searching indeed.

'So,' he said. 'Any of you gentlemen speak French?'

Mallory frowned. 'German,' he said. 'Greek.'

Andrea yawned and covered his mouth with a gigantic hand, still covered in bandages from the abrasions he had sustained holding onto the iron rungs of a ladder under the flume of water from the bursting Zenitsa dam.

'I do,' said Dusty Miller.

'Fluent?'

'I had a job in Montreal once,' said Miller, his eyes blue and innocent. 'Doorman in a cathouse.'

'Thank you, Corporal,' said Jensen.

'*Il n'y a pas de quoi*,' said Miller, with old-world courtesy.

'We've found you some interpreters,' said Jensen.

Mallory sighed inwardly. He knew Jensen. When Jensen wanted you aboard, you were aboard, and the only thing to do was to check the location of the life jackets provided, and settle in for the ride. He said, 'If you don't mind me asking, sir, why do we need to speak French?'

Jensen grinned a grin that would have looked impressive on a hungry shark. He walked across the bronze carpet to the huge ormolu desk, bare except for two telephones, one red, one black. He said, 'There is someone I want you to meet.' He picked up the black telephone. 'Sergeant,' he said. 'Please send in the gentlemen in the waiting room.'

Mallory gazed at the veining on a marble pillar. Aircraft were droning overhead, flying air support for the troops advancing north from the wreckage of the Gustav Line. He lit another cigarette, the taste of the last one still bitter in his mouth. He wanted to sleep for a week. Make that a month –

The door opened, and two men came in. One of them was a tall major with a Guards moustache. The other was shorter, stocky and bull-necked, with three pips on his epaulettes.

'Major Dyas. Intelligence,' said Jensen. 'And Captain Killigrew. SAS.'

Major Dyas nodded. Captain Killigrew fixed each man in turn with a searching glare. His face was brick-red from the sun, and something that Mallory decided was anger. Mallory returned his salute. Andrea nodded and, being a foreigner, got away with it. Dusty Miller remained horizontal in his chair, acknowledging Killigrew by opening one eye and raising a bony hand.

Killigrew swelled like a toad. Jensen's ice-blue eyes flicked between the two men. He said quickly, 'Take a seat, Captain. Major, do your stuff.'

Killigrew lowered himself stiffly onto a hard chair, on which he sat bolt upright, not touching the backrest.

'Yah,' said Dyas. 'You may smoke.' Mallory and Miller were already smoking. Dyas ran his hand over his high, intellectual forehead. He could have been a doctor, or a professor of philosophy.

Jensen said, 'Major Dyas has kindly agreed to brief you on the background to this . . . little job.' Mallory leaned back in his chair. He was still tired, but soon there would be something to override the tiredness. The same something he remembered from huts in the Southern Alps, after a gruelling approach march, two hours' sleep, and waking in the dark chill before dawn. Soon there would be no way to go but up and over. Climbing and fighting: plan your campaign, grit your teeth, do the job or die in the attempt. There were similarities.

'Now then,' said Dyas. 'To start with. What you are about to hear is known to only seven men in the world, now ten, including you. Other people have the individual bits and pieces, but what counts is the . . . totality.' He paused to stuff tobacco into a blackened pipe, and applied an oil well-sized Zippo. 'June is going to be an important month of this war,' he said from inside a rolling cloud of smoke. 'Probably the most important yet.' Miller's eyes had opened. Andrea was sitting forward in his chair, massive forearms on his stained khaki knees. 'We are going to take a gamble,' said Dyas. 'A big gamble. And we want you to adjust the odds for us.'

Miller said, 'Trust Captain Jensen to run a crooked game.'

'Sorry?' said Dyas.

Mallory said, 'The Corporal was expressing his enthusiasm.'

'Ah.' Another cloud of smoke.

Mallory could feel that jump of excitement in his stomach. 'This gamble,' he said. 'A new front?'

Dyas said, 'Put it like this. What we are going to need is complete control of the seas. We're good in the air, we're fine on the surface. But there's a hitch.' Killigrew's face was darkening. Looks as if he'll burst a blood vessel, thought Mallory. Wonder what he's got to do with this.

'Submarines,' said Dyas. 'U-boats. There has been an idea current that between airborne radar and asdic and huff-duff radio direction finding, we had 'em licked.' Another cloud of smoke. 'An idea we all had. Until a couple of months ago.

'In March we had a bit of trouble with some Atlantic convoys, and their escorts too. Basically, ships started to sink in a way we hadn't seen ships sink for two years now.' The professorial face was grim and hard. 'And it was odd. You'd get a series of explosions in say a two-hundred-mile circle, and you'd think, same old thing, U-boats moving together, wolf pack. But it wasn't a wolf pack, because there was no radio traffic, and the sinkings were too far apart. So then they thought it was possibly mines. But it didn't seem to be mines either, because one day in late March HMS *Frantic*, an escort destroyer, picked up an echo seven hundred miles off Cape Finisterre. There had been two sinkings in the convoy. The destroyer went in pursuit, but lost it.' He returned to his pipe.

'Nothing unusual about that,' said Mallory.

Dyas nodded, mildly. 'Except that the destroyer was steaming full speed ahead at the time, and the submarine just sailed away from her.'

'Sorry?' said Miller.

'The destroyer was steaming at thirty-five knots,' said Dyas. 'The U-boat was doing easily five knots better than that.'

Miller said, 'Why is this guy telling us all this stuff?'

Mallory said, 'I think Corporal Miller would like to know the significance of this fact.'

Jensen said, 'Excuse me, Major Dyas.' His face wore an expression of strained patience. 'For your information, U-boats have to spend most of their time on the surface, running their diesels to make passage and charge their batteries. Submerged, their best speed has so far been under ten knots, and they can't keep it up for long because of the limitations of their batteries.' His face was cold and grim, its deep creases as if carved from stone. 'So what we're faced with is this: the English Channel full of the biggest fleet of ships ever assembled, and these U-boats – big U-boats – carrying a hundred torpedoes each, God knows they're big enough – travelling at forty knots, under water. We know Jerry's got at least three of them. That could mean three hundred ships sunk, and Lord knows how many men lost.'

Miller said, 'So you get one quick echo. Not much of a basis for total panic stations. How fast do whales swim?'

Jensen snapped, 'Try keeping your ears open and your mouth shut.'

It was only then that Mallory saw the strain the man was under. The Jensen he knew was relaxed, with that naval quarterdeck sang-froid. Piratical, yes; aggressive, yes. Those were his stock in trade. But always calm. As long as Mallory had known Jensen, he had never known him lose his temper – not even with Dusty Miller, who did not hold with officers. But this was a Jensen balanced on a razor-honed knife's edge.

Mallory caught Miller's eye, and frowned. Then he said, 'Corporal Miller's got a point, sir.'

'Whales,' said Dyas. 'Actually, we thought of that. But one has been ... adding up two and two.' His mild voice was balm to the frazzled nerves under the frescoed ceiling. 'Another escort reported ramming a large submarine. Then a Liberator got shot up bombing two U-boats escorting a third that bore signs of having been rammed. They were huge, these boats, steaming at thirty-odd knots on the surface. The Liberator reported them as damaged. But when we sent more aircraft out to search for them, they had vanished.

'They were reckoned to be in no state to dive, so they were presumed sunk. Then there was a message picked up – doesn't matter what sort of message, doesn't matter where, but take it from me, it was a reliable message – to say that the Werwolf pack was refitting after damage caused by enemy action. Said refit to be complete by noon Wednesday of the second week in May.'

It was now Sunday of the second week in May.

The painted vaults of the ceiling filled with silence. Mallory said, 'So these submarines. What are they?'

'Hard to say,' said Dyas, with an academic scrupulousness that would have irritated Mallory, if he had been the sort of man who got irritated about things. 'The Kriegsmarine have maintained pretty good security, but we've been able to patch a couple of ideas together. We know they've got a new battery system for underwater running, which stores a lot of power. A lot of power. But there've been rumours about something else. We think it's more likely to be something new. Development of an idea by a chap called Walter. They've been working on it since the thirties. An internal combustion engine that runs under water. Burns fuel oil.'

Miller's eyes had opened now, and he was sitting in a position that for him was almost upright. He said, 'What in?'

'In?' Dyas frowned.

'You can't burn fuel oil under water. You need oxygen.'

'Ah. Yes. Quite. Good question.' Miller did not look flattered. Engines were his business. He knew how to make them run. He knew even more about destroying them. 'Nothing definite. But they think it's probably something like hydrogen peroxide. On the surface, you'd aspirate your engine with air, of course. As you submerged, you'd have an automatic changeover, a float switch perhaps, that would close the air intake and start up a disintegrator that would get you oxygen out of something like hydrogen peroxide. So you'd get a carbon dioxide exhaust, which would dissolve in sea water. Or so the theory goes.'

Jensen stood up. 'Theory or no theory,' he said, 'they're

11

refitting. They must be destroyed before they can go to sea again. And you're going to do the destroying.'

Mallory said, 'Where are they?'

Dyas unrolled a map that hung on the wall behind him. It showed France and Northern Spain, the brown corrugations of the Pyrenees marching from the Mediterranean to the Atlantic, and snaking down the spine of the mountains the scarlet track of the border. He said, 'They were bombed off Cabo Ortegal. They couldn't dive, so they wouldn't have gone north. We believe that they are here.' He picked up a billiard cue and tapped the long, straight stretch of coast that ran from Bordeaux south through Biarritz and St-Jean-de-Luz to the Spanish border.

Mallory looked at the pointer. There were three ports: Hendaye, St-Jean-de-Luz, and Bayonne. Otherwise, the coast was a straight line that looked as if it probably meant a beach. He said, 'Where?'

Dyas avoided his eye and fumbled at his moustache. Since he had been in the room, he had found himself increasingly unnerved by the stillness of these men, the wary relaxation of their deep-eyed faces. The big one with the black moustache was silent and dangerous, with a horrible sort of power about him. Of the other two, one seemed slovenly and the other insubordinate. They looked like, well, *gangsters*. Dashed unmilitary, thought Dyas. But Jensen knew what he was doing. Famous for it. Still, Mallory's question was not a question he much liked.

He said, 'Well, Spain's a neutral country.' He forced himself not to laugh nervously. 'And we've got good intelligence from Bordeaux, so we know they're not there.' He coughed, more nervously than he had intended. 'In fact, we don't know where they are.'

The three pairs of eyes watched him in silence. Finally, Mallory spoke. 'So we've got until Wednesday noon to find some submarines and destroy them. The only difficulty is that we don't know where they are. And, come to that, we don't actually know if they exist.'

Jensen said, 'Oh yes we do. You'll be dropped to a reception committee –'

'Dropped?' said Miller, his lugubrious face a mask of horror.

'By parachute.'

'Oh my stars,' said Miller, in a high, limp-wristed voice.

'Though if you keep interrupting we might forget the parachute and drop you anyway.' There was a hardness in Jensen's corsair face that made even Miller realise that he had said enough. 'The reception committee, I was saying. They will take you to a man called Jules, who knows a fisherman who knows the whereabouts of these U-boats. This fisherman will sell you the information.'

'Sell?'

'You will be supplied with the money.'

'So where is this fisherman?'

'We are not as yet aware of his whereabouts.'

'Ah,' said Mallory, rolling his eyes at the frescoes. He lit yet another cigarette. 'Well, I suppose we'll have the advantage of surprise.'

Miller pasted an enthusiastic smile to his doleful features. 'Gosh and golly gee,' he said. 'If they're as surprised as we are, they'll be amazed.'

Dyas was looking across at Jensen. Mallory thought he looked like a man in some sort of private agony. Jensen nodded, and smiled his ferocious smile. He seemed to have recovered his composure. 'One would rather hope so,' he said, 'because these submarines have got to be destroyed. No ifs, no buts. I don't care what you have to do. You'll have carte blanche.' He paused. 'As far as is consistent with operating absolutely on your own.' He coughed. If a British Naval officer schooled in Nelsonian duplicities could ever be said to look shifty, Jensen looked shifty now. 'As to the element of surprise . . . Well. Sorry to disappoint,' he said, 'but actually, not quite. Thing is, an SAS team went in last week, and nobody's heard from them since. So we think they've probably been captured.'

Mallory allowed the lids to droop over his gritty eyeballs. He knew what that meant, but he wanted to hear Jensen say it.

'In fact it seems quite possible,' said Jensen, 'that the Germans will, in a manner of speaking, be waiting for you.'

Killigrew seemed to see this as his cue. He was a small man, built like a bull, with a bull's rolling eye. He rose, marched to the centre

13

of the room, planted his feet a good yard apart on the mosaic floor, and sank his head between his mighty shoulders. 'Now listen here, you men,' he barked, in the voice of one used to being the immediate focus of attention.

Jensen looked across at Mallory's lean crusader face. His eyes were closed. Andrea was gently stroking his moustache, gazing out of the window, where the late morning sun shone yellow-green in the leaves of a vine. Dusty Miller had removed his cigarette from his mouth, and was talking to it. 'Special Air Squads,' he said. 'They land with goddamn howitzers and goddamn Jeeps, with a noise like a train wreck. They do not think it necessary to employ guides or interpreters, let alone speak foreign languages. They have skulls made of concrete and no goddamn brains at all – can I help you?'

Killigrew was standing over him with a face of purple fire. 'Say that again,' he said.

Miller yawned. 'No goddamn brains,' he said. 'Bulls in a china shop.'

Mallory's eyes were open now. The veins in Killigrew's neck were standing out like ivy on a tree trunk, and his eyes were suffused with blood. The jaw was out like the ram of an icebreaker. And to Mallory's amazement, he saw that the right fist was pulled back, ready to spread Miller's teeth all over the back of his head.

'Dusty,' he said.

Miller looked at him.

'Miller apologises, sir,' said Mallory.

'Temper,' said Miller.

Killigrew's fist remained clenched.

'You're on a charge, Miller,' said Mallory, mildly.

'Yessir,' said Miller.

Jensen's voice cracked like a whip. 'Captain!'

Killigrew's heels crashed together. His florid face was suddenly grey. He had come within a whisker of assaulting another rank. The consequence would have been, well, a court-martial.

Mallory ground out his cigarette in a marble ashtray, his eyes flicking round the room, sizing up the situation. God knew what kind of strain the SAS captain must have been under to come that close to walloping a corporal. Jensen, he saw, was hiding a keen curiosity behind a mask of military indignation. Without apparently taking a step, Andrea had left his chair and moved halfway across the room towards Killigrew. He stood loose and relaxed, his bear-like bulk sagging, hands slack at his sides. Mallory knew that Killigrew was half a second away from violent death. He caught Miller's eye, and shook his head, a millimetre left, a millimetre right.

Miller yawned. He said, 'Why, thank you, Captain Killigrew.' Killigrew stared straight ahead, eyes bulging. 'Seeing that there fly crawling towards my ear,' said Miller, pointing at a bluebottle spiralling towards the chandelier, 'the Captain was about to have the neighbourliness to swat the little sucker.' Jensen's eyebrow had cocked. 'I take full responsibility.'

Jensen did not hesitate. 'No need for that,' he said. 'Or charges. Carry on, Captain.'

Killigrew swallowed. ''ssir.' His face was regaining its colour. 'Right,' he said, with the air of one wrenching his mind back from an abyss. 'Our men. Five of them. Dropped Tuesday last, with one Jeep, radio, just south of Lourdes. They reported that they'd landed, were leaving in the direction of Hendaye, travelling by night. They were supposed to radio in eight-hourly. But nothing. Absolutely damn all.'

Once again, Miller caught Mallory's eye. Jeep, he was thinking. A Jeep, for pity's sake. Have these people never heard of road blocks?

'Until last night,' said Killigrew. 'Some Resistance johnny came on the air. Said there'd been shooting in some village or other in the mountains twenty miles west of St-Jean-de-Luz. Casualties. So we think it was them. But there was a bit of difficulty with the radio message. Code words not used. Could mean the operator was in a hurry, of course. Or it could mean that the network's been penetrated.'

Mallory found himself lighting another cigarette. How long since he had drawn a breath not loaded with tobacco smoke? He was avoiding Miller's eye. They were brave, these SAS people. But Miller had been right. They went at things like a bull at a gate. That was not Mallory's way.

15

Mallory believed in making war quietly. There was an old partisan slogan he lived by: if you have a knife you can get a pistol; if you have a pistol, you can get a rifle; if you have a rifle, you can get a machine gun –

'Thank you, gentlemen,' said Jensen. 'I'm grateful for your cooperation.' Dyas and Killigrew left, Killigrew's blood-bloated face looking straight ahead, so as not to catch Miller's sardonic eye.

'So,' said Jensen, grinning his appallingly carnivorous grin. 'Think you can do it?' He did not wait for an answer. 'Look,' he said. 'You may think this is a damn silly scheme. I can't help that. It could be that a million men depend on those submarines not getting to sea. I'm afraid the SAS have made a balls-up. I just want you to find these damn things. If you can't blow them up, radio a position. The RAF'll look after the rest.'

Mallory said, 'Excuse my asking, sir. But what about the Resistance on the ground?'

Jensen frowned. 'Good question. Two things. One, you heard that idiot Killigrew. They may have been penetrated. And two, it may be that these U-boats are tucked up somewhere the RAF won't be able to get at them.' He grinned. 'I told Mr Churchill this morning that as far as I was concerned, you lot were equivalent to a bomber wing. He agreed.' He stood up. 'I'm very grateful to you. You've done two jolly good operations for me. Let's make this a third. Detailed briefing at the airfield later. There's an Albemarle coming in this afternoon for you. Takeoff at 1900.' He looked down at the faces: Mallory, weary but hatchet-sharp; Andrea, solid behind his vast black moustache; and Dusty Miller, scratching his crewcut in a manner prejudicial to discipline. It did not occur to Jensen to worry that in the past fourteen days they had taken a fearsome battering on scarcely any sleep. They were the tool for the job, and that was that.

'Any questions?' he said.

'Yes,' said Mallory, wearily. 'I don't suppose there's a drop of brandy about the house, is there?'

An hour later the sentries on the marble-pillared steps of the villa crashed to attention as the three men trotted down into the square, where a khaki staff car was waiting. The sentries did not like the look of them. They were elderly, by soldier standards – in their forties, and looking older. Their uniforms were dirty, their boots horrible. It was tempting to ask for identification and paybooks. But there was something about them that made the sentries decide that it would on the whole be better to keep quiet. They moved at a weary, purposeful lope that made the sentries think of creatures that ate infrequently, and when they did eat, ate animals they had tracked down patiently over great distances, and killed without fuss or remorse.

Mallory's mind was not, however, on eating. 'Not bad, that brandy,' he said.

'Five-star,' said Miller. 'Nothing but the best for the white-haired boys.'

After Jensen's villa the Termoli airfield lacked style. Typhoons howled overhead, swarming on and off the half-built runway in clouds of dust. Inevitably, there was another briefing room. But this one was in a hut with cardboard walls and a blast-taped window overlooking the propeller-whipped dust-storm and the fighters taxiing in the aircraft park. Among the fighters was a bomber, with the long, lumpy nose of a warthog, refuelling from a khaki bowser. Mallory knew it was an Albemarle. Jensen was making sure that the momentum of events was being maintained.

Evans, one of Jensen's young, smooth-mannered lieutenants, had brought them from the staff car. He said, 'I expect you'll have a shopping list.' He was a pink youth, with an eagerness that made Mallory feel a thousand years old. But Mallory made himself forget the tiredness, and the brandy, and the forty years he had been on the planet. He sat at a table with Andrea and Miller and filled out stores indents in triplicate. Then they rode a three-tonner down to the armoury, where Jensen's handiwork was also to be seen, in the shape of a rack of weapons, and a backpack B2 radio. There were also two brass-bound boxes whose contents Miller studied with interest. One of them was packed with explosives: gelignite, and blocks of something that looked like butter, but was in fact Cyclonite in a plasticising medium – plastic explosive. The other box contained primers and time pencils,

17

colour-coded like children's crayons. Miller sorted through them with practised fingers, making some substitutions. There were also certain other substances, independently quite innocent but, used as he knew how to use them, lethal to enemy vehicles and personnel. Finally, there was a flat tin box containing a thousand pounds in used Bradbury fivers.

Andrea stood at a rack of Schmeissers, his hands moving like the hands of a man reading Braille, his black eyes looking far away. He rejected two of the machine pistols, picked out three more, and a Bren light machine gun. He stripped the Bren down, smacked it together again, nodded, and filled a haversack with grenades.

Mallory checked over two coils of wire-cored rope and a bag of climbing gear. 'Okay,' he said. 'Load it on.'

In the briefing hut, three men were waiting. They sat separately at the schoolroom tables, each of them apparently immersed in his own thoughts. 'Everything all right?' said Lieutenant Evans. 'Oh. Introductions. The team.' The men at the tables looked up, eyeing Mallory, Andrea and Miller with the wariness of men who knew that in a few hours these strangers would have the power of life and death over them.

'No real names, no pack-drill,' said Evans. He indicated the man on the right: small, the flesh bitten away under his cheekbones, his mouth hidden by a black moustache. He had the dour, self-contained look of a man who had lived all his life among mountains. 'This is Jaime,' Evans said. 'Jaime has worked in the Pyrenees. He knows his way around.'

'Worked?' said Mallory.

Jaime's face was sallow and unreadable, his eyes unwilling to trust. He said, 'I have carried goods. Smuggler, you would say. I have escaped Fascists. Spanish Fascists, German Fascists. All die when you shoot them.'

Mallory schooled his face to blankness. Fanatics could be trustworthy comrades; but that was the exception, not the rule.

'And that,' said Evans quietly, 'is Hugues. Hugues is our personnel man. Knows the Resistance on the ground. Practically encyclopaedic. Looks like a German. Don't be fooled. He was at Oxford before the war. Went back to Normandy to take over the family

18

chateau. The SS shot his wife and two children when he went underground.'

Hugues was tall and broad-shouldered, with light brown hair, an affable pink-and-white Northern face, and china-blue eyes. When he shook Mallory's hand his palm was moist with nervous sweat. He said, 'Do you speak French?'

'No.' Mallory caught Miller's eye, and held it.

'None of you?'

'That's right.' Many virtues had combined to keep Mallory, Miller and Andrea alive and fighting these past weeks. But the cardinal virtue was this: reserve your fire, and never trust anyone.

Hugues said, 'I'm glad to meet you. But . . . no French? Jesus.'

Mallory liked his professionalism. 'You can do the talking,' he said.

'Spent any time behind enemy lines?' said Hugues.

'A little.' There was a wild look in Hugues' eye, thought Mallory. He was not sure he liked it.

Evans cleared his throat. 'Word in your ear, Hugues,' he said, and took him aside. Hugues frowned as the Naval officer murmured into his ear. Then he blushed red, and said to Mallory, 'Oh dear. 'Fraid I made a fool of myself, sir.'

'Perfectly reasonable,' said Mallory. Hugues was fine. Pink and eager and bright. But there was still that wild look . . . Not surprising, in the circumstances. A Resistance liaison would be as vital as a guide and a radio operator. Hugues would do.

The last man was nearly as big as Andrea, wearing a ragged, oddly urban straw hat. Evans introduced him as Thierry, an experienced Resistance radio operator. Then he drew the blinds, and pulled a case of what looked like clothing towards him. 'Doesn't matter about the French,' he said, 'you can stick to German.' From the box, he pulled breeches and camouflage smocks of a pattern Mallory had last seen in Crete. 'I hope we've got the size right. And you'd better stay indoors for the next wee while.'

It was true, reflected Mallory wryly, that there would be few better ways of attracting attention on a Allied air base than wandering around wearing the uniform of the Waffen-SS.

'Try 'em on,' said Evans.

The Frenchmen watched without curiosity or humour as Mallory, Miller and Andrea pulled the German smocks and trousers over their khaki battledress. Disguising yourself in enemy uniform left you liable to summary execution. But then so did working for the Resistance, or for that matter operating behind German lines in British uniform. In occupied France, Death would be breathing down your neck without looking at the label inside your collar.

'Okay,' said Evans, contemplating the Feldwebel with Mallory's face, and the two privates. 'Er, Colonel, would you consider shaving off the moustache?'

'No,' said Andrea, without changing expression.

'It's just that –'

'SS men do not wear moustaches,' said Andrea. 'This I know. But I do not intend to mix with SS men. I intend to kill them.'

Jaime was looking at him with new interest. 'Colonel?' he said.

'Slip of the tongue,' said Mallory.

Evans looked for a moment faintly flustered. He strode busily to the dais, and unrolled the familiar relief map of the western part of the Pyrenees. There was a blue bite of Atlantic at the top. Along the spine of the mountains writhed the red serpent of the Spanish border.

'Landing you here,' said Evans, tapping a brisk pointer on what could have been a hanging valley above St-Jean-Pied-du-Port.

'Landing?' said Mallory.

'Well, dropping then.'

Miller said, 'I told Captain Jensen. I can't stand heights.'

'Heights won't be a problem,' said Evans. 'You'll be dropping from five hundred feet.' He smiled, the happy smile of a man who would not be dropping with them, and unrolled another larger-scale map with contours. 'There's a flat spot in this valley. Pretty remote. There's a road in, from Jonzère. Runs on up to the Spanish border. There'll be a border post up there, patrols. We don't want you in Spain. We've got Franco leaning our way at the moment, and we don't want anything to happen that would, er, make it necessary for him to have to show what a

20

beefy sort of chap he is. Plus you'd get yourselves interned and the camps are really not nice at all. So when you leave the drop site go downhill. Jaime'll remind you. Uphill is Spain. Downhill is France.'

Andrea was frowning at the map. The contours on either side of the valley were close together. Very close. In fact, the valley sides looked more like cliffs than slopes. He said, 'It's not a good place to drop.'

Evans said, 'There are no good places to drop just now in France.' There was a silence. 'Anyway,' he said briskly. 'You'll be met by a man called Jules. Hugues knows him.'

The fair-haired Norman nodded. 'Good man,' he said.

'Jules has been making a bit of a speciality of the Werwolf project. He'll brief you and pass you on. After that, you'll be on your own. But I hear you're used to that.' He looked at the grim faces. He thought, with a young man's arrogance: they're old, and they're tired. Does Jensen know what he's doing?

Then he remembered that Jensen always knew what he was doing.

Mallory looked at Evans' pink cheeks and crisp uniform. We all know you have been told to say this, he thought. And we all know that it is not true. We are not on our own at all. We are at the mercy of these three Frenchmen.

Evans said, 'There is a password. When anyone says to you, "*L'Amiral*", you will reply "*Beaufort*". And vice versa. We put it out on the BBC. The SAS used it, I'm afraid. No time to put out another one. Use with care.' He handed out bulky brown envelopes. 'Callsigns,' said Evans. 'Orders. Maps. Everything you need. Commit to memory and destroy. Any questions?'

There were no questions. Or rather, there were too many questions for it to be worth asking any of them.

'Storm Force,' said Miller, who had torn open his envelope. 'What's that?'

'That's you. This is Operation Storm,' said Evans. 'You were Force 10 in Yugoslavia. This follows on. Plus . . .' he hesitated.

'Yes?' said Mallory.

'Joke, really,' said Evans, grinning pinkly. 'But, well, Captain

21

Jensen said we might as well call you after the weather forecast.'

'Great,' said Miller. 'Just great. All this and parachutes too.'

TWO

Sunday 1900–Monday 0900

'Ladies and gentlemen, sorry, *gentlemen*,' said Wing-Commander Maurice Hartford. 'We are now one hour from drop. Air Pyrenees hopes you are enjoying the ride. Personally, I think you are all crazy.'

Naturally, nobody could hear him, because the intercom was turned off. But it relieved his feelings. Why, he thought, is it always me?

It had been a nice takeoff. Six men plus the crew, not much equipment: a trivial load for the Albemarle, droning up from Termoli, over the wrinkled peaks of the Apennines, and into the sunset. The red sunset.

Hartford switched on the intercom. 'Captain Mallory,' he said, 'why don't you pop up to the sharp end?'

Mallory stirred in his steel bucket seat. He had slept for a couple of hours this afternoon. So had Andrea and Dusty Miller. An orderly had woken them for a dinner of steak and red wine, upon which they had fallen like wolves. The Frenchmen had picked at the food; nobody had wanted to talk. Jaime had remained dour. Hugues, unless Mallory was much mistaken, had developed a bad case of the jitters. Nothing wrong with that, though. The bravest men were not those who did not know fear, but those who knew it and conquered it. On the aeroplane, the Frenchmen had stayed awake while Andrea made himself a bed with his head on the box of fuses, and Miller sank low in his bucket seat, propped his endless legs on the radio, and began a snore that rivalled the clattering thunder of the Albemarle's Merlins.

Mallory had slept lightly. What he wanted was ten days of unconsciousness, broken only by huge meals at four-hour intervals. But that would have to wait. Among the rockfalls and avalanches of the Southern Alps, and during the long, dangerous months in Crete, he had learned to sleep a couple of inches below the surface, a wild animal's sleep that could give way to complete wakefulness in a fraction of a second.

He clambered out of his seat and went to the cockpit. The pilot gestured to the co-pilot's seat. Mallory sat down and plugged in the intercom.

'Cup of tea?' said the pilot, whose ginger moustache rose four inches above his mask, partially obscuring the goggles he wore to keep it out of his eyes.

Mallory said, 'Please.'

'Co-pilot's having a kip.' The pilot waved a thermos over a mug. 'Sunset,' he said, gesturing ahead.

There was indeed a sunset. The western sky was full of an archipelago of fiery islands, on which the last beams of the sun burst in a surf of gold. Above, the sky was dappled with cirrus. Below, the Mediterranean was darkening through steel to ink.

'Red sky at night,' said the pilot. 'Pilot gets fright.'

The plane bounced. Mallory captured a mouthful of tea and hot enamel. 'Why?' he said.

Quiet sort of chap, thought Hartford. Not bashful. Just quiet. Quiet like a bomb nobody had armed yet. Brown eyes that looked completely at home, completely competent, wherever they found themselves. A lean, tired face, motionless, conserving energy. Dangerous-looking blighter, thought Hartford, cheerfully. Lucky old Jerry.

'Weather,' he said. 'Bloody awful weather up there. Front coming in. All right for shepherds. Shepherds walk. But we're flying straight into the brute. Going to get very bumpy.'

'Okay for a drop?'

Hartford said, 'We'll get you down.' Actually, it was not okay for a drop. But he had orders to get these people onto the ground, okay or not. 'Tell your chaps to strap in, could you?' He pulled a dustbin-sized briar from his flying-suit pocket, stuffed it with tobacco, and lit it. The cockpit filled with acrid smoke. He pulled back the sliding window, admitting the tooth-jarring bellow of the engines. 'Smell that sea,' he said, inhaling deeply. 'Wizard. Yup. We'll go in at five hundred feet. Nice wide valley. All you have to do is jump when the light goes on. All at once.'

'Five hundred feet?'

'Piece of cake.'

'They'll hear us coming.'

The pilot grinned, revealing canines socketed into the holes they had worn in the stem of the pipe. 'Not unless they're Spanish,' he said.

They hit the front over the coast, and flew on, minute after endless minute, until the minutes became hours. The Albemarle swooped and plunged, wings battered by the turbulent upcurrents. By the dark-grey light that crept through the little windows, Mallory looked at his team. Andrea and Miller he took for granted. But the Frenchmen he was not so sure about. He could see the flash of the whites of Jaime's eyes, the nervous movement of Thierry's mouth as he chewed his lips from inside. And Hugues, contemplating his hands, hands with heavily-bitten fingernails, locked on his knees. Mallory felt suddenly weary. He had been in too many little metal rooms, watched too many people, wondered too many times how they would shape up when the pressure was on and the lid had blown off . . .

The Albemarle banked steeply to port, then starboard. Mallory thought there was a new kind of turbulence out there: not just the moil of air masses in collision, but the upward smack of waves of air breaking on sheer faces of rock. He looked round.

The doorway into the cockpit was open. Beyond the windscreen the flannel-coloured clouds separated and wisped away. Suddenly Mallory was looking down a valley whose steep sides rose out of sight on either side. The upper slopes were white with snow. There was a grey village perched up there – *up* there, above the aeroplane. A couple of yellow lights showed in the gloom. No blackout: Spain, thought Mallory –

A pine tree loomed ahead. It approached at two hundred miles an hour. He saw the pilot's shoulders move as he hauled on the yoke. The tree was higher than the plane. Hey, thought Mallory, we're going to hit that –

But the Albemarle roared up and over. Something slapped the deck under his feet. Then the tree was gone, and the aircraft was banking steeply to port, into the next valley.

25

Mallory got up and closed the door. There were some things it was not necessary to see. Pine trees were, what? A hundred feet high? Maximum. Mallory decided if he was going to be flown into a mountain, he did not want to see the mountain coming.

It went on: the howl of the wind, the bucket of the airframe, the bellow of the engines. Mallory fell asleep.

Next thing he knew the racket was still there, and someone was shaking his shoulder. He felt terrible: head aching, thoughts slow as cold oil. The Albemarle's bomb-aimer was pushing a cup of tea in his face. Benzedrine, he thought. No. Not yet. This is only the beginning.

He had woken into a different world: the sick-at-the-stomach world of dangerous things about to happen. He badly wanted a cigarette. But there would be no time for cigarettes for a while.

A dim yellow light was burning in the fuselage. Bulky camouflage forms swore and collided, struggling into their parachutes and rounding up equipment.

'Five minutes,' said the bomb-aimer with repellent cheerfulness, when he had finished checking the harnesses. 'Onto the trench.'

'Trench?' said Miller.

The bomb-aimer indicated a long slot in the floor of the aircraft. 'Get on there,' he said. 'Stand at ease, one foot either side.' He pointed at a pair of light bulbs. 'When the light goes green, *shun*!'

'Gee, thanks,' said Miller, and shuffled into position. The first light bulb flicked on: red.

Hugues was behind him. Hugues' mind would not stay still. It kept flicking back over the past two years, with the weary insistence of a stuck gramophone record. After the SS had done what they had done to his family, he had not cared if he lived or died. Then Lisette had come along. And in Lisette, he had found a new reason for living . . .

On a night like this, a reason for living was the last thing you needed. Remember what they taught you in school, he thought. Keep it buttoned up. Don't let anything show –

Lisette. When shall I see you again?

Fear prised his mind apart and climbed in. Fear became terror. His bowels were water, and icy sweat was pouring down him.

First, there was the parachute descent, and of course it was possible that the parachute would not open. Then, even if the parachute did open, that big thin man Miller had two boxes balanced in front of him – *attached* to him, for the love of God! – full of explosives. So they were all dropping out of this plane, six humans and a land mine, in a lump. Jesus. He would be all over the landscape. He would never see Lisette –

Underfoot, he felt a new vibration, like gears winding. The trench opened. The night howled in, black and full of wind. He felt stuck, trapped, cramped by this damned harness, Schmeisser, pack, equipment.

A hand landed on his shoulder. He looked round so fast he almost overbalanced.

It belonged to the big man who did not speak, the bear with the moustache. The big face was impassive. A reflection of the little red bulb swam in each black eye. One of the eyes winked. *Jesus*, thought Hugues. He knows what I'm thinking. What will he think of me?

But surprisingly, he found that the fear had lessened.

Jaime was not comfortable either, but for different reasons. He had the short legs of the mountaineer. In his mind, he had been tracking their route: up the Valle de Tena, then north, across the Col de Pourtalet. He had walked it himself, first with bales of cigarettes, then with mules bearing arms for the Republican cause in the last days of the Spanish Civil War. He reckoned that now they would be coming down on Colbis. He did not like the feel of the weather out there. Nor did he like the fact that they were flying in cloud down a fifty-degree hillside at two hundred miles an hour. Feet on the ground were safe. Mules were safer. He wanted to get back on the ground, because his legs were aching, straddled over the trench, and he could feel the fear radiating from Thierry, slung about with his radios, straw hat stuffed in his pack, his big face improbably healthy in the red light –

Thierry's face turned suddenly green.

Shun.

Six pairs of heels crashed together. The static lines ran out and tautened. The hold was empty.

Through the bomb doors the bomb-aimer glimpsed points of

yellow light forming a tenuous L. He said into the intercom, 'All gone.' The pilot hauled back on the stick, and the clouds intervened. The Albemarle banked steeply and set its nose for Italy.

The ground hit Mallory like a huge, wet hammer. There were lights looping in his eyes as he rolled. A rock made his ears ring. He got rid of the parachute, invisible now in the dark, flattened himself against the ground, and worked the cocking lever of the Schmeisser, taut as an animal at bay. For a moment there was the moan of the wind and the feel of grit on his cheek. Then a voice close at hand said, 'L'Amiral.'

'Beaufort,' he said.

There was shouting. Then more lights – a lot of lights, a ridiculous number – in his eyes. He levelled the Schmeisser. The lights wavered away, and someone shouted, 'Non! Non! L'Amiral Beaufort. Welcome to France, mon officier.'

Unnecessary hands pulled him to his feet. He said, 'Where are the others?'

'Safe.' A flask found his hand. 'Buvez. Drink. Vive la France!' He drank. It was brandy. It drilled a hole in the cold and the rain. People were lighting cigarettes. There was a lot unmilitary of noise, several bottles. A dark figure materialised at his side, then another.

Miller's voice said, 'Any minute now someone is going to start playing the goddamn accordion.'

'All here?' There were grunts from the darkness. There were too many people, too much noise, not enough discipline. 'Hugues.'

'Sir.'

'Tell these people to put the bloody lights out. Where's Jules?'

There was a conversation in French. Hugues replied, his voice rising, expostulating. 'Merde,' he said finally.

'What is it?'

'These idiots. These goddamn Trotskyite sons of –'

'Quick.' Mallory's voice brought him up sharp as a choke-chain.

'Jules is held up in Colbis. There was an incident with your forces last week. The Germans are nervous.'

That would have been the SAS, thought Mallory, charging around like bulls in a china shop.

28

'But Colbis is only in the next valley. We will take you there, when we have transport. There is a problem with the transport. They don't know what. A lorry will come soon, they say. *Franche-ment*,' said Hugues, his voice rising, 'I do not believe these people. They are like the Spanish, always *mañana* –'

'Ask them how soon.' And calm them down, thought Mallory. Calm them down.

'They say to wait,' said Hugues, not at all calm. 'It is seven miles to the village. There may be patrols. There is a cave they know. It is dry there, and German patrols do not visit it. They say it will be a good place to wait. The lorry will come to collect you, in one hour, maybe two.'

Mallory looked at his watch. Raindrops blurred the glass. Just after midnight. Monday already. And they were being told to wait on a mountain top in the rain, and the Werwolf pack was leaving at noon on Wednesday.

He said, 'Where's this cave?'

'I know it,' said Jaime's voice.

Mallory sighed. Patience. 'Let's go,' he said.

Andrea appeared at his side. Mallory felt the comfort of his gigantic presence. 'This is not good,' said the Greek, under the babble of excited talk from the escort.

'We will make it better,' said Mallory. 'Hugues. Tell these people to be quiet.'

Hugues started shouting. The crowd fell silent. They started to walk in the lashing rain.

Jaime set a cracking pace up the valley, towards Spain, follow-ing a track that wound through a field of tea chest-sized boulders which had fallen from the valley's sides. The map had been right; those sides were not so much slopes as cliffs. From the rear, Mallory could hear Hugues' voice, speaking French, raised in viol-ent argument with someone. Mallory was beginning to worry about Hugues. Staying alive behind enemy lines meant staying calm. It was beginning to sound as if Hugues was not a calm person. He called softly, 'Shut up.'

Hugues shut up. The procession became quiet.

Mallory said to Miller, 'What was that about?'

'He was looking for someone. Someone who's not around.'

29

In ten minutes the valley floor had narrowed to a hundred yards, and the sides had become vertical walls of rock, undermined at their base, hidden in inky shadows. 'Here,' said Jaime's voice from the dark. A flashlight beam illuminated a dark entrance.

Andrea materialised at Mallory's side. 'Bad place,' he said. The cave had no exit except into the valley. And the valley was more a gorge than a valley. It felt bad. It felt like a trap. 'Hugues,' said Mallory, without looking round. 'Tell these people that this is no good.'

Mallory turned. 'Hugues,' he said. 'Tell these people –'

He stopped. There were no people. Hugues was a solitary dark figure against the paler grey of the rocks.

Hugues said, 'They have left.'

'Left?' said Mallory.

'Gone to look for the transport. Also, there was a . . . person I wished to see who did not arrive. That was why I had a discussion – yes – an acrimonious discussion.' His voice was rising. 'These people are frankly peasants –'

Andrea said, 'Enough.'

Hugues stopped talking as if someone had flipped a switch. Mallory said to Andrea and Miller, 'We're stuck with this. We need the transport. If we move, they'll lose us. We'll have to wait. Take cover.'

Andrea and Miller were already fading into the dark, taking up positions not in the cave, but among the rocks on the valley floor.

The night became quiet, except for the sigh of the wind and the swish of the rain, and the drowsy clonk of a goat bell from inside the cave.

This is all wrong, thought Mallory. We have been inadequately briefed, and we are dependent on a Resistance organisation that seems completely disorganised. It sounds as if the SAS have already compromised us. If the enemy comes up the valley there is no way out, except into an internment camp in Spain.

Mallory lay and strained his ears into the wet dark rain, wind, goat bells –

And another sound. A mechanical sound, but not a motor. The sound of metal on metal, gears turning. The sound of a bicycle.

30

There was a sudden crash. The old sounds returned, with behind them the noise of a back wheel spinning, ticking to a stop.

Mallory waited. Then he heard the brief, otherworldly *bleep* of a Scops owl.

Mallory had as yet heard no Scops owls in the Pyrenees. But there had been plenty in Crete, where he had served his time with Andrea.

Something moved at his shoulder: something huge, blacker than the night. Andrea said, 'I found this,' and dropped something on the gritty ground beside him, something that drew breath and started to croak.

Mallory allowed the muzzle of the Schmeisser to rest gently in the hollow under the something's ear. He said, 'Quiet.'

The something became quiet.

Mallory said, 'I am a British officer. What do you want?'

The something said, 'Hugues.'

'Good God,' said Mallory.

The something was a woman.

The woman got her voice back. She batted at Mallory with her hands. She was strong. She said, '*Laisse-moi,*' in a voice both vigorous and tough.

Out in the dark and the rain, Hugues' voice said, '*Bon Dieu!*' Mallory thought he could hear something new in it: shock, and awe. He heard the uncoordinated stumble of Hugues' boots in the dark. 'Lisette!' cried Hugues.

'Hugues!' cried the woman. '*C'est bien toi?*'

Then Hugues was embracing her. The fear was gone now. All the terrible things were gone. All Hugues' life, people had taken what he loved away from him, for reasons that seemed excellent to them but incomprehensible to him. They had taken away his parents and sent him to a stupid English school. They had taken away Mireille and the children because he was a saboteur. And then he had met Lisette, in the Resistance, and become her lover. When SOE had flown him out in the Lysander, he had thought that that had been the end of Lisette, too.

But here she was. In his arms. As large as life, if not larger.

'My darling,' he said.

31

She kissed him on the cheek, murmuring what sounded like pet names. Then Mallory heard her tone change. She sounded frantic about something.

'*Merde*,' said Hugues, in his new, firm voice. 'We must leave. Now.'

Mallory said, quietly, 'Who is this?'

'Lisette,' said Hugues. 'A friend. A *résistante*.'

'Is she the person you wanted to see who did not arrive?'

'Yes. She is an old friend. She knows the people on the ground in the region. It is an excellent thing that she has found us. Providential. She says there are sixty Germans coming up the valley.'

'Three lorries,' she said. Her accent was heavy, but comprehensible. 'The ones who reached Jonzère told me they caught two of your reception committee, found them with parachutes.'

'How long ago?'

'Half an hour,' said Lisette. 'At the most. They told me to warn you.'

Mallory's stomach felt shrivelled like a walnut. One and a half hours in France, and the operation was as good as over. He pushed the thought into the back of his mind. 'Jaime!' he said.

Jaime appeared out of the night. 'Lisette,' he said, without surprise.

'*Bonjour*, Jaime.'

Briskly, Mallory explained the position.

Jaime said, 'We must go to Spain. It is over. Finished.'

In his mind Mallory saw a soldier, pack on his back, seasickness in his belly and fear in his soul, squashed against the steel side of a ship by a thousand other soldiers. And suddenly, without warning, something stove in the side of that ship, smashed the soldier like an egg, and the cold green water poured in.

Once Mallory had been in a little steel room on a ship in the Mediterranean, checking grenades. There had been a bang. Someone had said, 'Torpedo.' Then the room had started to fill up with water, and the ship with screams, quickly cut off. Mallory had been one of four survivors. Four out of three hundred.

If the Werwolf pack got out intact, there could be a thousand such ships.

Mallory said, 'No other way?'

'None.' Jaime seemed to hesitate. 'Except the Chemin des Anges.'

'What's that?'

'Nothing. A goat track, no more. It runs from Jonzère, at the bottom of the valley, up the ridge, in the manner of the old roads. The pilgrims used to use it, the men with the cockle shells in their hats, bound for Santiago de Compostela, when there were bandits in the mountains. It is a dangerous road. It killed almost as many pilgrims as the bandits did.'

'Where is it?'

Against the dark sky Jaime's small shoulders appeared to shrug. He pointed upwards. 'On the spine of the hill. Here it runs three hundred metres above the valley. Above the cliff. Then it turns over the mountain and down to Colbis. There were pilgrims' inns in Colbis. But we can't go to Jonzère, to the start of the track. It'll be full of Germans –'

'We'll go up the cliff,' said Mallory, as if he were proposing a walk in the park.

There was a second's silence. Then Jaime said, 'To join the Chemin des Anges here? That is not possible.'

Mallory said, 'It is necessary.'

The chill of his voice silenced Jaime for a moment. Then he said, 'But you do not understand. Nobody can climb those cliffs.'

'That is what the Germans will think. Miller?'

Miller had been sitting on a boulder. He knew what Mallory was going to say, and he found the knowledge depressing. 'Yep?'

'Round up the people. Andrea and I are going up the cliff. We'll do a pitch, belay and drop you a fixed rope. Make sure everyone comes.'

Miller pushed his SS helmet back on his head and looked up. For a moment it was like being in a tunnel. Then, far overhead, clouds shifted, and there appeared between the two cliff-masses a thread-fine crack of sky. The wind was blowing up the valley. He could hear no lorries. The dark bulk that was Mallory slung a coil of wire-cored rope over his shoulder and walked towards the cliff. Wearily, Miller rounded up Hugues and Lisette, and Jaime, and Thierry the radio operator, and assembled the stores, and the radio, and the two wooden boxes of explosives, under the cliff. Mallory and Andrea seemed to vanish into the solid rock. The group at the cliff foot sat huddled against the icy rain. From above came the infrequent sound of a low word spoken, the clink of hammer on spike, the scuff of nailed boot on rock. The sounds receded quickly upwards. Human goddamn flies, thought Miller, gloomily. Personally, he had no suckers on his feet, and no plans to grow any. He stood up, cocked his Schmeisser and moved fifty yards down the valley in the rain. Someone had to stand sentry, and the only person on the valley floor Miller trusted was Miller.

Fall in with bad companions and what do you get?

I tell you what you get, he told himself, settling into a natural embrasure in the rock and preparing for the first of the sixty Germans to come round the corner.

You get problems.

There had been times in Mallory's life when he would have enjoyed a good crack at a limestone cliff in the dark. On a cold morning, perhaps, in a gorge in the Southern Alps, when you had got up at one in the morning, the stars floating silver and unwinking between the ice-white peaks of the range.

This was not one of those times.

This was a vertical slab of rock he could barely see. This was climbing by Braille, running fingers and feet over the smooth surface looking for pockmarks and indentations, tapping spikes into hair-cracks, standing with the tip of a boot-toe balanced on a foothold slim as a goose-quill.

But Mallory knew that there is a greater spur to climbing a cliff in the dark than a wish to dwell in the white Olympus of the high peaks. It is to get you and your comrades away from three lorry loads of Germans.

So Mallory climbed that sopping wall until his fingernails were gone, and the sweat stung his eyes, and the breath rasped in his tobacco-seared throat. And after fifty feet, he found a chimney.

It was a useful chimney, the edge of a huge flake of rock that would in a few hundred years separate from the face of the cliff and slide into the gorge. Mallory made a belay, called down to

Andrea, and went up the chimney as if it had been a flight of stairs.

At first the chimney was vertical. After thirty feet it started to trend leftward. Then suddenly there was a chockstone, a great boulder that had rolled down the cliff and jammed in the chimney. It formed a level floor embraced on two sides by buttresses of rock, invisible from the bottom of the valley. It was more than Mallory had dared hope for. Fifty people could have hidden up there while the Germans rumbled up the valley and flattened their noses against the Spanish border. Over which they would assume the Storm Force had fled –

Mallory felt a sensation he hardly recognised.

Hope.

Don't count your chickens.

Jaime was the first to arrive. He was carrying the bulky, square-edged radio pack. Jaime was a useful man on a mountain. There was a pause, and Andrea came up, carrying the second rope. 'All at the base of the chimney,' he said. 'Stores too.'

'Good,' said Mallory, belaying the rope and letting the end go.

Now that there were two ropes, things started to move fast. Thierry came up one, breathing in a high, frightened whimper, his straw hat crammed over his eyebrows. The second rope seemed to be taking a long time. 'It's the woman,' said Andrea. 'She doesn't have the strength in her arms.' Mallory saw his huge back dark against the sky as he bent to the rope. She was a big woman; there were not many fat people in wartime France, but she was one of them. She must have weighed ten stone. But Andrea hauled her up as if she had been a bag of sugar, set her on her feet, and dusted down her bulk.

'*Merci*,' she said.

Andrea's white teeth flashed under his moustache. He had the smile of a musketeer, this Greek giant. Even now, with the rain lashing down and Germans in the valley, Lisette felt enveloped in a protective cloak of courtesy and understanding. Andrea bowed, as if she had been a lady of Versailles, not a shapeless bundle of overcoats crouched on a cliff ledge. Then he let the rope go again.

Hugues came up, too breathless to complain, and went to

Lisette's side. Mallory had a nagging moment of worry. Hugues' priorities had to be with the operation, not his girlfriend. Mallory did not know enough about this woman. And he did not know enough about Hugues. For the moment, if her information was good, she had saved their bacon. But if Mallory's instincts were right, she was going to be a distraction. And distractions had no place on an operation like this. On this operation there was a single priority: find and destroy the Werwolf pack.

Hugues would need watching.

Mallory turned away, and hauled up the boxes of explosives and a couple of packs. The rain was turning even colder, developing a grainy feel. Mallory thought, soon it will be snowing. His hands were cracked and sore, and the plaster had peeled off the reopening wounds. God knew how Andrea must be feeling. But the stores were up, stacked on the edge of the boulder, and Miller was on his way up, but with no rope yet. Must get a rope to him; Miller was no climber.

The wind moaned and died. Andrea said, 'Listen.'

There was a new sound in the raw, snow-laden air. Lorry engines.

All the way up the bottom forty feet of the cliff, Miller had been feeling the void snapping at his heels. The wind was freezing, but inside his uniform a Niagara of hot sweat was running. His knees felt weak, his hands shaky. Miller had been raised on the flatlands of the American Midwest. One hold at a time, he told himself. Don't look down. Don't think of the sheer face down there –

Miller patted the cliff above his head, groping for chinks and crevices. Mallory must have found some. But as far as Miller was concerned he might as well have been trying to climb a plate glass window. Both ropes were in use . . .

Hurry, please, thought Miller politely. For forty feet down, things were happening. On the wind from the valley came the sharp whiff of exhaust. He looked up.

The cold, slushy rain battered his face. What he could see of the cliff was black and shiny, the chimney a dark streak rising to the chockstone. He had seen Mallory in a chimney, his shoulders one side, his heels the other, gliding his way skyward with that weightless fluency of his. Miller's limbs were too lanky for that, and his body wanted to plaster itself against the rock, not sit out over the emptiness as Mallory did, applying weight where it was needed, on fingers and toes –

Without a rope there was no way of getting to the chimney.

He pressed his face into the rock. The earthy smell of wet stone filled his nostrils. There was a lightening of the walls. Headlights down the valley.

He moved his hands again. The rock was rough, but there was nothing you could hold on to. Not unless you were a human fly like Mallory. Can't go up, thought Miller. Can't go down. So you just stand here, and hold on, and try not to follow that voice in your head that is telling you to shout and scream and keel gently out and back and plummet into space.

There were lights under his feet, and the gorge was churning with engines. A voice above him said, 'Rope coming!'

The lorries were directly below him now. By the grind of their engines they were moving at a slow, walking pace. Searching. *Nobody looks up.* It is fine. Nobody ever looks up. Particularly not up sheer cliffs.

Not even Germans. No matter how thorough they may be.

You wish.

The rope nudged his face, cautiously. Miller said a quiet, polite thank you. Then he wound his hands into it and began to climb.

'He's coming up now,' said Andrea, in his soft, imperturbable voice.

They were standing at the back of the ledge formed by the chockstone. Its edge was a horizon now, backlit by the glow of the lorries' headlamps. Against the edge was something hard-edged and square. The radio.

'Move that,' said Mallory to Thierry.

Thierry started forward, shuffling, his great bulk moving against the lights. He was tired, thought Mallory. Tired and frightened, in a wet straw hat.

If he had been less tired himself, he might have prevented what happened next.

Thierry scooped up the radio and slung it over his shoulder. As he turned, his foot hit something that could have been a tuft of grass but was actually a rock. The rock went over the edge.

It whizzed past Dusty Miller's head. At the base of the chimney it bounced, removing a fair-sized boulder. By the time it hit the valley floor it was a junior landslide. It landed with a roar fifteen feet to the right of the second truck in the convoy. Small stones pattered against the passenger door of the cab.

The truck stopped. A searchlight on the roof sent a white disc of light sliding across the black face of the cliff.

Miller was fifteen feet from the top, sweating, his breath coming in gasps. Clamp a hand on the rope. Pull up, shoving with feet. Clamp the other hand. There was shouting down below. Clamp the other hand. The hands like grey spiders against the cliff. They could have belonged to anyone, those hands, except for the pain, and the heavy thump of his heart.

And suddenly the other hand was not grey, but blazing, brilliant flesh-colour, and every fibre of the rope stood out in microscopic detail. And Miller was a moth, kicking on the pin of the searchlight.

A rifle cracked, then another. Chips of rock stung his face. His back crawled with the expectation of bullets. Ten feet to go. It might as well have been ten miles.

But there was a burst of machine-gun fire from above, and the searchlight went out, and suddenly the rope in his hands was alive, moving upwards like the rope of a ski tow. And he looked up and saw a huge shape, dim above the cliff, shoulders working. Andrea.

Andrea pulled him up those last ten feet as if he had weighed two hundred ounces instead of two hundred pounds. Miller hit the dirt in cover, rolled, and unslung his Schmeisser. Trouble, he thought. I am not a goddamn human fly, and as a result we are in it up to our necks, and sinking.

Beyond the boulder the cliffs were brilliant white. In their light he could see Andrea cocking a Bren.

'I'll cover you,' said Andrea, in his unruffled craftsman's voice. 'Grenades?'

Miller and Mallory each took two grenades from their belt pouches and pulled the pins. 'Two, three,' said Mallory. '*Throw.*'

There was a moment of silence, broken only by the metallic clatter of the grenades bouncing down the cliff, two left, two right. The world seemed to hold its breath. They would be setting up a mortar down there; taking up positions, radioing for reinforcements. Though, in a gorge like this, radio reception would be terrible –

Then the night flashed white, and four explosions rang as one, followed by a deeper explosion. Andrea crawled to the edge of the ledge. The lights had gone out. There was a new light, orange and black: a burning lorry. The firing lulled, then began again.

Mallory said, 'Cover us for ten minutes. We'll meet you at the top.'

Andrea's head was a black silhouette against the orange flicker of the gasoline fire. The silhouette nodded. For a moment his huge shoulders showed against the sky, the Bren slung over the right. Then he faded into the rocks. The five other men and Lisette gathered up the packs. Jaime said, in a voice apparently unaffected by fear, 'There is a path. A little higher.'

'Miller,' said Mallory. 'We don't want those trucks to get back. Or anywhere with anything like decent radio reception. Anything you can do?'

Miller shrugged. 'I'll give it the old college try,' he said. His hands were already busy in the first of the brass-bound boxes. He felt for one of the five-pound bricks of plastic explosive, laid it on the ground, latched the first box and unlatched the second. The second box was thickly lined with felt. Unclipping a flashlight from the breast pocket of his smock, he used it to select a green time pencil: thirty seconds' delay. Delicately he pressed the pencil into the primer and looked at the radium-bright numerals on his watch. Then he snapped the time pencil, yawned, and carefully lit a cigarette. By the time he had pocketed his Zippo, twenty-five seconds had elapsed. He took the brick in both hands and heaved it out and over the vehicles in the valley below.

Miller really hated heights. But nice, safe explosives were familiar territory. It felt great to be back.

For the space of a breath, there was darkness and silence in which the sound of Germanic shouting rose from the valley, mixed with the scrape of steel on rock as they set up the mortars.

39

Then the night turned white, whiter than the searchlights, and Mallory was blasted against the cliff by a huge metallic *clang* that felt as if it would drive his eardrums together in the middle of his head.

'Go,' he said, the sound small and distant behind the ringing in his ears.

They began to file up the cliff: Mallory in the lead, then Jaime, Lisette, and Hugues, with Miller bringing up the rear. Andrea climbed the fifty-degree face behind the chockstone until he found another boulder. There he stopped, unfolded the Bren's bipod, and rested it on the stone.

Fires were still burning on the valley floor. The flames cast a flickering light on torn rock and twisted metal, and many still bodies dressed in field-grey. There were three trucks. Two of them were burning. The other lay like a crushed beetle under a huge slab of rock prised away from the gorge wall by the force of the explosion. At the far side of the gorge, three grey figures were draped over the rocks beside what had once been a mortar.

One of the figures moved.

Andrea pulled the Bren into his shoulder, and fired. The heavy drum of the machine gun echoed in the rocks. The grey figure went over backwards and did not move any more.

Then there was silence, except for the moan of the wind and the patter of sleet on rock.

Andrea watched for another five minutes, patient, not heeding the icy moisture soaking through his smock and into his battle-dress blouse.

Nothing moved. As far as he could tell, the radio sets were wrecked, and there were no survivors. But of course there would be survivors. He had no objection to going down and cutting the survivors' throats. But if he did, it was unlikely that he would be able to rejoin the main party.

Andrea thought about it with the deliberation of a master wine maker deciding on which day he would pick his grapes: perhaps a little light on sugar today, but if he waited a week, there was the risk of rain . . .

Naturally, the Germans would assume that the force that had attacked them had gone on to Spain.

Andrea took a final look at the flames and the metal and the bodies. He felt no emotion. Guerrilla warfare was a job, a job at which he was an expert. His strength and intelligence were weapons in the service of his comrades and his country's allies. He did not like killing German soldiers. But if it was part of the job, then he was prepared to do it, and do it well.

To Andrea, this looked like a decent piece of work.

He slung the Bren over his shoulder and began to lope rapidly up the steep mountain. It had begun to snow.

It was a wet snow that fell in flakes the size of saucers, each flake landing on skin or cloth or metal with an icy slap, beginning immediately to melt. They slid into boots and down necks, becoming paradoxically colder as they melted. Within ten minutes the whole party was soaked to the skin. And for what seemed like an eternity, there was only the rasp of breath in throats, the hammer of hearts, and the sodden rub of boots against feet as they marched doggedly up the forty-five-degree slope in the icy blackness. Miller's mind was filled with anxiety.

He said to Andrea, 'What do you think?'

Andrea knew what he was being asked. 'They will think we have gone to Spain.'

'Perhaps.'

'And they will send out patrols. In case we have not gone to Spain.'

'Exactly.'

One foot in front of the other. Hammering hearts. Sore feet. Soon they would have to stop. Food was needed, and warmth. But they were walking away from food and warmth, upwards. Into unknown territory. Where they had been assured Jules would be waiting, somewhere warm and dry. Assured by Lisette.

Mallory was having to rely on people he did not know. And that made Mallory nervous.

Mallory said quietly, 'We'd better watch the rear, in case anyone drops out.'

Andrea stepped to one side. The walkers passed him: Jaime in the lead, Miller, Thierry. Then, a long way behind, too far, Hugues and Lisette: Hugues hunched over Lisette, apparently half-carrying her, their shapes odd and lumpy against the white snow, like a single, awkward animal. Andrea could hear Hugues' breathing.

'You all right?' he said.

'Of course,' said Hugues, in a voice whose cheerfulness even exhaustion could not mar.

Andrea frowned. Then he fell in behind, and kept on upwards.

It felt like an eternity. But in reality it was only a little more than an hour before Jaime emitted a bark of satisfaction, and said, '*Voilà!*'

The ground had for some time been rising less steeply. Between snow flurries, Mallory saw a silvery line of snow lying across the black-lead sky: the ridge. Between the walkers and the ridge was what might have been a narrow ledge, running diagonally upwards, its lines softened by six inches of snow. Jaime kicked at the downhill side with his foot, revealing a coping of roughly-dressed stone. 'The Chemin des Anges,' he said.

The path was easy walking, following the contours, skirting precipices over which Miller did not allow his eyes to stray. They followed it up and onto the ridge.

Lack of effort let them feel the chill of their sodden clothes. They paused to let Lisette and Hugues catch up. Mallory took his oilcloth-wrapped cigarettes from the soaking pocket of his blouse, and gave one to Miller. Their faces were haggard in the Zippo's flare. Hugues and Lisette approached.

Hugues said, 'Lisette needs food. Rest, warmth –'

'Don't be stupid,' said Lisette's voice. She sounded weak, but resolute.

'But my darling –'

'Don't you darling me,' she said. 'Can we go on?'

Mallory said nothing. It was possible to admire this woman's spirit. It was less possible to admire the speed at which she moved. Too slow, thought Mallory. It was all getting too slow, and there was a hell of a distance to travel before they even got to the start line.

His watch said it was 0200 hours. He said to Jaime, 'How long?'

'Two hours. All downhill. The slope is not so bad now.'

Mallory could hear Hugues' teeth chattering. There was a thin, icy wind up here, and the snow was colder. 'Any shelter before then?'

'In ten minutes. A shepherd's hut. There will be nobody.'

'We'll stop for twenty minutes.'

'Thank God.'

The shepherd's hut had a roof and three walls, facing providentially away from the wind. The floor was covered in dung-matted straw, but it was dry, and after the snow it was as good as a Turkish carpet. They burrowed into the filthy straw, smoking, letting their body heat warm their soaking clothes. Jaime produced a bottle of brandy. Lisette was half-buried in the straw next to Hugues. When Mallory shone his flashlight at her, he saw her face was a dead grey. He took the brandy bottle out of Thierry's hand and carried it over to her. 'Here,' he said.

The neck of the bottle rattled against her teeth. She coughed. 'Thank you,' she said, when she could speak.

Mallory said, 'It was a good thing you found us.'

'Love,' said Hugues. 'It was the power of love. A sixth sense –'

'There was a little more to it than that,' she said, dryly. 'Hugues, you are getting carried away.'

'Yes,' said Mallory, warming to her toughness. 'So how did you do it?'

She shook her head. Her shivering was lending a faint seismic movement to the straw. 'They were talking, the *résistants*. One of them I knew. They said the radio signal arranging your drop mentioned that you were carrying money, I don't know if it's true. They made a deal with a German officer. They are demoralised, some of these Germans in the mountains here. And of course the *résistants* too; some of them are no more than bandits. The German was to kill you. Then he was to give them the money and collect a medal, I guess.' Her teeth gleamed in the pale reflection from the snow outside. 'I saw them come back to warn the officer. I knew where they had come from. So I got on my bicycle, and fell off in the right place. And it didn't work out for those pigs.'

'Thank God,' said Hugues, fervently.

Mallory found he was smiling. 'Thank you,' he said. He got up, his weary knees protesting. It looked as if there was a new addition to the party. A brave addition, but a slow one. He hoped that

43

Hugues would get his ardour under control, and start acting human again. He said, 'We're moving out.'

An hour and a half later Jaime led them down a snowy path and into the trees above the village. There was another barn-like building in the trees.

Jaime opened the door and said, 'Wait in here.'

Mallory said, 'Where are you going?'

'To find some friends.' There was a fireplace. Jaime struck a match, lit the piled kindling, and threw on an armful of logs. 'Be comfortable. Dry yourselves.' His eyes were invisible in the shadows under his heavy eyebrows.

Mallory's eyes met Andrea's. He did not like it. Nor, he could tell, did Andrea. But there was nothing he could do.

Jaime disappeared into the night. Lisette sank down in front of the fire and began to pull her boots off.

'Outside,' said Mallory.

She looked at him as if he was mad.

'What if Jaime comes back with a German patrol?'

'*Mais non,*' said Thierry.

'Jaime?' said Lisette. 'Never. He hates Germans.'

Hugues' face was pink and nervous. 'How do you know?' he said. 'How does anyone know? The Germans arrived at the drop site within half an hour. Someone betrayed us –'

'I told you what happened,' said Lisette. 'Now for God's sake –'

'Outside,' said Hugues.

Something happened to Lisette's face. '*Non,*' she said. '*Non, non, non, non.* I am staying.'

'And I also,' said Thierry, his big face the colour of lard under the straw hat.

'*Women,*' said Hugues.

'I am not *women*!' snapped Lisette. 'I am someone who knows Jaime. And trusts him.'

'*Ah, ça!*' said Hugues. 'Well –'

'But perhaps you trust your friends more,' said Lisette.

And when Hugues looked round, he saw that where Mallory, Miller and Andrea had been standing were only wet footprints.

*　　*　　*

44

Out in the woods Miller lay and shivered in a pile of sodden pine needles, and thought longingly of the warm firelight in the barn. He had watched Hugues storm out, heard the slam of the door. Then nothing, except the icy drip of rainwater on his neck, and the mouldy smell of pine needles under his nose.

After half an hour, the rain stopped. There was silence, with dripping. And behind the dripping, the wheeze and clatter of an engine. Some sort of truck came round the corner, no lights. Miller sighted his Schmeisser on its cab. Three men got out. As far as Miller could see, the truck was small, and not German.

A voice said, '*L'Amiral Beaufort!*'

Another voice said, '*Vive la France!*'

The barn door opened and closed.

Mallory saw Hugues come out of the bush in which he had been hiding, and walk across to the barn. Hugues knew these men, it appeared. That was Hugues' area of speciality. So Mallory got up himself, and went in.

The men Jaime had brought wore sweeping moustaches and huge berets that flopped down over their eyes. They carried shotguns. Two of them were talking to Hugues in rapid French. Mallory thought they looked a damned sight too pleased with themselves.

'There are no Germans in the village,' said Jaime. 'But there is a small problem. It seems that Jules has had an accident. A fatal accident, they tell me. He was shot at Jonzère, last night.'

Mallory stared at him. 'How?' he said.

'A matter of too much enthusiasm,' said Jaime.

Hugues ceased his conversation and turned to Mallory. He said, 'Or to tell the truth, a mess.'

Jaime shrugged. He said, 'The *résistants* heard we had landed. There was an idea that we were a regiment, maybe more, because there were only two survivors from the German patrol in the gorge. So Jules heard all this and went to Jonzère to stop these hotheads getting themselves killed. But he was too late. They were firing on the Germans, and the Germans were firing back, and they got themselves killed, all right. And Jules got himself killed with them.'

Hugues blew air, expressing scorn. 'It is not as it is in the north. These mountain people have too many feelings and too few brains.'

It was Jules who had known the man who knew where the Werwolf pack were being repaired. Without Jules, the chain was broken.

Mallory said, with a mildness he did not feel, 'So how are we to continue with the operation?'

'Ah,' said Jaime. 'Marcel has a surprise for you, in Colbis.' He did not look as if he approved of surprises.

'Marcel the baker?' said Hugues.

'That's the one.'

Hugues nodded approvingly. 'A good man,' he said.

Mallory had the feeling that he was sitting in on gossip about people he did not know. He said, 'I need information about the Werwolf pack, not bread.'

'*Voilà*,' said Jaime. 'Marcel proposes breakfast in the . . . in his café. Then he will provide you with transport to where it is you wish to go. He has another Englishman there, you will be glad to hear, who may have information.'

May, thought Mallory. Only may. He took a deep, resigned breath.

'Oh, good,' said Miller, edging towards the fire. 'And the dancing girls?'

'You may find some dancing girls.'

'Breakfast would be fine,' said Miller.

Mallory beckoned Jaime over. The men with the berets followed him as if glued to his side. 'Why are there no Germans in the village?'

One of the men with the berets grinned, and spoke quickly. Jaime translated. 'Because they are all in Jonzère. First, fighting. Now, trying to catch some bandits before they arrive in Spain.' There was more talk in a language that was not French. Basque, Mallory guessed. 'This man says there has been a battle. Many Germans have been killed. There may be reprisals. It is said there was an Allied army in the mountains. In the next valley.'

Mallory raised his eyebrows. 'An army,' he said. From regiment to army, in the space of three minutes.

'Yes,' said Jaime, solemn-faced in the dim light of the torch. 'And they say it is lucky that we were not involved, being so few, and one of us a woman.'

Mallory looked at Jaime hard. Was that the ghost of a wink? Andrea's face was impassive. He had seen it too. His great head moved, almost imperceptibly. Nodding. Suddenly, Mallory found himself perilously close to trusting Jaime.

Mallory hardened his heart. 'Now you listen,' he said. 'I am grateful for your offers of hospitality. But I don't want to go into the village, breakfast or no breakfast. I want our transport out here, and I want to get up to the coast. The more time we spend in the mountains, the messier it's going to get, the bigger the rumours. We want to do this quick and quiet. I don't like rumours and reprisals, or battles. I want intelligence, and I want transport, and I want them before daylight. Tell these people to tell Marcel.'

Jaime said, 'I don't know –'

Mallory said, 'And make it snappy.'

Jaime looked at the steady burn of the deeply-sunken eyes over the long, unshaven jaw. Jaime thought of the cliff that nobody could climb, that this man had climbed; of three burned-out lorries in the pass; and the pursuit on a wild goose chase towards the Spanish border. This was not a man it was easy to disobey. Perhaps he had underestimated this man.

'*Bon*,' he said.

'And now,' said Mallory, when the men in berets had gone outside, 'Thierry. Time to tell the folks at home we've arrived.'

Thierry nodded. He looked big and pale and exhausted. His head moved slowly, as if his neck was stiff, the big jowls creasing and uncreasing, stray strands of straw waving jauntily over the burst crown of his hat. He began to unpack the radio. Miller was in a corner, stretched out full-length on the straw, humming a Bix Beiderbecke tune. Andrea was relaxed, but close to a knothole in the door, through which he could keep tabs on the sentries. Mallory leaned his head against the wall. He could feel his clothes beginning to steam in the heat from the fire.

He said to Hugues, quietly, 'What do you know about this Marcel?'

'Jules' second-in-command,' said Hugues. 'It is an odd

structure, down here. Security is terrible. But they are brave men.'

'And we trust them?'

Hugues smiled. He said, 'Is there any choice?'

Mallory kept hearing Jensen's voice. *It seems quite possible that the Germans will, in a manner of speaking, be waiting for you.*

Damn you, Jensen. What did you know that you did not tell us?

It was raining again, a steady rattle on the roof of the barn. On the mountain it would be snowing on their tracks. Perhaps their tracks would be comprehensively covered, and the Germans would not be waiting for them. Perhaps they would be lucky.

But Mallory did not believe in luck.

Thierry said, 'Contact made and acknowledged.'

'Messages?'

'No messages.'

Mallory closed his eyes. Sleep lapped at him. Despite the fire he was cold. Two hours later, he was going to remember being cold; remember it with nostalgic affection. For the moment, he lay and shivered, dozing.

Then he was awake.

A lorry engine was running outside. He gripped his Schmeisser and rose to his feet, instantly alert. He could see Miller covering the door. Andrea was gone. What –

The door crashed open. A man was standing there. He was short and fat, with a beret the size of a dinner plate, and a moustache that spread beyond it like the wings of a crow. His small black eyes flicked between the Schmeisser barrels covering him. He grinned broadly. 'Gentlemen,' he said. 'Colbis welcomes its allies from beyond the seas. *Allons, l'Amiral Beaufort.*'

Mallory said, 'Who are you?'

'My name is Marcel,' said the man. 'I am delighted to see you. I am only sorry that you had some little problems last night, of which I have already heard.' He bowed. 'My congratulations. Now, into the lorry. It will soon be light, and there are many eyes connected to many tongues.'

Outside, a steady rain was falling. In the grey half-light black pines rose up the steep hillside into a layer of dirty-grey cloud. The lorry was an old Citroën, converted to wood-gas, panting and fuming in the yard. '*Messieurs*,' said Marcel. 'Dispose yourselves.'

Mallory closed the Storm Force into the canvas back of the lorry, and climbed into the front. Marcel ground the gears, and started to jounce down a narrow track that snaked through the dripping trees. 'Quite a fuss,' said Marcel. 'The Germans have met an army of *maquisards*, it is said. Oh, very good –'

Mallory said, 'I am looking for three submarines.'

'Naturally,' said Marcel. 'And I know a man who will take you to them. We must meet him now. At breakfast.'

'A man?'

'Wait and see,' said Marcel, hauling the lorry round a pig in the road.

The trees had stopped. They were crossing open meadows scattered with small, earth-coloured cottages. Ahead was a huddle of houses, and the arched campanile of a church. Nothing was moving; it was four-thirty in the morning. But Mallory did not like it.

'Where are we going?'

'Breakfast, of course. In the village.'

'Not the village.' Villages were rat-traps. In the past eight hours, Mallory had had enough rat-traps for a lifetime.

Marcel said, 'There are no Germans in Colbis. No collaborators. It is important that we go into the village. To see this person.'

'Who is this person?'

'As I say,' said Marcel, with a winsome smile, 'this will be a surprise.'

Mallory told himself that there was no future in getting angry. He said, 'Excuse me, but there is very little time. I do not wish to commit myself to a position from which there is no retreat.'

Marcel looked at him. Above the jolly cheeks, the eyes were hard and knowing: the eyes of a lieutenant whose commanding officer had been killed in the night. Mallory began to feel better. Marcel said, 'This person you must meet cannot be moved. Believe me.'

Mallory gave up. He pulled his SS helmet over his eyes, checked the magazine of his Schmeisser, and leaned back in the seat. Slowly the lorry wheezed out of the meadows and wound its way through streets designed for pack-mules into the centre of Colbis.

There was a square, flanked on its south side by the long wall of the church. In the middle were two plane trees in which roosting chickens clucked drowsily. There was a *mairie*, and a line of what must have been shops: butcher's, baker's, ironmonger's. And on the corner, a row of tall windows streaming with rain, with a signboard above them bearing the faded inscription *Café Des Sports*.

''Ere we are,' said Marcel, cheerfully. ''Op out.'

Boots clattered on the wet cobbles. The etched-glass windows of the café reflected the group of civilians and the three Waffen-SS with heavy packs and Schmeissers; the civilians might have been prisoners. It was a sight to cause twitched-aside curtains to drop over windows – not that there was any visible twitching. The German forces of Occupation in the frontier zone were remarkably acute about twitched curtains.

Grinning and puffing, Marcel hustled his charges into the café, and shepherded them up through the beaded fringe covering the mouth of a staircase behind the bar. Miller's nostrils dilated. He said, 'Coffee. Real coffee.'

'Comes from Spain,' said Marcel. 'With the señoritas and the oranges. Particularly the señoritas. Come up, now.'

Miller went up the stairs. Mallory was behind him. Miller stopped, dead. Mallory's finger moved to the trigger of his Schmeisser. At the top of the stairs was a large landing overlooking the square. The landing had sofas and chairs. Too many doors opened off it. It smelt of stale scent and unwashed bodies.

Miller said, 'It's a cathouse.'

Mallory said, 'So you will feel completely at home.'

They had been walking most of the night. Mallory was soaking wet and shivering. His hands felt raw, his feet rubbed and blistered inside the jackboots. He wanted to find the objective of the operation, and carry the operation out while there was still an operation to carry out.

And instead, they were attending a breakfast party in a brothel.

'Village this size?' said Miller. 'With a *cathouse*?'

It should have meant something. But the smell of the coffee had blunted Mallory's perceptions. All he knew was that he had to get hold of some, or die.

It was light outside, cold and grey. But inside on the sideboard there was coffee, and bread, and goat's cheese, and a thin, fiery brandy for those who wanted it. Mallory drank a cup of coffee. He said to Marcel, 'You said there was someone here.'

Marcel nodded. 'He will be sleeping. Another croissant? I make them my own self.'

'We'll wake him.'

Marcel shrugged, and opened one of the doors off the landing.

The smell of sweat and perfume intensified. It was a bedroom, decorated in dirty pink satin. On the bed was a man in khaki uniform, lying on his back like a crusader on a tomb. Bandages showed through the unbuttoned waistband of his battledress blouse: bandages with rusty stains. On the chair beside the bed was a beret bearing the winged-hatchet badge of the SAS.

Mallory glanced at the pips on the epaulette. He said, 'Morning, Lieutenant.'

The man on the bed stirred and moaned. His eyes half-opened. They focused on Mallory. They saw a man in a coal-scuttle helmet and a Waffen-SS smock, carrying a Schmeisser.

'Hiding up in a brothel,' said Mallory. 'All right for some.'

The man's hand crawled towards his pillow. Mallory's hand beat him to it. His fingers closed on metal. He came out with the Browning automatic. 'Relax,' said Mallory.

The Lieutenant glared at him with berserk blue eyes. His face was white, with grey shadows. Pain. He was badly wounded. 'SOE,' said Mallory. 'We've come to bail you out.' Inwardly, his heart was sinking. This would be one of Killigrew's men. One of the gung-ho shoot-em-up boys who had been dropped and got themselves lost. Who had probably compromised the operation already. Things were in a bad enough mess without a wounded SAS man to slow them down. A badly wounded SAS man, by the look of him. Perhaps he could be smuggled over the border into Spain.

'How do I know that?' said the Lieutenant.

'Admiral Beaufort will tell you,' said Mallory. 'So did a little man called Captain Killigrew.' He opened the buttons of the SS smock. 'And this is British battledress. Seemed tactless to wear it on the outside, somehow.'

'Who told you I was here? Marcel –'

'Marcel was very discreet,' said Mallory, soothingly.

Slowly, the blue eyes lost their berserk glare. The wariness remained. 'Killigrew,' he said. 'Yes. When did you get in?'

'Albemarle, last night,' said Mallory. There was no time for chitchat. 'I need to know what happened to you.'

'Landed on a bit of a plateau . . . near here,' said the SAS man. He obviously wanted to give as little away as possible. 'Brought a Jeep.' A Jeep, thought Mallory. A full-size actual Jeep. On parachutes. Amazing. But that was the SAS for you. 'Heading for the coast. Ambushed. Other chaps bought it. I took a bang on the head and a bullet in the guts.'

Mallory said, 'How did it happen?'

'Driving down a track,' said the SAS man. 'Next thing we knew, there were two Spandaus. One either side of the road. Don't remember much after that. The Resistance brought me here.' There was a shake in his voice. He was very young.

'So it was a road block?' said Mallory.

'Not much of one.'

Mallory nodded. Give me strength, he thought. Conning your way through a checkpoint behind enemy lines, SAS style. Two grenades and put your foot down. 'Where were you going on the coast?'

'Doesn't really matter,' said the Lieutenant. This was his first operation. It was just like school, on the Rugby XV. You went for it, and sod the consequences. Your own team tactics were your own team tactics, and you kept them to yourself. The only thing different about war was this damned bullet. He did not let his mind stray too close to the bullet, in case the pain made him sick again. It felt the size of a cricket ball, down there. And it hurt. Was hurting worse, lately . . . He concentrated on his dislike for this old man in the Waffen-SS uniform who had burst in and dropped a few names, and thought that gave him a license to pump him, take over the operation, grab the glory. Let him find out for himself.

The old man's face was close to his. It had a broad forehead and very young brown eyes; eyes like old Brutus, who taught Latin at Shrewsbury and climbed Alps in the summer hols. The eyes seemed to remove the Lieutenant's reserve the way a tin-opener would take the lid off a tin. The old man said, 'Where were you going and who were you going to see?'

The Lieutenant summoned up his undoubted toughness. 'Doesn't matter.'

The eyes hardened. The old man said, 'Don't be childish. There's very little time.'

The Lieutenant gritted his teeth. He desperately wanted to tell someone. It would be less lonely, for one thing, and he was really, terrifyingly, lonely. But a secret was a secret. 'I'm sorry,' he said. 'I don't . . . I'm not authorised.'

Mallory allowed his eyes to rest on this lieutenant. He really was absurdly young. His was the berserker's bravery, frenzied and unbending. If the Gestapo got their hands on him, he would break like a twig.

Mallory sighed inwardly. He got up, opened the door and put his head out. There seemed to be a party going on. He said, 'Andrea.'

The huge Greek padded across from his seat overlooking the square. His shoulders seemed to blot out the light in the little room. Mallory said, 'If you won't tell me, tell the Colonel.'

The SAS man frowned. He saw no colonel. He saw an unshaven giant with a huge moustache. He saw a pair of black eyes, eyes like the eyes on a Byzantine icon, that understood everything, forgave everything. 'Colonel?' he said.

'Andrea is a full colonel in the Greek army.'

'How do I know that's not another bloody lie?'

Andrea sat down in the pink plush armchair. Suddenly the SAS man felt weak, and ill, and about fourteen years old. 'You are frightened,' said Andrea.

'I bloody well am not,' said the Lieutenant. But even as Andrea spoke, he could feel it draining away, all the team spirit, the gung ho, war-as-a-game-of-rugby. He saw himself as he was: a wounded kid who would die in a dirty little room, alone.

'Not of dying,' said Andrea. 'But of yourself, of failing. I also am frightened, all the time. So it is not possible to let myself fail.'

He did not sound like any colonel the Lieutenant had ever heard. He sounded like a man of warmth and common sense, like a friend. Careful, said a voice in the Lieutenant's head. But it was a small voice, fading fast.

Andrea's eyes alighted on a crude wooden crutch, a section of pole with a pad whittled roughly to the shape of an armpit. 'Yours?' he said.

'I'm going to use it,' said the SAS man. 'I can get around all right.' It was not altogether a lie. He could move. It was just that when he moved, he could feel that bit of metal in his guts twisting, doing him damage. But that was not the point. The point was fighting a war. 'Couple of days,' he said. 'Get into the hills.'

'Why don't you come with us?' said Andrea, tactfully. This boy and his crutch would not last an hour in the mountains. He could see it in his face. 'We will take you with us,' said Andrea. 'And you and I, and Miller and Mallory, will finish this operation.'

The Lieutenant's eyes moved back to the first man, the thin one. 'Mallory?' he said. He saw newspaper front pages pinned to the board behind the fives courts. On the front pages were pictures of this man, with a pyramid of snow-covered rock in the background. *That* Mallory. He came to a decision. He said, 'Jules told me. Guy Jamalartégui. At the Café de L'Océan in St-Jean-de-Luz. We would have told you. But . . . there's been a lot of German activity. Radio silence, except in emergency. Jerry's very quick.'

Mallory nodded. Radio detector vans would not be the only reason. The SAS liked to keep their intelligence to themselves, particularly when it was information that might help Jensen and SOE.

'Thank you,' he said. 'Thank you very much.' Sounds of revelry were percolating through the door. 'Now. Can I get you some breakfast?'

Once the shock had worn off, Miller had almost started to enjoy himself. The coffee was undoubtedly coffee, and the bread was still warm from the oven, and while he was not a goat cheese enthusiast, in his present frame of mind he would have cheerfully eaten the goat, horns and all. And by the time he had finished eating, there had been stirrings behind some of the doors. At the Cognac stage, his glass had been filled by a dark girl in a red silk nightdress, and Miller was beginning to be reminded that while occupied France might be occupied, it was still France.

He lay back in his chair, and listened to the rattle of French and Basque from the *maquisards*, and sipped his Cognac. A corner of his mind was on the girl in the red nightdress. But most of it was out there in the square, patrolling the darkness under the trees and in the corners. Soon the village's eyes would start opening and its tongues would start wagging. It was time they were out of here. The girl in the red nightdress ran her fingers through his crewcut. Miller grinned, a lazy grin that to anyone who did not know him would have looked completely relaxed. Which in a way, he was. Because Mallory thought it was okay to be here. So it was okay. In a life that had contained about ten times more incidents than the average citizen's, Miller had never met a man he trusted more than the New Zealander.

He was not so sure about the Frenchmen. Jaime was sitting in a corner, coffee cup between his hands. Jaime seemed at least to know his way around. Now he was watching Hugues, who was fussing round Lisette. A lifetime spent in places where personality carried more weight than law had made Miller acutely sensitive to the way people got along. Miller had the distinct feeling that Jaime did not have a lot of time for Hugues.

Miller had his own doubts about Hugues. Sure, he knew his way round the Resistance. But he was an excitable guy. Lotta fuss that guy makes, thought Miller. And a lotta noise, too much noise. Lisette, now. They were stuck with Lisette. She was slow; she carried too much weight. But she was one tough cookie –

Jesus.

Lisette had been removing her outer clothing. She had been wearing an overcoat, two shawls, and a couple of peasant smocks of some kind. They had made her look like a football on legs. Dressed up like that, she had bicycled up a steep valley road without lights, climbed a vertical cliff and force-marched fifteen precipitous miles without sleep.

What dropped Miller's jaw on his chest was not what she had done. It was the fact that she was just about the same shape without the winter clothes as with them. Face it, thought Miller.

If you were Hugues, and Lisette was your girl, you would maybe feel a tad over-protective yourself.

Because the reason Lisette looked like a gasometer on legs was that she was at least eight months pregnant.

Somewhere a telephone rang, the tenuous ring of a hand-cranked exchange. Down the hall someone answered it, and started shouting in frantic Basque. Miller became suddenly completely immobile, listening. The voices had stopped. Cocks were crowing. Otherwise there was silence.

But behind the silence were engines. Lorry engines, a lot of them.

In the French frontier zone at this particular time in history, there was only one group of people who had a lot of lorries, and the fuel to run them.

Miller grabbed his Schmeisser and yanked the cocking lever. The girl in the red nightdress seemed suddenly to have vanished. Marcel the baker was standing up, smiling from a face suddenly grey and wooden. The engines were in the square now: four trucks with canvas backs. The trucks stopped. Soldiers were pouring out of the backs, soldiers with coal-scuttle helmets and field-grey uniforms, their jackboots grinding the wet cobbles of the square.

A staff car rolled into the square. A tall, black-uniformed officer got out, said something, and pointed at Marcel's lorry. Two soldiers bayoneted the tyres. The lorry settled on its rims.

As Mallory put his head out of the SAS man's door, Andrea's hand went out and grabbed Marcel by the shoulder. Marcel was a big man, but Andrea held him at arm's length with his feet off the ground. He said, 'What are these troops doing here?'

Marcel's face was a mask of horror. 'I don't know . . . I was assured . . .'

In Mallory's mind, gears rolled smoothly and a conclusion formed. 'It's an SS brothel,' he said. 'Isn't it?'

Marcel's face turned a dull, embarrassed purple. 'It is a cover,' he said. 'A good cover. Now, gentlemen . . .'

Andrea dropped him. Marcel rubbed his shoulder. He said, 'Follow me, please.' His voice was calm and urbane: the voice of the perfect host. Already the girls had cleared away the traces of the breakfast. He pointed into the SAS man's room. One of the girls was holding open the door of the wardrobe. The wardrobe had no back. Instead, a flight of steps led down into darkness.

Mallory trusted Marcel. But someone had betrayed them. Who?

Andrea went to help the SAS man off the bed. The SAS man pushed him away, reached for his makeshift wooden crutch and hauled himself moaning to his feet. As Miller brought up the rear, he could hear the battering of rifle butts on the café's front door.

More rats in more traps, he thought. And all for a cup of coffee and a girl in a red nightdress.

Maybe the coffee had been worth it, at that.

The back of the wardrobe slammed behind them. They went downstairs and out into a small yard, wet and empty under the sky. At the back of the yard was a shed, the lintel of its door blackened by smoke. There was a powerful smell of baking bread.

From over the wall came guttural shouts, and the barking of dogs. '*Vite*,' said Marcel, shooing them into the shed.

The shed was a bakehouse. There were two bread ovens. The one on the left was shut. The one on the right was open. In front of the oven door was a big stone slab. On the slab lay a metal tray, six feet long by four feet wide. A small, one-eyed man in a dirty apron did not even glance at them. 'On the tray,' said Marcel. 'Two at a time.'

'Where are the others?' said Mallory.

'In the brothel. They speak French, *bien entendu*. Their papers are good. *Vite*.'

Miller jumped up onto the tray, and lay with his boxes on the big wooden paddle. Mallory climbed up beside him. 'When the tray stops, roll off,' said Marcel. 'Cover your faces.'

Mallory could hear German voices. A trap, he thought. Another, smaller trap. After this trap, absolutely no more –

He was lying on the tray with his pack on his stomach. He covered his face with his hands. Someone shoved the paddle. A ferocious heat beat on the backs of his hands. He thought of the parabolic brick roof of the oven, smelt burning hair. *The ammunition*, he thought.

But the heat was gone, and they were shuffling off the paddle and onto a stone surface that was merely warm. Mallory raised his head. It was dark, black as ink. After six inches his forehead hit the roof. There seemed to be air circulating.

The tray returned, bearing Andrea and the SAS man. The SAS man was breathing hard and tremulous as Andrea shoved him off the tray. Somewhere, stones grated. That's it, thought Miller. You've got your bread oven, circular, made out of bricks. And there's a little door in the back of it, and we've been pushed through, and now they've closed the door –

Scraping noises emanated from the oven.

– and now they are going to bake a little bread.

He tried to raise his head, to see where the air was coming from. He hit the ceiling. Eighteen inches high, he thought. And nothing to see. Buried alive.

He put out his hand, touched his brass-bound boxes. On the way, his hand touched Mallory's arm.

The arm was rigid, vibrating with what must have been fear.

No. Not Mallory. Mallory was cool as ice. Mallory had scaled the South Cliff at Navarone, when Miller had been mewing with terror at its base.

All right, thought Miller. But down in the middle of every human being there is a place kept locked tight, and in that place lives the beast a person fears most. But sometimes the locks go, and the beast is out, raging in the mind, taking over all its corners.

Mallory's beast was confined spaces.

Dusty Miller stared at the invisible ceiling six inches above his nose, and listened to the sounds coming through the brick wall of the oven. There was a brisk crackling, and a sharp whiff of smoke. They had lit a fire in there, to heat the oven for the next batch of baking. How long do we have to stay in here? he thought. What if Mallory can't take it?

He began to sing. He sang softly, 'Falling in loaf with loaf is like falling for make-believe –'

'Shut up,' hissed the SAS man.

'This is not well bread of you,' said Miller.

'For Christ's *sake* –'

58

'I'm oven a lovely time,' said Miller. 'And you're baking the spell – '

Mallory knew it was the torpedoing all over again: the little metal room with four men jammed together, the thunder of the terrible blue Mediterranean pouring into the hull, four faces in six inches of air under the steel ceiling, the air bad, hot, *unbreathable* – and Mallory was going to die, of suffocation, certainly, but first of terror . . .

Someone seemed to be talking. Talking complete drivel, in a soft Chicago drawl. Beyond the drawl, far away, there were other voices. German voices.

Miller.

The terror went. Mallory found himself thinking that there were worse things than small spaces. Dusty Miller's puns, for instance.

Miller felt Mallory's hand prod him sharply in the side. He shut up. Mission accomplished.

Suddenly a dog was barking close at hand. Much closer than the far side of the fire in the oven. The compartment where the four men were hiding filled with the scritch of claws on stone. The air holes, thought Miller. There must be air holes, and the goddamn dog's smelt us through them.

They lay looking up at the ceiling they could not see, in the dark that was full of the clamour of the dog. The little cell behind the oven grew steadily hotter. They began to sweat.

At the front of the ovens, Marcel was sweating too. His apron was smeared with flour and the ash of the bracken stalks he used to fire the oven. But he was not thinking about baking. He was looking at the SS officer who was leaning against the doorpost, slapping the barrel of his Luger into the palm of his black leather glove. The SS officer was smiling with great warmth, but his stone-grey eyes were the coldest thing Marcel had ever seen. 'Where are they?' said the officer.

'Pardon?' The yard was full of soldiers. A dog-handler came through, dragged by an Alsatian on a choke-chain. The Alsatian's tongue was hanging out, and it was panting eagerly.

The officer said, with patient friendliness, 'The dog has come from the brothel above the café. It is following the scent of some-one who was sitting in one of the chairs in the brothel. The scent leads straight to your oven. Why do you think this would be?'

The oven was burning well now. Smoke was pouring out of the door, crawling along the ceiling of the shed and billowing up at the rainy sky above the yard. Marcel pointed into the oven door at the incandescent glow of the burning bracken. 'What are these imaginary people?' he said. 'Salamanders?'

The smile did not waver. The SS man said, mildly, 'If these people are imaginary, why would the dog be so interested?'

'A mystery.'

The SS man said, 'I have the strong impression that there are people in this village who have no business here.'

Marcel said, 'What gives you this impression?'

The SS man smiled, but did not answer. His eyes slid over the bakehouse. He said, 'And what is inside the other oven?'

Marcel yawned. 'Who knows?'

'It is in my mind,' said the SS man, fingering his long, Aryan chin, 'to pull this oven to pieces.'

'*Non*,' said Marcel, his eyes discs of horror. 'My livelihood. Georges. In the oven. What is in the oven, in the name of God? Tell this gentleman.'

'*Pains Flavigny*,' said the one-eyed man.

'Ah!' said Marcel, his face cracking into a large grin. '*Voilà!*'

'*Bitte?*'

'Georges is from Alsace,' said Marcel. 'So he bakes from time to time *pains Flavigny*, whose vital ingredient is aniseed, beloved of dogs. They do not sell so well, of course. But you know how it is. One must keep the staff happy. It is so hard, in a war, to find –'

The SS man allowed the barrel of his pistol to swing gently towards Georges. 'Open the oven,' he said.

'But the *pains* –'

'Open it.'

'They will be destroyed.'

The officer's finger moved onto the trigger. Georges shrugged. He said, 'It is a crime. But if you insist.' He flicked up the catch on the door and shoved in a small wooden paddle. When he

60

brought it out there was a cake on the end, round and brown.
'Not yet cooked,' he said. 'See, *nom d'un nom*. Sacrilege. Ruin. It
is sinking. They will all be sinking.'

The SS officer took the cake and crumbled it in his glove. The
dog jumped up, lathering his hand with its tongue. He kicked it
in the stomach with his jackboot. It shrank away, yelping. Delicately, he sniffed the crumbs. They smelt powerfully of aniseed.
'Excellent,' he said, still smiling. He turned, and walked out into
the yard. 'The dogs have led us astray, I fear. But there are other
methods of arriving at the truth.'

Marcel had followed, wiping his hands on his apron. *'Pardon,
monsieur?'*

'Your countrymen have been very stupid,' said the SS man.
'Stupid as pigs. There are rules. We both know that. Rules have
been broken. In Jonzère last night, there was fighting, with
deaths. You people must learn that laws are to be obeyed. I fear
you will find the lesson painful.' The smile. Marcel stood smiling
uncertainly back, his insides congealed with terror, watching the
icy eyes. 'There is a way of making it less painful. There are British
agents in this village,' said the SS man. 'When I find them, I will
leave.' He walked through the baker's shop, and into the square,
and rested a negligent hand on the tonneau of the staff car.
'Feldwebel!'

A sergeant crashed to attention.

'Knock on the door of each house in this square,' he said.
'Politely. Whoever answers the door, bring them out into the
square, and request them to stand . . .' the cold eyes checked,
then settled on the long, blank north wall of the church, 'against
that wall. While you are doing that, I want a Spandau set up
under the trees.'

Marcel's face had turned as white as his flour. He said, 'What
are you doing?'

'Fighting a war,' said the officer. 'When we have these people
out here, we shall shoot one every ten minutes until I am told
the truth. Your bread will be burning, baker.' He smiled. 'You
had better go.'

61

THREE

Monday 0900–1900

Miller had been with the Long Range Desert Force, so he had been hot all right. But nothing on the parched ergs or the wind-blasted scarps of the Sahara had prepared him for the heat behind that bread oven.

He kept talking. He could feel that Mallory needed to be talked to. It was not easy to talk while being cooked, but it must, he thought, be a lot easier to talk while you were only hot than while you were hot and in a state of flat panic. Andrea talked too, reminiscing in a low rumble about the cave in Crete where he and Mallory had resided. And all the time the heat grew, hotter and hotter, searing the skin. There were smells, too: wood smoke and baking smells, with over it all another baking smell that Miller recognised but did not want to mention. It was the smell of confectioner's almonds; the smell of gelignite cooking in its box.

There was a consolation, thought Miller. A small one. If the gelignite set off the Cyclonite, it was going to take some Germans with it. Not to mention the village of Colbis, and a fair-sized chunk of the northern Pyrenees –

A new sound floated through the wall: a harsh judder, dulled by layers of stone. The sound of a machine gun.

Mallory knew he had won. He had beaten his glands, or what-ever it was that weakened the knees and liquefied the guts. The machine gun had taken him into the outside world. He was think-ing ahead now. 'We're going to need transport to St-Jean-de-Luz.'

'Transport?'

'It's thirty miles by road. The submarines sail the day after tomorrow, at noon. It's too tight to march.'

'Bicycles?'

There was a silence. They were all thinking the same: a pregnant woman and an SAS man with a bullet in the guts were no good on bicycles. A ruthless man who wanted to move fast would leave such impediments behind. Mallory did not know if he was that ruthless. Luckily, there was no chance of his being tested. The SAS man and Lisette knew too much to be allowed to fall into enemy hands.

Like it or not, they were along for the ride.

The SAS man had been lying very still, conserving energy in the heat, listening to the three men talking. Chattering was for girls and wimps and other classes of humanity despised by the SAS. Now he said, 'There's a Jeep.'

A Jeep. Presumably with Union Jacks all over it, two-way radios, heavy machine guns, mobile cocktail bar and sun lounge. You could not beat the SAS. Not unless you were the enemy.

'Well, well,' said Miller. 'This is excellent news.'

Mallory said, 'Where?'

'In the barn at the back of the bakery. It's the Jeep they dropped with us. Under the bracken. Marcel told me they brought it in.'

Mallory said, 'Thank you, er . . .'

'Wallace.' Miller was surprised to feel a hand reach across him. He shook it. It shook his back. So that's all right, he thought. We've been introduced, and now he's lending us his car. And we're walled up in an oven, cooking.

Goddamn limeys.

There was a new sound outside: a voice, at one of the air holes. Marcel's voice. 'You must come out,' said the voice.

'We'll take the Jeep.'

'Yes.' The voice sounded strained. 'You must go away from here. You know where. Your comrades are by the barn. Go soon.'

'Just open the door.'

'Yes.'

A pause. There were movements, felt in the walls rather than heard. Someone was raking the fuel out of the oven. The door separating them from the oven opened, admitting a scorching blast of air. 'Tray coming in,' said Marcel's voice.

Afterwards, Mallory could not remember how they got out. There was a hellish blast of heat, and a smell of burning hair, and then they were standing in the bakehouse, surrounded by large, beautiful volumes of space.

'The barn,' said Marcel. He looked suddenly thinner, and his face was a bad greyish colour. 'Follow me.'

Andrea gave Wallace his shoulder. They went into the yard and through a green door. The barn was half-full of bundles of dry bracken stalks. *'Allons,'* said Marcel, and began tearing with more frenzy than effect at the faggots on the right-hand side. 'Here.'

They began pulling the bundles away. After a couple of minutes the rear bumper of a vehicle emerged from the bracken.

'Hey,' said Miller. 'SAS, we love you.'

The vehicle was a Jeep, but not just any Jeep. There was no cocktail bar, and no sun lounge, but they were about the only amenities missing. Mounted in the rear were a pair of Brownings. There was another pair mounted on the hood in front of the passenger seat. The ammunition belts were still in place.

'Here are the other passengers now,' said Marcel. 'They have been in bed. Perhaps sleeping, perhaps not.' He made a sound that might have been a laugh.

Thierry, Hugues and Jaime lurched into the barn. Thierry's hat had a slept-in look. Hugues' eyes were snapping, and he was chewing his lips. He said, 'Where is Lisette?'

There was a spreading of hands and a shrugging of shoulders. Jaime said, 'She is tired. Sleeping. It is best we leave.' His face was grim. 'She has good false papers. She will be safe there.'

Perhaps he was right, thought Mallory. He had better be. There was no time to dig her out wherever she was resting. It was a hitch, but not a setback.

Hugues said, *'Non, merde –'*

'Jaime is right,' said Marcel. Another burst of Spandau fire sounded from the square. He looked as if he was going to cry. He said, 'Please. Be quick. Someone will talk.'

'Talk?'

'They are shooting people. One every ten minutes.' His face collapsed. He put his hands to his eyes.

Hugues said, 'For God's sake, be a man.'

Marcel looked at him vacantly. His cheeks were wet with tears. He said, 'The first person they shot was my mother.'

Hugues went red as blood, then pale.

'God rest her soul,' mumbled Andrea.

Mallory said, 'She has died that others may live. We thank you for her great courage. And yours.'

Marcel met his eye firmly. He said, '*Vive la France.*' He took a deep breath. 'For her sake, I ask that you complete your mission.'

'It will be done.'

He shook Mallory's hand. Andrea put his great paw on his shoulder.

Hugues said, 'I leave Lisette in your care.'

'I am honoured,' said Marcel. 'Now you must go. Then I can make them stop.'

'How?'

'I will tell the girls to say they saw you.'

'The girls?'

'They are friends with some of the Germans. The Germans who come to this brothel. That is why they leave us alone. Used to leave us alone. The Germans will not hurt the girls.'

Mallory said, 'How do we get out?'

'Drive ahead,' said Marcel. 'The entry is beyond the bracken.'

Hugues said, 'I must say goodbye to Lisette.'

'You must go,' said Marcel. 'Please.' He rummaged in a crate, came back with four bottles of Cognac. 'Take these. Go.'

'*Non,*' said Hugues, his voice rising. 'The child –'

He did not finish what he was going to say because Andrea had reached out a crane-hook hand and gripped his shoulder. Andrea said, 'Like this brave Marcel, you are a soldier,' and pushed him into the back of the Jeep.

Hugues said, shamefaced, 'Tell her I love her.'

Marcel nodded dumbly.

'Miller,' said Mallory. 'Drive on.'

'By the square?'

Mallory turned upon him his cool brown eyes. 'I think so,' he said. 'Don't you?'

The Jeep's engine started first time. They lifted Wallace into the back and climbed aboard as best they could. The engine sounded very loud in the confined space. It would sound very loud in the village, too; there were no other engines running in Colbis.

Miller slammed the Jeep into four-wheel drive. The engine howled as he stamped on the throttle. He let out the clutch. The Jeep plunged into the dried bracken, and kept on plunging. The brittle fronds piled up against the windscreen and spilled into the back. Miller saw daylight, and aimed for it. Covered in a haystack mound of bracken, the Jeep shot out of the barn doorway and into the lane, turned on two wheels, and turned right again. At the end of the lane was a slice of the square, with plane trees. In the slice of square, three SS men were crouched round a Spandau. 'Civilians keep down,' said Mallory, cocking the Brownings on the bonnet and flicking off the safety catches. 'Open fire.'

The Spandau gunners did not enjoy shooting innocent civilians. It was, frankly, a disagreeable duty, only marginally better than cleaning latrines. But *Befehl ist Befehl*. Orders are orders.

They were sitting there, ignoring the two clusters of bloody pockmarks on the church wall above the crumpled bodies of their first two victims, and concentrating on the third victim, the priest's housekeeper, a thin, slope-shouldered old woman, standing stiffly to attention in a flannel dressing gown. The machine gunners were looking grim and efficient, because they were dying for a smoke. The sooner they got this over with, the better –

From the back of the square came a clatter like a giant type-writer. Something hammered the Spandau into the air and sent it spinning, tripod and all, across the square. Ricochets whined into the sky. Two of the machine gunners performed sudden ragged acrobatics and fell down. The third had enough time to spin round and think, *machine-gun fire*, and see a haystack with four wheels howling out of an alleyway, the muzzle-flash of machine guns dancing in the hay, which seemed to be catching fire. Then a succession of hammers walloped the last gunner in the chest and his legs lost their strength and his mouth filled with blood. And as his head bounced limply on the pavé of the square he saw his comrades, drawn up in lines, start tumbling like corn before the scythe, and heard the *whoomp* of a petrol tank exploding.

Then the machine gunner's eyes grew dim, and he died.

Miller yanked the Jeep's steering wheel to the right. The main road out of the square gaped in front of him. The clatter of the Brownings was a mechanical thunder in his ears. Something was burning, with a smell that reminded him of burning tumbleweeds when he had worked a summer in the Kansas oil fields. It was not tumbleweed, of course. It was bracken, set on fire by the muzzle-flashes of the heavy machine guns. It was dry as tinder, that bracken. Mallory and Andrea were still firing short sharp bursts. Miller yelled, 'Get it off!'

From the square there came a higher, sharper crackle: rifle fire. A bullet spanged off the Jeep's suspension and moaned away skyward.

Mallory said, calmly, 'Fire low.'

A patrol of Germans had appeared in the road ahead. The Brownings thundered. More bullets cracked over the Jeep. Then the Germans were down, rolling, and the suspension was jouncing as the wheels went over the bodies. The street behind had vanished in a pall of grey-white smoke. The houses were thinning. The crackle of the bracken was a roar.

'Get rid of it!' yelled Miller.

Hugues' coat was smouldering as he unfolded himself from the bed of the Jeep. He was coughing, his eyes streaming. He began to kick blazing faggots of bracken onto the road. Jaime was doing it too, and Thierry, who was making small, frightened prodding movements, clearing his precious radio first.

'St-Jean-de-Luz,' said Mallory, over the slipstream. 'Which way?'

'Up the road,' said Jaime. 'Then there's a track.' He brushed burning bracken from his sleeve. '*Merde.*'

There were strips of blue sky between heavy squalls of cloud. The last of the bracken lay fuming in the road, receding fast. Ahead the pavé stretched, polished black and gently curving. It was the main road out of the valley. A road crawling with

Germans – Germans who would by now have found out by radio that a unit of the British army was on the loose in a Jeep. At least, Mallory hoped they would think they were a unit of the British army. That way, there might be no civilian reprisals.

But how had the Germans known to come to Colbis?

It seems quite possible that the Germans will, in a manner of speaking, be waiting for you.

Mallory said, 'Where were you hiding in the village?'

'They spread us round,' said Jaime. 'Me, I was in the brothel. In bed. In the most innocent way, of course.'

'But they searched the brothel.'

'My papers are in order,' said Jaime. His face was dark and closed. 'What have I to fear?'

Mallory nodded. Unanswered questions buzzed around his ears like flies.

'Left,' said Jaime.

Left was a track that turned off the main road, crept along the side of a mountain and into a wood. The Jeep ground through a deserted farmyard and onto a road of ancient cobbles.

'The back way,' said Jaime. 'Arrives close to St-Jean-de-Luz. The main road goes down the valley and joins the big road to St-Jean-de-Luz at the foot of the mountains. This one takes us over a hill, into a valley, then over another hill, and down to St-Jean. But it is only good for mule or Jeep. It's a small road. It doesn't run over the frontier, so the Germans don't pay much attention to it.'

They sat three in the front, four in the back. The SAS man was white, and his eyes were closed. When the Jeep hit a boulder, the muscles of his jaw tautened with pain. For an hour the Jeep moaned upwards into the mountains. Jaime and Hugues were talking quietly in French.

Suddenly, Hugues started shouting. His face was purple, contorted with rage. He got his fingers round Jaime's neck and his knees on his chest, and he picked the small man's head up and slammed it against the bodywork, and pulled it back, and was going to do it again when Andrea's hands closed, one on each arm, and, without apparent effort, detached his hands. Jaime rolled away, coughing and retching. Hugues struggled futilely in Andrea's grip, still shouting.

Mallory said, 'Shut up,' in a voice that cracked like a rifle bullet.

Hugues shut up.

'What's the problem?'

Hugues' eyes were the size of saucers. 'Lisette,' he said.

'What about her?'

'She's not in the village. She was supposed to be in the village, asleep. But not so. Jaime says he saw her. She was taken away. By a German in a leather overcoat. Gestapo.' He put his face in his hands.

Mallory's stomach was hollow with apprehension. He said, 'Is this true?'

Jaime's face could have been carved from yellowish stone. He said, 'It's true.'

Hugues sat up, suddenly. 'We must go to Bayonne,' he said. 'Immediately. Without delay. With the guns we have, the explosives, we can get into Gestapo HQ –'

Mallory said, 'How much does Lisette know about this operation?'

'She knows we are going to St-Jean,' said Hugues. 'But she will never talk.'

Jaime said, 'Everyone talks.'

'*Non!*' shouted Hugues, losing control.

'She is pregnant,' said Jaime. 'What do you think they will do to the child?'

Hugues' anger evaporated. He seemed to grow smaller. He covered his face with his hands.

Mallory said, 'How did this happen?'

Jaime looked straight ahead, his face without expression. 'I saw from the window of the *bordel*. She was led out. They put her in a big car, and drove away.'

'Why didn't you tell us earlier?'

'There is a thing we must do. The mother of Marcel has died for this thing. So has Jules, at Jonzère, and others. It is war. I kept quiet so our decision could not be . . . influenced.' He looked at Hugues, then back at Mallory. 'You would have done what I did.'

Hugues said, 'Only a monster –'

'Shut up,' said Mallory.

Of course Jaime was right. The object of the operation was to destroy submarines, not chase Gestapo cars across the northern foothills of the Pyrenees. By pretending that Lisette was in Colbis until she was definitely beyond help, Jaime had prevented a worse crisis.

Not that it could be much worse for Lisette.

Mallory tried not to think about what would be happening to Lisette. He said, 'She'll talk.'

'Not for two days,' said Jaime. 'That is the rule. She will hold out for two days to give us time to get clear.'

Thierry cocked his straw hat over his eye and delivered himself of an offensively cynical chuckle. 'The Germans know this also. They will be very persuasive.'

Hugues said, 'Jesus.' His face was grey and bloodless.

'But relax,' said Thierry. 'If the Gestapo ask the wrong question, they will get the wrong answer. How will they ask the right question?'

Mallory knew that in Gestapo HQ at Bayonne, there would be people who could make you beg to be allowed to tell them everything you knew, without a question being asked. He said to Hugues, 'There is nothing we can do. I really am very sorry.'

Hugues looked at him with haunted eyes. 'Old women have lived their lives,' he said. 'Soldiers protect their country. Who can use my unborn child as a weapon of war? What has this poor child done?'

Andrea said, 'These are questions you must ask a priest.' Mallory did not look at him. The Greek had found the bodies of his parents in the river at Protosami. They had been shot by Bulgarian soldiers, then lashed together and thrown to the fish. Andrea knew about total war. So had his parents' killers, until they had died, very suddenly and all at once. 'But the time for asking such questions is when the war is finished. For now, we must only obey orders and fight, because if we think, we go crazy.'

There was no more talking after that.

The Jeep ground on, up and over the mountain, away from

the great hazy prospect of the valley. Hugues had opened one of the bottles of brandy Marcel had loaded into the Jeep. His blue eyes turned pink and glassy. A shoulder of wooded hillside interposed itself between the road and the valley. The sun came out from between the shredded clouds. Flies buzzed round Wallace's bloody tunic. The track left the trees and wound across a marshy saddle between two peaks. High overhead, a pair of vultures hung in the blue. There were no Germans, no sign of the war raging out there in the world. As the road started downhill again, Dusty Miller saw a glittering blue line beyond a notch in the whaleback hills. The sea.

'Progress,' he said. 'And about goddamn time, too.'

But the road dipped down again, into the first rank of the chestnut forests, and the blue line disappeared. As the Jeep ground on downhill, Miller's spirits suffered the small but definite dip that with him passed for extreme gloom. They were nearing the coast at last. There was two-thirds of a tank of gas left in the Jeep. Keep on driving, and whatever happens will happen –

But there was a hell of a way to go, through Indian country, to a destination at best uncertain.

'One kilometre now, a big road,' said Jaime, rising from his gloomy silence like a diver from a lake. 'Road to the frontier. Patrolled, I guess.'

'We'll take it quietly,' said Mallory. 'Go on five hundred yards. Turn off the engine. Freewheel.'

The Jeep rolled down the track, silent except for the twang of its springs and the sniffing of Hugues. A light breeze sighed in the chestnuts. It was a beautiful spring morning, quiet except for the song of birds in the trees.

And the guttural voices that drifted up from the road.

Mallory tapped Andrea on the shoulder. The big Greek nodded. He jumped down from the Jeep and started down the track. His gigantic shoulders seemed to merge into the trees in a way not entirely attributable to the camouflage smock he wore. Watching him Hugues shivered, recalling the warm, padded but horribly powerful hands that had pulled him off Jaime as if he had been a light blanket.

His eyes slid to Jaime, to the stony face of the man who had

71

lost him Lisette. Sometimes, being a soldier was impossible.

He looked away. Looking at Jaime hurt his eyes.

Andrea moved down the track quickly and quietly. When he could see the dark glimmer of the road below him he cut into the trees, placing his feet carefully among the ferns and dry leaves. He passed through the forest with the faintest of rustles, more like a breeze than a twenty-stone human. At the edge of the trees, he stopped.

The road was pavé, the square, polished cobblestones of France. Twenty yards to his left was a sandbagged enclosure with a single embrasure from which projected the muzzle of a machine gun. Beside the enclosure, a bar painted in red-and-white stripes blocked off the road. The machine gun was pointing to the right, north, towards France, and, coincidentally, the stretch of road across which the Jeep would have to travel to rejoin the track on the far side, where it dived into the forests at the foot of a tall mountain plated with grey rock.

Andrea absorbed all of this in perhaps ten seconds, checking off a mental list of options. Then he walked quietly back into the trees and inside the wood along the side of the valley, passing above the checkpoint.

From above, he saw that the machine gun was unmanned. Its three-man crew and two other soldiers were lying on the grassy bank of the road, smoking. One of them was telling what Andrea recognised as a dirty joke he had overheard in the town at Navarone. Swiftly, he walked fifty yards through the wood, parallel to the road, in the general direction of Spain. Then he slung his Schmeisser across his stomach, pulled his helmet down over his eyes, and walked out onto the pavé.

At the sound of his boots, the men on the bank looked up. They saw the biggest Waffen-SS they had ever seen, moving light-footed towards them, eyes invisible under the helmet. They had never seen an SS man with a moustache before. Being honest Wehrmacht footsloggers, they did not like the SS, and they did not like moustaches. So the sergeant who had been telling the joke pretended not to see this one until he was on top of them. Then he looked up. 'What the hell do you want?' he said. 'A shave?'

*　　*　　*

The men in the Jeep on the hillside heard nothing. A thrush was singing. A pigeon crashed out of a chestnut tree. Otherwise, there was silence, a silence that reminded Mallory of the silence on the far side of an operating theatre door. Andrea would be doing his horrible worst. After five minutes, mingled with the thrush's song came the metallic cry of a Scops owl.

Mallory said, 'Drive.'

Miller started to drive. This time he used the engine, because there would be no enemies alive to hear it.

Andrea was waiting by the road, wiping a long, curved knife on a tuft of grass. On a grassy bank nearby, five men in grey uniforms were staring at the sky. There was a lot of red among the yellow and white flowers on which they lay. But it was too early for poppies.

Andrea clambered into the Jeep. Miller gunned the engine.

Up the road, a figure in field-grey stumbled out of the trees, buttoning his trousers. When he saw the Jeep, he shouted, 'Halt!'

Mallory straightened his helmet and gripped his Schmeisser. He said, 'I'll deal with him.' But the brandy Hugues had drunk was heating up his mind. The sky and the trees and the mountains were swimming. It was difficult, being a soldier, obeying orders. When it meant that this woman, the woman you loved, Lisette . . . her fingernails, he thought, her teeth. They pull them out with pliers. And the baby –

In the centre of his vision, something new was moving. Something grey. A German soldier.

Hugues knew he had made himself look foolish in front of these granite-faced soldiers. But in his mind was a newborn baby, and a man with a pair of pliers in his hand. He heard Lisette scream. Because the man was walking, not towards Lisette, but towards the baby –

The man who was a German, like the soldier.

Of course he would have to be killed. And it should be Hugues who killed him, to redeem himself in the eyes of the soldiers.

And suddenly there was a gun in his hand, and his finger was on the trigger, and the gun was jumping, and the air was full of the clatter of the Schmeisser.

The bullets went high. Somebody snatched the weapon out of

his hands. The soldier flung himself to the ground and rolled out of sight into the ditch. His rifle fired three times. The last shot smacked into the Jeep. 'Let's go,' said Mallory, quietly.

The Jeep roared across the road and up the track on the far side. After two hundred yards, Andrea said, 'Stop here.'

The Jeep stood at the bottom of a long, steep incline. Andrea swung his legs over the side. He plucked the Bren from the back seat, slung it over his shoulder as if it had been a twenty-bore shotgun, and loped away down the track.

He did not have far to go. This side of the valley was armoured with big, grey plates of limestone on which nothing grew. He found a slab that overlooked the road, cast himself flat behind it, and raised his head in time to see the field-grey figure scuttle like a rabbit into the horseshoe of sandbags that was the machine-gun emplacement. The emplacement was full of shadows, but Andrea knew what the man would be doing as surely as if he could see him. There would be a field telephone in there, and the man would be using it to call for reinforcements.

Carefully, Andrea trained the Bren on that shadow-filled horseshoe and adjusted the backsight one notch up. Then he fired four single shots into the lip of the sandbags, spacing them like the four pips on the four of spades. Then he stood up, quickly.

Down in the machine-gun emplacement, the shadow was punctured by something that might have been a grey tortoise, or a steel helmet. The man interrupted his telephone call to defend his life. Andrea watched the tin helmet move as the eyes searched for him. The eyes found him. The helmet became a human figure, struggling to haul the heavy machine gun round on its mount. Andrea watched clinically, without hatred. Should have stayed on the telephone, he thought, with the detached disapproval of a craftsman watching a bodger. Fatal mistake. The Bren's sight settled on the tin helmet. The huge finger squeezed the trigger.

The burp of the machine gun rolled round the cliffs and precipices of the valley. Down in the emplacement, the little figure flung its arms wide, jerked upright, fell over the sandbag parapet, and lay still. Even before the echoes had died, Andrea was striding back uphill.

He smelt petrol before he saw the Jeep. As he came over the

hill the other men were out of the vehicle. 'Problem solved,' said Andrea.

'We've got another problem,' said Mallory. Andrea noticed a curious woodenness in the faces round the Jeep. 'We've got a bullet in the petrol tank. Did your friend have time to contact his headquarters?'

'No way of telling,' said Andrea. 'Gas all gone?'

'All gone.'

Mallory, Miller and Jaime got behind the vehicle. Andrea lent his shoulder. The wheels started to roll. Miller twitched the wheel. The Jeep gathered speed, bounced on a boulder, and disappeared with a metallic crash into a ravine.

Thierry had been squatting by his radio, tinkering with the tuning dial. Mallory said, 'Radio silence from now on, please.'

Thierry nodded. He shouldered the pack. 'How far?'

'Twenty kilometres to the sea,' said Jaime. 'There is one ridge in between. A high ridge.'

Miller yawned and shouldered his brass-bound boxes. 'Nice to stretch your legs after a drive in the country.'

Andrea said, 'I'll help Mr Wallace.'

The SAS man was upright. His face was the colour of wood ash, with dark circles under his eyes. He said, 'I'm all right.'

Andrea said, 'Come,' and walked towards him, hands out.

Wallace raised his crutch and held it against Andrea's breast-bone. He said, 'I can manage.'

Andrea said, 'Sometimes it is the bravest man who surrenders.'

But Wallace was in a corner, his eyes hardening, getting that berserk look. He said, 'No SOE bastard tells me what brave men do.' His hand was going to the automatic in the holster at his side.

Andrea shrugged and turned away. For a moment his eyes caught Mallory's. There was no expression in them, but Mallory knew him well enough to see he was worried. They were on an island of limestone in a sea of Germans. There was more to worry about than regimental pride.

'Don't want you holding us up,' said Mallory.

The SAS man snapped, 'Nobody's going to hold you up.' He recollected himself. 'Sir.'

Mallory shrugged. 'Jaime first,' he said. 'March.'

They marched.

Things had improved, Mallory reflected.

There were too many of them, one of them was drunk, another wounded, and they had no transport. But they had a destination. That was the plus side.

On the minus side, there was a trail of dead Germans stretching back across the Pyrenees. But there was nothing to be done about that.

Except keep going.

The track climbed from the valley floor, rising steeply and trending northward. It was a good track, built for mules, with wide steps separated by six-inch copings of stone. The vegetation was sparse. The limestone plates lower in the valley continued, less broken up here, until they were walking up a dry gorge between huge, overhanging crags. Wallace plodded on, wincing at each grind of his crutch against rock, the flies buzzing and crawling round the blackened dressing on his belly.

At first it was hot. But the sun grew hazy behind veils of cirrus, and by eleven the sun had gone in and a black edge of cloud had crept across the sky. The adrenaline of the pursuit was gone, oxidised in the weariness of a night without sleep. Life was the slog against gravity, one foot in front of the other, up the interminable mule-steps along the dry valley towards a horizon that always gave way to another, higher horizon. Jaime moved at the steady, straight-legged pace of the mountaineer. Thierry plodded on under the weight of the radio, sweat running down his great jowls, darkening the collar of his shirt and the band of his straw hat. Hugues let his head roll on his neck, stumbled a lot, and would not speak when spoken to. And Wallace kept struggling grimly on, crutch grinding on the stones, face contorted with pain and effort.

By noon it was cold and spitting with rain. Another front was coming in from the Atlantic. Mallory said, 'How far to the top?'

'One hour,' said Jaime. He squinted his small black eyes at the lowering clouds. 'Soon we will need shelter.'

'Why?'

'Snow,' said Jaime. 'I know a cave.'

'No more caves,' said Mallory. 'We must go on.'

'This is a . . . particular cave,' said Jaime. 'Twenty minutes more.'

'Particular?'

'There will be a storm,' said Jaime. 'For now, we should save our breath for the road.'

'On,' said Mallory. 'Twenty minutes.'

There was a crash and a clatter. Wallace had fallen. He was not moving. Andrea squatted by his side, hand on his forehead. He looked up at Mallory. His face, normally unreadable, was worried. 'Fever,' he said.

'Can you carry him?'

'Of course.' Andrea picked the SAS man up, slung him over his shoulder, and began to march. The rain started, then stopped again. The cloud was still high, but patches of dirty mist were hanging in the crags, and the air was damp and raw on their faces.

The floor of the gorge rose until they were walking on a bare slope of limestone. It steepened to forty-five degrees. Mallory could hear Andrea's breathing.

'At the top,' said Jaime.

At the top of the slope was a cliff. In front of the cliff was a little plateau that narrowed into a curious little gully, like a gorge in embryo. The gully went back into the cliff, steep-sided, and ended abruptly in a tangle of boulders.

'In here,' said Jaime. 'Behind the rocks.'

Mallory paused at the top of the slope, listening to the breath in his throat, the pound of the blood in his ears.

And another sound.

'Get into the cave,' he said. 'Quick.'

They began to run, slithering on the loose flakes of limestone that carpeted the ground. They had all heard it: the steady drone of an aeroplane engine.

They were not going to make it to the cave. 'Down!' roared Mallory.

They fell on their faces between the boulders. The droning intensified. The Fieseler Storch observation plane came slowly up the path. Between two boulders, Mallory was close enough to see the glint of the observer's binoculars as the plane circled over the little plateau.

The Storch flew on, down the other side of the mountain. Slowly and with great effort, the Storm Force dragged itself into the cave.

The entrance was little more than a crack in the rock, but inside it became a room-sized chamber, with a floor of broken stones and goat droppings, and a ceiling that faded upwards into shadow. The walls were smooth, as if they had been worn by water. There was no water now, except for a few drips from the roof. A cold draught blew from the inside of the cave, bearing the musty smell of stone.

Thierry said, 'Did they see us?'

Mallory shrugged out of his pack. 'No way of telling,' he said. 'Twenty minutes. Then we move on.'

Andrea caught Mallory's eye, and slipped back out of the entrance.

'If they had seen us, they would have turned back the way they had come, and made their report.' Thierry's eyes were anxious under the brim of the straw hat. 'Do you not think?'

'Sure,' said Mallory, not because he was sure, but to keep him quiet. 'Food.' He began rummaging in his pack, pushing out cans of sardines and blocks of chocolate.

'Brew up?' said Miller.

'Not yet,' said Mallory casually. 'Take a look at Wallace, would you?'

Wallace was lying on the stony floor. Andrea had put a pack under his head. The flesh had fallen away from his face, so the nose and cheekbones looked as if they would burst through the skin. He seemed to radiate a dry heat. His eyes were open, but were dull and glazed. 'Hurts,' he said.

Miller crouched at his side. 'Just a little prick,' he said. 'As the actress said to the bishop.' He pushed a morphine syrette into the ice-white skin of the SAS man's dangling upper arm. Wallace moaned and stirred, and said something in a high, incomprehensible voice. Then his eyes closed. Miller unbuttoned the tunic and started to unwrap the bandages on the stomach.

When he had unwrapped them he sat very still for a moment,

face immobile. Then he lit a cigarette and took a deep, soothing drag.

The wound was by no means soothing. It was a crater on the right-hand side of the belly; a crater puffed at the edges to an unhealthy redness that shaded to yellow. A faint odour rose from it, the smell of a meat-safe the morning after a hot night. And that was only the outside. It looked as if the bullet had been travelling from right to left. It had passed behind the abdominal muscles. It was still in there, somewhere. Miller had no means of finding out what damage it had done, and very little inclination to do so.

He rummaged in his first-aid box and pulled out a can of sulfa powder. He sprinkled a heavy dusting on the entrance hole, and applied fresh dressings. While Andrea held Wallace up, he rebound the bandages so it looked neat and white and tidy.

Mallory said, 'How is he?'

Miller lit a new cigarette from the stub of the old one. 'Could be lucky,' he said, without conviction.

'Nothing you can do?'

'You can sit there with your mouth open and wonder how the hell he managed to climb a three-thousand-foot mountain,' he said. 'Otherwise, I've packed it with sulfa. I may also pray a little.'

Mallory nodded. The weeks of effort were telling on Miller. His eyes were sunk deep in his head, and they held a manic gleam. Miller had always had an over-developed sense of humour, but now it was developing an edge colder than bayonet steel.

'But I tell you something,' said Miller. 'If he can climb with a stomach like that, he can probably bloody well fly as well.' He rummaged in his pack, pulled out a can of sardines and ate the fish in concentrated silence, using a knife.

Mallory sat down, let his aching limbs relax, and ate some sardines of his own. He was exhausted. Forty-eight hours from now, the Werwolf pack was due to sail. They were going to have to keep moving.

But if they left Wallace, he would die.

Drowsily, he debated with himself. They had already left Lisette. Why not leave Wallace?

If the Storch had spotted them, they would find him here. And he would talk.

Mallory found himself dozing. He sat up quickly, took a Benzedrine out of his pack and swallowed it.

Hugues was nodding over his bottle of brandy. Mallory leaned over and took it out of his hand. He washed the pill down with a fiery gulp and passed the bottle on to Jaime. Andrea was going to have to carry Wallace.

He looked around the grey, cheerless shadows. Andrea was not there. He would be standing sentry. Mallory climbed stiffly to his feet and went to the mouth of the cave.

The gully stretched away like a corridor roofed with sky. In the ten minutes they had been inside, the roof had become lower, changed from black to soft grey. And from out of the grey, whirling on the eddies of a bitter wind, there floated billions of snow-flakes. Already the outlines of boulders in the gully were melting and fusing under the chill, white blanket. Of Andrea there was no sign.

Jaime appeared at his side. He said, 'Now only one small hill to the sea.'

'How far?'

'Twelve kilometres.'

'It's snowing.'

'Not down below. Snow up here, rain down below.' Jaime laughed. The brandy had given his eyes a mischievous glitter. 'We can go the inside way, if you want.'

'What do you mean?'

Jaime took his arm, led him back into the cave, and pointed at its shadowy inner recesses. 'Once this was where a river came out of the cliff. The river is still in there, but it has found new ways out. Now it arrives in the valley close to the Hendaye road. And in other places, they say, it springs from the hill. I once met a man, Norbert Casteret, who told me he had walked inside this mountain. He was a great bore. In great detail he told me: shafts, waterfalls, and the rest.'

'Fascinating,' said Mallory. The Benzedrine was making his ears ring in the intense, snow-muffled silence. There was only Wallace's stertorous breathing, and the drip of water from the cave

80

roof. And now that Jaime came to mention it, something else, something more a vibration than a sound, as if far away, something hugely powerful was roaring and thundering. A waterfall, for instance.

Mallory's muscles tensed and his palms sweated. Caves and water ... Not fear, he told himself. Only the Benzedrine. He looked at his watch. They had been here fifteen minutes. Time they were moving on. He said to Jaime, 'Moving out in three minutes. The outside route.'

Hugues and Thierry groaned, stretching their cold-stiffened limbs. Miller gathered his pack and his precious boxes. Mallory shouldered his own pack and his weapons. He went once again to the mouth of the cave and down the gully, and looked onto the little plateau. It was empty, except for snowflakes. Where the hell was Andrea?

Then something moved in the snow: a giant moustache, and a pair of black eyebrows that grew larger. Mallory realised that he was looking at Andrea; Andrea wearing a white snow smock, carrying the Bren.

Andrea said, 'My Keith, we have a German patrol.' He spoke calmly, but he was moving fast.

Mallory's ears sang in the silence. 'How many?'

'Perhaps thirty.'

At the edge of the plateau, a ragged line of dark shapes was materialising in the snow. The shapes of German soldiers. And with the soldiers, other shapes, from which came the sound of whining and baying.

Dogs.

There was no point in trying to draw the men away from the cave: the dogs would not be distracted, even if the handlers were.

Andrea stared at him. He said, 'I'll go up the hill and draw them off.'

'No,' said Mallory. He hated saying it. But the dogs would not be drawn. 'Back to the cave.'

Andrea said, 'But the cave is a trap.'

'There's a back entrance.'

One of the figures in the snow shouted. The line stopped.

Andrea sighed, and took aim with the Bren. The machine gun's stammer fell flat in the soft white world. One of the figures buckled and collapsed.

Mallory slid back into the gully. The Schmeisser chattered in his hands as Andrea fell back past him. Bullets smashed rocks above his head. He felt stone-chips sting his cheek, and the trickle of blood. He was moving back towards the cave mouth, Andrea firing past him, covering him. As he arrived at the cave mouth, four figures in field-grey appeared at the end of the gully.

Suddenly, Mallory and Andrea were inside the cave, and Mallory's Schmeisser was bucking in his hands again. Next to him, Andrea was fumbling in his belt. His arm came over, and a grenade was tumbling through the air like a little dark egg, bursting with a big, flat *slam* in the mouth of the gully. There were screams. But there were a lot of bullets coming in now, spanging off the cave mouth and zipping into the dark interior.

The Benzedrine was chewing away in Mallory's mind. *How did they find us?* Dogs. Or the Storch. It did not matter. Either they broke out now, or the patrol would call up reinforcements. Reinforcements were probably on the way already.

Outside, there was a big, steady hammering, and the entrance droned with stinging shards of stone. Reinforcements or no reinforcements, there was at least one heavy machine gun out there. Mortars next.

Mallory thought about what a mortar bomb would do in the mouth of the cave. He saw the air full of razor-sharp chunks of steel and the shrapnel of blasted rock, the ceiling falling in –

The ceiling falling in.

'Miller,' he said. Miller came. Mallory spoke to him. Miller nodded, trotted back into the shadows.

Mallory called over his shoulder. 'Jaime. The exit?'

'Found it,' said Jaime.

Oh, God.

Andrea was crouching behind a boulder. He caught Mallory's eye. His face was the same old face, large and impassive above the sweeping black moustache. But there was something about the set of the big, unshaven jaw that shocked Mallory. Andrea had walked alone from Greece to Bulgaria, through the heart of occupied *Mitteleuropa*. He was a full colonel in the Greek army, and with that army had suffered defeat. With him, Mallory had spent eighteen months behind German lines in Crete, stared death right between the eyes on Navarone and in the Zenica Cage. But in all that time, Mallory had never seen this expression on his face. Up here, five thousand feet above sea level, in a dank cave near the summit of this tilted sheet of limestone, Andrea's face was . . . *resigned*.

Mallory found that his muscles were tense as boards, and in his mind something was scrambling and scuttling, like a terrified animal. He made himself think of the Channel covered with ships, the ships crammed with men, and among them giant submarines swimming swiftly, undetectable, laden with torpedoes. A Spandau burst punched into the cave wall above his head.

He said to Andrea, 'Jaime has found the back way.'

Andrea's face relaxed. Resignation gave way to the expression that with Andrea conveyed anything from polite curiosity to frenzied enthusiasm. 'Then we should take it,' he said. 'Soon.'

Four minutes later Miller was alone, standing among the boulders at the back of the cave. The entrance was a narrow white window, pointed at the top. The rest of it was dark, black as ink, in contrast to the glare of the snow outside.

Miller filled his eyes with that glare, and tried for three seconds not to think about anything but daylight, and sky. But his right hand was chilled by the stone-flavoured draught blowing from the crack in the cave floor on his right – the crack down which his companions had vanished, and down which he must vanish himself, now that his preparations were complete –

A sleet of bullets lashed through the entrance, and the air was deafening with ricochets. The snow beyond the entrance was suddenly peopled with grey figures, running, firing as they came. Miller fired a burst of his Schmeisser into that brilliant white lancet. Then he lowered himself into the crack, and started to climb down the doubled rope into the dark.

The first two Germans flattened themselves against the walls outside the entrance. They pulled the string fuses on two stick grenades, and flung them into the cave mouth. There was a hollow *boom*, and smoke rolled out. There was no sign of life from the black interior. They threw in two more grenades, to make sure, and waited for the bang.

They did not get it.

What they got was a thunderous roar, and a sheet of flame that lashed out of the entrance and melted the snow for fifty feet, and picked up the men who had thrown the grenades and fired them like cannonballs out of the gully and onto the plateau, where they lay under a sheet of rock fragments that fell out of the sky like hard rain. Where the cave had been was a raw cleft in the mountainside, half-filled with fuming scree.

'*Gott*,' said the Feldwebel. 'What are they putting in the grenades, nowadays?'

'Whatever it is, it's done the job,' said the Sturmbannführer. 'Now pick up those men and for God's sake let us get out of this snow.'

Miller was twenty feet down the crack when the big explosion came. A blast of hot air frizzled his eyebrows and the doubled rope in his hands became two separate ropes. He thought, in one compressed moment: one kilo of plastic with a thirty-second time pencil will not only blow up a limestone cave, but cut a wire-cored climbing rope.

Then he had landed with a crash on wet stone, and a big pain in his leg was filling the world, and dust was in his lungs, and stone was falling on his head.

He became aware that he was lying in a place lit by yellow torch light, and that the stones falling on his head were small, and the pain in his leg was ebbing. Bruised, not broken, he thought. He groped for a cigarette in the breast pocket of his blouse, and lit it. The smoke rose vertical in the torch light. Before, there had been a draught.

He said, 'Looks like the roof fell in.'

'Quite,' said Mallory, in a voice perhaps a shade lighter than usual. 'Thank you, Dusty.'

And now all we have to do is get out of here, thought Miller, and find some submarines.

Mallory lit a cigarette himself. The entrance to the shaft had been narrow – almost too narrow for Andrea. Down here it had widened out. It was better down here, as long as you did not think of all those billions of tons of rock around you, the dynamited entrance –

His heart was going like a rivet gun. He could hardly breathe for all that rock up there, sitting on his chest –

Panic later, he told himself. Once you have done the job. For now, there are six men depending on you. The Benzedrine made that sound like a good thing. He took a deep breath. 'Flashlights off,' he said. 'Use one at a time, only when moving.' The light went out. Darkness descended, thick and suffocating as wet velvet. 'Jaime,' he said. 'Your friend Casteret. What did he tell you?'

'It was two years ago,' said Jaime.

'Try to remember.'

There was a pause, in which he could almost hear the wheels spinning in Jaime's brain. 'He entered the cave,' he said. 'The shaft. A river. He said there are many passages: the river made one way out, then found a way to another, lower down, then another. So the mountain is full of holes like a Gruyère, some blocked, some flooded. There is a route, because Casteret found it. But it took him many days.'

'That's it?'

'That's it.'

Many days. In this darkness. Mallory could hear his own breathing, very loud. 'So if we head downhill, we can't go far wrong.'

'Maybe,' said Jaime.

'Very good,' said Mallory. 'I'll lead. Hugues and Andrea, carry Wallace.'

They made a sort of sedan chair out of a couple of webbing straps and Wallace's crutch. Mallory stood up, flexing his stiff limbs. He turned on his flashlight.

It began.

The beam of the flashlight showed a water-smoothed gallery heading steeply downwards. It was high, the gallery, so high in places that the flashlight failed to touch its roof. Once, it had been a runnel of acid rainwater, dissolving its way through a seam of limestone. The water had gone now, leaving a bed of grey pebbles down which they walked as if down the gravel drive of a house in the suburbs of hell.

They went two hundred yards like this, downwards at an angle of perhaps forty degrees, heading west by Mallory's compass. Then the gallery took a turning to the right.

Mallory was pointing the flashlight down at the ground. Suddenly there were two flashlight beams, one where he was pointing it, and another on the roof of the gallery, which was low here. The reason that it was on the roof was that it was being reflected by the black pool that spanned the gallery from side to side before it sloped down into the water.

Dead end.

Mallory's heart was thumping in his ears. In front of them, the roof ran down into the water. Behind them, the cave was sealed.

Trapped.

Dusty Miller saw the flashlight stop. He heard the drip of water, the rasp of the stretcher-bearers' breath. He remembered the panic-stricken rigidity of Mallory in the bread oven. He fumbled in his breast pocket, and lit a cigarette.

'For Christ's sake,' said Hugues, in a voice a good octave too high. 'You will use up the air.'

'Plenty of air,' said Miller, languidly, for Mallory's benefit. 'There used to be a howling draught up that shaft, remember?' He heard Mallory grunt, as if he did not trust himself to speak.

'And this is a most commodious cave by cave standards. Did I ever tell you about the time I was working the Go Home Point amethyst mine back in Ontario? Little tiny shaft, and we get a flash flood. So there is me, a half-ton of dynamite, and as it turns out a rabid skunk, one hundred foot under the Canadian Shield, and that sucker is filling up quicker'n a whore's bidet –'

'Some other time,' said Mallory.

Miller could hear his voice was back to normal. 'Sure,' he said. 'Well, seems to me there must be some place above that water for all that air to have been coming from, before we blew the cave.' He took a last drag on his cigarette. It made a bright shower of sparks as he threw it away. 'So it ain't the air we have a problem with, it's the cigarettes, and I guess they need smoking right up, because I have a feeling I am going to get real wet.' He walked forward, eyeing the swim of the flashlight beam in the water and unbuttoning his tunic.

'Take a rope,' said Mallory.

'Sure.'

Miller's body was long and pale, corded with stringy muscle in the dimness. He tied the rope round his waist in a bow line, took the waterproof flashlight in his hand, and stepped into the pool.

The water was so cold it burned. He set his teeth and walked on. The gravel under his feet sloped down sharply, continuing the forty-five degree slope of the cave's floor. Within three paces the water was up to his chest, and he was gasping for breath. Within four, he was swimming, the coldest swimming he had ever done. He swam hard, hoping that he was right, that there was a way through here, between the gallery roof and the water, for the draught to blow –

But perhaps the draught had come from somewhere else, a hole in the rock high in the roof, invisible. Perhaps this was a blind-ended hole, deep as the mountain was high, full of this icy water.

What a way to go, thought Miller. Drowning in mineral water. I promise that if I get out of this, I will never drink anything but brandy again.

He clamped the flashlight between his teeth and dived.

Back on the gravel beach Mallory saw the light fade in the dark water, then vanish. He tried not to think of the cold under there, the pressing down of the roof, the ridges of stone that could catch you and keep you under there while you drowned, in the middle of miles of rock –

But the coils of rope moved slowly through his fingers and into the water. Miller was making progress –

The rope became still.

He's in the air again, Mallory told himself.

But the rope remained still for a minute, then two. Mallory's mind told him that it was normal, there was an explanation. But deep down, that creature was raving at him: he's stuck, he's drowned, for Christ's sake –

Mallory found he had seized the rope and was tugging at it, hauling for all he was worth, and the bight of it was thrashing the black pool. Andrea was at his side, saying something soothing, but he could not hear what –

And suddenly a flashlight clicked on, and a voice said, 'Colder 'n the nipple on a witch's tit in there.' Miller's voice.

For a second, Mallory felt deep shame.

'It's like the bend in your toilet bowl,' said Miller. 'There's a little uphill the far side, stalagmites, stalactites, the whole shebang. I put the rope on a stalactite. Or 'mite, whichever. Anyways, it's cold and wet, but once you get to the other side you can breathe.'

Mallory put the shame behind him. There was a lot to do, and he needed a clear mind to do it with.

Miller wrapped his battledress in his waterproof cape, and went back through the icy water. The rest of them came after him, one by one, dragged under the low roof, breath held, clothes and weapons wrapped against the water, Andrea bringing up the rear. On the far side, they stood and shivered in the tomb-like cold. Wallace was the most worrying. 'Work your arms,' said Mallory. 'Circulation.'

Wallace raised his arms weakly, let them fall again. Miller bent over him, tugging his tunic over his arms. He was too weak to dress himself. 'Physical jerks,' he said, and tried to grin. Even the grin suffered from lack of muscle power.

They sat and drank soup brewed on a pressure stove, and checked their weapons. Miller put his oil can down by the edge of the water, and went over the lock of his Schmeisser with a corner of pullthrough. When he had finished the gun, he looked down again at the oil can.

It had been six inches from the water's edge. Now the water's edge was lapping against its base.

Up in the world, there was wet snow and rain. Down here in the underworld, the waters of the earth were rising.

Best not tell Mallory.

After five minutes, Mallory stood up. 'Okay,' he said. 'We're off.'

The gallery ran downhill again. There were a couple more pools, neither of them more than waist-deep. Hugues marched through the blackness head down, hands in pockets, shoulder aching under the pressure of Wallace's crutch. When he brushed against

Wallace's hand it felt cold as marble. It was obvious to Hugues that this man was going to die. Why carry him, when they had abandoned Lisette? It was folly, madness. Hugues was a soldier. He accepted that in war there were sacrifices to be made. But some things were too precious to sacrifice. Like the life of the woman you loved, and your unborn child. Deep under the mountain, Hugues was making promises to himself. If I live, he was thinking, things will be different. From now on, I will take care of the things I can see and touch with my own eyes and hands. From now on, it is not the big causes I will fight for. From now on, it will be the people I love.

If there is a from now on.

The brandy throbbed in his head. He marched on, detesting Mallory and Miller and this Greek killer Andrea, their cold, sunken eyes, the hard jokes they made, the way they did not care about individual people, thought only of their operation –

Andrea's boot trod on his heel. He was out of step, stumbling, panting for breath, the blood roaring in his ears.

Not just the blood.

Ever since they had been inside the mountain, the air had been tremulous with a faint rumble. Now the rumble was gaining in intensity. At first it was a long, uniform growl. Then the growl had become a roar that shook the ground underfoot and vibrated in the still air of the gallery. After perhaps a mile the gravel underfoot had become finer, and the ground had started to rise. At the top of a low mound the gallery was suddenly blocked by a wall of rock.

The beam of Mallory's flashlight wavered up the wall to a crack of darkness at its summit. The crack was a foot wide, the roar as loud as a bomber's engines. He put a foot on the wall and began to climb.

It was only twenty feet high, but running water had smoothed away the footholds. It took him a careful five minutes to get to the top. And when he did, he wished he had not.

When he put his head through the crack, the thunder of falling water was like a hand that grabbed his head and shook it. He shone his torch into the darkness. The beam lanced into emptiness. He put his head into the racket, and looked down.

Once, the wall must have been the sill of a waterfall. Now the river had found a lower channel, and the place where the waterfall had been was now a cliff, smooth as ivory, falling away below beyond the reach of his flashlight beam, plummeting like a gigantic mine shaft into the bowels of the earth. From the depths rose the bellow of falling water, and a fine mist of spray that chilled Mallory's face.

Curiously, this hellish hole in the world made Mallory feel better. It might be underground, and dark as the inside of a bank safe. But it was an open space; a problem that with a small stretch of the imagination could be regarded as a problem in mountaineering.

Mallory called for Miller and Andrea. They looked over the edge, and went back to the bottom of the sill. Miller said, 'Holy cow,' in a voice not altogether steady.

'We've got two ropes,' said Mallory. 'I'm going to put them together, double. If I find anything useful, I'll pull twice. Send Wallace down first. You'll have to show the other three how to rappel.'

'Ideal place to learn,' said Miller.

Mallory knotted the first two ropes together, slung the last coil over his shoulder, and went over the edge.

The wall was as smooth as it looked: no purchase for feet. He kept his weight well out, rope over shoulder and up between his legs, walking down the wall. By the time he came to the first knot he was walking in complete darkness. Miller's flashlight was a faint yellow glow far above. The roar of water surrounded him like a thunderstorm. He unclipped his own flashlight and shone it downwards.

Sixty feet below, the beam met something black and gleaming, muscular as the back of a giant slug. For a moment he could not work out what it was. Finally, the truth filtered through. It was a waterfall. A river, a big river, was pouring out of a ragged hole in the side of the shaft, tumbling down into a blackness too deep for the flashlight to penetrate. The roar numbed his mind. He saw a sudden picture of himself suspended like a spider on a string of gossamer, hung in this dreadful shaft. He blanked it out.

The shaft would have been a pothole: a whirlpool a million

90

years old, a spinning auger of carbonic acid sinking its way slowly into the limestone. After the river had gnawed its way down a hundred and fifty feet, it had joined forces with another seam of water, and adopted its course as its own. The new waterfall emerged to his left, almost at right angles to the wall he was descending.

There should be a ledge. Where the old waterfall had been supplanted by the new, there should definitely be a ledge.

He knew he must be getting to the bottom of the second rope. The wall was still smooth. To his left, he could feel the wind of the down-rushing water, falling God knew where. The spray of it had soaked him to the skin. He felt cold and weak. What if there was no ledge, only this smooth wall falling direct to the bottom?

Something touched his back. He almost shouted with the shock. He was lying on his back on a ledge. He shone his flashlight. The ledge was four feet wide, twenty feet long, piled with boulders, crusted white with limy deposits, and shining with water. When he shone his light over the edge, he still saw nothing. There was only the black water rushing past with its mind-numbing roar.

He pulled the rope twice, hard. Then he sat with his back against the wall, and shivered, and gnawed some chocolate.

Wallace came down first, lowered by Andrea. Then there were two loads of packs and weapons and radios, then Thierry and Hugues. Somehow, Thierry had kept his hat. Hugues had had a bad descent: there was blood on his face. Then there were Jaime and Miller, who Mallory imagined would be swearing vigorously, and finally Andrea, leaping down the wall like a huge cat.

When they were all down, Mallory stood up, flexed his aching fingers, looped the ropes over a lime-cemented boulder, and went over the edge again.

This time it was easier. There were footholds, of a sort. Twenty feet after the halfway mark he entered a place where his flashlight, instead of making a yellow disc on black water, created a sort of white halo, as if in fog. The noise was more like an avalanche than a waterfall. There was wind, too, irregular flumes of draught that splattered limestone-tasting water in his face. And suddenly he was standing on dry land again.

This time it was not a ledge. This time the plunging roar of water told him that he was at the base of the waterfall, standing on a beach.

He tugged the rope twice. Then he flicked the flashlight on again, and began to grope his way round the beach. It was a broad horseshoe of broken boulders surrounding a thrashing pool of water. The waterfall must have been twenty feet across and ten feet thick, a solid column of water plunging down two hundred feet and hammering the pool to froth. The pool itself had a circular motion, like a giant bath plug –

Mallory's heart thudded unpleasantly in his chest. He walked round the piled boulders to one margin of the waterfall. Then he went all the way back round, as far as the other margin.

If he had expected anything, it had been that the river would turn horizontal at the base of the waterfall, and make its way out through the side of the mountain. But there was no horizontal passage.

The shaft was a tube. The reason the water in the pool was spinning like a bath plug was because it was finding the way out, as water will . . .

Straight down.

Mallory sat on a boulder. Carefully, he fished in his blouse pocket for the oilcloth bag with his cigarettes and lighter. He put a cigarette in his mouth, and lit it.

The draught blew the lighter out. He relit it, but the cigarette was soaked.

Soon, the others began to land on the beach. Mallory's flashlight was dim yellow, the batteries gone. It went out. He flicked his lighter. The petrol caught.

The draught blew it out again.

He sat down, and concentrated on shivering.

Miller came down third, after Wallace, with his eyes shut, cursing. For a man who loathed and despised heights, it struck him that he had been doing an unfair quantity of mountaineering these past few weeks. When he reached the beach, he moved away from the base of the rope; having avoided death by falling, he had no desire to be flattened by a plummeting Frenchman. A gleam of yellow light showed him where Mallory was sitting. Miller flicked on his own flashlight. He was on his last set of batteries. He saw what Mallory had seen: there were no exits. He shivered, too. The reason he shivered was because of the wind –

The wind.

He flashed his torch at Mallory. Mallory's face looked pinched and white. He looked like a man who had wrestled for a long time with a monster, and had discovered that despite his best efforts the monster was not yet dead.

Two packs arrived down the rope. Miller flicked his torch over them, and onto Wallace. Wallace's face had the corpse-look, grey and sunken, but he raised a hand. Miller let the torch beam slide over his bandages. The wound did not seem to be bleeding any more.

Miller suddenly stopped thinking about Wallace. The beam of his flashlight had touched the margin of the water. Five minutes ago, there had been a brick-sized stone by Wallace's foot. Now there was no stone.

Not that the stone had gone – brick-sized stones do not evaporate. What had happened was that the stone was under water.

The water was still rising.

It was not a military problem. But then Miller was not in any strict sense of the word a military person. In fact, having enlisted in the RAF and been posted to the cookhouse, he had simply walked away from his unit; not out of cowardice, but because he wanted to use his talents somewhere they could damage the enemy, not potatoes. He had been astonished when someone had informed him that this constituted desertion. But by then he had been behind enemy lines, causing Rommel severe headaches as a member of the Long Range Desert Force. And nobody had got round to court-martialling him.

But as he stood on that black and shrinking beach, Miller was thinking of a time before the Long Range Desert Force. It was not a time he was particularly proud of, but it was a time when he had caused the maximum possible mayhem using the minimum possible resources.

It had been during Prohibition. For reasons best left undiscussed, even with himself, Miller had found himself in Orcasville, a small white clapboard town on the southern shore of Lake Ontario. It was into Orcasville's pier that a Canadian bootlegger called Melvin Brassman was wont to bring his cargoes of hooch. None of which would have posed any problems for Miller, except that Brassman's boys were causing a lot of trouble in the town, culminating in the rape of three girls, one of them the minister's daughter, and the burning of the warehouses of two merchants Brassman saw as rivals. Having committed these acts of mayhem, Brassman's men had let it be known that any rival rumrunners would be treated as hostile, rammed, and sunk by the steel ex-tug *Firewater*, in which they plied their trade.

It was Brent Kent, one of the burned-out merchants, who had called in Miller, then dynamiting pine stumps in the Finger Lakes region. Kent had laid his problem before Miller, stressing the need for a swift, untraceable, no-blame vanishment of the *Firewater*. There were no explosives in the town, or at least none that could not be traced.

But Miller was more than a demolitions man. Miller was a practical chemist.

Miller had taken possession of an old but superficially sea-worthy steam barge, which he had enigmatically christened *Krakatoa*. He had painted the exterior a pleasing royal blue, and let it be known that he was off to Canada to pick up a cargo of hooch. With great puffings and clankings, he and the *Krakatoa* had set off from the Orcasville quay. Just out of sight of land he had stopped the engine, and waited. After twelve hours, he had attended to the *Krakatoa*'s real cargo.

This consisted not of liquor, but several dozen barrels of tallow, and a similar number of carboys of sulphuric and nitric acids. Descending to the deck of the hold with an axe, Miller staved in the tallow barrels. Then, carefully, he uncorked the acid carboys and let their contents gurgle into the barge's ancient wooden bilges. After that, he rowed clumsily away in a dinghy, and was collected by the mayor in his catboat. When they arrived ashore, Miller was observed to be the worse for liquor, bragging in a foolish manner about the large quantity of Canadian whiskey bobbing at anchor offshore, which, landed at nightfall, would wreck the Brassman booze market for good and all.

These braggings swiftly reached the ears of Brassman's Orcas-ville lieutenant, who made certain long-distance telephone calls. That night, a night of full moon, the *Firewater*, steaming out of the north, saw the low silhouette of the *Krakatoa* at anchor, and took anticompetitive action. The *Krakatoa* was known to be rotten. The *Firewater* screwed down her regulator, achieved ramming speed, and ran her down.

What the *Firewater*'s master had not bargained for was Dusty Miller. When Dusty had rowed away, the barge had exuded a sour smell and a greenish chemical cloud. Now, twelve hours later, the acids swilling in her hold had compounded with the fatty fractions of the tallow, and formed a new substance.

So the rotting wooden barge into which the *Firewater*'s bow had knifed at twelve knots was not a rum ship. It was a rotting wooden barge that contained ten tons of impure and highly unstable nitro-glycerine.

The explosion that vaporised the *Firewater* also broke most of the windows in Orcasville, and woke the Mayor of Toronto eighty miles away. Miller left town the following morning, and the town reglazed. There was no further trouble from Melvin Brassman.

Hugues came down the rope. He saw by the dim and pearly light of a single torch that the American, Miller, had gone off to a section of beach opposite the waterfall, a section where, to judge by the boulders piled up against the face of the cliff, there had been a rockfall of some kind. Hugues shivered in the chill wind that was blowing from the direction of the rockfall: a wind that reminded him of the outside world. *Merde*, thought Hugues, gazing into the dark. This is not a war in which anything will be solved. And certainly not by these stupid old men who have brought me to the bottom of this well to die.

The light at the other side of the pool seemed to become suddenly animated, bobbing like a drunken firefly. He stared at it dully. Someone was walking, running, *racing* towards him. A hard body whacked him off his rock and onto the wet ground, and he was struggling, indignant, his mouth full of limy pebbles, while a voice, Miller's voice, bellowed over the thunder of the fall, 'Cover your ears!'

Suddenly, Hugues was given a vision. The shaft became a vast tube of grey rock, the waterfall a silver column falling out of a sky roofed with more rock, every ridge and ledge and pebble razor-sharp, illuminated by a huge flash of light. The noise of the water was momentarily replaced by a new noise, so loud as hardly to resemble a noise at all.

It was the noise of the five pounds of gelignite that Dusty Miller had packed into the rockfall at the point where the draught had been strongest.

When the rock fragments had ceased to fall Miller walked back across the beach, and examined the scene of the explosion. It was a neat job, though he said it himself. The boulders had separated like a curtain. At the focal point of the explosion was a ragged gap perhaps two feet square, through which the wind howled in a jet like water from a fire hose. Miller sniffed at it hopefully, trying to detect the herbs and aromatic plants of the maquis.

It smelt of damp Norman churches.

Can't win 'em all, thought Miller. He shone his torch through the hole. There were jumbled boulders, and beyond them the hint of space: a previous bed of the river. Quick, now, before the water rose far enough to spill down the channel. He walked along the beach to Mallory, directed his torch at his hand and gave the thumbs-up sign. The stony rigidity of Mallory's face relaxed. They assembled the loads and shared them out. Then Miller led the way into the hole in the rockfall. Andrea was the last in. As he stepped up to the hole he found he was walking in water.

The new passage was another tube of water-smoothed rock. The wind was strong in their faces. Mallory looked at his compass. They were heading north. They must have crossed the mountain by now. Mallory was tired, and hungry, and cold, and his feet had been wet for so long that they felt like raw sponges. But they were heading in the right direction. In the gale that was making him shudder with cold he detected the breath of freedom.

Provided there was an exit.

The passage was flattening out. Hugues stumbled. Andrea trod on his heels again; Andrea, who walked with the stolid regularity of a machine. Hugues was exhausted. He wanted to drop his end of the crutch from which Wallace was hanging, stop, rest his blistered feet, sleep in the dark.

Behind him, Andrea's voice said, 'I'll take him for a while.'

Hugues thought, he understands, this one. He understands exactly how weak I am, the way my mind will not be still, but must keep chewing at these questions that have no answers. There was something almost diabolic about that. Hugues felt naked, exposed.

To prove Andrea wrong, he said, 'I'm fine.'

The stretcher party plodded on in the dark. The last torch was turning yellow. There was no sound but the harsh rasp of breathing, and the rustle of water over rock.

Andrea did not want to say anything, but the water in the passage was definitely getting deeper.

It had started as a wetness on the floor. Now it was shin-deep, and it seemed to be rising faster. He thought of the waterfall. He imagined all that water pouring down here. He imagined it pouring down into a chamber with a small exit, making a pool that spread back into the tunnel, a pool that would fill the tunnel up. That would be a problem for the operation, thought Andrea methodically. If they drowned, the operation would not be completed. It would be best if that did not happen.

Mallory walked on. The water shone under the now orange beam of his flashlight, chuckling merrily downhill.

The flashlight became an orange point, and went out.

Mallory lit his Zippo and held it above his head. The flame flickered in the rush of air.

Ahead, the tunnel broadened and became a flat sheet of water that led to a blank wall of rock. Above, at the height of a cathedral roof, a shaft led upwards. It was down this shaft that the wind was howling. The lighter went out. In the darkness left by its flame it was possible to see at the top of the shaft, bright as a diamond in the cold black velvet of far underground, a speck of light.

An unattainable speck. For as their eyes adjusted to the dim glow they saw that the chamber in which they were standing was roughly the shape of an inverted funnel, with the shaft as the spout.

Mallory's mountaineering exploits had covered the newspapers of the Empire. But even master mountaineers do not have suckers on their feet.

Mallory felt a presence by his side. Miller raised his own lighter. The sheet of water was a pool, fed by the knee-deep torrent underfoot. Stalactites threw angular shadows across the ceiling, and stalagmites stood neck-deep in the pool. Beyond each stalagmite was a little writhing in the water.

'It's flowing,' said Miller. 'Must be going somewhere.'

This time he was so wet that there was no point in taking his clothes off. He tied the rope round his waist and waded in.

The first thirty feet was no more than knee-deep. Then, suddenly, the bottom sank away, and he was swimming, treading water rather, swept along by a fierce current in a narrow trench. At the rock wall ahead.

And he knew he had miscalculated.

He opened his mouth to shout, realised it was too late, and grabbed a deep breath of air instead. Then he went under.

The current was like a hand, grabbing him, tearing him down. He went headfirst, felt himself crash against a big rock. Then his shoulders were in a tight opening, too narrow for him to get through, and the current was forcing water into his nose, trying to get it into his lungs. He wriggled convulsively, got free, hit another rock with a bang that made his ears ring. He was in a pipe, a pipe of rock that was such a tight fit that he could not move his arms or legs. The shove of the water was huge. You goddamn idiot, he told himself. You can get away with it once, twice, ten times. But diving into God's waterworks is asking for trouble.

And trouble is what you got.

His chest was bursting. The blood was hammering in his ears, and his head was roaring and juddering like that waterfall back there. Thirty more seconds of this, and he was going to be dead. And then those other guys would be dead. And then those submarines would go through that invasion fleet like three red-hot pokers through a pound of butter.

Chest full of air, oxygen turning to carbon dioxide. Going to suffocate you.

Make yourself smaller.

Breathe out.

Miller breathed out. The contraction of his chest shrank his girth by a fraction. The tunnel's grip slackened. The water hauled him along the pipe, and slammed him into a hole through which his head only just fitted, and poured into his nostrils and gaping mouth.

Now he was going to die.

He was going to die with his head in daylight.

Daylight?

With the last of his strength, he writhed like an eel. And suddenly, whatever it was that was holding his right shoulder had given way, and he was through, out, beyond it all, flat on his back in a cheery little brook that was gurgling down a wooded valley under the five o'clock sky, from which a little snow was falling, but only a little.

He breathed twice, big breaths, with coughing. He looked back at the hole in the hill, a hole no bigger than a badger sett, as it burst out and expanded into a raw rent big enough for a bear, or even Andrea. The flow of water seemed to have lessened. He had broken the bottleneck. There might even be air in the tunnel now. He gave the two pulls on the rope.

It was cold in the little valley. The snow had not settled, but white skeins drifted in a half-hearted manner from heavy black clouds sailing in on the westerly breeze. They inspected and cleaned the weapons, fumbling with cold, water-wrinkled fingers. Jaime found some dry branches and knocked up a fire that burned with hardly any smoke. Andrea made soup. Thierry crammed his straw hat on his head, unpacked his radio, and began to inspect the parts.

Miller took Wallace a can of soup. None of them looked in the best of health, but Wallace looked terrible. His skin was like grey paper, but burning hot to the touch. His eyes were glazed. When Miller tipped some soup down his throat, he vomited immediately.

His wound looked pale and bloodless because of its perpetual rinsing in water. But the yellow edges looked yellower, and the

99

red puffiness angrier. There was swelling, and a nasty putrid ooze. 'Hurts,' he said.

'Bloody awful mess you are,' said Miller. 'Sooner we get you under a roof the better.'

Wallace opened a dull and rheumy eye. 'Lea' me,' he said.

'Leave you my ass,' said Miller, sticking in the morphine syrette and squeezing the tube. 'We'll get a dressing on that. Still hurt?'

'Can't feel a thing,' said Wallace.

'Sure,' said Miller, as if that was the right answer. 'Just get a new dressing on that for you.' He smeared damp sulfa on the wound, bandaged it up again, and covered Wallace with a more-or-less dry blanket.

Mallory said quickly, 'How is it?'

'Looks like it's going wrong,' said Miller, grim-faced. 'Plus shock, I guess. I don't know why he's still alive.'

Mallory's deep-sunk eyes were bright and distant. It was a mystery to him why any of them were still alive. 'We'll take two hours' rest,' he said. 'Jaime knows where we are. The Germans think we're dead. Andrea, get your head down.'

He watched as Miller spread a groundsheet over Wallace, rolled himself up in his poncho, and went immediately to sleep. Andrea was sitting with his back to a tree, eyes invisible. Asleep, awake, nobody knew, and nobody would ask. Jaime and Hugues were asleep. Only Thierry was awake, a large, crouching figure, fiddling with his radio, testing it after its immersion.

Mallory said, 'That thing working?'

He had moved close to Thierry quietly; Mallory knew no other way of moving. Thierry looked up sharply. His fingers moved a switch. An indicator light went out.

Mallory bent and looked at the set. The light had been the TRANSMIT light. He felt the short hairs bristle on his neck. He said with a new, dangerous quietness, 'Thierry. What are you doing?'

'Testing the equipment,' said Thierry.

Mallory said, 'Just as long as you're not transmitting.'

'I heard what you say,' said Thierry irritably, squashing the straw hat over his face and leaning back against a boulder. Mallory walked to the end of the valley. The snow had stopped. Between the squalls

100

of black cloud deep ravines of blue were appearing. There was real warmth in the gleam of sun that lanced down into the trees. Warmth was what was needed. Particularly, it was what Wallace needed. In four hours it would be dark, and it did not seem likely to Mallory that Wallace would survive a night in the open.

And Wallace was not the only worry. Mallory guessed that they were at best halfway down the mountain. They still had to get down into the valley and walk to the sea, where this Guy Jamalartégui was waiting for them. Whether or not the Germans believed that they had died in the collapsed cave beyond the ridge, the roads to the sea would be heavily patrolled.

Mallory eased his sodden feet in his boots, and squeezed his cracked and abraded hands, to change the nature of the pain. The Benzedrine was wearing off. He felt weary and irritable. What they needed was to get dry. Being dry would change everything.

He was too jumpy to rest. He patrolled the wood, walking downhill until the trees started thinning.

Below him a meadow dropped steeply into the smoky blue deeps of the valley. The sun was out again. He could feel its warmth on his face. This far down the mountain the snow had melted as quickly as it had fallen, and the meadow grass was a brilliant green space in which swam constellations of wild flowers, falling away to a hazy gulf in which a village lay like a group of toys, and beyond it a shoulder of mountain, more heavy black clouds, and the metal sheet of the sea.

But Mallory was not looking at the view. He had faded back into the shadow of a stand of pines. He had his binoculars at his eyes. His grey-brown face was stony under the stubble on cheeks and jaw.

In the disc of the glasses the lower slopes of the meadow were lousy with grey mites. The sun gleamed off windscreens: the windscreens of half-tracks and lorries, and of an odd, boxy van with a steel loop on its roof, like the frame of a giant tennis racket.

A radio-direction-finding van.

It came upon Mallory like a flash of revelation: not a flash of lightning, but the dull, red blink of the TRANSMIT light on Thierry's radio.

Thierry had not been checking the equipment. He had been transmitting.

Things began tumbling into place. That damn silly straw hat that Thierry insisted on wearing, rain or no rain, had nothing to do with vanity. It was an identification mark. *Don't shoot the man in the straw hat*, the orders would have said. *The rest, kill them. Not the man in the hat.*

In a manner of speaking, Jensen had said, they will be waiting for you.

Courtesy first of the SAS. And now Thierry.

A short mile away, at the foot of the meadows, three armoured cars had begun to grind uphill, hub-deep in the lush spring grass, leaving tracks like railway lines. Mallory faded back into the woods.

At the gully, everyone was asleep except Thierry, who was still squatting in front of his radio like a lard Buddha. Mallory did not look at him. Andrea was snoring heavily. Mallory shook him by the shoulder. He said, 'I think you should shave off your moustache.'

Andrea said, 'Wha –'

'Quick.'

Andrea's hand went to his upper lip. For the first time since Mallory had known him there was uncertainty in his eyes. 'No,' he said.

Mallory said, 'The Germans are coming. Five hundred men. Armoured cars. Listen.'

Andrea listened. He hung his head. Then, finally, he nodded. Reluctantly, he pulled a razor from his pack and began hacking at the luxuriant growth on his upper lip. 'Twenty years,' he said.

But Mallory was gone, waking the others.

Within two minutes the upper lip was bare, except for a black stubble that matched the rest of his face. A new Andrea stood up: an Andrea clean-shaven, olive-skinned, with a nose increased and cheeks enlarged by the lack of moustache. And there was something else on his normally impassive countenance. Andrea would shave his moustache in the name of duty, but that did not mean he was going to be happy about the man who had caused his loss.

Andrea was angry.

Up on his rock Thierry was beginning to be nervous. People were stirring in the camp, when there should have been no stirring. He looked at the steep walls of trees on either side of him, the valley, the stream babbling out of the mountain. These people would fight to the death. He could imagine the chug of machine guns, the blast of mortar bombs. He was working for the Germans to keep himself safe, not expose himself to danger. A stupid straw hat would not save him from Spandau rounds or shrapnel.

Thierry found that he was on his feet, and that his feet were moving, sidling away towards the woods. He found he was yearning with his whole being for the anonymous shade of the trees. The sky was a bright, hopeful blue beyond those green leaves. His mission was over; there was no shame in running. He would collect the money Herr Sachs of the Gestapo had promised him, buy a bar, listen to dance music, run a couple of girls upstairs; and the sky would never, ever be anything but blue again.

There was no more sidling, now. He was running in earnest, his great bulk crashing through wild raspberries and chestnut saplings. From the corner of his eye he could see someone coming after him. His bowels were loose with terror. He thought he could hear engines now, and the crash of jackboots in the undergrowth. Holding the identifying straw hat on his head with one hand, he shouted, '*Hilfe! Hilfe!*'

The hat and the shouting must have slowed him down. He knew that something had smacked him hard from behind, on the left-hand side of the rib cage. He pitched forward. A voice in his ear said, 'This is from Lisette, animal.' He thought, surprised, that was Hugues, the stupid Norman. What happens now?

There had been something wrong with the blow on his ribs. It hurt too much. It hurt very badly indeed, as if there was a red-hot iron bar in there. A heart attack? thought Thierry. The doctor had warned him: lose weight. But to die of a heart attack in a war. How stupid, thought Thierry, covered in cold sweat. How very stupid. Perhaps one can recover –

He tried to breathe. But his lungs were full of liquid. He coughed. Something poured out of his mouth.

Blood.

In front of him loomed the blank face of the blond Norman, Hugues. He was doing something to a knife. Cleaning it with a handful of chestnut leaves.

He stabbed me, thought Thierry, in a panic. With a knife. I may die.

He died.

The SS men in the armoured car stopped on the edge of the wood, and waited. The Gestapo were manoeuvring the third detector van into position, so the position of the radio could be pinpointed exactly. The terrorists could then be surrounded, and methodically crushed.

The SS men in the armoured car were ready to wait for as long as it took.

For there were rumours in circulation that made it sound very unwise to take any risks with these people. They had, it appeared, already accounted for almost a hundred men. The logical way of dealing with them was massive force. And massive force, thank God, was what was being applied to the problem.

The SS Obersturmführer was not like other men. He turned and watched scornfully as the grey straggles of soldiers marched doggedly up the mountain, and curled a lip. His men might welcome this great application of force. But it looked to the Obersturmführer like taking a sledgehammer to crack a nut. There were only five or six men, terrorists, Frenchmen, British: mongrels, members of inferior races. In the Obersturmführer's view, it was time to get them out of the way, and get on with the war.

At that point, five men walked out of the edge of the wood; or rather, four men walked, carrying a fifth on an improvised stretcher. Three of the walkers and the man on the stretcher were wearing British battledress. Behind them, walking at a safe distance, was a fat, dark man, holding a Schmeisser trained on his companions, with two more Schmeissers slung round his neck. As planned, he was wearing a straw hat.

He looked up at the armoured car. His dark eyes took in the Obersturmführer's black uniform with the lightning-flashes on the collar of the tunic. He said, in heavily-accented German, 'Three English and two French bastards.'

The Obersturmführer allowed a clammy blue eye to rest on the man. He was disgustingly unshaven, and his clothes were too small and too wet. His accent sounded French, but not quite French. The Obersturmführer said, 'There were supposed to be six of them.'

'One of them is inside the mountain,' said the man in the straw hat. 'And ever more shall be so.'

'Good,' said the SS man. The chilly eyes flicked across the bedraggled group of Englishmen and their two French companions. He jumped down from the armoured car. 'Werner and Groen. Bring the Spandau. Altmeier, radio Search HQ and tell them that the problem has been dealt with.' He gazed clammily upon the prisoners. Herr Gruber, the Chief of the Gestapo in St-Jean-de-Luz, might want to interrogate them. But Herr Gruber was a civilian, an expert at pulling out women's fingernails; he knew very little about the wars fought between man and man. The Obersturmführer sniffed. There was only one cure for vermin. 'A clean death,' he said. 'It is probably more than you deserve. *Komm.*'

They set up the Spandau twenty-five yards away from the armoured car, pointing at a low cliff of limestone. Thirty or forty Wehrmacht soldiers in field-grey hung around, watching. 'Good,' said the Obersturmführer to the man in the straw hat. 'Now tell them to dig.'

'Dig?'

'Not too deep,' said the Obersturmführer. 'Thirty centimetres will suffice.'

Two SS men unstrapped spades from the back of the armoured car, and threw them at the men. Mallory began to dig. So did Hugues and Miller. Wallace, on his knees, picked feebly at the spongy soil. The Wehrmacht men looked disgusted, and began to drift away.

'Good,' said the Obersturmführer ten minutes later, contemplating the shallow pit. 'Tell them to undress.'

They undressed, slowly. The last of the soldiers in field-grey had gone. They hated the revolting tricks of the SS. A man who was a man could not watch this kind of thing. The execution party and its victims were alone under the birdsong and the dripping green trees by the little cliff at the margin of the wood.

There were the three men round the Spandau: the Obersturm-führer, and two more SS. Facing them, white-skinned and goose-pimpled in the low sun, were the prisoners. Mallory said in German, 'What about a cigarette?'

The man in the straw hat said, 'Give them a cigarette.'

The Obersturmführer said, 'For a traitor, you are a generous man.'

The man in the straw hat walked across to Mallory, gave him a cigarette, and lit it for him. The Obersturmführer had a sudden feeling that there was something wrong with the transaction.

It was the last feeling he ever had about anything.

Because as the man in the straw hat lit the cigarette for the man with no clothes on, he must have passed over the Schmeisser as well. And suddenly the Schmeisser was firing a long burst at the Spandau crew, who seemed to make a sitting jump backwards and lay twitching, gazing at the sky with sightless eyes. That left the Obersturmführer, his Luger halfway out of his holster. The Schmeisser turned on him. The firing pin clicked on an empty chamber.

The Obersturmführer started to run.

He ran well for a man wearing breeches and jackboots, but not well enough for a man running for his life. Deliberately, Andrea reached into his belt and pulled out a knife. Silver flashed in the sun. The figure in the black uniform stopped running suddenly and collapsed in an untidy tangle of arms and legs. His cap rolled away and came to rest against a thistle. The breeze fluttered his close-cropped yellow hair.

Andrea pulled his knife from the nape of the Obersturmführer's neck and wiped it on the wet grass, waving away the flies that were buzzing over the wound. Already Mallory and Miller were stripping the uniforms from the bodies of the SS men. The Obersturmführer's uniform more or less fitted Mallory.

They tumbled the corpses into the graves they had dug for themselves. They drove back to the little valley and loaded the gear and Miller's boxes into the armoured car. Mallory sat bolt upright, head out of the turret, face grey and unshaven. 'Go,' he said.

Miller put his foot on the throttle. The armoured car jounced down the hill, through the remnants of the Wehrmacht force. The field-grey soldiers looked away. They knew what those Totenkopf bastards had been up to on the mountain.

Up on the edge of the wood the air was silent, except for the buzz of the flies over certain dark patches on the fresh-turned earth, and the whistle of a griffon vulture wheeling high between two clouds.

Down in the valley, the armoured car turned onto the pavé, and began to clatter officiously towards St-Jean-de-Luz.

FOUR

Monday 1900–Tuesday 0500

The inhabitants of St-Jean-de-Luz paid very little attention to an SS armoured car; they saw too many of them. Mallory stared straight ahead at the thickening houses. He said to Jaime, 'We need a safe place. Not a cave this time.'

Jaime nodded. On the outskirts of the town he said, 'Halt here.'

Miller turned the armoured car down a track, through a rusty iron gate with a chain and a padlock bearing a swastika seal. Jaime cut the chain, let them in, and hooked the broken links closed behind them.

Beyond the gate was a farmyard. It looked as if it had been abandoned in a hurry. The farmhouse windows were open, the remnants of shutters flapping in the breeze from the sea. The cattle-sheds were empty too. 'The Nazis took the people,' said Jaime. 'The men to forced labour. Later, the women were sheltering *résistants*. They also went. Nobody has come here since.'

Mallory walked round the place. It had an evil, septic smell. There was mouldy hay in the mangers and dried manure still in the cowshed gutters. In the house, the bedclothes were still on the beds, and in the kitchen a saucepan full of mould stood on the cold stove. It was like a house visited by a plague.

But Mallory was less interested in the house than in the exits. The exits were fine. The house stood in a grove of ilex in open fields, plentifully laced with deep, useful ditches. The nearest house was two hundred yards away; the wall it turned on the farm was blank and windowless. And best of all, they were behind an iron gate with an apparently unbroken Nazi seal.

They drove the armoured car into the barn and heaved the door shut. They sat on the broken chairs round the kitchen table and lit cigarettes, while the fleas from the floor attacked their ankles. The westering sun made yellow shafts in the curling smoke. Mallory could have slept for a year.

Hugues said, 'We must go to the café.'

Mallory nodded. Hugues' face was pouchy with exhaustion. Mallory wished he trusted him more. It would be dangerous in the café. He said, 'What if Lisette has talked?'

'If she has talked, she has talked,' said Hugues. 'That is a risk I will take.'

After Colbis, Mallory had begun to think of Hugues as a weak link. But then he had seen him run down Thierry, a Thierry screaming for help, about to break cover under the eyes of the Germans. It had been a nasty job, a job Mallory had been glad he had not had to do himself. Hugues had done it.

And under the one eye of the SS Spandau, standing by the graves they had dug themselves, it had been the same. Certainly, Hugues was frightened. But he was a man who had the courage to face down his fear. And that, in Mallory's book, was the true bravery.

But Hugues' courage was not the issue. The issue was to find out the whereabouts of Guy Jamalartégui.

I am sorry, thought Mallory. But brave or not, I cannot trust you, not one hundred per cent. Once you are out from under our eyes it will be too tempting to bargain for Lisette's life, and the life of your unborn child.

Mallory looked into the veil of smoke surrounding the head of Miller, sprawled in a chair with his boots on the table, and caught his eye. 'I'll go along,' said Miller. 'I could just about handle a drink.'

Ten minutes later they were walking towards the port of St-Jean-de-Luz. Miller made an improbably tall Frenchman, loping along in a black beret and a blue canvas workman's suit whose trousers flapped round his calves. He had found the clothes in a wardrobe at the farm. They stank of rats. His papers, however, had been supplied by SOE and were in order. Hugues was dressed in the sweater and corduroys in which he had clambered through the mountain, and another beret. They were dirty and unshaven. They were chewing raw garlic, and they had rubbed dirt into the cracks and scrapes on their hands. They were convincing peasants on their way from the fields to the café.

St-Jean-de-Luz could almost have been a town outside the war zone. The golden evening light held the particular sparkle that comes from proximity to large expanses of water. The inhabitants were out enjoying the weather. A dark-haired girl haughtily ignored Miller's wink. Miller sighed, and wished he had a cigarette. But all he had was blond tobacco, and smoking blond tobacco in this town would be like hauling up the Stars and Stripes and running out the guns.

The Café de l'Océan was strategically sited on the crossing of two narrow alleys in the Quartier Barre, north of the harbour. At the end of the alley Miller saw two grey-uniformed Germans with a motorcycle combination parked on the quay under a crowd of squalling gulls. They looked as if they were having a pleasant seaside smoke. Soon, an SS armoured car and six men would have failed to respond to signals enough times for there to be noise and fuss. But not, Miller devoutly hoped, too soon.

Outside the café, Hugues looked up and down the alley with the air of a conspirator in a bad play. 'Get in here,' said Miller, not unkindly, and shoved the door open for him.

The Café de l'Océan was a room twenty feet on a side, with a bar across the inside corner. It contained some thirty men, five women, and a fug of cigarette smoke. Two field-grey Germans were playing draughts at a table in the corner. Seeing them, Hugues stiffened like a pointer at a grouse. Miller knocked his arm and said, 'Camouflage.' He hoped he was right.

Hugues swallowed, his Adam's apple bobbing in his throat above the frayed collar of his shirt. He elbowed his way up to the bar, next to an elderly gentleman with a beret, a large grey moustache and red-and-yellow eyeballs. He said to the fat man behind the bar, 'A Cognac for me, and a Cognac for my friend the Admiral.'

The barman had eyes like sharp currants. '*L'Amiral Beaufort?*'

'That's the one.' A fine sheen of sweat glazed Hugues' pink-and-white features. The BBC had sent the password down the line. But it was always possible that something would have gone astray,

110

that this impenetrable barman, whom he knew to be a *résistant*, would refuse to make the next link in the chain.

But that was all right, now.

The barman gave them the brandy, and scribbled a laborious bill with a stub of pencil. Hugues passed a glass to Miller, said, '*Salut*,' and looked at the bill. Pencilled on the paper were the words *Guy Jamalartégui – 7 Rue du Port, Martigny*. Hugues pulled money from his pocket and passed it to the barman with the bill. The barman put the money in the till, tore the bill into tiny fragments, and dropped the fragments in the wastepaper bin.

'*Bon*,' said Hugues. '*On s'en va?*'

Next to him, a voice said in a hoarse whisper, '*Vive la France!*' Hugues' heart lurched in his chest. The voice belonged to the man with the grey moustache. He turned away.

'I saw the paper. He is a good man, Guy,' said the man with the moustache. His breath smelt like a distillery. 'A very good man. Permit me to introduce myself. I am Commandant Cendrars. Perhaps,' he said, 'you have heard of me?'

Hugues' eyes flicked to the Germans at their draughts game. He smiled, an agonised smile. 'Alas no,' he said. 'Excuse me –'

'*Croix de Guerre* at the Marne,' said the old man. 'A sword long sheathed, but still bright. And ready to be drawn again.' He put his head close to Hugues. A silence had fallen around him. Cendrars' alcoholic rasp was singularly penetrating, his attitude visibly conspiratorial. 'I am not the only one. There are others like me, waiting the moment. The moment which is arriving. Arriving even now. The great fight for the resurrection of France from under the Nazi heel. We are not Communists, *monsieur*. Nor are we Socialists, like the *résistants*. I trust you are not a Communist. *Non*. We are simple Frenchmen –'

'Excuse me,' said Hugues. 'It will soon be curfew.'

Cendrars said, with a significant narrowing of his orange eyes, 'In the mountains today, it is said that they killed six SS.'

The silence had become intense: a listening silence. Miller drained his glass, grabbed Hugues firmly by the arm, and marched him out into the alley. 'What was he saying?'

'Madness,' said Hugues. 'Stupid old bastard. Stupid old Royalist *con* –'

'No politics,' said Miller. 'Home, James.'

They started to walk.

Miller kept a little behind Hugues. He did not like this Cendrars. He liked even less the fact that the news about the killing of the SS on the mountain was already gossip in the town. Germans did not sit still and mourn dead SS men. There would be searches and reprisals –

In front of him, Hugues stopped dead. He was talking to someone: someone small, in a woollen hat and a big overcoat. He had thrown his arms round the small person, was embracing this person, making an odd baying noise that might have been laughing but sounded a lot more like crying. It was a weird and dreadful noise, the sort of noise guaranteed to attract attention. It caused Miller to pull the beret down over his eyes and start his feet moving in a new direction.

Suddenly, the person said in French, 'For God's sake, shut up.' Hugues leaped back as if shot. His face was amazed, mouth open.

'Be a man,' said the small figure.

The small figure of Lisette.

Miller said, 'Hugues. We have to go.'

'You have to go,' said Lisette.

This is all we need, thought Miller.

Hugues stared at her. He did not understand the words she was saying. Through his tears of joy, her face looked luminous, like an angel's. He had forgotten he was a soldier. He was a man, and this woman was bearing his child. There was nothing else he needed to know. Now they could be happy for ever.

'Free,' he said.

'Correct,' said Lisette. 'Now for God's sake get moving.'

'Moving?'

Miller cleared his throat. Lisette looked as good as new. Not a mark on her. Eight months pregnant. Blooming with health.

That was bad. That was very bad.

Miller said, 'They told us that you were taken to Gestapo HQ in Bayonne.'

'I was,' said Lisette. She looked up and down the alleyway. It was empty, except for the deepening shadows of evening. 'They let me go. Because of the baby.'

Her face was the same as ever: pale, aquiline, with the dark-shadowed eyes and transparent skin of late pregnancy. This was not a woman who had been tortured.

Miller said, 'What happened, exactly?'

'They asked me what I knew, how I came to be in that village. I said I was visiting, that I knew nothing. They ... well, they seemed to believe me. They said that a woman in my ... condition would not tell them lies, out of respect for her unborn child.' Her face split in a white grin that sent the shadows scuttling for cover. 'Of course, I agreed.'

'Sure you did,' said Miller. 'How did you find us here?'

'I knew you were heading for St-Jean-de-Luz. It is a known thing that if you require information in St-Jean, you will find it in the Café de l'Océan.'

'Is it?' Miller did not like this. In fact, he hated it. No Gestapo man had ever been worried about an unborn child, let alone an unborn child whose mother had been apprehended in a raid on a Resistance stronghold. The only reason the Gestapo would have let Lisette out was so they could follow her to her friends.

Miller said, 'I have to go.'

'You?' said Hugues.

Miller said, 'We have a military operation here. It seems to me that this town is going to get real hot, real soon. And we have to be moving right along.'

'So Lisette accompanies us.'

Miller looked at him with a face grey as concrete, 'It is whoever has accompanied Lisette from Bayonne that gives me the problems.' He watched Hugues' face. He saw the frown, the struggle. He knew what the answer was going to be. Hugues had abandoned Lisette once in the name of duty. He would not do it again.

Lisette said, 'You must go.'

Hugues said, 'No.'

Miller turned away and started to walk, hands in pockets, stopping himself from running, keeping to a stolid peasant shuffle, heading towards the farmyard.

He heard footsteps behind him: one pair of short legs, one pair of long. In a pane of glass he saw their reflection. Hugues had his arm round Lisette's shoulders and an agonised expression on his face. The steps slowed and halted. Miller walked on, faster, heading for the edge of town.

God damn it, thought Miller. Hugues had seen the address pencilled on the bill at the Café de l'Océan. And it would not take the Germans long to get it out of him.

It was a mess. A five-star, copper-bottomed, stinking Benghazi nine-hole latrine of a father and mother of a mess.

The houses were thinning. A truck engine clattered on the road ahead. Miller faded gently off the verge and into some bushes. A lorry load of soldiers rolled by, blank-faced under their coal-scuttle helmets. Hugues and Lisette had not jumped into the hedge. The lorry stopped alongside them with a wheeze of brakes. An officer climbed down from the cab. Miller heard him bark, *'Papiers?'*

In Miller's pocket was an identity card, work permit, ration card, tobacco card, frontier zone permit, and a medical certificate signed by a Doctor Lebayon of Pau explaining that chronic lumbago had prevented him from being deported to Germany as a forced labourer. Miller derived a certain sense of security from carrying them, but he knew that a detailed cross-examination about his maternal uncles or the colour of Doctor Lebayon's beard would scupper him, quick.

He hoped that Hugues and Lisette were in the sort of mental state that permitted clear thinking. He doubted it.

Quiet as a shadow, he slid away through the bushes. Ten minutes later, he was back in the farmyard.

Mallory said, 'Where's Hugues?'

Miller told him.

Mallory lit a cigarette. Then he dropped it on the floor and stamped it out, and shouldered into his webbing. 'We're off,' he said.

'Off where?' said Miller.

'Martigny.'

'What if they talk?'

'They talk,' said Mallory. 'The Germans will react. If they don't react, nobody's talked.'

And if they do, thought Miller, gloomily, we're dead.

Again.

* * *

There was a peak in the Southern Alps that had done this to him: Mount Capps, a treacherous peak, full of crevasses and rotten rock, its upper slopes decorated with snow fields that in the morning sun fired salvoes of boulders and later in the day became loose on their foundations and came slithering down like tank regiments, roaring and trailing plumes of pulverised rock and ice.

Mallory had left his base camp on the third day of the climb, leaving Beryl and George, his companions, waiting. He had bivouacked in the lee of a huge rock, halfway up an ice field, and spent a cold, restless night among the cracks and booms of the refreezing ice.

He had woken at four, and gone out. The sky had been clear, the peak of Mount Capps a peaceful pyramid of pink-tinged sugar icing over whose slopes Venus hung like a silver ball. It was a beautiful morning.

Mallory had walked ten feet away from the tent, into the cover of the rocks he used as his lavatory. He dropped his trousers.

A rumble came from the mountain. Feathers of snow fluttered away from the rocks. The rumble became a roar. He looked back at his tent.

A fifty-foot wall of snow and ice and rock thundered across his field of vision. It must have been moving at two hundred miles an hour. The icy breath of its passage slammed him against the rocks.

Ears ringing, he dragged himself back on his feet.

In the tent had been his pack, with spare ropes, food, extra clothes, sleeping bag.

The tent was gone. In its place was a deep, rubble-filled scar in the mountainside. All he had left was the rope he had taken to the rocks, his ice axe, and the fact that he had been climbing mountains since his tenth birthday.

Mallory buckled his trousers. Beryl and George were down there, waiting for him. They had spent six weeks planning this expedition. Nobody had ever climbed the southeast face of Mount Capps.

Mallory had thought at four o'clock that December morning, nine thousand feet above sea level: Beryl and George and the rest

115

of the team are counting on you. It is not just your life. You have
responsibilities. So you get killed going up. On this mountain you
are just as likely to get killed going down. Three hours to the
summit, then nine hours to base camp.

If you are going to die, you might as well die advancing as die
retreating.

So he had shouldered his single coil of rope and his ice axe,
and made it back to base camp in eight hours.

Via the summit.

The papers had said he was a hero. As far as Mallory was
concerned, he had done the job, and not let the team down, and
that was enough.

And now the team were out there on the south coast of England, hundreds of thousands strong, waiting to embark on the
transports.

It was a job with risks. But that did not make it any less of a
job.

They left quickly across the fields, Andrea carrying Wallace. There
had been very little sleep: enough to make men groggy and dazed,
but not enough for anything approaching rest. As they tramped
through the orchards and fields of young corn it was raining
again, and a blustery wind clattered branch against branch.

The town lay in darkness under the evening sky. Night fell as
Jaime led them round its southern fringes, crossing darkened
roads, climbing a couple of low ridges and scrambling down ter-
races. Engines were roaring in St-Jean-de-Luz. On the other side
of the bay the Germans were moving. there was no way of telling
where, or who against. All they could do was hope that the movements had nothing to do with Hugues and Lisette.

One step at a time.

'Wait here,' said Jaime.

They had arrived on a cobbled lane that headed steeply downhill. At the bottom of the lane water flexed like a sheet of metal.

Jaime drifted off into the dark.

Mallory said, 'Andrea. Recce?'

Andrea put Wallace down behind a wall, in what might have
been a potato patch, and gently pressed a Schmeisser into his

hand. Wallace's head was buzzing with fever and morphine. At first, he had thought that these people were SOE bunglers, rank amateurs. Now he had changed his mind, or what was left of it. They were the coolest, most matter-of-factly competent team he had ever met up with. It was something that he would never have admitted to himself if he had been a well man. But frankly, they were a lot better than any SAS he had ever seen.

Think rugby. Think of a team that has trained itself not by running up and down the pitch and practising, but by playing first-class matches, and winning. Team spirit was for children. These men were in a different league.

Wallace wanted to live up to their standards. But it was hard to know how. He knew enough about wounds to know he was bad; really bad. Behind the morphine he was cold, except for the big, throbbing lump in his stomach. The lump seemed to be getting bigger, sending sickly fingers of poison into the rest of his body. Should have rested it, he thought. Should have stayed in the brothel.

But staying in the brothel would have meant a German bullet, probably with torture first.

There had been torture, bouncing along those dark, wet passages underground, metal twisting in his belly, burning up with fever, all those weeks – was it only hours? – ago. But it was a torture you could come through, if you were one of a team of grown men.

Hell of a life. Wallace felt the fever-taut skin of his face stretch in a grin. You think you're doing fine in the children's team, with the bombs and the Jeeps and the old gung ho. Then you get into the men's team, and for a minute or two you feel like a man.

And after that, what?

Andrea went quietly over the back garden walls of the village. Somewhere a dog began to bark. Soon all the dogs were barking. In one of the houses a man flung open a window and swore. A light drizzle fell. At the base of the hill – more a cliff, really – the sea shifted silver under the sky.

But for the lack of lights, it could have been peacetime. Somewhere in Andrea's mind there appeared the memory of a wedding, long tables with bottles, laughter and tobacco smoke rising into the hot Aegean night, the moon coming up out of deep blue water. This place could have been like that. And would be again.

But the memory was small, as if seen through the wrong end of a telescope, shrunk not by lenses, but by years of war. It was suffocated by the picture of his parents' bodies, bloodless on the shingle bank of the river. It was suffocated by a choir of death-grunts, and hundreds of night-stalks on which Andrea had not been a full colonel in the Greek army – had hardly indeed been human; had been a huge, lethal animal with a mind full of death.

Andrea slid over the last of the garden walls, and walked across the field that led to the edge of the low cliff. There was a jetty at the bottom of the village, a crook of stone quay in whose shelter a couple of dinghies shifted uneasily on outhaul moorings.

The rain swished gently down. Andrea watched, patient as stone.

And was rewarded.

Down there in the lee of a shed at the root of the quay, a match flared, illuminating a face under the sharp-cut brim of a steel helmet, silhouetting a second helmet.

The rain fell. The dogs were still barking. Andrea returned the way he had come.

Mallory, Miller and Jaime were already under the wall.

'Pillbox on the hill opposite,' said Mallory. 'Covers the harbour.'

'Two sentries,' said Andrea. 'On the quay. No pillbox this side.'

'No soldiers in the village,' said Miller. 'This Guy's house is the third house up from the quay.'

'Bring Wallace,' said Mallory.

The dogs were still barking as the five of them went over three walls and came to the back of a cottage. A dog lunged at Andrea, yelling with rage. Andrea laid a great paw on its head and spoke quietly to it in Greek: soothing, earthy words, the words of a man used to working with animals. The dog fell silent. Very quickly, Mallory opened the back door. Miller and Jaime were well into the room before the man at the table even realised they were there.

He was small and thin, with a bald, brown head, a much-broken nose and crooked yellow teeth. There was a spoon in his right hand, a wedge of bread in his left. He was eating something out of a bowl.

He looked up, mouth hanging open, eyes shifting, looking for ways of escape and finding none. He took a deep breath, and prepared to speak.

'We are friends of Admiral Beaufort,' said Jaime. 'Monsieur Guy Jamalartégui?'

The black eyes narrowed. The mouth closed and recommenced chewing. The head nodded. The mouth said, 'Have you brought the money?'

'We have.'

Jamalartégui said, 'There are a lot of you. Only one person will speak at a time. There are Germans.'

'Four in the pillbox. Two on the quay,' said Mallory. 'Is that all?'

Jamalartégui nodded. 'Unless we get a patrol.' He looked vaguely impressed. Andrea laid Wallace in a chair by the stove. Wallace was breathing badly. His face was bluish-white.

For a moment there was silence, except for the wheeze of the cooking range and the rattle of rain against the windows. There was a smell of garlic and tomatoes, wine and wood smoke.

'Jaime,' said Mallory. 'Interpret.'

Jamalartégui dug thick glass tumblers and bowls out of the cupboard by the range, and spread them on the table. 'The Germans steal the meat,' he said. 'But there are eggs, and many fish in the sea.' He got up, and threw onions, peppers and eggs into a frying pan. The room filled with the smell. '*Piperade*,' he said.

Then there was silence.

Mallory ate until he could eat no more. Then he mopped his plate with bread and refilled his wine glass. He said to Jaime, 'Tell him he has some information for me.'

'I am a poor fisherman,' said Jamalartégui, after Jaime had spoken. 'One does not eat without paying.'

'What is a meal, without conversation?' said Jaime. Mallory did not understand the words, but he understood the tone of

119

voice. He reached into his pack, took out the watertight box, and opened it. In the dim yellow light of the oil lamp it was packed with sheets of white paper, bearing a copperplate inscription and the signature of Mr Peppiatt, Chief Cashier of the Bank of England. 'One thousand pounds,' said Mallory. 'For the information, and transport to the site.'

The old man's eyes rested on the five-pound notes. They glittered. He opened his mouth to haggle. 'Take it or leave it,' said Mallory.

'I take half now,' said Guy, through Jaime.

'No.'

'Perhaps you will not like the information I will give you.'

'We shall see. Now talk.'

'How do I know –'

Mallory stiffened in his chair. 'Tell him that it is the duty of a British officer not to abuse the hospitality of an ally.'

Jaime spoke. Guy shrugged. Mallory watched him. This was the moment: the crucial moment, when they would know whether they were on a military operation or a wild-goose chase. The moment for which many people had died.

There was a silence that seemed to last for hours. Mallory found he was holding his breath.

Finally, Guy said, '*Bien*.' Mallory let his breath out. Guy began to talk.

'It is like this,' said Jaime, when he had finished. 'He has seen these submarines. They are at a place called San Eusebio.'

In his mind, Mallory searched the map. The coast of France south of Bordeaux was straight and low-lying: a hundred and fifty miles of beach, continuously battered by a huge Atlantic surf. The only ports of refuge were Hendaye, St-Jean-de-Luz, Bayonne, Capbreton and Arcachon: all shallow, all unsatisfactory for three gigantic submarines. He did not remember seeing any San Eusebio on the map. So we have been looking in the wrong place, he thought. All those people have died in vain.

He said, 'Where's that?'

'Fifty kilometres from here.' Mallory felt the blood course once again through his veins. All they needed to do was pinpoint the place and call in an air strike. The bombers would do the rest. Even if the submarines were in hardened pens – unlikely, or he would have heard of them – there were the new earthquake bombs –

'In Spain,' said Jaime.

Mallory felt cool air in his mouth. His jaw was hanging open. He said, 'Spain is a neutral country.'

Jaime's dark Basque face was impassive. He shrugged. 'But that is where they are. To be in a neutral country could be a convenience, *hein*? And Franco and Hitler are both of them Fascists, *c'est pareil*.'

Mallory said, 'Neutral is neutral.'

'But submarines are submarines,' said Andrea, quietly.

And as he so often did, Andrea made everything clear in Mallory's mind.

For a moment he was not in this fisherman's cottage, with the gale nudging the tiles, and the stove hissing, and the sentries on the quay and the pillbox on the hill. He was back in that briefing room in the villa on the square at Termoli, hot and cool at the same time, tracing the veins in the marble of the columns. It had sounded like a throwaway line then: *You'll be absolutely on your own*, Jensen had said.

But of course, that was what Jensen had to say. Jensen could not order an operation against a neutral country.

There would be no RAF. No support of any kind. The Storm Force was absolutely on its own.

'What the hell is this about?' said Miller.

'We get to blow up some submarines,' said Mallory. 'Very, very quietly.'

'Oh,' said Miller, with the air of a man saved from a great disappointment. 'Is that right? I thought maybe Spain being nootral and all, you know? Fine.'

Mallory poured himself more wine, and lit a cigarette. It was at times like this that he knew he would never be anything but a simple soldier. Jensen had stuck knives between German ribs, and slipped bromide in the wine of Kapitän Langsdorff of the pocket battleship *Graf Spee* the night before she was scuttled. But

121

he was also a diplomat; it was rumoured that he had been offered the crown of Albania, and to many Bedouin chieftains he was the official voice of the British Empire.

This business bore all the hallmarks of Jensen at his devious best. And perhaps the imprint of another hand, more powerful, normally seen clamped round a huge Havana cigar.

Spain's neutrality was at best idiosyncratic. Twenty thousand Spaniards were fighting for Hitler on the Russian Front. The German consulate in Tangier – a Spanish possession – monitored Allied shipping movements in the Straits of Gibraltar. And Spanish wolfram provided a vital raw material for German steelworks.

But the British ambassador in Madrid, Sir Samuel Hoare, was prepared to ignore all this hostile activity in the name of keeping lines of communication open. He had set his face firmly against SOE operations in Spain, for fear of being compromised.

So Hoare would have been kept in the dark about the Storm Force. This operation was not just to prevent a repaired Werwolf pack carving a terrible swathe through an invasion fleet in the Channel. It was to send a signal over Hoare's head to Franco. To tell the Spanish dictator that the Allies knew just how far he was bending the rules, and to give him an object lesson as to the kind of thing he could expect if the rule-bending continued.

As long as Storm Force achieved its objectives.

If it failed . . .

Mallory lit another cigarette, and tried not to think of being paraded through the streets of Madrid as a saboteur, an infringer of the rights of a neutral state.

Out of the question.

Damn you, Captain Lord Nelson Jensen.

He ground out his cigarette in his wine glass. He said, 'We'll be needing a map.'

Hugues and Lisette had been having a difficult evening. The inspection of their papers by the roadside had passed off well enough: the Germans seemed to be in too much of a hurry for more than a perfunctory cross-examination of an obviously pregnant woman and her lover. There was, after all, a dead SS patrol in the mountains, and justice to be done.

But Hugues was rattled. Was it possible that Lisette was a traitor? Knowingly, no. Unknowingly . . . yes, it was possible.

Hugues made his decision. The operation must continue without them. He took Lisette by the arm. They turned back, towards the middle of town. They had been a pair of lovers out for a stroll, and had been overtaken by the rain and the approaching curfew. What could be more natural than that they should now head home?

'Where do we go?' said Lisette.

Hugues forced a smile. 'To make contact with our other friends,' he said.

So they walked back to the Café de L'Océan, and Lisette sat gratefully at a table while Hugues ordered two *coups de rouge*, and wondered what the hell they did next.

The Café had emptied out. It was blowing half a gale now, and flurries of wind agitated the puddles in the road leading down to the port. But the Commandant was still at the bar, speaking in a low, warlike voice to the barman, who was looking sceptical. He glanced round at Hugues, caressed his strawberry nose at Lisette, and returned to his conversation.

A hundred metres away, on the quay, two men in raincoats were talking quietly in German. 'She went in,' one of them said. 'The man with her.'

'Did she make any other contacts?'

'Not that I saw. I lost her for twenty minutes.'

'*Scheisse*,' said the taller of the two men. 'It'll be curfew in a moment, and we'll lose her completely. I think it is time to start our hare.'

'Pardon?'

'Flush her out, and see where she runs.'

'Ah.'

They walked into the house of M. Walvis, the undertaker, who was a nark for the Milice, the Vichy police. The taller of the two picked up the telephone and jiggled the cradle. When the operator answered, the man said in his heavily-accented French, 'Give me the garrison commander.'

There was a pause while the switchboard operator plugged him in on her board. Then a harsh German voice said, '*Wer da?*'

'Café de l'Océan,' said the man. 'Immediately.' He hung up.

The garrison commander hung up too. At the telephone exchange, the operator released the breath she had been holding while she listened to the conversation, and reached for her plugs.

Two minutes later, the telephone at the Café de l'Océan rang. A woman's voice said, 'Fire at the Mairie.'

'*Merde*,' said the man behind the bar. '*Les boches arrivent.*'

Hugues had been expecting this moment, he realised. But now that it was upon him, he was paralysed. Being with those soldiers had taken away his willpower.

Not that willpower was any help, in a situation like this.

He stood irresolute, sweating. 'Lisette,' he said. 'Hide yourself.'

'No need,' said the barman, wiping his fat hands on his gigantic apron. 'Our friend in the telephone exchange gives us ten minutes' warning.' He poured himself a small Cognac. 'Drink?'

The Commandant twirled his moustache, and accepted a Cognac for himself. 'At moments like this,' he said, 'it is vital to steady the nerves.'

Hugues was beside himself. '*Non*,' he said. Was this walrus-faced cretin seriously proposing to sit here and wait to be shot? These were *résistants*. If Lisette was found in their company, she would be arrested again. And there was the matter of his papers. His papers would never stand up under detailed scrutiny –

A roaring and clanging sounded in the street outside. With a squeal of tyres, an ancient fire engine skidded to a halt on the cobbles. The Commandant finished his drink and said, 'All aboard!' Leaping into the passenger seat, he clapped a huge brass helmet on his head.

'*Allez-y*,' said the barman.

Hugues stared at him. The barman made shooing movements with his fat hands. '*Vite*,' he said. Lisette's hand grasped Hugues'. 'Come,' she said. The Commandant was beckoning with arthritic sweeps of his arm. She hustled Hugues out and into the cab. The fire engine took off.

There seemed to be seven or eight other men on the engine, all elderly. 'Where are we going?' said Hugues to the Commandant.

'The hour has come,' said the Commandant. 'We go to assist our friends the English.'

'No,' said Hugues. 'You must not.'

'And why?' roared the Commandant, alcoholically. 'Every man on this engine has fought for *la patrie* at the Marne. We are ready to fight and die. For the glory of France. Not for your damned Lenin, *nom d'un nom* –'

Hugues said, 'It must be said that I am not a Leninist.' Stupid old man, he was thinking. Café firebrand –

'Sir,' said the Commandant, drawing himself up. 'I am a soldier. We are all soldiers, and we are fighting an honest war, face to face with the enemy, honourably, not hole-in-corner. Seventy men, hand-picked, will at dawn be rallying to the house of Guy Jamalartégui. The time has come.'

Hugues opened his mouth to tell him that he should keep his childish fantasies to himself. But Lisette got there before him. She said in a conciliatory voice, 'You cannot do this.'

The Commandant raised a hoary eyebrow that fluttered with the speed of the hurtling engine. 'Cannot? Madame, I must tell you that at the Marne, I and thirty of my comrades held our redoubt for three days against a regiment of Boches. Nothing has changed.'

'Mon Commandant,' said Lisette. 'I will place confidence in you. What I am about to tell you is of the highest importance, a great secret.' The parts of the Commandant's face not concealed by the slipstream-whipped expanses of his moustache were pinkening with pleasure. 'You will endanger an important Allied mission.'

'My little cabbage, I thank you,' said the Commandant. 'I accept your secret. Do not bother your pretty head with it further. And if you please, Mademoiselle, do not speak to me of fighting and other things you do not understand. A woman's place is in the bedroom and the kitchen.' He pinched her cheek. 'Leave this to the men.'

The crack of Lisette's palm on his ear was audible even over the sound of the bell. *'Vieux con!'* she said. 'Buffoon! At least do not arrive in your stupid fire engine.'

'Monsieur,' said Hugues. 'This lady has only this morning escaped the clutches of the Gestapo, while you have been in the café since lunchtime.'

The fire engine was bowling along the southern side of the

port. It was raining. From some secret locker in the back, one of the ex-*poilus* had hauled out rifles of ancient design. 'We also fight, who sit in the café,' said the Commandant sulkily, rubbing his ear. On the far side of the harbour, a few fishing boats were tied up at the town quay. Behind them, two large grey trucks were moving through the twilight.

'Look,' said Hugues, pointing. 'They are following us. I beg you. You are endangering this British operation. Secrecy is vital –'

The Commandant said, as if scoring a debating point, 'It is you that they are following.'

Lisette said, '*Mon Commandant,* the end result will be the same.'

'I will not skulk,' said the Commandant. 'I am not listening to you.'

The road left the shore and began to wind uphill between small houses. '*Bien,*' said Lisette, between clenched teeth. 'In that case, there is only one solution.' She reached forward, twitched the key from the fire engine's ignition, and flung it as far as she could into the bushes that lined the road.

'Now run,' said Lisette.

She jumped from the cab. Hugues went after her. She ran well, for a woman who was eight months pregnant. My God, thought Hugues, this is certainly a remarkable woman. He had never loved her as much as he loved her then.

For they were free, she and he. She had left the Commandant, that old fool of a Commandant, to divert the pursuit. The Commandant would get himself killed, and the knowledge of Guy Jamalartégui's address would die with him. And he and Lisette and their child could go to Rue du Port in Martigny, safe from pursuit, and reunite themselves with the English. And Lisette and the child would be safe again.

War was war. But Lisette was what mattered.

It was getting dark; it was after curfew, and the port of Martigny would certainly be guarded. But what other option was there?

At the top of the hill he paused and looked back the way they had come. Three broad-bottomed veterans of the Marne were head down in the bushes, looking for the keys. Beside him, Lisette was making a peculiar sound, as if she was weeping.

But she was not weeping. She was laughing.

Hugues took her hand and started walking uphill at a brisk clip. After five minutes there was firing behind them. Good, thought Hugues. So far, so good.

'Nice place,' said Dusty Miller. 'Sea views. Sheltered bathing.'

They were looking at an Admiralty chart spread out on the scrubbed pine planks of the kitchen table of Guy Jamalartégui. It showed a coastline, steep-to, indented with small, stony coves exposed to the huge bight of the Bay of Biscay. But in the centre of that stretch of coast was something different.

In the times when the world was molten and rocks flowed like water, a huge geyser of liquid stone had forced itself through and at an angle to the other strata. Now, that great irruption of granite formed a peninsula that flung a protecting arm round the bay of San Eusebio. The arm was marked Cabo de la Calavera.

At its entrance, the bay was not more than a hundred yards wide; but inside, it broadened into a two-mile oval of water, deepening to twenty fathoms. The village of San Eusebio was on the landward side of the bay. On the tip of the peninsula, the chart said FORTALEZA: fortress. Below the fortress were buildings, with a note that said CHIMNEY CONSPIC.

'There is a fort overlooking the entrance to the harbour,' said Guy, through Jaime. 'The Germans have put new guns. There is a magazine in the fort, well defended, *vous voyez*, I suppose for the ammunition of the guns and the torpedoes of the U-boats. Also, there is a line of fortifications here.' He put a cracked and filthy thumb across the neck of the peninsula at its narrowest point. 'This is the only way onto the Cabo. There are ancient fortifications, originally against the Arabs, and now also new ones from the Germans, I think. To seaward, the cliffs are high. The land slopes from the seaward side towards the harbour, so that there is a beach of sand looking across towards the town. On this beach there is much barbed wire, and a quantity of mines. These defences run from the inland end of the fortifications along to the buildings of the old sardine factory. There are also two merchant ships in the harbour, which arrived with supplies, ostensibly from Uruguay. These ships discharged their cargo at the fish factory quays. Now they are anchored off the factory. They have many machine guns on their decks, to cover the waters of the harbour.'

'So where are the U-boats?'

Guy shrugged. 'This is a very big fish factory,' he said. 'There was an American, a Basque who made a lot of money in the Pacific salmon fishing, and wanted to help his home town. He built four quays, with a dry dock, and many boats, and wanted to make a big sardine fishery. Naturally, it failed. There were not enough sardines in those years, or ever, on that scale: this was a madman, an American, need one say more? But the buildings are there still. It is a perfect place to make repairs on a ship, or a submarine, *bien entendu*.' He drew with a matchstick, extending a puddle of red wine on the table. He drew four quays like the tines of a fork, forming three bays parallel to the shore. The innermost quay ran along the base of the rock. On the crosspiece connecting the tines, he hatched in a group of sheds. 'There are the quays, the buildings, even the cranes. And it is an easy place to defend.'

Mallory's eyes rested on the chart and the spidery puddle of wine beside it. It was indeed an easy place to defend; and a difficult one to attack. But there were glimmers of light. The brightest was the fact that it was in a neutral country. He said, 'What size is the garrison?'

Guy shrugged. 'It is not a good place to visit, to count soldiers. Perhaps five hundred. Some Wehrmacht. A certain number of SS. The crew from the U-boats. And the technicians, the dockyard people who make the repairs. They came in from Germany, they say, on these so-called Uruguayan ships in the harbour. Perhaps two thousand men in total. They are under the command of a man of importance. A man with a black uniform, I am told. A general, I think; or an admiral. SS or Kriegsmarine, nobody could tell me.'

'They get their supplies from the ships,' said Mallory. 'Where do they get their power?'

'They brought it with them,' said Guy. 'Behind the *fortaleza* is a little town of wooden huts where the men live. Between the huts and the *fortaleza* is a building that was once the laundry. Now they have installed many diesels, with generators. Naturally, it is heavily guarded. There is also a magazine, in a cave in the rock.'

128

Andrea had been sitting back in his chair, eyes closed, as if asleep. Now he said, 'You know a lot about this place, *monsieur*. How?'

'My friends work on the fishing boats out of San Eusebio. They tell me.'

'There is still fishing at San Eusebio?'

'But naturally,' said Guy. 'It is a port in a neutral country. There is a railway, to take the fish to San Sebastian. The town, it was destroyed by the Fascists. But the quay is a good quay. And the customs . . . well, there is always a need for money, so close to the border.'

Andrea said, 'What does that mean?'

'There are those who have business with the inhabitants. Business not strictly legal, and for which the cooperation of the customs is important.'

Jaime cleared his throat. 'This I know to be true,' he said.

'You know this place?' said Andrea.

'In the course of business,' said Jaime. 'I did not know about these submarines, of course. For me, it was only a useful harbour for cigarettes, wine, commodities of this kind. There was only a little of the town left standing, after these Fascist bastards had finished with it. I have business contacts there.'

'Had,' said Guy.

'*Pardon?*'

'You are speaking of Juanito,' said Guy. 'It was Juanito who told me all these things. Two months ago.'

'I was last at San Eusebio four months ago,' said Jaime, his eyes on Andrea. He was deeply conscious of what Andrea could do to a traitor. He wished passionately for Andrea to be quite certain that he was not holding out on him.

Andrea nodded. He said, 'This knowledge will be useful.'

'*Bon*,' said Guy. 'So Juanito was found on the Cabo. He had been there two, three times before. This time he was selling Cognac to the troops. The Germans caught him. They hanged him from the top of the *fortaleza*. He is still there, what the gulls have left of him. On the flagpole. *Pour encourager les autres*.' His eyes strayed to the tin of bank notes. 'So this is a dangerous game.'

Andrea nodded, his great neck creasing and uncreasing like a seal's. 'In war,' he said, 'there is unfortunately a great deal of danger.'

There was silence, except for the sough of the wind in the tiles. The Frenchmen seemed improbably interested in their hands. Andrea's presence occupied the room like a ticking bomb. Mallory waited. This was the crucial moment: the moment when the running stopped, and the troops had a chance to draw breath and reflect; reflect on the fact that now they had deliberately and with their eyes open to walk out over the abyss, and jump. The time for hot blood was passing. The time for cold blood had begun.

Mallory let Andrea's presence sink in for a moment, as he had done so many times in so many small, hushed rooms these last eighteen months. When the silence had gone on long enough, he said, 'And the seaward defences?'

The change of subject earthed the tension in the room like a lightning rod. Guy laughed, a short, scornful laugh. 'Round the quays they have put anti-submarine nets. Beyond the nets are the cliffs,' he said. 'Eighty metres. And at the bottom of the cliffs, the sea, with waves that come all the way from America.'

'No fortifications?'

Guy's eyebrows rose under his beret. He smiled, the smile of a man who has the welcome sensation that he is once more on familiar ground. *'Mon Capitaine,'* he said. 'With such cliffs and such seas, fortifications are not necessary. Only four months ago, Didier Jaulerry was blown onto the base of the cliff, under the fortifications. He drowned, with his crew. His boat is still there, what is left of it. You can see it at half-tide.'

Mallory nodded. He said, 'What time of tide was it when he went ashore?'

'High water. A spring tide.'

'And the boat is still there, you say.'

Guy's mouth opened and closed again. *'Monsieur.* You are not –'

Mallory did not seem to hear him. He was looking at the chart, rubbing the stubble on his chin with a meditative thumb. At its narrowest, the neck of the peninsula was no more than a hundred yards wide. It would unquestionably be fortified.

'What are the cliffs made of?' he said.

'Granite,' said Guy. 'But rotten granite. Many birds nest there.'

'And at the bottom of the cliff?'

Guy looked at him as if he was mad. 'Rocks. The sea. A big sea, with big waves. Listen,' he said. 'If I were you, I would think about the town. It is destroyed, this town. I told you. In the Civil War, the Republicans held out there. The Fascists burned everything. So there are not too many people, and those who remain live like rats in the ruins. No food, no water. Now that would be your place to land. If you could pass the fortifications in the harbour, you could make an attack . . .'

Guy fell into an uncomfortable silence. These men gave him the idea that he said too much, too lightly; that he was a child in the presence of his elders, babbling. 'So,' said Mallory, finally. 'Your boat.'

Guy's eyes moved to the flat tin box of bank notes under Mallory's hand.

'You will be paid as we land,' said Mallory.

'But, *monsieur* –'

'These are the conditions. And of course, you will be inspired by the idea that you are helping make a world in which it will be possible to spend this money.'

'*Ah, ça,*' said Guy, shrugging with a smuggler's realism. War was part of politics. Money was money; money was different.

'Agreed?'

'Agreed.'

'When can we leave?' Mallory watched him with his cool, steady brown eyes.

Guy was not an impressionable man. But he found himself thinking, thank God this one is not my enemy. 'There will be water in the harbour at four o'clock,' he said. 'The sentries do not pay big attention then. The hour will be too early, the port too small. They will be half-asleep. Be in hiding near the quay. When it is time for you to come aboard, I will show lights for five seconds, by accident.'

'And if there are Germans watching?' said Andrea.

Guy smiled, a weary smile, the smile of a man who has already gone further than he intended and sees no way of getting back to safety. 'I am sure you will know what to do with them,' he said. 'And once you are aboard . . . well, we are a fishing boat.

131

We are one hour from the border here. I shall fly the Spanish ensign. The Germans will respect a neutral flag on the high seas, in territorial waters. It is not the same as the things that happen in secret on the Cabo de la Calavera.'

Andrea nodded. Guy was glad he had nodded.

'Thank you,' said Mallory, and reached for the bottle of wine. From the direction of St-Jean-de-Luz there came the sound of gunfire, mingled with explosions. Mallory lay back in his chair and listened to the clatter of the rain on the roof, the bluster of the gale at the windows, and closed his eyes. Miller and Jaime were already snoring; Wallace was quiet. The gusts seemed to be losing their force, becoming more widely separated. Miller will be happy about that, thought Mallory. And so will I. Miller hated the sea as much as Mallory hated confined spaces. Mallory did not hate it, but he did not understand it, and did not want to –

Then he was asleep.

When he woke up, it was dark. He had been asleep for no longer than four hours, by the taste in his mouth and the ache of his head. There was a voice in the darkness near him: Andrea's voice.

Andrea said, 'There are people outside.'

Knuckles rapped the door. A voice said, *'L'Amiral Beaufort.'* Hugues' voice.

Guy said, *'Entrez.'*

Hugues came in. Lisette was with him. She looked round at the grey, fleshless faces, pouched and deep-shadowed in the yellow lamplight. She said, *'Bonjour.'*

'Bonjour,' said Mallory, urbane and polite.

There was a silence.

Finally Hugues said, 'Miller has told you, I think. Lisette was released. We have evaded pursuit. For some hours we have been hiding in a barn above the village. I kept watch. You can see the road from there. Nobody approached. The Germans have lost sight of us.'

Mallory rested his head on the back of the chair. Hugues looked pale and nervous. Lisette was holding his hand. 'There was shooting,' said Mallory.

'The Commandant and his men,' Hugues explained. 'They are

132

clever, those ones; clever and stupid, at the same time. They will occupy the Germans.'

Mallory nodded. Once again, he had the feeling that events were moving beyond his control. But at least Guy's boat was a means of getting them back in hand.

The wind had become a series of squalls now. Between the squalls there was calm, except for the distant rustle of the sea.

'Guy,' he said, as if he were proposing a game of tennis. 'I think it is time you went to fetch your boat. And the rest of us should move out of here. How long?'

Guy said, 'I could be alongside in half an hour. There will not be much water. But maybe there will be enough.' He pulled a large, tarnished watch from the pocket of his greasy waistcoat. 'At four-thirty.' He cleared his throat. 'As I said, it will be important for you to be discreet.'

'Zat right?' said Miller.

'*Monsieur*,' said Guy. 'I assure you. The sentries may be sleepy, but they make reports at five minutes to every hour, via a field telephone. I suggest you be very careful.' Guy smiled, a nervous, perfunctory smile. He slid out of the back door and into the night.

Mallory looked at his watch. It was half-past two. Once again he was in a room, with his back to the sea, relying on other people to get him out of trouble. He hoped it would be the last time. He said to Andrea, 'Bring Wallace. We'll get out of here.'

Hugues said, 'What will you do about the Commandant?'

Mallory had the sensation that he had not slept enough. He said, 'The Commandant?'

'The Commandant will be arriving before dawn, he said. With seventy men.'

'The Commandant was drunk,' said Lisette.

Hugues sighed. 'I know this Commandant,' he said. 'He will arrive at dawn.'

Wallace said, 'You'll have a rearguard then.'

Lisette said, 'Commanded by the Commandant? You're crazy.'

Wallace said, 'The Commandant is retired. I am a serving officer. I'll take command.'

Mallory turned his head, and looked at the papery face, the glassy, fever-bright eyes.

'I'm not up to a ride in a boat, sir,' said Wallace. 'Maybe one of these chaps can get me to Spain when the fuss dies down.'

Jaime said, 'It is possible. Certainly, these old fools need orders. But *monsieur* cannot stay in Guy's house. The Boche will destroy it.'

'Hold on,' said Mallory. 'Seventy men arriving at dawn?'

'Commanded by a drunk,' said Hugues.

Mallory looked at Wallace. He would be no good in a boat. His only hope was to rest, and get over the border later, in discreet silence.

Mallory said, 'We will send you the Commandant. We will tell him that you are his commanding officer. You will tell him to go home, and collect you when the fuss has died down.'

'Yes, sir,' said Wallace.

Hugues looked at him, then at Mallory. 'The barn where we stayed is quiet. There is a loft. You can see the road, the harbour. It's a good command post.'

Mallory looked at the transparent face, the cracked lips, the glittering eyes. He walked across the room and shook Wallace by the hand. 'Best of luck, Lieutenant,' he said. 'It's been good having the SAS along. We wouldn't have got this far without you.'

Wallace grinned. 'I think you probably would,' he said.

Mallory said, 'I'll send up the Commandant.' Then he beckoned Miller, and said, 'Help Lieutenant Wallace up to the barn.'

They separated, leaving Mallory with the memory of a hand-shake that had been no more than a touch of icy bones.

'Brave man,' said Andrea.

Lisette was watching them. She nodded. There were tears on her face.

Miller's steps faded on the path.

Wallace was gone.

Miller threaded across the dark vines and potato-ridges. He carried his burden up the road, into the barn and up the stairs. In the loft, he propped Wallace on the dusty, sweetish-smelling mow. 'No smoking,' said Miller.

'Sure,' said Wallace. 'Thanks.'

'Good luck,' said Miller, arranging three canteens of water within reach.

In the yellow light of the lantern, Wallace looked like an Old Master painting: wounded soldier, with pack, Bren, Schmeisser, grenades and sulfa powder. His face wore a faint smile; a weird, faraway smile, Miller thought. 'Give my regards to England,' he said.

'You'll be there before us,' said Miller, cheerily. 'You can buy me a bourbon at the Ritz.' He went down the stairs in two strides of his beanpole legs, and paused by the door. The view from the barn was excellent. The village lay spread out at the end of its road. Nothing moved in the potato-ridges. The night was still: the wind had dropped flat, and the stars were out. In the loft, Miller heard Wallace stir, a stifled moan of pain. Then hinges creaked.

Miller walked onto the road and down towards the houses. After fifty yards he glanced back. When he had carried Wallace up, the shutters of the loft had been closed. Now, a shutter stood open. From that open shutter Wallace would command a view of the road leading down to the quay.

Miller raised a hand in salute, and walked quietly down to the village.

Hugues said to Mallory, 'Lisette will come on the boat.' Mallory watched him from under his heavy brows. The eyes were tired, but they seemed to Hugues to see everything. 'If we leave her, she may talk,' said Hugues. 'And there are often women on fishing boats. She will be . . . camouflage.'

A pregnant woman, thought Mallory. A hell of a member of a penetrate-and-sabotage expedition.

Lisette did not know where they were going, or why. But if she was picked up, she would talk, all right. This time, the Gestapo would make sure of that.

If she had not talked already.

He said, 'Bring her along.'

It was twenty to four by the time Miller got back to Guy's house. There was one dirty glass and one plate on the table. There was no sign that seven men and a woman had spent part of the night

135

there. Mallory was waiting, pack on back, Schmeisser in hand. Miller shouldered his boxes. The Storm Force filed out of the back door, across the garden walls, until they came out onto the field at the top of the cliff from which Andrea had watched the sentries. The wind had dropped flat. The water was smooth as satin, the swells slopping against the jetty with a small roar. One of the rowing boats was gone from the outhaul. From out of the hazy darkness of the bay there came the pop and thump of ancient diesels as the fishing fleet got ready for the tide. Of the sentries there was no sign.

Mallory said to Andrea, 'We'll wait till the sentries give their all-clear at 0355. Then we'll take care of them. That'll give us half an hour to get clear.'

'Half an hour?' said a voice at his side. '*Monsieur*, you have my personal guarantee that you will have all the time in the world.'

Mallory spun round.

'*Mon Capitaine*,' said the figure, in a gale of old Cognac. 'Permit me to introduce myself. Le Commandant Cendrars. At your service.'

'I was telling you about the Commandant,' said Hugues. 'A valuable *résistant*.'

'Pardon me,' hissed the Commandant, shirtily, in French. '*Chef de la Résistance* of the region –'

'*Ah, ça!*' said Hugues, scornfully.

Mallory cut off whatever it was he was going to say next. 'Commandant,' he said. 'I am most grateful to you. Hugues, please interpret. Tell the Commandant that his arrival is most timely. I am exceedingly grateful to him for his assistance. I am putting him under the command of Lieutenant Wallace, Commander of His Majesty's rearguard. Rearguard HQ is the barn above the village. He is to report there immediately for orders. I would remind him that stealth and silence are of the essence.'

The Commandant became still. Down on the rain-blackened quay, a figure was marching slowly: one of the German sentries. The other sentry would be in the command post, standing by the field telephone for the 0355 report. The Commandant said, 'A rearguard action, *hein*? Under the command of a lieutenant? I must say –'

'Hey!' said Miller. 'Get out of there!' Dark figures were crouching over the pile of equipment on the ground. 'Mind your own damn business –'

Next to his head, something exploded, shockingly loud in the still, starlit predawn. It took him several heartbeats to work out that it had been a rifle going off. 'In the army of the Marne, we do not sneak past the Boche,' bellowed Cendrars. 'We shoot him.' And he fired again.

The German sentry, surprised by the bullet that had smacked into the granite coping of the quay three metres from his right foot, had dived from view. The second shot hit the empty quay.

Miller found that he was on the ground, his Schmeisser cocked and ready in his hands, his heart thumping. You goddamn maniacs, he was thinking.

Mallory saw the Frenchmen still standing against the sky, obvious targets for the machine gunners in the pillbox on the hill opposite. Wallace, he thought, you are on your own.

Perhaps that is what you wanted.

Miller and Andrea had disappeared, as he would have expected. He said, 'Andrea?'

'I'll organize the pillbox,' said Andrea's voice from the darkness.

'Good. Miller?'

'Here.'

'Sentries.'

He looked at his watch. The hands were at five to three. The wires would be humming with the sentries' yelps: *we are under fire, send reinforcements*. The Commandant could not have chosen a worse moment if he had tried.

There was a moment's eerie silence, in which it was possible to imagine that nothing had happened. Then, on the summit of the hill that rose on the other side of the valley in which the village lay, a stabbing flame began to flicker. The Germans in the pillbox were taking an interest.

The sound of the machine gun came a split second later, with the whip of large-calibre bullets. One of the Commandant's men went over like a skittle. The rest of them lay down, old bones creaking. *'Merde!'* said the Commandant. 'What is that?'

Hugues was lying beside Lisette, clutching her hand. He said, wearily, 'You foolish old men, why will you not obey orders?'

Jaime felt something that might have been a breeze pass by him, except that it was no breeze, because breezes do not talk; and this breeze said, 'Come down in five minutes. Bring the equipment,' in the unmistakable voice of Captain Mallory.

Andrea went down through the village and up the hill the other side at a steady jog, conserving energy. The pillbox was directly above him now, its tracers flicking across the top of his vision. He paid them no attention. He had seen the pillbox before night had fallen. This far south, and next to a friendly neutral neighbour, invasion was not a serious fear. So it was not one of the impregnable strong points that you found in Crete, designed to stand days of siege. It was merely a concrete box with a steel door and a slit from which the machine gun could enfilade the bay and the quay.

Something was moving out at sea: something that might have been a fishing boat. Its exact outline was hard to determine, because there was a haziness at sea level, a pale vapour like kettle-steam on the dark face of the waters.

Andrea slowed to a walk. There would be a sentry. He put his face close to the ground and saw the silhouette of a man crouching against the hillside. The silhouette looked nervous, flinching at the occasional bullet that whizzed raggedly overhead from the heroes of the Marne on the hilltop opposite.

The sentry was indeed watching that hilltop. It had taken a lot of wangling to get down here onto the Spanish border, where nothing ever happened. He had no idea what had got into these Resistance idiots. Reinforcements would soon be arriving from St-Jean. There would be shootings and burnings in the morning. Meanwhile, this was annoying.

Or perhaps something worse. Rumours of invasion from England were growing in force, no matter how savagely the SS and Gestapo suppressed such defeatist talk. The sentry felt a dull foreboding. Still, if you were going to survive this damned war, Martigny was the place to be stationed –

A forearm like a steel bar clamped across the sentry's windpipe. The knife went in and out once, fast as a snake's tongue. Andrea lowered the body to the ground, put the helmet on his own head, and walked softly to the pillbox door. He took three grenades from his blouse, cradling them like eggs in his vast hand. He pulled the pins from the grenades. He held two of them, levers closed, in his left hand. The other he held in his right hand. He waited for a pause between bursts of fire. Then he banged on the steel door with the grenade.

'Hey!' he shouted, in his fluent German. 'Where is your damned sentry?'

Muffled voices came from within.

'This is Sturmbannführer Wilp!' roared Andrea in a voice hoarse with Teutonic rage. 'This is an exercise. Open up!'

The door opened. The man who opened it saw a large shape topped with a coal-scuttle helmet silhouetted against the stars. He said, *'Was?'*

Andrea kicked him down the stairs and threw the grenades after him. He was already fifty yards down the hill by the time the gun-slits spouted flame and the flat, heavy explosion rolled across the bay.

The sentries were not the Third Reich's finest. By the time Mallory and Miller arrived on the quay, they were in the guard post with the door shut, yelling at each other and into their field telephone, and someone was yelling back.

Mallory hoped Guy would be quick. There were a lot of German soldiers within five miles, and they would all be here in a very short time.

The guard post had once been a net shed. It had a stable door, in two parts. Mallory kicked both parts open. The Germans by the telephone looked round. They had wide, flabby faces, and looked well over fifty. They made no movement towards their rifles. Instead, their hands went up in the air.

'Key,' said Mallory.

The elder of the two handed him the key.

'Rifles on the ground,' said Mallory. The weapons clattered to the flagstones. 'Kick them over here.' He picked up the rifles. Then he smashed the telephone and closed the door. If by some miracle the Commandant of the St-Jean-de-Luz garrison had not been informed of his sentries' screams down the telephone, he could hardly fail to ignore an exploding pillbox. The lorries would already be on the road.

'Now listen,' said Mallory. 'This is a British army operation. It has nothing to do with the Resistance. We are about to board one of our submarines and withdraw. The civilian population have not been involved. Do you understand?'

The sentries nodded, dazed, their eyes shifting from the lean and haggard face, down the SS smock to the Schmeisser, unwavering in the hard, battered hands.

'You will inform your commanding officer,' said Mallory. 'This has been a commando raid, to demonstrate our capabilities. Tell him to remember what we can do.'

The sentries nodded. Their minds would be full of the icy winds of the Russian Front. But the message would have got across.

Mallory and Miller went out onto the empty quay. Mallory padlocked the door.

There was a dampness in the air, mixed with the faint, industrial reek of high explosive from the pillbox. It was quiet, except for the sploosh of the waves and the nearby thud of the fishing boat's engine.

And in the far background, on the edge of hearing, the sound of lorry engines.

The reinforcements were arriving.

Hugues scrambled down the cliff onto the quay, with Jaime and Lisette and Miller's boxes. Andrea was back, too. The fishing boat was coming out of the horizon, masts moving across the stars in the handle of the Plough.

Mallory noticed that the lower stars of the Plough's share had disappeared. He checked it off on a mental list. In the middle of all these disasters, that was something that could be useful.

He said to Jaime, 'Where are those old men?'

'Preparing for a final stand.'

'Go and tell them that for every German they kill, ten Frenchmen will be shot in reprisal. Tell them that this is a British army operation, and that the British army is withdrawing. Tell them that I have informed the sentries accordingly. Make it quick.'

Jaime nodded, and trotted up the cliff. Hugues said, 'For God's sake, where is this fishing boat?'

A dark shape came out of the murk. The fishing boat glided alongside. Andrea said, 'We won't get far without air support.'

It was a joke. It was a joke that was too true to be good. If lorry loads of Germans soldiers arrived on the quay now, they would have no trouble sinking Guy's boat. Machine guns, grenades, mortars, they would do the job.

If they arrived on the quay now.

Mallory thought of Wallace, the look in those china-blue eyes. Wallace was a berserker.

Good luck, Wallace, thought Mallory.

The fishing boat was a dark hulk alongside the quay now, the sound of its engine a clanging thump like the beat of a metal heart. The lorry engines were nearly as loud, approaching the top houses of the village.

'*Bon*,' said a small figure in Guy's voice, but higher than usual. 'All on boat. Quick, quick.'

Jaime had materialised out of the night, panting. 'I told them,' he said. They went aboard. The propeller churned water under the transom. The bow swung out and steadied on the strip of absolute blackness between the sea and the stars. For a moment the land astern lay dark and quiet, the houses of the sleeping village draped across their valley under the stars.

Then the valley erupted like the crater of a volcano.

In the cab of the lead lorry, the Hauptmann had been tired and bored. The bloody Resistance were having one of their fits. Whoever had knocked off the SS patrol in the mountains had in the Hauptmann's opinion done a good job. It was just that the Hauptmann wished that, having shot the bastards up, they had gone to ground, instead of making a bloody nuisance of themselves in the suburbs of St-Jean-de-Luz and scaring the wits out of his sentries in hopeless little shallow-water ports like Martigny. Until someone had hammered on his door, the Hauptmann had been entertaining Big Suzette in his billet. Suzette might be large, but she was a person of surprising skill. And instead of testing those skills to the limit, the Hauptmann was sitting half-drunk, very tired, and in a state of aggravated coitus interruptus in a truck at the head of a column of three other trucks, one hundred men in all, on the way to sort out a bit of local difficulty in Martigny, on pain of transfer to the Russian Front.

Sod it, thought the Hauptmann.

The lead truck rounded a corner in the lane and started down-hill, into the beginning of the valley, where the houses began. There was an old barn a hundred metres down the road on the right. The Hauptmann paid it no attention, because he was peering at the southern side of the valley, where the pillbox stood. The pillbox should have been heavily engaged, if there was real trouble. But the pillbox was silent. As the truck drew level with the barn it seemed to the Hauptmann that the gun-slits of the pillbox were illuminated by a dull orange glow that waxed and waned. But the brandy was playing monkey's tricks with his eyesight –

A tight cluster of Bren rounds blew the windscreen in with a hellish jangle of broken glass. The driver went halfway out of the window and collapsed like a wet rag. The lorry slewed sideways across the lane, demolishing a wall and coming to rest against a boulder. One of the men in the back saw a jabbing flicker of flame in the open shutter under the roof of the barn by the roadside. As he opened his mouth to point it out, a line of bullets stitched across his abdomen. The last bullet hit one of the stick grenades at his belt. The explosion that followed set fire to the lorry's gas tank. Men spilled out of the three lorries following, and took up positions in ditches and behind potato-ridges. There was obviously a considerable force in the barn. A machine gunner slammed his weapon on the ground in the lee of a ruined pigsty and fumbled for the trigger. He was a badly shaken man, partially blinded by the flames of the burning lorry. His first long burst went wild, the tracers striking sparks from the coping of the quay and whip-ping out over the water of the harbour. For a moment, half the weapons in the squad fired after his tracers, and the black water of the port was churned to foam. Then a Feldwebel who had been invalided home from the Eastern Front and knew what he was doing started screaming orders, and the squad turned its attention to the shutter under the barn roof.

There must be at least a company in there, thought the squad, hugging the ground and pouring in fire. The black opening became silent. The squad's firing lulled. A man got up and scuttled in with a grenade. A hoarse, agonised bellowing came from the shutter, followed by the burp of two sub-machine guns. The streams of bullets started low and went high, almost as if the men firing them were too weak to hold the muzzles down. The man with the grenade ran into the first burst, and fell down. The Germans opened up again.

This time, the machine gunner put an accurate stream of bullets through the open shutter, one in three of them tracer. A light was then seen inside, yellow and blue, and volumes of smoke obscured the sky. The hay was on fire. And suddenly against that light there appeared the figure of a man; a man crawling on one hand and two knees. In the hand he was not using to support himself he held a Schmeisser, which he fired until it was empty.

Now they could see him, they shot him quickly, and he fell to the ground in front of the barn, which was burning well now as the last year's hay rose in the draughts. The flames spread quickly to the rafters.

The Germans kept on shooting. They had killed one man, sure. But there was no possibility that only one man could have done so much damage.

So they poured lead into the burning barn, the flames dazzling their eyes, until the ridge went and the roof fell in, and a fountain of orange sparks rose at the cold and hazy stars. And when the place was merely a heap of glowing ashes and there was no possibility of anyone being left alive, someone went and looked at the body that had come out of the shutter.

He was lying on his back. His face was peaceful, pale, with a trickle of blood from the corner of the mouth. He was wearing a beret, with the flying hatchet of the SAS. The two privates next to the body were almost too frightened to touch it.

'Doesn't look very healthy,' said one of them.

'That's because he's dead,' said the other one.

The battledress blouse was open. The bandages round the belly shone black and wet in the flames. 'Ach,' said one of them. 'Stinks.'

'Brave man,' said the first German. 'To fight like that with his guts hanging out.'

'Bloody idiot,' said the second. He bent and closed the eyes, which were blue, and berserk, and open.

It was four o'clock by the time they got the burning truck out of the lane and moved on down to the quay. This time, nobody was taking any chances.

But when they got down to the sea, there was only the sloosh of the ripples against the quay, and the smooth expanse of the harbour at high water, lightening now with the dawn.

Guy Jamalartégui did not see the huge bloom of flame at the top of the valley. From the wheelhouse window, he was saying, in broken English, '*Messieurs*, '*dames*, welcome to the *Stella Maris*. And now, *Capitaine* Mallory, it is a question of my money –'

Then the guns started up, and Jamalartégui stopped.

One moment the water was dark and smooth. Then it was churning with tracers from the fusillade following the first wild burst the German machine gunner had fired after Wallace had shot up the lorry. The air was whining like injured dogs, and a flock of hammers slammed into the wheelhouse. Guy said, 'Oh,' a curious, breathy sound, as if the air was coming out of more places than his throat. He fell on the deck with a crash like a bag of coal. There were more tracers, but random, whizzing into the air like fireworks, passing over the spidery masts of the *Stella Maris*, dimming and vanishing.

Miller knelt by the body and felt for the pulse in the scrawny neck. He said, 'He's dead.'

Mallory looked down at them through eyes sore with sleeplessness. He realised that it was getting light. He could see Miller, crouched on the deck, his bony knees by his ears. And down there beside him in a pool of something that looked black but was not black, was Guy. A Guy who was no longer breathing; whom that random burst of fire from the hill had caught fair and square across the rib cage.

Mallory stepped over the body. He took the wheel. From the chart he recalled that the shore of the bay ran southwest. So he steered southwest, aiming at the horizon, as the light grew.

144

The engine thumped on. The sea was black like an asphalt parade ground, the horizon clogged with pale haze.

Andrea fingered the upper lip where his moustache was meant to be, and reached for the bottle of Cognac, and took a long swig. 'No rocks, my Keith, if you please,' he said. 'Only peace and quiet.' Then he lay down in the lee of the wheelhouse.

Mallory kept the bow southwest and motored for the horizon, waiting for the drone of engines, aircraft or marine, that would mean that after all this time, it was all over.

After three or four minutes, he realised that there was something wrong with that horizon. It should have been a knife-sharp line. Instead it looked lumpy and ragged, as if it was made of grey wool. And suddenly the grey skein ahead rose and touched the sky, and the air was wet on his face, and he realised the truth. The *Stella Maris* had sailed into thick fog.

The world was a round room, with walls of grey vapour. It was a room that moved with the *Stella Maris*, southwest. It was a room impenetrable by ships and aircraft, except by accident. A most fortunate room.

As long as you did not mind being off a rocky shore in tides of unknown strength, not knowing where you were going.

FIVE

Tuesday 0500–2300

The sun rolled up, a blood-coloured disc above the ramparts of vapour. From somewhere – astern, possibly, it was hard to tell – heavy explosions thumped across the water. They sounded to Mallory like blasting charges.

Andrea said, 'Wallace was a good man, my Keith.'

Mallory nodded. His eyes hurt with peering into the fog. Wallace had done his duty; more than his duty. Now he was another offering on the altar of war. Unlike most such offerings, his death had not been in vain. Mallory felt sadness, and gratitude.

And puzzlement.

Wallace had not had any high explosives with him. It was unlikely the Germans would have used such explosives to winkle one man out of a hayloft.

It must be Cendrars and his men. They must have got their hands on some quarry explosive, and be slugging it out with the Germans. Mallory profoundly hoped that he was wrong. A pitched battle between the Germans and the heroes of the Marne would only bring down horrors on the civilian population. But he turned his face resolutely away from such speculations. What mattered was what lay ahead, in San Eusebio.

The light grew. They wrapped Guy in a tarpaulin and weighted his feet with a chunk of old scrap iron from the *Stella Maris'* noxious bilges. Jaime took off his beret and said a couple of Basque prayers. Hugues said, '*Vive la France!*' The body pierced the black surface of the sea with scarcely a ripple, and was gone.

The sea was getting to Mallory. In the globe of fog it was quiet, and grey, and solitary: an oasis in the desert of battle and violence that he wandered like a Tuareg. But Mallory disliked the peace of the sea in the same way a Tuareg might find an oasis cloying. It produced in him a nervous sickness, the sickness that the Tuareg might feel under green palms among people he did not know, as he watered his camels and longed to return to the real life of furnace winds and red-hot sands. Mallory experienced a moment of longing for the rock and ice of mountains: hard mountains whose habits he understood. Mountains in which he was not the hunter and the destroyer; mountains in which the only enemies were the failure of finger and foot to cling to hold, or human will to continue upwards.

He looked down at Andrea. The Greek was lying by the wheelhouse, smoking, watching the oily heave of the sea. He felt Mallory's eyes on him. He looked up. 'This is a most disgusting ocean,' he said.

Mallory nodded.

'These tides,' said Andrea. 'They are a thing of barbarians. How can men make ideas when the world they inhabit is being dragged here and there by the moon? It is for this that you are so restless, you of the North.'

Mallory laughed. They had escaped from a burning village and were on their way to attack a fortified rock. And Andrea was complaining about the tides.

But when he looked again at Andrea's face, he saw something that stopped his laughing. Despite his claims to the contrary, Andrea was not afraid of men or bullets, night or war. But unless Mallory was very much mistaken, Andrea was afraid of the cold black waters of the Atlantic.

He lit a cigarette. There was a breeze now, enough to whip the smoke away. The sun had gone, and the sky was a leaden grey. Mallory wedged himself into the corner of the wheelhouse. Twelve hours, he thought. He took inventory.

The *Stella Maris* was forty-five feet long. She had a tall mast at the front end and a short mast at the back end, which probably made her a ketch. There were what looked like sails on the booms, which Mallory devoutly hoped they would not have to use. There was a big fish-hold amidships, a dirty little fo'c'sle, and an engine room abaft the wheelhouse. The engine was a single-cylinder Bolander hot-bulb diesel, with a rust-caked flywheel the size and weight of a millstone. In the bullet-shattered wheelhouse was a compass of unknown accuracy, and the bloodstained Admiralty chart Guy had spread on his kitchen table all those weeks – hours – ago. The *Stella Maris* was thumping southwest through the fog at something like five knots, Mallory estimated. They should have moved out of French waters into Spanish. There would be patrol boats.

He offered a cigarette to Andrea. Andrea took it and lit it, scowling from under his black brows at the grey and sunless sea. 'A cold hell,' he said. He began to rummage restlessly in lockers. He found a new bottle of brandy, sniffed it, took a swig, and passed it to Mallory. One of the lockers was full of flags. He pulled out a yellow one. 'Quarantine,' he said. 'For when you have disease on board.' His white teeth showed in his black and bristly jaw. 'Or when you have goods to declare. This flag has never been used, I think.'

He's beaten it, thought Mallory. Andrea was not one to let irrational fears occupy space more profitably reserved for rational fears, like fear of failure in the face of the enemy. 'Guy said there was a Spanish flag,' he said.

Andrea rummaged some more, and came up with a red-and-yellow ensign. It was big, for easy visibility, and looked as if it had done long, solid service. Mallory gave Andrea the wheel, walked out of the wheelhouse and ran the ensign up to the top of the mizzen mast.

So now the *Stella Maris* was a Spanish boat, and all they had to worry about was motoring full ahead into the cliffs of Northern Spain.

The wind was definitely freshening. Ahead, the fog was becoming pale and ragged, and the slow Atlantic heave of the waves was taking on a sharper, more urgent feel.

Behind the wheelhouse, Miller stirred and opened his eyes. He lay for a moment, watching the Spanish flag snapping in the crisp breeze. Then he sat up and lit a cigarette. '*Buenos dias*,' he said. 'Coffee?'

'If you please,' said Mallory.

Miller stumbled down a flight of steps into the grease-varnished galley. From its door there emerged the smell first of paraffin, and then of coffee. He brought Mallory and Andrea mugs, well dosed with condensed milk and brandy. 'Nice as this is,' said

Miller, eyeing the sea with scorn and dislike, 'how long does it last?'

'At least till nightfall.'

The *Stella Maris* thumped on, rolling heavily in the swell from the west. The fog was thinning in the breeze, piling into banks. One particularly heavy bank hung to the south, a heap of grey vapour that should, if Mallory's dead reckoning was right, hide the land. Miller drank another cup of coffee and smoked two cigarettes in quick succession. His bony face, already pale with exhaustion, was turning greenish under the eyes. Mallory said to Andrea, 'Better let him steer,' and lay down on the bench at the back of the wheelhouse.

Sleep came immediately, deep as a lake. It all went: the submarines, fog, the approaching cliffs of Spain.

It was a peaceful sleep: not the two-inches-below-the-surface doze of action, but a deep, heavy coma, a sleep of the interregnum between the confusions of the Pyrenees and the task waiting on the Cabo de la Calavera. Watching him, Andrea saw the broad forehead smoothed of the tensions of the last three days, saw the knots at the hinges of the jaw relax. Rest well, my Keith, he thought. You have brought us a long way, but you have only brought us to the beginning.

Mallory dreamed. He dreamed he was in a place in the mountains, in a valley of grey stone through which a glacier inched. He dreamed that there were great birds wheeling in the sky that were not birds, but aeroplanes: Stukas. The Stukas were diving, dropping their bombs, which were bursting around him in red flowers of flame. But Mallory felt nothing, heard nothing, because he was separate from it all. A voice told him, 'You are in the ice.' Wallace's voice. And Mallory realised that it was true. He was encased in a huge block of clear ice, which was saving him from the bombs. But at the same time it was preventing him from feeling anything, and that was bad –

Then someone was shaking him, and he was coming up out of that ice, his mind clicking into awareness that something had changed. The engine was still panting, the boat still rolling. But he seemed to be wet, and there was a new sound: a shrill wailing, an ululation, the sound of the Stukas –

He swung his feet to the deck, eyes searching the sky. There were no Stukas. There were only clouds, arranged in long squalls, their bellies trailing rain. Against them, the *Stella Maris'* masts described jerky loops. Her stub nose rose and fell like a blunt wooden hammer, walloping the troughs into spray that came back down the deck in bucketfuls. The wailing was the wind in the rigging.

'Land, er, ho,' said Miller.

As Mallory stood up he saw the fog bank, smaller and lighter now, shift and writhe. Then a great hand of air seemed to grab it and wrench it aside.

Five miles away, across a grey and gnarled sea, the black cliffs of Spain stood high and clear. Through his glasses Mallory could see a bay, with a cluster of grey houses, and on one of the head-lands, the ruins of what might have been a fortress. He took a bearing and checked the chart. 'Forty miles to go,' he said. Miller nodded, without enthusiasm. Miller did not like the sea. As far as he was concerned, four miles would have been better; a lot better, even if there were two SS regiments at the end of it. 'Get Jaime on deck,' said Mallory.

Miller went below. Mallory kept the boat's head to the sea, blinking the spray out of his eyes. It had almost been better in the fog. He felt horribly exposed, out here in the clear grey breeze. And by the feel of it, they would be here all day; the *Stella Maris* was making four knots at best, labouring over these humpbacked seas like a weak-hearted charwoman climbing a flight of stairs.

Jaime appeared on deck, bleary-eyed. He squinted around him, said, 'That's Cabo del Lobo. Long way to go.'

'What about patrol boats?' said Mallory.

Jaime shrugged. 'They make big trouble on the border. This far down the coast, maybe they don't bother. Either way, they like money.'

'Stay on deck,' said Mallory.

Jaime nodded. He said, 'One thing. If you stay out here, people will be suspicious. You're a fishing boat. So we go in under the cliffs, no? That way, you are fishing. And nobody can see you from the land. And if we do get a problem, we throw some lobster pots in the sea.'

150

Mallory said, 'You know a lot about this.'

Jaime grinned, the grin of a man in his element. 'Frontiers are my business,' he said.

Mallory nodded. Without Jaime, they would not have found the Chemin des Anges, or the cave system. Without Jaime, they would have been dead.

The *Stella Maris* closed the shore. Across two hundred yards of grey and lumpy sea the cliffs reared three hundred feet into the grubby sky swept by the white motes of innumerable seabirds. Miller did not like the look of them at all. At least when their caïque had blown into the south cliff at Navarone it had been decently dark. If Miller was going to get smashed to bits, he would rather not get smashed to bits in broad daylight.

Hugues was on deck, looking as nervous as Miller felt. 'Is okay,' said Lisette, showing her white teeth. 'Jaime has sailed this route many times.'

'I didn't know you were a fisherman,' said Miller.

Jaime grinned, his dark eyes glinting under his beret. 'There are many people in the cigarette fishery,' he said. 'Sometimes you fish from a mule, sometimes from a boat.'

'It is not only lobsters you find in the pots here,' said Lisette.

Through the horrid queasiness of his belly, Miller thought that he saw in her something new, a confidence that she had not had in France. Of course, getting away from the Gestapo and into neutral territory would tend to improve your confidence, particularly if your guide in neutral territory was Jaime.

A sharp-crested hill of water swept under the *Stella Maris'* bow and dropped her into a trough. For a moment, Miller was once again weightless. To seaward a great hole had appeared in the sea, floored with weedy rock. 'Caja del Muerto,' said Jaime. 'Dead man's chest.' The waters closed over the rock with a boom, sending a depth-charge burst of ice-white spray a hundred feet into the wind.

For the next two hours the *Stella Maris* ground on down the inshore channel, invisible from the land. Mallory began to regain confidence. He went to Miller, who was lying in the scuppers alongside the wheelhouse, and said, 'Four hours' sleep. Then check your gear, and I'll brief the team.'

Miller groaned and dragged himself to the fo'c'sle, where Hugues was snoring on his bunk. He rolled into the bunk underneath, and passed out.

Mallory leaned against the wheelhouse, apparently watching the gulls on the cliffs. He had been thinking about Guy's chart of the Cabo de la Calavera and the harbour of San Eusebio. The approach was from the town quay, across the harbour, through the beach defences onto the Cape and into the U-boat repair docks. That was obvious.

Far too obvious.

The tide would be low, just after dark. The beach would be exposed and easy.

Far too easy.

Mallory lit a cigarette, and rested his head against the wheelhouse doorpost. There were features of the San Eusebio chart that had been making him think hard about cliffs; particularly if, as seemed likely, the wind fixed itself in the west.

'*Capitaine*,' said Jaime in a new, sharp voice, and pointed.

Mallory followed his finger.

Halfway to the horizon was the silhouette of a grey launch. As Mallory watched, the silhouette foreshortened until he could see the moustache of foam on either side of the bow.

He felt the muscles of his stomach clench and become rigid. San Eusebio seemed suddenly a long way away.

'Well,' he said, calm as a goldfish pond. 'I suppose it's time we hauled the pots.'

El Teniente Diego Menendez y Zurbaran was in a vile mood. It was not being posted to this wet green corner of Spain; he had fought hard for the Nationalists in the Civil War, so he had no objection to the sight of Basque towns in ruins and Basque children starving. It was worse than rain and Basques. A week ago, he had been told in an unpleasant interview with Almirante Juan de Sanlucar, his cousin and commanding officer, that he was to double his patrols and increase his vigilance generally. The Teniente had pointed out that his vigilance was as always at maximum, and that the patrol boat, known to its crew as the *Cacafuego*, was operating all the hours its ancient engine and weary rivets could stand. Sanlucar had assumed a dour, bellicose look, and told him that instructions from above did not take account of such objections. It was the will of . . . someone very exalted (here Sanlucar's lips framed the words *el Caudillo*) that patrols on the stretch of coast for which the Teniente was responsible should be greatly increased.

At the framing of the Dictator's august title, never lightly spoken aloud, the Teniente's heart had started to bang nastily in his chest. At first he had interpreted it as a general rebuke for his laxity; the pay of a Naval officer was scarcely a living wage in this dreary province of surly people and expensive food, so he had fallen into the habit of accepting the voluntary contributions of the smuggling fraternity. But he realised that there was more to it than that after a conversation with Jorge, his bosun. Jorge had observed military activity on the Cabo de la Calavera, and had approached the sentries on the gate, who were dressed in the uniforms of the First Zaragoza Regiment, to offer them the services of certain Basque women he maintained in the Calle Brujo in Bilbao. The soldiers had chased Jorge away, cursing him in a language that was not Spanish. Jorge had expressed to the Teniente the opinion, based on certain military vehicles and black uniforms he had half-glimpsed through the heavily-fortified gate that cut off the neck of the peninsula, that the garrison on the Cabo de la Calavera was German.

And thirty-six hours ago, just before this patrol, the Teniente had been notified that his bow gun crew was to be replaced, as were the port and starboard machine gunners. When the replacements had turned up, they had been German.

The Teniente had nothing against Germans. He disliked them only insofar as he disliked everyone except himself. But their presence on Cabo de la Calavera made him nervous, and their presence at his guns insulted his pride. He valued Spain's neutrality, because it meant his life was not in danger. He needed his bribes. And he had not taken kindly to standing on that worn patch of carpet in front of the Almirante's desk in Santander, being subjected by the Almirante to a diatribe on the importance of duty under the cold grey eyes of an obvious homosexual from the German Embassy in Madrid. This coast was the Teniente's

153

personal patch. The fact that his superior officers' new jumpiness was obviously German-inspired made him feel, insofar as such a feeling was possible for a Fascist, frankly bolshy.

So it was with no great sense of mission that he bore down on the familiar black hull of the *Stella Maris*, hauling lobster pots under the cliff.

He paused a hundred feet away, snarling at Paco the coxswain to keep the boat steady. The *Stella Maris* was head to wind, fat and black as ever. There were a couple of unfamiliar faces: two men who might have been northern Portuguese or even German, tall and lean, wearing singlets despite the cut of the west wind. They lurched uneasily on the *Stella Maris'* splintery deck; it looked to the Teniente as if they were not used to hauling lobster pots. But they were hauling all right. And back in the wheelhouse – it looked as if something had happened to the wheelhouse – Jaime Baragwanath was waving and grinning from under his beret. There seemed to be a woman with him.

The Teniente knew Jaime of old, as a fixer and a smuggler. He brought coffee out of Spain to France, and in the other direction the wines of Bordeaux, to alleviate the suffering caused by *vino negro*. If Jaime was personally on board the *Stella*, she would be carrying a high bulk, high value cargo, like wine.

The Teniente was partial to a few bottles of claret of an evening. Normally, he would have taken his cut at the landing. But he saw in the *Stella Maris* a way to impress his new gunners – and thus, he suspected, the Almirante – with his zeal.

The Teniente lit a thin black cigar and tilted his cap rakishly over his right eye. Plucking the brass megaphone from its clips on the bridge, he put its oxide-green business end to his mouth. 'Halt!' he shouted. 'I am boarding you.' On the foredeck, the crew of the 75-mm gun swivelled their piece to cover the *Stella*.

Mallory put a couple of loops of tail-line round a samson post, and tied it off with a knot that had more to do with rock faces than boats. He shuffled aft at a fisherman's slouch. He said to Jaime, 'What is this?'

'Routine inspection,' said Jaime, his dark face still, avoiding Mallory's eye. 'This officer takes bribes. He's used to seeing the *Stella* under the Spanish flag, as long as he get money. He maybe want some money. Or maybe some tobacco, drink, who knows?'

'Jaime knows,' said Hugues.

Mallory ignored him. He said, 'Does he normally point guns?'

'Not normally.' Jaime frowned at the men on the *Cacafuego's* foredeck. 'He's got new gunners.'

Mallory nodded and grinned, a simple fisherman's grin, full of salty good nature, for the benefit of anyone watching from the gunboat. His eyes were not good-natured. They checked off the rusting grey paint of the bow, the two blond men balancing easily on the deck by the breech of the 75-mm gun. The Captain was on the bridge. Aft of the bridge, another two men stood at machine guns. Spandaus. Spandaus were light guns, but they could still unzip a boat the size of the *Stella*. A 75-mm gun could blow her right out of the water.

But the guns were not the main problem. The main problem was the array of radio aerials between the two masts.

In his mind, he followed the trail of wreckage back into the Pyrenees. If the *guarda-costa* sent out a signal about unusual occurrences off the Vizcayan coast, any German with a map and eyes to see would be able to grasp the general direction of this dotted line of mayhem.

There was only one solution.

Mallory trotted forward and shouted down the main hatch. Jaime started yelling at the patrol boat in Spanish. The patrol boat was yelling back. Mallory cast off the tail-line of the lobster pots. Then he went aft to the wheelhouse. He said to Lisette, 'Get down, please.' He politely took the wheel from Jaime, spun it hard-a-starboard, and drove the *Stella Maris* straight at the patrol boat's mid point.

The Teniente started screaming into the megaphone. That was a mistake. By the time he had realised screaming was no good, the *Stella Maris* was twenty feet away. The 75-mm gun banged once. The shell screamed past the *Stella's* wheelhouse and burst on the black cliff face two hundred yards behind. The Spandaus opened up, bullets fanning across the sky as the gunboat rolled. Then Andrea and Miller came out of the *Stella's* forehatch like jack-in-the-boxes. Andrea hosed the gun's crew with Bren bullets. They disappeared. Hit or not, it did not matter, as long as they were away from the gun. Miller took the Spandau crews. By the time he had finished his burst, the *Stella Maris* was in a trough, the gunboat on a wave. The patrol boat's grey side came down with a rending crash on the *Stella*'s stem, and stuck there. The gunners on the patrol boat could not depress their sights far enough to bear on the *Stella*. Andrea had the Bren going by now, hammering a tight pattern of bullets into the patrol boat's hull, at the place where the radios might be. Miller pulled the pins out of four grenades. He tossed them up the patrol boat's side, heard them rattle down her decks, and heard the *blat* of their explosions in the wind. The two boats hung together in the form of a T, bashed and wrenched by the short inshore chop, the *Stella*'s bow borne down by the patrol boat's side. There was a hole in that side. The *Cacafuego*'s plates were no thicker than a tin can: a rusty tin can –

A wave came under. The *Stella* pitched away from the gunboat at the same time as the gunboat rolled away from the *Stella*. The gunboat's plates gave with a wrenching groan. The two boats came apart, the *Stella*'s bow rearing high as Mallory took her round and away.

'Fire!' screamed the Teniente. His ears were ringing from the grenade explosions. The radio aerials were gone, streaming in the breeze. The Teniente heard the bullets clang and whizz, and felt an odd sogginess in his ship's movements. 'Fire!' he screamed again. The *Stella Maris* was twenty yards away now. He saw the Spandau crews sprawled over their guns, and the foredeck by the 75-mm swept clean of men. He found that his feet were wet, and realised that his ship was sinking. He had been sunk by the *Stella Maris*. He opened his mouth to scream for help.

Then he thought of what his cousin would say when he told him that his armed patrol boat had been sunk by a bunch of smugglers.

The Teniente realised that the time had come to die.

He stood to attention, and shut his mouth.

The patrol boat rolled and sank in the space of twenty seconds. There was a tremendous eructation of bubbles. An oar came to the surface. Then nothing.

'*Jesus*,' said Jaime, pale to the lips.

Mallory turned his eyes away from the satiny patch of water where the patrol boat had been. Andrea's eyes were blank. The blankness had very little to do with shock, or the violent sinking of a *guarda-costa* with half a dozen crew. He and Mallory were both calculating whether the *guarda-costa* had announced its attentions on the radio before it had tried to come alongside the *Stella Maris*.

Mallory said, 'Full ahead, I think.'

Andrea nodded, and lowered his great bulk into the engine room.

The Bolander took on a more urgent thump. Mallory cut the tail-lines free from the bow. The *Stella Maris* heaved on westward, the wind cold in Mallory's face.

Jaime came on deck with Lisette. She looked pale. She had reason to look pale. Jaime said, '*Capitaine*, I need a word.'

Lisette watched them walk to the wheelhouse, watched Mallory's straight back, the precise step. Even on this filthy boat, that one walked like a soldier.

Jaime said, 'That was not normal.'

'Sorry?'

'I know this man,' said Jaime. 'The officer commanding the *guarda-costa*. He is a bastard, but a careful bastard. He would never stop the *Stella*. He takes money from smugglers, but not on the sea. Only in the bar, after they have gone ashore. The only reason he stopped us is because someone told him stop any ship.'

'So the Werwolf pack hasn't left,' said Mallory. 'Good.'

Jaime said, 'Was it necessary to kill those people?'

Mallory was not interested. 'There's a war on.'

'So you kill these men. Life into death. Like a mule turning food into shit.'

'War is nasty like that,' said Mallory. 'The reason we are here is to destroy submarines.'

Jaime grinned, a grin that held a horrible irony. 'Perhaps it is just that I do not like to destroy a useful trading partner.'

'There will be better trading after we have won the war,' said Mallory. 'Now, there are some things I need to know about the Cabo de la Calavera.'

*   *   *

By the middle of the day the sky was whitening under a veil of cirrus, and Miller had been sick fourteen times. Andrea was taking his spell at the pump; Andrea never got tired. Mallory came down into the fish-hold.

'Briefing,' he said. 'Ready for this?'

Andrea nodded, impassive behind his three days' growth of beard. Miller would have done the same, but nodding required energy, and he was saving his energy for when he really needed it.

Mallory said, 'There's a cliff on the seaward side of this Calavera place. Guy said it's not climbable. So the Germans won't be watching it. With luck.'

There was a silence, filled with the pant of the engine and the distant boom of waves on rock.

Miller said, 'If it's climbable, what do we do?'

Mallory lit his sixtieth cigarette since dawn. 'Climb it,' he said.

Miller shook his head weakly. 'Ask a silly question,' he said.

'We'll go over the side after dark,' said Mallory. 'In the dinghy. Jaime and Hugues and Lisette will take the *Stella* on into the harbour. They'll look like fishermen in to make repairs. The Germans have put big defences on the harbour side of the Cabo. As far as I can see, there's very little on the seaward side, because they've decided the cliffs will do the job. We'll go up in the dark, get ourselves some uniforms. Dusty, you'll want to check your equipment. We'll all need to shave. Questions?'

Miller listened to the boom of waves on rock. He said, 'How do we get from the dinghy onto the cliff? Seems to me that the sea has all these waves on it.'

Mallory flattened the chart on the filleting table. 'The sea's coming from the west.' He pointed to the northerly bulge of the shore. 'In behind here there's a wreck; Guy's friend Didier Jaulerry's fishing boat, went up the beach four months ago. Jaime says that with the sea from the west, you sometimes get a smooth patch in the lee of the wreck.'

'Sometimes.'

'During the bottom half of the tide. Till about 2100 hours tonight.'

Andrea said, 'It's not full dark at 2100.'

'It is at 2130.'

Miller said, 'But what if the waves are breaking clear over that wreck at 2130?'

Mallory folded the chart briskly, and stuck it in the pocket of his battledress blouse. 'Oh, I expect we'll manage,' he said.

There was more silence. There was a lot to hope for. They had to hope that the *guarda-costa* had not got a radio message off, and that the dinghy would not be spotted by the Germans or smash against the cliff, and that the *Stella Maris'* remaining complement would escape notice in San Eusebio.

The wind went up, and so did the waves. Lisette put her swollen ankles out of her bunk, and moved towards the filthy galley. Hugues stopped her. 'I'll cook,' he said. 'You rest.'

She looked at him with the dark-shadowed eyes of late pregnancy. He saw hostility and frustration. He said, 'What is it?' and tried to put his arm round her.

She pulled away. 'You're right,' she said. 'I'm tired.' She turned her face to the wall. Hugues went grim-faced into the galley and rummaged in the boxes that lined the bulkhead. Half an hour later, smoke was issuing from the chimney, and the smell of frying onions mingled horribly with the stench of the *Stella*'s fish-hold. And in an hour, a stew of tomatoes, hard chorizo, onions and potatoes was steaming in a blackened tureen. Jaime pulled a bottle of suspiciously good red wine out of a locker. Mallory, Andrea and Miller sat themselves at the table in the saloon. Mallory and Andrea ate hard and long. There was no talk. This was the grim refuelling of war machines. At the end, Andrea poured another tumbler of wine, lit a cigarette and leaned back against the fishing boat's side, eyes closed, humming a Greek tune full of Oriental runs and quarter-tones. Mallory looked across at him, the massive neck running into the colossal shoulders, the face peaceful in repose. He looked at Miller, smoking, pale-green under the eyes, in front of his largely untouched plate of stew. They looked like fishermen: tired fishermen, who smoked too much and drank too much when they could get hold of it. They looked like the kind of fishermen you would expect to find aboard this leaky boat with no bloody fish in the hold, and a smuggler, and an eight-months-pregnant woman, and the man who had got her pregnant.

They did not look like the cutting edge of a Storm Force whose task it was to climb a two-hundred-and-fifty-foot cliff in the dark, penetrate a strong and watchful garrison, and destroy the submarines of the Werwolf squadron.

Still, thought Mallory. Nobody would have believed the distance they had come to arrive at this point. But here they were. It was just a matter of carrying on: dividing the big problem into small, manageable problems, and solving them, one by one, with the tools at his disposal.

And a hell of a lot of luck.

Miller said, 'I guess I'll go turn in.' He shambled forward to the bunks.

When they were alone, Andrea said, 'What do you think about this?'

Mallory had known the Greek long enough to realise that he did not want an opinion, but a discussion. Mallory was in command of the expedition – there was no argument about that. But Andrea was a full colonel in the Greek army as well as one of the most dangerous and experienced guerrilla fighters in the Mediterranean. To fight at his most lethally efficient, Andrea needed to understand the situation.

Mallory said, 'It's a good place to keep some submarines.'

'Some hidden submarines.'

'That's right.'

'Good security.'

'That's right.'

'And that patrol boat. That was part of the security?'

'The gun crews looked German.'

'True.' Andrea stroked the place where his moustache should have been. 'And that was a routine patrol.'

'Sorry?'

'Not based on specific information.'

Mallory shrugged. 'No way of knowing,' he said.

'Quite.'

'Do we trust all these people?'

Mallory had been wondering the same thing. Jaime had a

smuggler's capacity for double-dealing. Hugues was brave, but he had an irrational streak a mile wide. And Lisette . . . well, Lisette under Storm Force control was safer than Lisette at large.

'We've got to,' he said.

Andrea nodded. There was a pause. Then he said, 'It seems to me that the Germans will have problems of their own.'

That had also occurred to Mallory. Spain was full of spies. To keep the occupation of Cabo de la Calavera secret, the garrison would be manned and supplied from the sea, or across the Pyrenees, by night. Either way, it would be a smuggling operation, with all the inconveniences attendant on such operations. And German efficiency or no German efficiency, it seemed likely that a garrison hastily convened and furtively supplied would be a less well-organised garrison than the garrison of, say, Navarone. Confusion would be to the Storm Force's advantage.

Andrea poured the last of the wine into the two glasses, and raised his to Mallory. 'My Keith,' he said. 'Victory, or a clean death.'

'And two days' kip to follow,' said Mallory.

He thought, in five hours, we will be on hard rock again, climbing. He raised his own glass and drank. Andrea swung his boots up onto the bench, put his head on his pack, and closed his eyes.

The door opened. Miller came in.

At first, Mallory thought he had been shot. His face was bloodless, his lips the colour of ashes. But he was walking well, braced against the heave of the *Stella Maris'* deck. In his hands he was carrying the big, brass-bound boxes that held his explosives and his fuses.

Mallory said, 'Sleep first. Check gear later.'

Miller shook his head. He did not speak: it was as if something had happened that had removed his voice. He lifted the boxes and placed them side by side on the gutting table. He unlatched them, opened the lids, and gestured at the contents.

If the Storm Force was a bomb, the personnel were the fuse and the casing and the fins. What was inside those two brass-bound mahogany boxes was the charge: the stuff that would do the job, blast those three Werwolf submarines into water-filled hulks and save the lives of all those men crammed into transports on the Channel.

Mallory looked into the boxes. His mouth became dry. His mind went back six hours, to the bay of St-Jean-de-Luz, the red ball of the sun hauling itself up through the fog, the heavy explosions coming from the land. He had thought that Commandant Cendrars' old soldiers had got their hands on some quarry explosive.

He had been wrong.

They had been fifteen minutes on the cliff at Martigny, while Andrea disposed of the pillbox and Mallory and Miller had explained their wishes to the sentries. During that fifteen minutes, the boxes had been in the care of Commandant Cendrars' enthusiastic veterans.

The veterans had profited from those fifteen minutes. Possibly their arsenal had been running low, or possibly they merely suffered from an enthusiastic lightness of finger. Whichever the case, the outcome was the same.

The brass-bound boxes that had contained the explosives and detonators that were going to blow the Werwolf pack to hell now contained, besides a few blades of wet grass and a couple of small stones, half a hundredweight of best Martigny mud.

There was a silence that seemed to last five years. It was Andrea who broke it. He yawned. 'Oh, dear,' he said. 'Now I must sleep.'

'Take the bunk,' said Miller, through lips numb with shock.

'Thank you,' said Andrea, and shuffled bear-like into the sleeping cabin. It was as if he understood Miller's sense of failure, and attached to it little enough weight to accept the offer of the bunk as full reparation.

Miller said, 'I let it out of my sight.' Never let your tools out of your sight. If you carry a gun, carry it at all times. Keep your knife strapped on, even in the bathtub. And never, ever, leave your Cyclonite and your detonators to be guarded by heroes of the Marne with the wind under their tails. 'We have grenades.'

'Ten grenades,' said Mallory. His knees felt weak. He was sweating. So this is how it ends, he thought.

Miller said, 'Four. We used eight on the patrol boat.' He was thinking again. 'Anyway, grenades won't work on U-boat pressure hulls.' But he did not say it nervously. He said it in a measured, judicious voice, like a prosecution lawyer assessing the chances of convicting a known murderer on circumstantial evidence. If grenades would not work, the voice implied, it would be necessary to find something else that would.

Mallory heard that new voice.

For a moment, he had felt it all slipping away from him. That was because in his exhaustion he had forgotten that this was Dusty Miller, who had destroyed the guns at Navarone and the dam at Zenica, not to mention an Afrika Korps ammunition dump with a Cairo tart's hairpins. Confidence began to tiptoe back into Mallory's thoughts.

'So I guess they'll have a magazine there,' said Miller. 'And they'll have to load the torpedoes some time. Your torpedoes take up most of the space on a U-boat. You couldn't refit with torpedoes on board, could you?' He folded his hands. 'So there's that. And then there's the engines. Those Walter engines. Hydrogen peroxide, you said. Fuel oil. Water. Interesting stuff, hydrogen peroxide.' He leaned his long back against the bulkhead, hands folded across his concave stomach, boots propped on the opposite bench, eyes closed. He seemed to be thinking.

Finally, Mallory could stand it no longer. 'What about hydrogen peroxide?' he said.

But Miller was asleep.

Mallory thought about waking him, then decided against it. If the Werwolf pack was sailing tomorrow at noon, would they not already have loaded the torpedoes? And what was so interesting about hydrogen peroxide?

He lit another cigarette. Relax, he told himself. Miller and Andrea were of the opinion that the operation was possible. So the operation was possible. Easy as that.

Within thirty seconds, Mallory, too, was asleep.

It was the gulls that were the first sign. All afternoon, after the turn of the tide, they had been thickening in the sky. When Mallory went on deck, groggy in the mind after too little and too shallow sleep, their cries filled the air.

The *Stella Maris* had moved out to sea again. A stiffish breeze was blowing from the northwest, and on it the gulls slid and balanced with frantic voices and perfect self-possession. The wind seemed to be blowing out of the sun, which had appeared pale and brilliant below the roof of grey cloud. It was twenty minutes before sunset, but there was no red in that sun. It glared like a big metal eye across the water, draining the colour from everything its rays touched, making the *Stella Maris* black and the seas grey, and the cliffs the dull non-colour of slate. And shining into the eyes of anyone watching from the land.

Mallory lit a cigarette, stuck it between the nicotine-stained fingers of his left hand, and pulled his Zeiss glasses out of their case. He panned the disc of vision across the crawling waves until he found the black line of the land: a flat black line, a continuous cliff, marred here and there by pillars of rock over which a mist of spray hung, silvering the towers of gulls. He moved the glasses to the west.

The line of the cliff suddenly rose into a rounded hump, sheer-sided. The sides plunged straight down into the sea. The structure looked like a steel helmet, or a skull. Cabo de la Calavera. The cape of the skull.

Mallory breathed smoke, and made a fine adjustment to the focus wheel.

On the crown of the skull, at the apex, a stubby white pencil jutted skyward: the lighthouse. The lighthouse was not showing a light. To the right of the lighthouse, on what might have been the skull's forehead, were square-edged masses, topped by a tower. The fortress: an efficient fortress, dug into the cliff to cover the entrance to the harbour of San Eusebio. He moved the disc of the glasses eastward, along the spine of the ridge.

There was a structure of some kind slung across what must have been the throat of the peninsula, but they were too far away for Mallory to see what it was. He could guess, though. It looked like a stone wall, probably with battlements and a moat. The Germans would have supplemented it with a line of fences and trenches. As far as he could tell, it stopped abruptly some distance above the sea – where the cliff became vertical, he guessed. The base of the cliff was a continuous line of white water.

Mallory walked aft. Jaime was at the wheel. Mallory said, 'You

164

have come out of some port. You are in trouble. You are making repairs to the engine. Do you know anybody in San Eusebio?'

'Only professionally.'

'That will do. Get estimates for repairs.' Mallory pointed at the radio set in the wheelhouse. 'That work?'

Jaime grinned. 'A smuggler's radio always works.'

'Keep it switched on. Now let's go ashore.'

'How are you getting ashore?' said Jaime.

Mallory said, 'We'll manage.' At this stage in the expedition, there was no sense in telling anyone on the *Stella Maris* any more than he needed to know. He looked at his watch. It said 2015. 'We'll get to you before 1500 tomorrow. Be alongside the fish quay. We'll sail immediately we're on board.'

'For where?'

Mallory looked pious. 'The Lord will provide,' he said.

Jaime looked at the black rock skull of the Cabo, with its cloud of gulls, tinted by the now-pinkening sun. 'A-okay,' he said. *'Bonne chance.'*

The *Stella Maris'* nose turned and settled on the brow of the skull. The sun was sinking fast now, and as it sank its pink turned to blood, dabbling the cloud-roof with crimson. 'Looks like hell,' said Jaime.

'Sorry?' said Mallory. To him it looked like a sunset, followed by a hard climb in the dark.

'No importa,' said Jaime.

Darkness fell.

An hour later, Mallory, Miller and Andrea were in the *Stella Maris'* dinghy, heaving up and down on the seven-foot swell rolling out of the Atlantic wastes. The pant of the *Stella's* engine was receding eastward. In the dinghy with the three men were the two coils of wire-cored climbing rope, three Schmeissers with five spare magazines each, and the grenades. They were dressed in Waffen-SS smocks, camouflage trousers and steel helmets. In the breast pocket of his smock, Mallory carried the special pitons Jonas Schenck had made for him in 1938, out of the rear springs of a Model A Ford. Anything else they needed they would have to find on the Cabo.

At least, that was the idea.

Miller sat in the bow of the boat, his knees close to his ears, clutching the lock of his machine pistol to keep out the wet. Miller was fairly sure that this was it: the end. He would not have minded, except that he did not wish the end, when it came, to have anything to do with the sea. Miller had had enough of the sea.

The dinghy rose and sank again, vertiginously, on a glossy black wave like the back of a man-eating animal. Andrea dug in the oars and took a couple of strokes towards the darkness above the booming white line that separated vertical rock from Atlantic ocean.

'There,' said Mallory.

In the line of white there was a break; the merest hint of a break, the sort of paling that would come of a wave whose force was spent before it hit the wall. Spent, for instance, by the wreck of a fishing boat once the property of a M. Jaulerry, impaled on the boulders at the base of the cliff.

Miller thought, we will at any rate have the advantage of surprise. And if we live, nobody will be as surprised as me.

Then Andrea gave a final heave and the dinghy went up on the back of another wave, as huge and black as the last. Only this one did not stay huge and black, but while the dinghy was on its crest turned white and foaming, insufficiently substantial to support the dinghy, which was falling, with the whole of the rest of the world, stern-first, in a cataclysm of water that made a sound like an earthquake, and had no bottom –

They found the bottom. They found it with a sudden splintering crash that knocked the seat from under Miller. He discovered that things previously available for holding on to were no longer available for that purpose. Then the wave had him, and he was rolling away somewhere, he could not tell where, except that he had a Schmeisser slung round him, a couple of kilos of negative buoyancy that were going to drag him a watery grave among the boulders at the base of the cliff, and he thought, so this is it.

But then something had him by the collar of his smock, and was dragging him in the opposite direction from the direction in which the water wanted to take him. And he was out of that black whirl, and on something hard and slimy that he realised must be the deck of the wrecked fishing boat. And Andrea's voice was saying into his ear, 'When we get ashore, check your weapon.' And things were back to normal.

Or what passed for normal, on the seaward side of the Cabo de la Calavera.

At the base of the cliff was a beach of boulders which had fallen from the crags above, forming a sort of glacis on which the waves beat themselves to white tatters. The fishing boat had hit this beach, been driven up to its summit, and landed wedged with a northeast–southwest orientation, its bow rammed against the main face of the cliff, which ran east–west.

Mallory, Andrea and Miller crouched for a moment on the slimy deck, tilted away from the hammer of the seas, feeling the concussion of the rollers in their bones. Then Mallory handed his Schmeisser to Andrea, slung one of the coils of rope over his shoulder, and stepped on nailed soles down the deck towards the ink-black rise of the cliff.

The first ten feet were boulders, slippery with bladder wrack, treacherous in the complete blackness, but by no means steep. Mallory went up carefully but fast, until his hands met something that was not seaweed. Lichen. Then a cushion of vegetation set in sand and peat that crumbled under his fingers. His fingers crawled above it, looking for a hold. They found loose rock. The cliffs of Cabo de la Calavera were not as solid as they looked.

He glanced downwards. The backwash of the breaking waves was a broad white road, cut aslant by the hull of the fishing boat. He felt wet on his face as a big wave hit.

He started to climb.

It was a bad climb. The rock down here was as rotten as cheese, and a sparse vegetation of moss and sea-thrift had taken hold in the cracks. Each hold meant a sweep with the fingers to remove loose soil, a gradual increase of pressure from the fingers until they bore his full weight, resting on at least two firm points while he tested a third, slow and sure, never committing himself. He went up the cliff inch by inch, chest sore from the cigarettes of the past three days, finger muscles burning, horribly aware of the clatter of loose stone down the cliff below him.

After five minutes the climbing became mechanical, as it always did: a delicate shifting of balance from hold to hold, working from the hips, so he seemed to float rather than crawl. And the part of his mind not filled with testing holds and balancing on rock went ahead, onto the Cabo. There were Totenkopf-SS up here, from what Guy had said. There would be Wehrmacht too. And Kriegsmarine, and dockyard workers. A force hastily assembled, wearing a diversity of uniforms, strangers to each other, probably in the final stages of preparing for departure. There would be confusion. Mallory devoutly hoped it would be a confusion he could exploit.

He was seventy feet up now. The wind was battering his ears, and the rumble of the seas had receded until it had become a dull, continuous roar. He reached out his hand for the next hold, fumbling like a blind man.

Suddenly he was no longer blind. Suddenly his hand emerged from the darkness, a pale spider groping its way across quartz and matrix towards the dark shadow of a hold. The cliff face had come into an odd, shadowed relief, a landscape of vertical hills and vales stretching down to a sea whose waves now looked not so much black as silver-grey.

And above the horizon of the cliff, where the sky had been a matt emptiness of squally cloud, there had taken place the change that had brought about all the other changes. The squalls had turned and separated. Between them fingers of deep black sky had appeared, specked with the needle-tips of stars. And into one of those bottomless chasms of darkness swam like a silver lamp a brilliant quarter moon.

Mallory froze, clinging to the face of the cliff. Far below, he saw white surf and the wreck of the fishing boat sheltering its tiny eddy of black water. He could distinctly see shattered wreckage from the dinghy spinning in the vortex. This was bad. Potentially, this was very bad. All it needed was a casual glance down the moonlit cliff. The Storm Force would be pinned down, brushed off the rock face like flies. And the Werwolf pack would sail at noon tomorrow, unmolested.

The wind blew, eddied, became for a second still.

Directly above Mallory's head, someone coughed.

Mallory's stillness intensified until it was like the stillness of the rock face itself. He turned his eyes upwards. The moon was sliding towards a lip of cloud. But before it went and darkness swept back over the cliff, he saw something he had not noticed before.

Up there on the cliff face was an overhang of rock too regular to be natural.

The coughing came again. There was a brief splash of yellow light. A little spark dropped past Mallory's head. A spent match.

Mallory eased his feet on their minute ledges, and leaned in against the cliff. He turned his face upwards and watched.

To his dark-accustomed eyes, the regular glow of the cigarette was as bright as a lighthouse. Against it, he analysed the little bulge of masonry projecting from the cliff. It was a half-moon of stone or concrete, a demilune, a strongpoint built out from a narrow ledge of the cliff. Mallory rested, recreating in his mind the fortifications of the Cabo. This would be the seaward end of the line of fortifications running across the neck of the peninsula.

The moon slid out again. By its light he could see the joins in the masonry. Not German, he thought. Older than this war.

Something gleamed in the moonlight: something shaped like a small funnel. The flame deflector on the muzzle of a light machine gun. The old Spanish defences had new tenants.

For the blink of an eye, Mallory took stock.

To his right, the cliff was sheer, but climbable. But the moon was painting it a brilliant grey. Figures climbing over there would be plainly visible from the demilune. To the left, the cliff looked even easier, the summit concealed behind a shoulder of rock. There was no way of telling what was on that summit. There was only one thing you could be sure of: even if the top was undefended, and you could arrive there without being seen, you would be the wrong side of the fortifications at the top, and there would still be the gates to get through.

So there was only one way.

Straight up.

He eased the commando knife in the sheath on his right hip, and began once again to climb.

The moon was swimming in a wider gulf now. But Mallory

169

climbed fast and efficiently, knowing that he was directly underneath the demilune, invisible. It took him ten minutes to cover the hundred feet: ten quiet minutes, choosing holds with a surgeon's delicacy, breathing slow and deep through his nose. This was the Mallory who had moved remorselessly up the southeast face of Mount Cook, above the Caroline glacier. A crumbling Atlantic cliff was a stroll in the park to this Mallory.

The base of the demilune was a bulge of masonry rooted in the natural rock. Mallory paused on an exiguous ridge ten feet underneath it. He collected his breath, then took off his boots and socks and hung them round his neck. The sea was a dull mutter two hundred feet below. Above, he could hear a pair of boots walking four steps left, pause, four steps right, pause. He stood for a moment, fingers and toes gripping their holds, balancing like a man on springs, waiting for the four steps left, two steps right –

He took a deep breath, and went up the final ten feet like a spider up a wall.

If you had asked him then or afterwards what holds he had used or what route he had followed, he would not have been able to say. It seemed to him that one moment he was poised below the emplacement, and the next he was alongside it, looking over a waist-high wall at the silhouette of a figure in German uniform. The figure had its back to him, at the far end of the four steps left. And there was a bonus, because the figure stayed there, shoulders bowed, helmet brim lit flickering yellow from below. Lighting another cigarette. Very soon after the last one –

Mallory loosened the knife in its sheath, put his left hand on the parapet of the demilune, his right on the ledge at its side –

Two things happened.

Mallory's right hand landed in a pile of twigs and dry seaweed and something warm and feathery that suddenly came alive and started to shriek in a high, furious voice. And the moon came out from behind its cloud.

For a split second, Mallory hung by his left hand on the wall, staring into the slack-jawed faces of not one, but two young German soldiers. Then he realised that he had no foothold, and fell, feet kicking air, to the full extent of his left arm. *Fool*, he told himself, feeling the crack of muscle and sinew, gritting his teeth against the agony of his clawed fingers on the rock of the parapet. He waited a split second that felt like a year, waited for the rifle butt to smash his fingers, waiting for the Germans to start yelling, alert the garrison –

His right hand was on the cliff face now, clawing for a hold, finding one. Somewhere he could hear the squawking of a frightened gull, the harsh breathing of young, panic-stricken Germans trying to work out a way of getting rid of this *thing* from the cliff, and forgetting that the easiest way of doing it was to yell and let their five hundred comrades do it for them.

Mallory had an idea.

He said, '*Hilfe.*'

He had learned his German at Heidelberg University before the war, and on the high crags of the Bavarian alps in the sunlit middle years of the 1930s. His accent was perfect; so perfect that the Germans hesitated.

'Get a hold of me,' said Mallory, in German. 'I fell.'

The soldiers were bamboozled with relief. This was not an enemy but a victim, a comrade in need –

The hesitation lasted the fraction of a second. That was enough for Mallory. He heaved himself up and halfway over the parapet. The Germans looked undecided. This was a Mallory undisturbed by seagulls. This was a Mallory who for eighteen months had lived wild as an animal in the White Mountains of Crete.

The Germans did not stand a chance.

Mallory drove his dagger through the first one's eye and into his brain. The second one opened his mouth to shout. Mallory drove his fist into his throat. He tugged the knife from the eye socket. As the body hit the ground the second German came at him, gasping. The man's momentum carried him on, over Mallory's shoulders and the parapet. Then he was hanging face down, caught by the toe of his boot, hooked on a small projection of the stone. If his vocal cords had been functioning, he would have been screaming.

Mallory felt an odd tugging sensation. He saw the German's boot slip, millimetre by millimetre, in the moonlight. Some part of the German had gone through the spare coil of rope Mallory carried on his shoulder. When he fell, he was going to take Mallory with him.

Mallory dived inside the parapet. The German emitted a quiet, rasping croak. The boot went over the edge. A crushing load came suddenly on the rope. It lifted Mallory. But the friction of the parapet stopped it dragging him over the edge.

Cautiously, Mallory found an end of the coil and belayed it to the iron steps set in the rock above the demilune. Then he wriggled out of the toils.

The rope ran out. He looked over the edge.

The part of the German that had caught the coil had been his neck. Mallory left him to hang while he tipped the first German over the edge. Then he began to untangle the rope.

'Okay, Schlegel?' yelled a voice in German from above

'Fine,' shouted Mallory. Thirty feet below the demilune, the corpse of the second German swung like a clock pendulum over the dizzy swoop of the cliff and the rock-smashed waves at its base.

The moon went in. Mallory let an end of the rope go. The hanging German became a patch of darkness falling through greater darkness to the ribbon of white below. He thought he saw a little splash. Then he finished untangling the rope, and let it drop to where Miller and Andrea were waiting. While they climbed, he put his boots and socks back on.

Five minutes later, Miller and Andrea were with him in the demilune, breathing heavily. He pulled up the rope, coiled it, clambered over the parapet and hung it in the branches of a stunted juniper in the cliff, out of sight below the base. By the time he got back, he could no longer hear their breathing.

'Ready?' he said.

The silhouettes of the two coal-scuttle helmets nodded.

Mallory looked at his watch. The radium-bright hands said 2215. He said, 'I'll meet you by the generators at midnight. Check the sentries on the repair sheds. Look at rotas, timings. And Dusty. Your department. Bangs and so on.'

'Sir,' said Miller.

'And if you could avoid getting caught?'

Andrea's teeth gleamed suddenly in the moonlight. 'But without my moustache, where shall I hide?'

Mallory laughed quietly. 'See you at midnight,' he said. He stepped lightly onto the parapet of the demilune, reached out a hand and a foot, and stepped onto the naked cliff.

For a moment, he hung there in the moonlight, poised easily on the apparently sheer rock wall. Miller closed his eyes and held onto the first of the iron rungs leading upwards from the demilune, his stomach weightless with vertigo. Climbing a rope was one thing. This human-fly business was another altogether.

When he opened his eyes again, the little cloud was passing away from the moon, and the face of the cliff was once more covered with light. But of Mallory there was no sign.

'Off we jolly well go,' said Andrea.

Andrea led the way up the iron rungs in the cliff face. It was a fifty-foot climb. At the top was a sort of stile in the parapet. Before he reached it, Andrea hooked an arm through the rung, brushed the worst of the cliff-dirt from his SS smock, and pulled back the cocking lever of his Schmeisser. This was easier than thrashing around in the Pyrenees. Here, you knew whom you could trust. It was the old team, without distractions: a well-oiled machine.

He stepped up onto the parapet, keeping his shoulders hunched to reduce his mighty bulk. He probably looked nothing like either of the men Mallory had killed. But it was elementary to suppose that if two men had clambered down a set of iron rungs to a stone gull's nest, below which was a precipice and some sea, then the two men who came back up the rungs were the same two men, even if they looked different.

He said, in his perfect German, 'Hell, it's cold down there.'

The parapet formed the edge of a sort of terrace ten yards wide, down a flight of stone steps from another fortified level. A line of ancient cannons stood rotting at their embrasures. At the end of the line of cannons were the silhouettes of two men with a machine gun. One of the men said, 'Bloody cold up here, too.'

Private soldiers, thought Andrea. No problem. 'Coffee,' he said.

'There's over an hour to midnight,' said one of the shadows. '*Befehl ist Befehl.*'

173

Andrea shrugged. He looked down over the edge. The moonlit precipice fell away sheer to the sea. No sign of Mallory. 'Hurry up, you.'

Miller came up and onto the terrace.

Andrea said, 'We'll get the coffee and take it down.' The note of authority in Andrea's voice had not escaped them. An officer. Officers had their reasons.

'*Marsch*,' said Andrea.

Miller in the lead, they stamped up the stone steps from the terrace to the summit level.

'Right *turn*,' said Andrea.

The two of them were marching along a flat plain, paved with stone, silvery under the moon. To their right, the parapet marked the edge of the cliff. Ahead and to the left, the ground sloped away and downwards into the black pit, beyond which guttered the few yellow lights of San Eusebio. Immediately to the left, cracks of light showed round the poorly blacked-out panes of what must be a guardhouse. Immediately behind them was an ancient battlement, topped with modern barbed wire, that looked as if it stretched from the cliffs to the beach facing the town.

They were in. In, but horribly in the open.

Somewhere in the guardhouse a bell rang and a man's voice began screaming: a parade-ground scream, a scream of military emergency requiring immediate action. Lights jumped on. The surface on which Andrea and Miller were standing was suddenly a harshly illuminated plain on which each was the focus of an asterisk of shadows. Men in jackboots were pouring out of doors, lining up shoulder to shoulder, distancing off, shuffling jackboot heels on the granite stones. Miller could feel the sweat now, not climbing sweat, but the sweat of being in the middle of five hundred Germans.

Andrea yelled, '*Shun!*' Miller crashed to a halt.

They were in, all right. But not all the way.

What they had not been able to see without the floodlights was straight: a second fence, running parallel with the wall, fifteen feet tall, topped with barbed wire strung between insulators, stretching from the rim of the cliff down to the black waters of the harbour. The area between the fences was a no-man's land, bathed in a pitiless grey-white light that limned every speck of grit, every button and buckle on the hundred-and-twenty German soldiers fallen in between the guardhouse and the sandbagged machine-gun posts on either side of the main gate.

Miller could feel a trickle of sweat on his forehead. Andrea was massive and silent at his side.

In the middle of the inner fence was another gate. The gate stood open. On either side were more machine-gun emplacements. The floodlights gleamed off the steel helmets by the guns.

Andrea's eyes flicked round the yard. The soldiers were Wehrmacht, not SS. His shoulders squared. In a voice of brass, he said, '*Marsch!*' Holding their Schmeissers rigidly across their chests, the two men tramped steadily across the paving. The gate loomed up ahead, a goal of darkness in the palisade of the fence. Miller could feel the mouths of the machine guns pouting at him from their emplacements. At his side, he could see that Andrea's helmet was tilted a fraction, and there was dirt on his camouflage smock. Must have been when he went up the cliff. Wehrmacht hated dirt. Almost as much as they hated SS . . .

Someone, thought Miller, had raised the alarm. It must have been those guys down by the cannons. They had waited for the intruders to walk right into the hornet's nest, and then stirred it up with a pole. They would be looking for two men in SS uniforms. And here were these two men, in wet, dirty SS uniforms, marching across the killing floor under the floodlights.

Miller marched on. A small seed of hope took root and began to grow. Nobody was doing anything about it. Maybe, thought Miller, this is an exercise. Or maybe they are so frightened of the SS that they will not even screw with the uniform. Maybe this is just a a regular night in a major military installation, and you have been skulking in the mountains so long you have forgotten.

Pace by pace, the sandbags reached out and funnelled them towards the black gate. Behind them, someone was bellowing orders. On the right, three privates and a Feldwebel were standing rigidly to attention. Miller could feel the Feldwebel's eyes flicking up and down: the eyes of a stickler, used to cataloguing a minute smear on the surface of a boot, a tiny flaw in the polish of a leather strap. And these SS guys were marching through his gate squelching with Atlantic and covered in half a cliff.

Andrea marched on, regular as a metronome, out of the gate area and away from the eyes and into the darkness beyond. The darkness that held the docks and those U-boats, waiting to slide out of the harbour and back into their black underwater world –

They were through. The lights were dimming, shaded by the brim of Miller's helmet. Made it, he thought. We have goddamn well made it –

The darkness was suddenly full of metallic noises. Ahead and to the left, brilliant suns of light came into being. A voice said, in English, 'Do not touch your guns. The hands out to the sides, if you please. You are completely surrounded.'

Miller squinted to one side of the light, but saw nothing. There could be one man or a hundred men back there. A hundred seemed more likely.

Slowly and reluctantly, he spread his arms out in an attitude of crucifixion.

So this is how it really ends, thought Miller.

Figures emerged from the dark, figures in SS uniform. The figures looped the Schmeisser straps over Miller's head and stood on tiptoe to disarm Andrea.

'Welcome, gentlemen,' said the SS Hauptsturmführer. His accent was very good. 'We have been expecting you.'

Then they marched them away.

SIX

Tuesday 2300–Wednesday 0400

They marched them through a little village of wooden huts, past a wire-fenced concrete building that throbbed with diesels. Living quarters, thought Miller, collecting information he would never use. Generator shed. Down on the left, the jackhammer rattle of riveting guns sounded, and the tame lightnings of arc welders flashed blue in the dark. Dockyard stuff. A privileged overview of the whole layout.

'*Halt!*' yelled the Hauptsturmführer in charge of their escort.

They were standing on a bridge in front of a gateway in a tall, windowless granite wall. The gate was studded with iron bolts. Above it were battlements. The sweat was cold on Miller's body, and his body ached. He was exhausted.

A wicket opened in the gate. The Hauptsturmführer stepped forward and showed a pass to the gatekeeper. There was a pause, with the sound of telephoning. Then the double gates opened, and a machine pistol jabbed Miller in the kidney. The squad marched in. The gates clashed to behind them.

They were in a yard, paved with granite, surveyed by the barrels of three machine guns sited on the battlements. Same old thing, thought Miller. 'No imagination,' he said.

'But very competent,' said Andrea, his eyes moving, mapping the yard. 'Thorough.'

'That's Germans for you,' said Miller. 'Thorough.'

The gun muzzle behind him jabbed him painfully in the kidney. 'Silence!' barked the Hauptsturmführer.

'Don't understand,' said Andrea.

'Don't speak German,' said Miller.

And for a second there was a small warmth in the notion that although they were in the hands of the enemy, mission not

177

accomplished and never to be so, they had something up their sleeves.

Two things. There was also Mallory, still at large.

A door opened in the wall opposite. This was not your studded oak, medieval style. This was your basic twentieth-century armour plate, four good inches of Nazi steel. It gaped wide, exhaling a stink of damp stone and sewage. Then it swallowed them in, and the door clashed to at their backs.

They went down granite stairs, through corridors with bomb-proof roofs and whitewash blistered with mildew. There was a spiral staircase like the entrance to a tomb. At the bottom, a corridor lit glaring white was lined with steel doors. One of the steel doors was open.

'In there,' said the Hauptsturmführer.

'We will take a look,' said Miller. 'If we don't like the linen, we will speak to the manager about –'

The soldier behind him smashed him on the ear with the barrel of his Schmeisser. Miller's head rang with pain. A jackboot shot him through the door. Andrea followed. The steel door clashed shut. Outside, jackboots tramped off down the corridor.

There was brilliant white light, and dirt, and silence.

The warmth had gone. They were in the stone bowels of the earth, and it was cold.

The silence was the worst part.

The room might have been designed as a magazine, or a cell. It had a domed roof, and no window. The floor was of granite flagstones, patched with concrete. There was a grating in one corner, presumably for use as a lavatory. From it there came a vile smell.

The silence was the silence of a place buried beneath tons of masonry and rock. It was the silence of a place with no secret passages, no hope of overpowering guards, no hope of escape. The silence of the tomb.

Mallory, reflected Miller, would have hated it.

Andrea yawned. He said, 'This is really most unpleasant.' Then, with the massive grace of an animal that refuses to be concerned about the future because it inhabits the perpetual present, he located a cleanish patch of floor, lay down, and closed his eyes.

They had left Miller his cigarettes. He pulled out the packet, found a dry one, and lit it.

Then he waited.

The hands on his watch ticked along to eleven-thirty. At eleven-thirty-one, a key clashed in the door, and five men came in.

Four of them were big Waffen-SS whose torsos strained at their camouflage smocks. The fifth was a man of about twenty-five, wearing civilian clothes: a blue double-breasted suit, with a stiff collar and a dark-blue tie. His hair was blond, with a wave. His mouth was a little red rosebud, his eyes blue slugs that crawled over the prisoners' faces.

He waved a handkerchief under his nose. 'Really,' he said, in prissy, faintly-accented English. 'They should do something about the smell.' He smiled, a cherubic smile. 'Gentlemen,' he said, 'I am Herr Gruber.' He snapped his fingers. 'Chair.'

One of the burly SS men trotted into the corridor, and returned with a hard chair. Herr Gruber flicked the seat with his handkerchief and sat down.

Miller and Andrea sat side by side, slouched against the wall. Miller yawned. Andrea watched Gruber with eyes that managed to be simultaneously hostile and condescending. In their travels in occupied Greece, both of them had had experience of the Gestapo. Neither of them understood why they were still alive. Herr Gruber was going to provide the answers.

Miller said, 'So can we help you? Only I am kinda sleepy, and –'

Gruber had made a gesture to one of the SS men. The barrel of the man's gun came round quickly, slamming into Miller's already bruised ear. The pain of the cartilage trapped between metal and skull was ferocious. Miller's eyes watered. He kept his anger down. Save it for later.

If there was a later.

'So,' said Herr Gruber. 'I understand that now you would like to kill me and these soldiers.' He smiled, his cherubic smile. 'And the SS is not what it used to be. So I expect you could probably do it. But I would point out that the odds against you are most impressive. Even if you were to escape this cell, you would quickly lose your own lives. Which if you listen to me may not be necessary.'

179

Gruber watched the two men closely. Normally, when he told prisoners that there was a road to survival, they could not wait to get onto it and start running, jostling each other off the edge if necessary.

Not these two.

Their faces were haggard under the weatherbeaten glow. They were old: forty at least, and looking older. Herr Gruber could hardly believe that these people had done what they were reputed to have done: evaded a regiment of Panzerjäger, murdered a platoon of SS, found this place. But they had done it. And Herr Gruber was absolutely delighted with their success, which had turned a run-of-the-mill secret weapon into something much more important. They had played, as the saying went, into his hands.

But as they sat there, the big one with the flat, black-eyed stare of a Byzantine icon, and the thin American with the blood running red from his ear into the collar of his tunic, they did not look like men who were playing into anyone's hands at all.

'You have come here to destroy certain weapons,' said Herr Gruber. 'Which of course we cannot permit, not only because we value these weapons, but because of the diplomatic problems this would cause for our friends in Madrid.' The smile did not falter. 'Soon we shall be leaving. And I think that we shall leave you behind us. You seem quite comfortable here. A rest will do you good after your busy time. After which I suspect the Guardia Civil will receive an anonymous call to say that some Allied soldiers have become . . . locked in what will certainly be perceived as an embarrassing position. I hope you will still be alive then.' The smile left his face. The lips were wet and shiny, the eyes icy. 'Though I doubt you will last long in a Spanish internment camp. The guards are trigger-happy. Also the food is neither wholesome nor plentiful, and there is much typhus.' The smile returned. 'And I doubt that anyone at the British Embassy will be too keen to see you again, after the embarrassment you will have caused them. Spain is, after all, a neutral country, and your presence will be held to constitute a most cynical violation of this neutrality.' He licked his lips. In his future he saw sunlit vistas of promotion, victory, universal success. 'Your diplomats are bringing pressure to bear on the Spanish government just now to stop our wolfram exports, and to withdraw Spanish troops from the Russian Front. Your visit here will I think change all that. In fact, it seems to me not unlikely that at the end of this little . . . adventure, Germany will have a new ally.' He sighed. 'There is only one disappointment, of course. That is that politics prevents me from having you shot out of hand.'

Andrea spat in the general direction of the grating. The Gestapo man tutted. 'Keep your spit,' he said. 'I think you will need it. Now. There is one thing. Your comrade. Where is he?'

Andrea said, 'Comrade?'

Miller looked across at him. In the American's posture the Gestapo man read the bitterness of defeat. Miller said to Andrea, 'What are you trying to prove?'

Andrea said, 'We have no comrade.'

Miller seemed to have developed a nasty twitch in his right cheek. His tongue ran round his dry lips. The Gestapo man spotted the signs of fear, an emotion he had had much practice recognising.

Miller said, 'There's no point.' He turned to the Gestapo man. 'Listen,' he said. 'He's –'

Andrea moved. He moved suddenly, but with the lumbering slowness of a bear, across the filthy floor to Miller. He grabbed Miller round the neck and pulled his head away from the wall, and the Gestapo man knew that next this big man was going to bash this thin man's brains out. That would have been a thing he would have enjoyed watching.

But it was important that it did not happen.

So he gestured to the guards. The guards grabbed one of Andrea's arms each, and pulled him off. It was not as difficult as the Gestapo man had feared. He might be big, but he was weak. These Mediterranean types. Hot blood, but no sinews.

Miller was rubbing his neck. 'Hey!' he whined. 'Ain't no call to beat up on a guy –'

'Insect!' hissed Andrea. 'Reptile!'

'Silence,' said Gruber. The Greek subsided.

The American said, 'The third guy. He's dead.'

'Come,' said the Gestapo man. 'Can you not do better than that?'

'It's the truth.'

The wet blue eyes were as blank as the indicator lights on a wrecked tank. 'How did he die?'

'He fell down the cliff.'

'What was he doing on the cliff?'

'Hiding.' Steady, thought Miller. The *Stella Maris* was in the harbour. No sense involving them. 'He'd led us round from the mainland. He placed the rope. He fell, poor bastard. Strangled himself. Take a look at the bottom of the cliff, you'll find his body. Then you caught us.'

The Gestapo man fingered his chin. Certainly it would be possible to fall on those cliffs. He said, 'It was not a clever thing to do, to enter by the cliffs. You made much noise. Naturally, you were caught.'

Miller hung his head. That was not what the Hauptsturmführer had said. The Hauptsturmführer had said they were expected, and Miller was inclined to believe him. 'Shucks,' he said.

'Quite so,' said Gruber. He stood up. 'Well. I cannot say it has been a pleasure meeting you.' He snapped his fingers. 'Chair.'

One of his SS men took the chair away. Herr Gruber walked across to Andrea, who was propped against the wall. 'Goodbye, Greek,' he said. The cane in his hand lashed out like a striking adder. It caught Andrea across the eyes.

Muscles swelled at the corners of the Greek's jaw. Then he smiled, a happy, white-toothed smile of anticipation. Blood ran from his heavy black eyebrows into the smile. 'For that,' he said, 'you will die.'

Herr Gruber smiled a superior smile, and strode out of the cell.

The door slammed. The lock clashed. The light went out. They were in darkness.

Miller said, 'Colonel?'

'Miller.' The voice sounded strangled.

'Can you see?'

'I can see.'

'More 'n' I can,' said Miller. A peculiar noise rattled in the vaulting of the cell.

They might be locked up in the dark, facing the imminent failure of their mission, the decimation of the invasion fleet, and a diplomatic disaster in Madrid.

But Mallory was out there somewhere. And Miller was laughing.

For Mallory, being alone on the cliff had been a sort of liberation. After all those days and weeks of little rest and occasional food, the feel of rock under feet and fingers and the freedom of the great vertical spaces acted like a tonic. He trusted the other two to reconnoitre the landward side and the submarine sheds. But he trusted only himself to reconnoitre from the seaward. There were some things he needed to look at on his own. Mallory was a team player, but Andrea was too big, and Miller got vertigo. There were times when solo climbing was what you had to do.

The moon slid behind a cloud. In the darkness, he began to move swiftly sideways across the face of the cliff. He had gone a hundred yards when he heard the commotion up above: a bell, a voice screaming, the clatter of boots on granite; then the faraway double tramp of jackboots, and a voice, Andrea's, yelling *Marsch!*

The boots stopped.

Mallory could hear nothing after that. But he did not need ears to tell him that this was trouble. He waited for the shooting to start. The shooting did not start.

He hung for a moment, waiting for a patch of moonlight to pass. The cloud returned.

Before he had been climbing diagonally upwards towards the parapet. But the sky above the parapet was glowing with a nimbus of ice-grey floodlights. So he headed low, towards the sea, acquiring the grammar of the crumbling stone through fingers and toes, keeping the bulge of an overhang between him and the parapet.

Soon the floodlights went out, and the Cabo de la Calavera was once again a domed and sinister lump of darkness against the sky. Whatever had happened had happened. Mallory took a deep breath. He knew that nobody would be there to meet him at the rendezvous by the generator sheds.

He was on his own.

Steady.

Worrying about Miller and Andrea was a waste of time. He kept his mind on the operation. One man needed to operate differently from three. Time spent on reconnaissance was time wasted now. He needed to penetrate the Cabo. He needed a weak spot.

He had one in mind.

He began to climb upwards.

Whatever Moor-hating grandee had built the *fortaleza* on the tip of the Cabo de la Calavera had chosen his spot well. The cliffs came sheer out of the sea – more than sheer, on some of the pitches. Mallory concentrated on the rock. Here on the sheer cliffs, it was less friable, and grass and sea-pink had failed to find a foothold. There were little cracks and corrugations that would have given pause to a fly with common sense. But Mallory was desperate. So Mallory went up the face, slow but sure, moving from the hips, gracefully, almost without effort. He worked his way steadily westwards, towards the point on which the *fortaleza* stood, working his way steadily higher. The clouds were thickening again, and the moon had gone. That was useful, even if it meant climbing by feel. The sea was a heavy murmur far below, the wind a tenuous hand pressing on his back.

After perhaps an hour, the wind brought him the stench of drains. When he next looked up, he saw the cliff above him had changed nature. It was no longer natural granite. It had become the outer wall of the *fortaleza*.

Mallory paused, standing on the sheer precipice connecting sky and sea. Cliffs were no problem, and masonry walls he could deal with. It was the transition between the living rock of the cliff and the cut stone of the fortress wall that would be the difficulty.

For where masonry met rock face, a heavy black line crossed the darkness of the wall. The outer face of the masonry was cantilevered out over the rock: machicolated, Mallory seemed to remember. Machicolation or cantilever, it boiled down to the same thing. What he had up there was a bloody great overhang. Mallory was solo, no rope, four spikes. Normally, he would have looked for another route to avoid an overhang. But this time, there was no going round.

Suddenly, Mallory was horribly tired.

He hung there for a moment. The smell of sewage was powerful in his nostrils. When he reached for the next hold, his right hand landed in a foul slime.

A foul slime that must have come from somewhere.

Suddenly, Mallory's weariness was gone. Thank God for Spanish sanitation, he thought. For medieval Spanish sanitation, invented by Arabs, bringers of civilisation to the European world.

And with a bit of luck, bringer of Mallory onto the walls of the Fortaleza de la Calavera.

He started to climb again, keeping to the left, out of the stream of sewage. In two minutes, he was up against the bottom course of the machicolations.

He could see the detail of the overhang now. It was like an inverted flight of seven steps, a foot each, angled outwards at forty-five degrees. Impassable without a rope.

But ten feet to Mallory's right, a vertical line of darkness broke the steps: a line perhaps two feet wide that was not a line, but a crevasse. To the designers of the *fortaleza*'s sanitation, it was the outlet from the castle garderobes. To a climber like Mallory, it was a practicable chimney in an impracticable overhang. The tiredness left him. There was a route here. In the face of a route, it was not possible to feel tired.

He crouched on a nearly invisible ledge and checked his spikes. He took his boots and socks off. He put his boots back on his bare feet, and pulled the socks over the boots. Then he swung himself round, face to the cliff, and started to move crabwise towards the chimney.

He knew he was under it from the stinging reek of urine and ammonia. He looked up, sighting against the sky with watering eyes. The slot in the machicolations reached out as far as the last two steps. If he could reach those last two steps, he would be able to get a hand up and onto the masonry of the vertical wall, and find a place to get a spike in.

Garderobe or no garderobe, it was a hideously difficult place. But the thought did not even occur to Mallory. It was a climbing problem, and climbing problems were there to be solved.

He reached in the pocket of his smock, checking his spikes and the leather-wrapped lead mallet he used as a hammer. Then he moved into the dreadful recesses of the chimney.

As he had suspected, it was a chimney of cut stone built out from the living rock. At first, he was climbing the slippery natural rock. When the rock gave way to masonry, he put his shoulders against one side, his feet against the other, and pushed.

The socks over his boots gave him a grip through the slime. The slime lubricated his shoulders as they slid up the cut stone blocks. Easy chimneying, if you could cut out the stench. He was moving outwards now, away from the face of the cliff, following the line of the machicolations. Once, the cliff's sheerness had been daunting. Any minute now, it was going to seem almost like home.

As long as he ignored the black hole above his head, and what might come down it.

Brace the shoulders. Keep the feet against the far wall, hard, so the socks bite through the film of filth and the boot-nails grind into the solid rock. Do it again. And again –

Mallory's helmet clanked against stone. He had run out of chimney.

He stood there, wedged shoulders and feet in that slot in the masonry, his breathing shallow. Two hundred feet below, white tongues of foam curled round jagged rocks and licked up the cliff wall.

Mallory fumbled in his pocket for a spike. Before the war, he would not have considered using spikes. Spikes were for Germans, during the assaults on the north face of the Eiger, the attempts on Kanchenjunga for the greater glory of the Third Reich. Mallory had on one occasion climbed the Big Wall on Mount Cook, removing the spikes left there by an unsportsmanlike German expedition. But in Zermatt he had met Schenck, an American blacksmith and climber who ran a forge in the back of his pickup truck. Schenck had seen a war coming, and foreseen the kind of things that someone would ask Mallory to do. He had forced on Mallory half a dozen of his specials: three-inch blades of steel cut from the rear springs of a Model A Ford, pierced to hold a loop of rope. When Mallory had demurred, Schenck had pointed out that whatever he thought about using a spike to beat a mountain, using a spike to beat a German was fine.

God bless you, Schenck, wherever you are, thought Mallory in his stinking chimney. He looped a spike's cord round his wrist. Then he reached up and out and round the last two steps of the overhang, running the spike's point across the stones like the point of a pencil until he felt the check that would mean a seam of mortar. Then, gingerly, one-handed, he began to tap it in.

He tapped slowly, with infinite caution, partly for the sake of quietness, but mostly because he had only four of those three-inch splinters of metal left, survivors of the original half-dozen. And much depended on these four: his life, Andrea's and Miller's, the lives of the invasion fleet. He tapped for a full two minutes, until he was sure. Then he put in another spike inside the chimney, level with his eyes. This one went in more easily; he was not working at arm's length, and the mortar in the gully, attacked by hundreds of years of carbonic acid from the rain and uric acid from the garrison, was softer than the mortar on the outside of the wall.

When it was in, he tugged at it stealthily. It held firm. Reaching up, he found the loop of rope on the head of the first spike, shoved his hand through, and applied weight, without loosening his grip on the walls of the chimney.

The spike held firm.

He took a deep breath. Then he gripped that loop of rope and swung his weight out over the abyss. For a moment he was dangling free, a spider hanging from a cornice, a little creature of flesh suspended by a metal spike and a loop of quarter-inch cord two hundred feet above the sullen moil of white surf in sharp black rock. Then he put his left leg up, searching for the spike he had driven into the side of the chimney.

He put the sole of his boot onto that spike, applied his weight like a man applying weight to the pedal of a bicycle, and straightened his leg until he was standing, his leg in under the overhang, his torso vertical, parallel with the wall of masonry that went up, up, into the black sky. His left hand went to his pocket, found another spike, placed it above the first, made the pencil-like scribbling movements until the point caught, burrowed it in the first millimetres until it held, brought up the hammer, and began to tap. The muscles of his right arm and left leg were yelling that they could not be expected to keep this up, that they were going to cause pain, and cramp, until Mallory bloody well stopped this abuse. Mallory forced himself to pay no attention. Tap the spike gently, take your time –

There was the smallest of small movements under the sole of his left boot.

And suddenly he was falling, the full extent of his right arm, until the loop brought him up with a crunch of armpit sinews, and he was dangling once again from the edge of the cornice above the hungry rocks below.

The spike under his foot had fallen out.

Falling, the reflex is to open the hands, make the fingers a feeble approximation of feathers of flesh, spread the limbs, try to turn a solid body into a gliding thing that will fly away from danger.

Mallory knew about reflexes. He knew that the only direction humans fly is vertically downwards. Even as he swung, he kept his left hand clamped around the hammer.

After what felt like ten hours but was more like ten seconds, the swinging stopped. Mallory hung there. *Rest*, his body told him. But he knew that as he hung, the strength would be draining out of him, the blood leaving that arm. The muscles of the right arm needed all the blood they could get. Even if using them meant that the spike up there would pull out of the wall, and drop him through all that air onto all those rocks.

Damned if you hang. Not necessarily damned if you don't.

Carefully, Mallory put the hammer into his pocket. Then he reached his left hand up to join his right, and pulled himself up like a gymnast chinning the bar.

The muscles crunched in his arms. His teeth bared in a rictus of effort. The blood roared in his skull.

But there were his hands, and the spike, and the blessed stones, level with his eyes.

He held on with his right hand, pulled a fold of his smock over the projection of the spike, and lowered himself until he was hanging by the methodical German canvas. Then, very carefully, he teased the last spike out of his pocket, and the hammer, and raised his arms above his head, and began to tap.

Two minutes later he was up, left hand holding the upper spike, right boot on the lower, right hand putting in the next spike. The overhang was a full two feet below: out of sight, out of mind. The wall of the fortress stretched above him, eighty-five feet of sheer masonry to the top of the tower. Mallory kept tapping the spike, not letting himself stop, because stopping meant reaction, and reaction meant the shakes, and the shakes were no good when you were balanced on two little stubs of steel, with no spares.

So Mallory did not stop. Mallory went on up.

It became a rhythm. Tap the spike. Test the spike. New hand. New foot. Shake out the bottom spike, move it to the top . . .

Keep climbing.

To the observer, Mallory would have seemed to drift up that wall in defiance of gravity. But of course there were no observers. The murmur of the sea receded. Small, thick-walled windows passed by to the left and right. Mallory ignored them. He heard the breath in his throat, the blood in his ears, mingled with the roar of the sea. *Tap the spike. Test the spike.* It had started to rain, a thin, persistent Atlantic rain, coming in with the wind on his back. The rain was a help. The reason he was climbing this stone oil drum was that anybody standing sentry on top of a tower rising three hundred feet above the sea would be watching half-heartedly at best. And this was the kind of rain that would turn half-heartedness into actual neglect of duty. *New hand. New foot.* Mallory had an idea that depended on the neglect of duty. *Tap the spike. Test the spike.*

Above, the tower was no longer a cliff losing itself in the dark. It was a wall, a sharp-cut semicircle of stone. Mallory was nearly at the top.

He paused, stuck to the wall like a fly, listening. The wind rushed round his ears, and the rain pulled a flat, mouldy smell from the stone. Above the drizzle of the rain he heard another noise: the tramp of booted feet.

Mallory waited.

The feet marched to and fro. The rain eased, then returned,

harder now. A voice above his head said, '*Scheisse.*' The footsteps changed sound, became muffled. There was the metallic click of a latch, a groan of heavy iron hinges. The sentry was taking shelter from the rain.

Mallory started climbing again. He was in a hurry now, but he did not let it alter the steady rhythm of his movements. The rain was becoming heavier, driving in hard and steady on the wind. After the sixth spike he found he could hook his fingers over the parapet. Then he was up, standing on the stone deck inside the battlements in his boots and socks, flexing his stiff fingers.

The top of the tower was flat, except for the turret with the staircase. Its door faced inland, away from the prevailing wind. On the roof of the turret were chimneys, emitting wood smoke, and a group of radio aerials. There were four aerials: three whips and a big shortwave array, and a flagpole. At the top of the flagpole something waved and bumped in the wind – something that was not a flag: a vaguely man-shaped mass against the clouds, but with a disgusting raggedness about the outline. Something that had once been Juanito the smuggler.

Mallory was cold and stiff from a dangerous hour crawling up a vertical wall. Now he felt an angry warmth spread through him, against a lunatic enemy who wanted to rip the world back into the Middle Ages.

His wool-padded boots thudded softly on the stones as he walked across the roof of the tower and flattened himself against the wall of the turret. He could hear a man coughing inside the door. Cigarette smoke wafted out through the keyhole. The sentry was alone.

Mallory waited with the patience of a hunting animal. The rain slackened.

The door opened.

The sentry never saw what hit him. There was a sudden, agonising pain in the left-hand side of his chest. Then there were no more thoughts.

Carefully Mallory wiped the blade of his knife on the dead man's tunic. He unstrapped the man's Schmeisser, and took the two spare clips from his bandolier. He went through the pockets and found the man's paybook. Then he dragged the corpse across the wet roof to the parapet he had climbed, and rolled it over.

It fell with no sound, the way Mallory would have fallen, if he had fallen. Mallory did not stay to watch it.

He took the rags of his socks off his boots. The rain had washed a certain amount of the sewage from his tunic. He squared his shoulders, and checked the Schmeisser with his rope-raw hands. Then he went through the door, closed it silently behind him, and started down the spiral stone stairs inside.

He smelt cigarette smoke, and old stone, and sewage on his tunic. After fourteen steps there was a Gothic-arched doorway, closed with an iron-studded door. A cardboard notice on the door said, in Gothic script, WACHSTUBE: guardroom. God bless the orderly German mind, thought Mallory, with renewed hope. It may yet be the saving of us all.

Beneath the guardroom was another door. From behind it came voices, and the clatter of Morse keys. Radio room. A new noise was coming from below, a busy, many-voiced buzz of ringing telephones and scurrying feet and shouted instructions; the noise of a human anthill, bustling. If the submarines were moving out at noon, this would be the sound of last-minute arrangements being made, repairs finished, evacuations planned. Mallory permitted himself a small, grim smile. It was the kind of bustle that could with a little thought be turned into confusion, and taken advantage of.

He rounded the last turn in the stairs.

Ahead of him was a corridor lined on one side with doors, and on the other with windows looking out onto a darkened courtyard. The corridor was lit with dim yellow bulbs. Mallory began to walk down the corridor at a measured sentry's tread, towards the stone balustrading round the stairway at its end. Cardboard signs labelled a navy office, a dock office, stores. Inside, men leaned over desks tottering with piles of papers, smoking and talking into telephones, and scribbling in the pools of light from their lamps. A German machine: dotting the last i, crossing the last t, before it closed itself down.

Two soldiers, pale men, clerkish, passed him. One of them wrinkled his nose and said, 'What a stink.' Mallory kept his face blank. The clerks accelerated away. Mallory tramped on, slow and steady, towards the stairs at the far end of the corridor, hiding in his measured tread the fact that he did not know where he was, or how to find what he was looking for. What Mallory needed was a clue, any clue. And in an operation like this, strolling tired and sore through the heart of an enemy installation, clues were not easy to come by.

Mallory arrived at the top of the stairs at the end of the corridor. A Kapitän of the Kriegsmarine was coming up. Mallory waited, crashed his heels together, extended a stiff right arm. *'Heil Hitler,'* he said.

The Kriegsmarine Kapitän touched a negligent hand to the peak of his cap, frowning at the wall, not looking at him. To a German, the uniform signified more than the man. And of course, there was the stink.

Mallory offered silent thanks to the *fortaleza's* sewage, which had let him in and was now keeping people away from him. He started to go down the stairs.

Then he was vouchsafed his clue.

Into the smell of sweat, and smoke, and sewage, and cold stone, had come another smell; a smell that transported Mallory for a split second back to Cairo three years ago, with the tinkle of fountains in marble patios, the murmur of staff officers with creased trousers and soft handshakes making assignations for drinks at Shepherd's Hotel while the front line troops died hot, flyblown deaths under the desert sky.

The smell of expensive Turkish tobacco.

It was rising up the stairs, a mere hint of it in the column of cold, wet air. Mallory followed it like a hound.

He went down the stone-balustraded steps, and found himself on a corridor identical to the one above, except that this one was blocked off halfway by a door; not studded, this door, but made of black oak, with elaborate wrought-iron hinges, their strapwork in the form of stylised olive branches. It was an elegant door, built to please the eye as well as turn aside weapons of war. From the orientation of the corridor, Mallory guessed that the rooms beyond would look south, over the harbour. Once, these would have been the Commandant's quarters.

The smell of Turkish cigarettes was stronger here.

These were still the Commandant's quarters.

As Mallory walked up to the door, it opened. An Obersturm-führer in the black uniform of the Totenkopf-SS marched quickly out, glanced at Mallory without curiosity, closed the door behind him, and marched on. In his hand was a sheet of paper, and on his face an expression of sulky haste. An odd, harsh voice pursued him. 'Within one hour!' it barked. It sounded as if there was something wrong with the speaker's throat.

'*Jawohl, Herr General,*' muttered the ADC, and disappeared down the stairs.

Mallory pushed the door open.

The smell of Turkish cigarettes rolled out to meet him. Ahead, the corridor continued to a Gothic window full of night. Moroccan rugs covered the flagstones. The air was warm, and the smell of damp stone had disappeared. The light came from a gilt chandelier. Pictures of Spanish saints adorned the walls: male saints, stripped to the waist, bearing the marks of torture.

Mallory was not concerned with the interior appointments. There were two doors each side of the corridor. Three of them were closed; it was inconceivable that they would contain anything as vulgar and tasteless as a sentry. The fourth was open.

It was a huge room, forty feet on a side, with a sofa, two armchairs, a coffee table. There was a vast fireplace, surmounted by the carved arms of a Spanish duke. At the far end was a Gothic solar window. In front of the window was a desk with two telephones, a green onyx desk set, a bell-push and an ashtray from which the smoke of a Turkish cigarette rose vertically into the still, warm air. Behind the desk was a man with a pointed head, bald on top but fringed with close-clipped grey-blond hair.

No sentries. How could there be no sentries?

If nobody could get into the castle, there was no need of sentries inside the castle. That was logical.

Mallory walked into the room and shut the door. The man at the desk did not look up. The lights of the room moved in the silver insignia of an SS General, the lightning-flash runes on the collar, the silver skull-and-bones below the eagle on the high-crowned cap on the desk. The thin fingers reached out for the cigarette. The sausage lips sucked, blew smoke. The eyes came up to meet Mallory's.

The eyes were the colour of water, set above high cheekbones in a fleshless face with a cleft chin. The Adam's apple moved in the neck. There was something wrong with the Adam's apple: a dent in the right-hand side, a groove the thickness and depth of a finger. An old wound, perhaps. Striated webs of muscle shifted in the wasted areas where the cheeks should have been. 'What?' said the General, in his thin, harsh croak. He clipped his cigarette into his right hand. Mallory saw the hand was artificial, an unlifelike imitation of hard orange rubber.

Mallory reached in his pocket for the paybook he had taken from the dead sentry, stepped forward to the desk and held it out to the General. The General waved it away impatiently, wrinkling his nose at the smell. Private soldiers did not roll in sewage, then burst into General's rooms and identify themselves. What on earth did this *Dummkopf* think he was doing? The orange rubber fingers of the prosthesis strayed to the bell-push.

Mallory plastered a foolish grin on his face, and swatted the artificial hand away from the bell. The General was looking up at him now. A ropy vein was swelling on either side of his neck. He ignored the hand with the paybook. He opened his mouth to shout.

The hand holding the paybook kept moving. The General ignored it. He was watching Mallory's face. The anger was turning to something else, something like puzzlement, or even fear. But the hand with the paybook had gone further than a hand with a paybook need go, and it had dropped the paybook and folded the fingers under a hard ridge of knuckle and accelerated until it was an axehead aimed at the ruined Adam's apple in that stringy neck.

Mallory put his whole weight behind that punch. It was designed to smash the larynx. But whatever the General saw in the brown eyes above Mallory's foolish grin made him move his head at the final split instant, so the knuckles caught him on the side of the neck, bruising the larynx instead of smashing it, and he went backwards out of the carved-gilt chair and into the bow of the window, groping for the flap of his holster as he fell.

Mallory scrambled over the desk after him, his boot-nails leaving tears in the red Morocco top. The General was halfway up to his feet, his back against the stone tracery of the window. Mallory covered him with his Schmeisser. He said, 'Put your hands in the air.'

The General said in a rasping whisper, 'Have you gone mad?'

'Do as you are told,' said Mallory.

'You are not a German soldier,' said the General.

Mallory said, 'No.'

The General's Adam's apple bobbed in his throat. Self-possession returned to the cold-water eyes. He said, 'If you shoot me there will be ten of my men in here before you can take your finger off the trigger.'

'And you will be dead,' said Mallory. 'What good will that do you?' He saw the flicker of calculation in the colourless eyes, and knew that this was not an argument that would work. It might have cut some ice with a junior officer. But for one of Heinrich Himmler's inner circle, there were more frightening things than death.

'So,' whispered the General, with a smile that was no more than a stretch of the lips over the teeth. 'We have been expecting you.'

'That was clever of you,' said Mallory. 'How?'

The General said, 'You will die wondering, I think.'

Mallory yawned. 'Pardon,' he said. It was the old chess game of lies and evasions. 'You captured two men,' he said. 'Where are they?'

The General's face had relaxed. Mallory had shown weakness. He was in control. His orange artificial hand rested on the red leather desk. 'Where you will shortly be,' said the General. The bell-push was six inches away. 'What are you trying to achieve?' This one will hang from piano wire, his brain hissed furiously. From a meathook. He has no idea of the extent of his presumption. But he will learn, kicking his life out on the hook with the cut of thin steel at his damned impudent neck.

'My objectives,' said Mallory. The barrel of the Schmeisser moved like a snake's tongue, and smashed into the General's good arm above the elbow.

The General pulled his hand back. The pain was abominable. The arm was definitely broken. He said, in a whisper unstable with agony, 'For this you will die.'

'Oh, quite,' said Mallory. 'Where are your prisoners?'

The General stood there, cradling his good hand with his orange rubber fingers to take the weight off the upper arm. Nobody had spoken to him like this since the SA purge in 1934. The pain was terrible. He wanted to shout, but his vocal cords were paralysed. He wanted to push the bell, but he was frightened that some other part of him would be broken. When would von Kratow the aide-de-camp be back? An hour. He had told von Kratow to leave him alone for an hour.

He was alone and helpless under those pitiless brown eyes. And he knew, with the sure instinct of the merciless, that the man behind those eyes had as little mercy as himself.

In that moment, he recognised him. The Abwehr had circulated the name, the description, holograph cuttings from the London *Times* and the *Frankfurter Zeitung*, from before the war. Cuttings with pictures of this face, those eyes, fixed without mercy on the next peak to be conquered.

He said in his rasping whisper, 'Mallory.' He breathed hard. 'You will all die together. It will not be an easy death.'

Mallory felt the sweat of relief flow under his stinking uniform. Andrea and Miller were still alive. He said to the General, 'Please. Take your clothes off.'

The General's brain felt starved of blood. He knew the things this man had done. He knew that he was in trouble. He said, 'No.'

Then he dived for the bell-push.

Mallory saw him go, as if in slow motion. He lashed out again with the barrel of the Schmeisser. It caught the General on his bone-white temple. His eyes rolled up. His body went limp and dropped to the Turkish carpet. His head hit the flagstones at the carpet's fringe with a loud, wet *crunch*. He lay still.

Mallory laid the Schmeisser on the desk. He stubbed out the cigarette in the ashtray, took another from the silver box, lit it, and inhaled deeply. He walked across to the door and quietly shot the big bolt. Then he crouched by the body on the floor, and took the pulse in the neck.

There was no pulse.

Mallory began to remove the uniform.

He pulled off the boots, the tunic, the breeches. He paused a moment, face immobile, eyebrow cocked. The uniform was bigger than the body. The General's corpse was white and fleshless, little better than a skeleton. Under the dead-black uniform, the man was wearing ivory silk French knickers.

Mallory began to unbutton his tunic. He thew his sewage-stained clothes behind the curtain, and climbed into the General's uniform.

It had been oversized for the General, but was about the right size for Mallory. He had climbed the castle tower without socks, and large areas of skin had come away from his feet. The General's socks were clean and made of silk, which was soothing; the General's mirror-polished jackboots were a size too tight, which was not. But Mallory's own boots were not the elegant boots of a General, so there was no help for it.

When he had finished dressing Mallory transferred the contents of his battledress pockets to the General's tunic and breeches. He caught sight of himself reflected in the glass of the window. He saw a tall, thin SS General, the hollow-cheeked face shadowed by the cap that came down far over the eyes, the unscarred neck hidden by the shirt collar. Unless he got too close to someone who knew the General well, he would pass. The Cabo de la Calavera force would be a scratch team. They would not know each other well.

You hope.

Stay in the shadows.

He took the cap off, and began to walk round the office. A door led to a room with a shortwave radio on a table.

Mallory went into the bathroom. He washed his hands and face. He changed the blade in the dead man's razor for a new one. He shaved: SS Generals do not have twelve hours' growth of stubble. As he shaved he thought about the way that the lights had come on after the landing, the instantaneous capture of Andrea and Miller. And what the General had said: *we have been expecting you.*

Mallory wiped the remains of the lather from his face, and decided that, disguise or no disguise, he could not face the General's violet-scented eau de Cologne. He walked back to the radio room, stiff-legged because of the pinch of the boots. Jensen had made sure his men were trained in the use of German equipment. He flicked on the power, and tuned the dial to the *Stella Maris'* frequency. '*Ici l'Amiral Beaufort,*' he said.

There was a wave of static. Then a little voice said, '*Monsieur l'Amiral.*' Even across the static it was recognisable as Hugues.

Mallory said, 'I have laid large explosive charges at the main gate. Am expecting reinforcements from the landward.'

Hugues said, 'What –'

Mallory hit his press-to-talk switch. 'Stay where you are,' he said. 'Ignore all further radio communications. Await arrival of main force, one hour. Acknowledge.' He lifted his thumb from the switch.

Static washed through the earphones. For a moment he thought Hugues had not received him. Then he realised that the silence would be the silence of confusion.

Or treachery.

'Acknowledge,' he said again.

'I acknowledge,' said Hugues.

'Out,' said Mallory, and disconnected.

Mallory hobbled back into the office. Very quietly he unbolted the door, walked back to the desk and pulled the body behind the curtain. Then he lit another Turkish cigarette from the box on the desk, and turned away from the door to face the window. It was dark out there. He waited five minutes. Suddenly, the night to the left whitened, as if many lights had come on. Mallory pressed the button on the desk. The door opened behind him. A voice said, 'Herr General?'

Mallory could see in the rain-flecked glass the reflection of a young SS officer, standing to attention with tremulous rigidity, eyes front. The officer would not be able to see Mallory's reflection. Mallory was standing too close to the glass. And of course, the officer was German, so he would notice uniforms, not faces.

At least, that was the theory Mallory was backing with his life. And Andrea's, and Miller's.

He said, in what he hoped was a replica of the General's harsh croak, 'There seems to be a problem by the gate. The lights are on. What is happening?'

'We have reports of enemy action.'

'What do you mean?'

'Intelligence,' said the voice.

Mallory said, 'Investigate this. Personally. Come back only when you have established the nature of this action, and neutralized it. Take all forces at your disposal. The whole garrison, if necessary.'

'But Herr General, the administration ... we depart at dawn . . .'

Mallory's heart seemed to stop beating. 'At what time?' he said.

'At dawn,' said the SS man, worried. 'The Herr General will remember . . . it was the Herr General who issued the order . . .'

'The time of dawn, idiot,' snapped Mallory.

'Of course.' The SS man sounded flustered. 'My apologies. 0500, Herr General.'

'So you will raise the general alarm,' said Mallory. 'And you will proceed to the gate.'

'But Herr General –'

'With all the men you can find.'

'But the work –'

'Silence!' barked Mallory. 'Leave only the sentries, and one man. I need to interview the prisoners. I shall require an escort. The rest to the gate. I hold you personally responsible.'

'But –'

'You will go out in the rain,' said Mallory, 'and confront the enemy! There is worse than rain on the *Ostfront*!'

He heard boot heels crash together. The officer said, '*Jawohl, Herr General*,' in a tight, offended voice. The uniform would be occupying the whole of his vision.

'Send the escort in five minutes,' said Mallory. 'Dismiss!'

The boot heels crashed again. The door slammed. Alarm bells started ringing, rackety and imperious. Mallory turned, stubbed out the cigarette, and lit another.

Five o'clock. The U-boats were sailing seven hours early. And the Storm Force had not even begun.

There was the stamp of many feet in the corridor outside: the General's staff, trotting off to the gate, scared witless by the prospect of the Russian Front. The footsteps faded. A double knock sounded on the door. Mallory turned back to the window. *'Komm!'* he cried.

A nervous voice said, 'Herr General.'

'We will visit the prisoners,' said Mallory. 'Lead the way.'

'The way?'

'You lead,' rasped Mallory. 'I will follow you. About *turn.*'

The soldier about turned. Mallory clasped his hands behind his back and hobbled out from behind the desk.

In the corridor, he sank his chin into his collar and strode stiffly after the private. Anyone watching would have seen the General, cap pulled low over his eyes, deep in thought, doing his rounds. But there were only clerks to watch. The alarm bells had sent the garrison clattering for the assembly points, and from the assembly points the Feldwebels had bellowed them to the ramparts on the peninsula.

The escort's boots rang in the vaulting and crunched grit on the stone stairs. The pain in Mallory's feet and the aches of his body were small, distant inconveniences.

He had radioed the *Stella Maris* with false information. Within five minutes, that false information had been relayed to the garrison.

Someone on the *Stella Maris* was a traitor.

Lisette was out of France, away from the long arm of the Gestapo. Hugues had his girlfriend and his child safe alongside him; if he betrayed the *Stella Maris* party, Lisette would be separated from him, and probably killed. Which left Jaime: Jaime the dark and silent, the smuggler, connoisseur of secret paths and byways.

Not that it mattered just now.

The soldier halted, with a stamp of his feet. 'Herr General,' he said.

They were in a long corridor lined with steel doors. White lights glared harshly from the ceiling. There was a smell of damp and mould. The sentry standing rigidly at attention outside the nearest door coughed. Mallory said, 'Key.'

The sentry was still coughing.

'Key!' rasped Mallory, holding out his hand.

The sentry said, 'Herr General,' and fumbled at his belt. He looked at Mallory's hand.

And Mallory's skin turned suddenly to ice.

For the sentry was frowning at that outstretched hand. The right hand. The hand of flesh and blood.

The hand that on the real General had been an artificial hand of orange rubber.

'Herr General,' said the sentry, with the face of one undergoing a nervous breakdown. 'This is . . . you are not the General.'

'The key,' rasped Mallory.

But under the brim of his cap he saw the man's hands going for the Schmeisser.

The cell had not changed. It was still cold, and it still stank, and it was still dark, dark with the absolute blackness of a pocket hewn from living rock. Midnight in the goddamn dungeons, thought Miller. Ghosts would be walking, witches doing whatever the hell witches do when it rains. As far as Miller was concerned, the ghosts and the witches could get on with it. Right here, midnight meant time for a cigarette.

He gave one to Andrea, put one in his own mouth, and lit them. The hot little coals began to glow in the dark, and for a couple of minutes there were warm points in this cold, evil-smelling universe.

But cigarettes end. And when they were finished, it was colder again, and lonelier, and worst of all, quieter.

What felt like two hours later, Andrea said, 'What time is it?'

Andrea would be thinking about the operation. Miller was thinking about it too. Miller wanted to get finished up.

Some chance.

He looked at the radium-bright hands of his watch. 'Five past twelve,' he said.

'Any minute now,' said the rumble of Andrea's voice. And although Miller knew it was a packet of bullshit, he felt for a moment that, any minute now, something might happen.

But nothing did.

Not for thirty seconds, anyway. After thirty seconds, the silence was broken by an odd noise.

It sounded like a jackhammer. It was not a jackhammer.

Someone was firing a machine pistol outside the cell door.

The door swung open. Brilliant light exploded into the darkness. A figure stood against the light, a black, angular silhouette. Andrea stared at it, dazzled. From the monochrome blur there emerged a spidery figure, jackboots set well apart, hands on hips, face invisible under the high-fronted black cap. It was the silhouette that stalked Andrea's dreams: the rusty-black silhouette that had stood against the sun on the low hill in Greece, with the blue Aegean twinkling like sapphires under the sky.

Under the hill had been the house of Andrea's brother, Iannis. It had been a small house, with a vine growing over a little terrace of red tiles, fanned by the small thyme-scented breeze that blew up from the sea.

By the time Andrea had got there, the damage had been done. His brother had been suspected of partisan activities, and captured in possession of British weapons. Under the pleasant green shade of the vine, the General had opened a bottle of Iannis' retsina and poured himself a glass. Then he had perched elegantly on the wall, gleaming boots crossed at the ankles, and watched the show.

The show had consisted of lighting the fire of charcoal on which the family had from time to time cooked an alfresco meal. Three Croatian SS had then brought Iannis' three daughters – Athene, six, Eirene, eight, and Helen, nine – out of the house. In the fire of charcoal they had burned off the girls' hands. When Iannis' wife had begun to scream, the General had had her hanged before the eyes of her husband and her still living children. Iannis they had left alive, nailing his hands to the house door against his attempts to claw out the eyeballs that had seen this thing, and wrench out the heart that was broken.

It was only after they had hanged the children beside their mother that Iannis had managed to tear his hands free and run, run like a maniac, eyes blinded with tears, to the brink of the high white cliff, and keep running, though his feet were no longer running on ground, but running on air, and he was falling down the glistening face of that cliff, falling happily, because he would see his children again, and his wife, and his parents, murdered by Bulgarians –

Five minutes later, Andrea had arrived, slowly, wearing a straw hat and leading a donkey in whose panniers were more weapons. Andrea had stood a moment, blank-eyed, watching. He saw the woman and the three children hanging from the vine that used to shade the evening drinking of ouzo. He saw the black-uniformed SS men, their thick red faces pouring rivers of sweat under the sun, laughing. The flames began to pour out of the roof of the house. He saw the silhouette of the General standing on the cliff, admiring a distant ruin, smiling complacently at the liquid-agate of the sun in the glass of retsina. He smelt burned flesh.

Then Andrea had seen nothing else.

When he could see again, there were five SS men dead at his feet. Them he fed to Iannis' pigs. The General he shot in the knees and threw into the privy to drown. He heard later from the people of the village that it had taken three days; not that he was interested. For Andrea had not waited. He had gathered together the bodies of his brother and his sister-in-law and his nieces, and given them to the priest for burial. Then he had left, to fight for his country on other fronts.

Andrea did not like SS officers.

He growled, and started forward, his gigantic hands unclenching.

The SS General dropped the Turkish cigarette he was smoking, and ground it out with a fastidious toe. He said, 'Unless you really like it here, I think we should leave.' And his voice was the voice of Mallory.

There was a moment's stunned silence, broken only by the sound of moaning from the corridor. Then Miller said, 'Personally, I find it damp.'

Andrea's eyes were pits of darkness. They moved from Mallory to Miller and back again. Then his teeth showed in a smile that was like the sun among thunderclouds. 'You should be careful about second-hand clothes,' he said. 'You could catch something really nasty. Like a knife in the guts.'

Mallory said, 'It is true that the owner wasn't very well when I left him.'

There were two bodies in the corridor. 'Get their clothes and their paybooks,' said Mallory. Andrea dragged them into the cell, and shut the door. 'And now?' he said.

Mallory looked at Miller. 'What do you need?'

What Miller really needed was his explosives back. But there was no use crying over spilt Cyclonite. 'Whatever,' said Miller. 'These guys will be carrying torpedoes. You can have a nasty accident with a torpedo. I guess I'd like to see the magazine.'

Andrea nodded gravely. During the weeks he had known Miller, he had learned to take this languid, flippant American very seriously indeed.

'I have a feeling,' said Mallory, 'that there might be a certain amount of confusion out there. So the sooner we get dressed, the better.'

Five minutes later, the SS General left the *fortaleza* by the main gate, escorted by two men in grubby Waffen-SS uniforms, one tall and wide, one tall and lanky, marching eyes front, with Schmeissers strapped across their chests. The sentries on the gate saluted. The General returned their salute with his left hand; the right, being artificial, he held rigidly at his side.

Once across the bridge over the moat, the party turned right, down a flight of wide, shallow stairs that led to a sort of crater in the shoulder of the headland. In the centre of the crater was a squat concrete bunker surrounded with barbed wire.

At a slow and stately pace, Mallory and his escort started down the stairs. There were few other people about. The welding torches still flickered their lightnings at the sky by the harbour, and riveters still rattled in the night. Somewhere, truck engines were rumbling; the evacuation was getting under way. But the armed men of the garrison were still apparently up by the main gate.

The garrison would not stay by the main gate for ever. Sooner or later, someone would decide that the threat might be based on faulty intelligence, or that it was not wise to leave the rest of the Cabo unguarded. Before that happened, there would be fifteen minutes, at best.

They were approaching the gate to the bunker. Seen close up, it was not so much a bunker as a fortified entrance, a steel door set behind a system of concrete baffles giving admittance to a low, tumulus-like mound, covered in salt-blasted turf. The entrance to the magazine.

The soldier at the gate stared straight ahead. 'Pass?' he said.

Mallory said, in the General's harsh whisper, 'Open the gate.'

'But Herr General –'

Mallory said, 'The weather in Russia is terrible at this time of year.'

The man's face paled under the floodlights. 'Herr General?'

'Perhaps when you get there you will send me a postcard,' rasped Mallory. 'Now if you would kindly open the gate?'

There was a split second of inner struggle. Then the sentry hauled open the gate in the wire, and Mallory walked through at his cramped, mincing hobble. The sentry must have pressed some sort of switch, because the steel door swung open with a hiss of hydraulics. Mallory and his escorts walked in without pausing. The steel door swung shut behind them. Ahead was a flight of spiral stairs, with at its centre the hoists that fed ammunition to the guns in the fort. Mallory looked at the faces of his companions. They were pale and expressionless, tired, but with a tension to their tiredness that was new. It came from the closing of that steel door.

They were inside now. There were no sandbags to hide behind, no shadows to skulk in. Their only protection against five hundred enemy soldiers was the thin cloth of their uniforms and the shape of the badges they wore. They were small, fragile machines of flesh and blood, armed with small guns. With those small guns and their bare hands, they had to destroy huge machines of steel. It was a nasty feeling; a naked feeling. A feeling from a nightmare.

But this was real. And this was the way it was going to be, from now on.

Down those stairs, Mallory told himself, were the tools for the job. Put Miller near explosives, and his bare hands could shatter an army. Everything was going to be fine.

Except my feet, thought Mallory, hobbling on. His feet felt as if they would never be the same again.

The shaft with the staircase descended into the bowels of the hill. Shells could be carried by hoist. But torpedoes were big, and heavy, and needed to travel horizontally. The floor of the magazine would be on the same level as the floor of the quay.

Miller stamped down the stairs at what he hoped was a convincing Wehrmacht stamp. It was costing him some effort to keep his appearance military. He was a fighter, Miller, but he would have been the first to admit that he was not much of a soldier. As they rounded the last twist of the spiral staircase, he felt a pleasurable anticipation. Once again, it was time to improvise.

At the base of the stairs was a flashproof door. Miller pushed the door open. They were in the magazine.

It was a big magazine. It stretched away in front of them, lit harshly by white bulkhead lights, a devil's wine cellar of grey concrete compartments, bins for shells, and bays for the trolleys that would roll the torpedoes down to the quays where the submarines waited, black and evil, crouching in the cold Atlantic.

Mallory looked at his watch. It was three forty-five.

Christ.

They went through the door, all three of them, and looked down the stark concrete perspective that was the magazine's central aisle. This was where they would find the wherewithal to sink three submarines and scupper the Nazis' last defence against the invading Allies.

But there was a problem.

The concrete bays and alcoves of the magazine contained a few crates. The dollies for the shells lay on their rails, and the torpedo racks, five hundred of them, stood padded with felt. But the crates were cracked open, the dollies burdenless, the torpedo racks bare. A gang of men was dismantling an electric motor.

But apart from the men, the magazine was empty.

They stood there, and watched, and let it sink in. The job was waiting. The tools were missing.

After a minute, Mallory began to hobble down the floor of the magazine, heading for the rails that would have taken the torpedoes to the quay.

The *Stella Maris* was lying on the outside of a raft of fishing boats against the quay wall of San Eusebio. Among the ruined buildings behind the quay, yellow dogs with feathered tails barked maddeningly in the rain. Hugues and Lisette were out of sight below. Jaime was on deck, propped in the splintered remnants of the wheelhouse, smoking. At his side a radio hummed gently to itself. There had been no signals. Jaime was not expecting any more signals.

Across the black water of the harbour, the sheds and quays of the old sardine factory on Cabo de la Calavera, which earlier had flickered with angle-grinder sparks and welder lightnings, were almost dark. It looked as if the work was complete. Now and then, a crane-jib caught the light as it swung. Loading up, thought Jaime. Not long now.

There was activity on the harbour too; the murmur of launches and lighters, moving out to the two five-thousand-ton merchantmen anchored in the deep water half a mile from the quay. On the move, thought Jaime. And who knew where it would all end?

'Slow,' said Mallory. 'Your work is very, very slow. Work faster.'

The Leutnant in charge of the embarkation of the magazine stores felt a hot anger at the injustice of it all. But it was not helpful to be angry with SS Generals. So he clicked his heels and ducked his head and said, 'As the Herr General wishes.'

'The Herr General does,' said Mallory. 'Now I wish to inspect the magazine.'

'Herr General?'

Mallory frowned. 'You speak German, do you not?'

'Herr General.' The man had just been rated for slowness. Leading a tour of inspection for some damned Nazi with a skull-and-bones hat was not going to speed things up. But a General was a General.

'Here were the shells,' said the Leutnant. 'All gone now, as per your orders. Here were the torpedoes. They are also gone, naturally.' He waved a hand at the tunnel leading down to the quay, and walked to another bin lined with empty racks. A pile of grey boxes stood on the floor. 'And in here, the small arms. A few only remaining. Grenades, mortar bombs. The last consignment will be leaving when the barge comes back alongside.' He clashed his heels together again, thumbs nailed to the seams of his breeches. 'I trust the Herr General is satisfied.'

Mallory eyed the three grey wooden boxes the officer had indicated. 'Quite satisfied,' he said. He looked round. Nobody was in sight. 'Andrea?'

The huge Greek took one step forward and crashed his jackboots on the concrete. His shoulders moved. There was a sound like a felling axe hitting a tree trunk. The German officer sighed, and fell down.

'Hide him,' said Mallory. 'Miller, boxes of grenades.'

Miller piled two boxes of grenades one on top of the other: ten grenades to the box, rope handles on either end.

'We'll go to the quay,' said Mallory. His face was the colour of dirty ivory. Exhausted, thought Miller.

Mallory fumbled in his pocket. There were three Benzedrine left in the little foil packet. He gave them out, one each. Benzedrine was not good for you, thought Miller, stooping to pick up the grenades. But then, nor was trying to climb aboard a U-boat to blow it up.

It was a long time since Miller had eaten anything. The pill worked fast. He could feel the strength pouring through him. These pills, thought Miller, dry-mouthed and sweating. You will feel terrible later.

Except that later was hardly worth worrying about, under the circumstances.

Miller laughed. Then he walked with his two companions into the throat of the tunnel that led to the quay.

SEVEN

Wednesday 0400–0500

The tunnel was fifty yards long, lit with the harsh white bulkhead lights installed all over the Cabo. Rails ran down each side, for the torpedo dollies. Down the middle was the walkway. There were men moving up and down the tunnel, moving at a fast clip. When they saw Mallory's uniform their eyes skidded away. Popular guy, thought Miller.

The three men began to march down the walkways, boots echoing. They had gone twenty yards when a voice behind said, '*Halt!*'

Mallory's heart walloped heavily. He thrust his all-too-real right hand into his tunic. Andrea's hands stole to the grips of his Schmeisser. Miller's hands were sweating into the rope handles of the grenade boxes. Mallory spun on the heel of his agonising jackboot.

He was looking at a small, bald man with rimless glasses and a prissy mouth, bulging out of a badgeless uniform. The small man was holding a book.

'*Was?*' said Mallory.

The small man was not impressed by the death's-head cap badge, the black uniform, the harsh croak of the voice. He pursed his lips. 'It is necessary to fill out the requisite forms,' he said. 'For the withdrawal of these weapons from the magazine. Otherwise, correct systems cannot be maintained.'

Mallory said, 'And you are the inventory clerk.'

'*Jawohl.*'

'Well, Herr Corporal,' said Mallory. 'Give me your book, and I will sign it.'

The clerk made tutting noises. 'Signature alone is not enough,' he said. 'You will naturally need a requisition form signed by the garrison duty officer.'

Mallory said, in a voice crammed with broken glass, 'Do you know who I am?'

The clerk moistened his small mouth with a grey tongue. 'Yess, Herr General. You are the garrison commander, Herr General.'

'And who signs the requisitions?'

'The duty officer.'

'By whose orders?'

'By your orders, Herr General.'

'So,' said Mallory.

The clerk said, 'I have my orders. The duty officer must sign the requisition.'

Mallory checked his watch. It said 0405. In fifty-five minutes the submarines were due to sail.

In fifty-five minutes, they could still be arguing with this clerk. The only thing stronger than the uniform was the system.

He said, 'Corporal, I compliment you on your attachment to duty. The duty officer is on the quay. You will accompany us there, please.'

'But –'

'Schnell.' Mallory's voice was a bark that admitted no contradiction.

The clerk, he had decided, was a blessing. An officious little blessing with rimless glasses, but a blessing nonetheless.

'Lead on, Corporal,' said Mallory, in a harsh purr.

The clerk led on.

The mouth of the tunnel was walled off. On one side was an opening for the torpedo dolly track. On the other was a sort of wicket gate for the pedestrian walkway. By the wicket gate was a species of sentry box. In the sentry box were two figures like black paper silhouettes: SS.

From the corner of his eye, Mallory saw that Andrea's hands had not moved from the grips of his Schmeisser. He wished he had a Schmeisser of his own. But he had a Luger, and the insignia of his uniform. That should be enough –

Except that the face above the uniform was not the right face.

He tugged down the peak of his cap.

The heels rang on. The SS sentries in the box had blank faces the colour of dirty suet. Their uniforms were rusty, their belts grainy, the folds of their jackboots cracking with salt. Their eyes were cold, and vicious, and restless. When they settled on Mallory's uniform, something happened to them, something that was not the other ranks' usual reaction to an officer's uniform. It was a look compounded of furtiveness and pride. Esprit de corps, thought Mallory. Oh, dear.

There were fifty SS men on the Cabo de la Calavera: the élite, keeping an eye on things for Himmler. They would know each other, all right.

But the only way onto the quay was through that night-black wicket by the sentry box.

Mallory shouted, 'Attention!'

The SS faces became blank and automatic. The General's uniform was doing its job. The boot heels ground concrete as Mallory, Miller, Andrea, and the magazine clerk marched on. The magazine clerk looked pleased with himself, proud to be part of something important and official. Mallory was profoundly grateful to him. The magazine clerk was credibility. The SS knew the magazine clerk.

They were close now: ten feet away. Mallory walked with his supposedly artificial hand in his breast, head bowed, as if in deep thought. Through the wicket came the smells of the sea, stirring the chill, leaden air of the magazine. The smell of the endgame.

The eyes were on them now, peripherally at least. In the corner of his vision Mallory could see the white, large-pored skin, the brown eyes seamed below with the marks of arrogance and cruelty. He could smell the uniforms, the sour smell of rain-wet black serge badly dried, leather on which polish was fighting a losing battle with mildew. He could smell the oil on the Schmeissers, the tobacco smoke, and garlic on their breath.

Then they were past, and Mallory was sweating –

'Herr General?' said a voice, a hard voice, cold, a little tentative: the voice of one of the black-clad sentries.

Mallory took another step.

'The Herr General will please stop,' said the voice.

'Quiet,' murmured Mallory, in English. Then he said, in his approximation of the General's bust-larynx rasp, 'What do you want?'

'If the Herr General would show us his pass?'

Mallory made a small, exasperated noise. 'Clerk,' he said. 'Show them your pass.'

The clerk's face was pink and shiny behind the rimless spectacles. He fumbled in his pocket.

'Quickly,' grated Mallory. 'Time is wasting.'

The SS man's eyes flicked at the clerk's pass. He handed it back. 'And now,' he said, 'the Herr General's pass.'

Something seemed to have removed the bottom of Mallory's stomach. There was a sort of icy purr in the voice, the sound of a cat about to stab a claw into a rat.

Miller put down the boxes of grenades. His hands were wet on the grips of his Schmeisser. He moved it casually, negligently, until it was covering the guard who was not doing the talking. The guard who was doing the talking had an odd expression on his face. Miller understood it.

It was the expression of a man who knew the General well, but who had been conditioned to respond to uniforms, not faces.

Miller knew that something bad was going to happen.

The SS man wet his lips with a grey tongue. He said to Mallory, 'Herr General, what is the Herr General's name?' His right hand was under the level of the desk. There would be an alarm button down there.

Miller thumbed the selector on the Schmeisser to single shot, and took up the first pressure on the trigger. Andrea, he noticed, had his hands off his gun. Andrea said, with a wide, despairing gesture of both spread palms, 'For God's sake, who do you think you are talking to?'

The SS sentry opened his mouth to reply. But he never got the words out, because Andrea's gesture had become something else, and his huge right had gone into the sentry's face, the heel up and under the nose, driving the bone into the brain, while the other hand, the left, had sprouted a knife that went in and out of the other sentry's chest, and in and out again. The two helmets clanged on the concrete.

There was a long, dreadful silence that lasted perhaps a second. Then something small scuttled past Miller. The clerk.

He stuck out a foot. The little man went flat on his face. His

212

spectacles skittered away on the concrete. The face he turned to Miller was the face of a blind mole. He said, 'Please.'

Miller looked at him. This was not an SS man. This man had all the malice of a ticket office clerk in Grand Central Station.

But this man could stop the operation dead.

Miller looked away.

There was a sound like a well-hit baseball. When Miller looked back, the magazine clerk was silent, face down, but breathing.

Andrea sighted along the barrel of his Schmeisser. 'Thought I'd bent it,' he said.

They dragged the clerk and the SS men out of sight behind the desk of the sentry box. The clerk was still breathing.

Then they walked onto the quay.

They were standing on the inshore end of the map the late Guy Jamalartégui had drawn beside the chart on his kitchen table with a matchstick and a puddle of wine.

The Basque-American who had donated the port to his sardine-fishing compatriots had not stinted. The quay was built of cut granite, on a scale that would have excited the respectful envy of a Pharaoh. The magazine entrance was set in the low cliff halfway down the long side of the innermost quay. Three more quays ran parallel to the first. There were rails set into the paving of the quays, designed presumably to carry waggonloads of sardines, first to the long sheds at the base of the quays for canning, and then to the sardines-on-toast enthusiasts of Europe.

Now, the black lanes of water between the granite fingers of the quay held no fishing boats; probably they never had. Instead, the long, sleek hulls and oddly streamlined conning towers of three great U-boats lay under the cranes.

Three men walked past, smoking, splashing in the puddles left by the night's rain. They were wearing baggy blue overalls, and had the hell-with-you air of dockyard mateys the world over. They paid no attention to Mallory and his two guards. Their task was finished. On the nearest submarine – presumably the one that had been reported rammed – a small gang of men was packing up what looked like oxy-acetylene welding gear. For the rest, what was going up and down on the cranes was definitely stores.

213

Mallory watched a tray of green vegetables and milk cans. Last-minute stores, at that.

More men in blue overalls drifted up the quay. There was a building up there, a green clapboard facade on a tunnel in the cliff. From it there drifted a smell of frying onions. The canteen, thought Mallory. The men going towards the canteen carried tool boxes. The men coming back had bags and bundles as well as the tool boxes. They had gone for a final meal up there, and picked up their possessions. At the far side of the harbour, launch engines puttered in the dawn; the engines of the launches ferrying the dockyard mateys out to the merchant ships waiting in the harbour, Uruguayan flags fluttering on their ensign staffs.

Mallory waited for another pair of workmen to walk past. They studiously avoided his eye, the way a skilled civilian technician of any nationality would avoid the eye of a murderer and torturer. The next pair came. One of them was a huge man, as big as Andrea.

That was what Mallory had been waiting for.

He said, 'You and you.'

The two men gave him the looks of schoolboys with permanently guilty consciences. One of them dropped his cigarette and stamped on it. The big man's cigarette dangled, unlit.

'Don't worry,' croaked Mallory. 'You have committed no crime.'

Their faces remained wooden.

'Smoke if you wish,' said Mallory. Another man was walking towards them, by himself. Mallory pulled out the General's lighter and lit the big man's cigarette with his left hand. 'There is one little job,' he said. 'Hey! You!'

The solitary man halted. Mallory pointed back at the magazine tunnel. '*Komm!*'

He marched into the tunnel. The lights were very bright after the grey predawn outside. The dockyard men were yawning and sullen. It had been a long night shift, and they wanted to get some food and climb aboard a merchant ship and go to sleep. They did not want to do any more jobs, particularly jobs for this whispering child murderer and his nasty-looking bodyguards. The big one said, 'What is it then?'

'Further,' said the SS General.

They were in the magazine tunnel. There were steel doors let into the wall, and a smell of new blood. The General pointed at one of the doors. 'In there,' he said.

The big man turned round. 'Why?' he said.

It was then he saw the bodyguards' guns, foreshortened, looking between his own eyes with their own deadly little black eyes.

'Take off your overalls,' said Mallory.

The big man was a bully. He was tired, and hung over, and hungry. Being told to undress had the effect on his temper of a well-flung brick on a wasps' nest. Nobody talked to him like that, SS General or no SS General. And word was that this SS General was a poof. 'Take 'em off yourself,' said the big man, and took a swing at the General's jaw.

He never saw what hit him. He merely had the dim impression that someone had loaded his head into a cannon, fired it at a sheet of armour plate, and dropped the resulting mess into a black velvet bag.

His two companions watched with their mouths open as Andrea dusted his hands, stripped the overalls off the big man's prone body, and loaded the tools back into their box.

'Strip,' said Mallory.

They stripped at a speed that would have won them first prize in an undressing contest.

'The door,' said Mallory.

Miller went to the steel door. It closed from the outside, with a latch. Inside was a locker with tins of paint, ten feet on a side.

'In,' said Mallory.

One of the men said, 'How will we ever get out?' He looked frightened; he was a civilian, caught up in something not his quarrel.

Mallory did not believe that a grown man could stand back from a war. As far as Mallory was concerned, you were on his side, or you were the enemy. He said, 'How do you get on those U-boats?'

'With a pass.'

'What pass?'

The man produced a much-folded card, seamed with oil.

'Anything else?'

'No. Who are you?'

Mallory went and stood so that his face was two inches from the German's. 'That is for me to know and you to wonder,' he said. 'I am going out there. I wish to move freely. If I am captured, I will not say a word about you, and that door is soundproof. So you have a choice.' He could feel the sweat running down inside his uniform, see the impassive faces of Miller and Andrea. Not much more than half an hour now. 'If you are telling me the truth, you have nothing to fear. If not, this locker will be your tomb.'

The man's throat moved violently as he swallowed. He said, 'There is ... in fact ... something else. A word.'

'Ah,' said Mallory.

'*Ritter*,' said the man. 'You must say *Ritter* to the gangway sentry.'

Mallory said, 'If you are not telling the truth, you will die in your underpants.'

'It is the truth.'

'Your overalls,' said Mallory, 'and what size are your boots?'

'Forty-two.'

Thank God, thought Mallory. 'Also your boots,' he said.

Five minutes later, three dockyard mateys were wandering down the quay towards the ferry. They were carrying much-chipped blue enamel toolboxes and smoking cigarettes. Their faces were surprisingly grim for men bound for Lisbon, home and beauty. But perhaps that would be because of the danger of submarines.

Outside the sheds at the root of the quay, the three men stopped.

Andrea looked up. The clouds had rolled away. The sky was duck-egg blue. Dawn was coming up, a beautiful dawn, above this press of people and their deadly machines.

Mallory said to Andrea in a quiet, level voice, 'We'll want the *Stella Maris* standing by.'

'I'll arrange that,' said Andrea.

Mallory looked down the first finger of granite. On either side were foreshortened alleys of water, with the bulbous grey pressure hulls and narrow steel decks of the submarines. There were two gangplanks down there, one leading left, the other right, a crossroads of quay and gangplanks. This was the access to two submarines. If you could get past the sailor at the base of each gangplank, rifle on his shoulder, cap ribbons fluttering at his nape in the small dawn breeze.

Mallory took a deep breath of the morning air, and tried not to think about the little steel rooms inside those pressure hulls, into which he must go with his grenades.

'Peroxide,' said Miller, sniffing.

'Sorry?'

'Hydrogen peroxide. Smells like a hairdressing parlour. Hunnert per cent, by the smell of it. Don't get it on you. Corrosive.'

Mallory said, 'What do you recommend?'

Miller told him.

'Fascinating,' said Mallory, taking a deep breath. 'I'll do the right-hand one. You do the left.'

Andrea said, 'Good luck.'

Mallory nodded. There was such a thing as luck, but to acknowledge its existence was to hold two fingers up to fate. What Andrea had to do was potentially even more dangerous than climbing around U-boats with a toolbox full of hand grenades.

Not that there was much to choose between the jobs. Dead was dead, never mind how you got there.

Mallory was not wasting time thinking about death. He was planning the next phase.

Andrea slipped away into the crowds heading for the ferries. Mallory and Miller started to walk down the quay towards the sentries. Miller had his hands in his pockets, and he was whistling.

Good lad, thought Mallory. What would it take to get you really worried?

Miller's thoughts were less elevated. The smell of peroxide had taken him back to Mme Renard's house in Montreal, to Minette, a French-Canadian girl with an educated tongue and bright yellow curls. There had been something about Minette, something she had shown him with two goldfish and a bag of cement –

Concentrate.

Down in his saboteur's treasure-house of a memory, he knew

that the catalyst for hydrogen peroxide was manganese dioxide. Manganese dioxide would separate the hydrogen from the oxygen, and make a bang next to which a hand grenade would look stupid.

Manganese dioxide was the obvious stuff.

Unfortunately, it was not the kind of stuff people left lying around.

He was at the bottom of the gangway. He grinned at the sentry and showed him his pass. 'Ritter,' he said, rattling his toolbox. 'Problem with lavatory. Two minutes only.'

The sentry said, 'Thank God you've arrived, then.'

Miller walked up the gangplank.

Andrea shouldered his way through the thickening crowd on the quay. There was a sense of urgency, now, and very little Teutonic efficiency about the milling scrum of men and soldiers. He made his way to the quay's lip.

And stopped.

The queue might be inefficient, but the embarkation procedures were well up to standard. There were four iron ladders down the quay. At the bottom of each ladder was a launch. At the top of each ladder was an SS officer with a clipboard. As each man arrived at the front of the queue, the SS man scrutinised his identity card, compared the photograph minutely with his face, and checked his name off the list. Only then was he allowed down the ladder.

Once the launches themselves had left the quays they did not hang about. They went straight alongside the two merchant ships anchored in the harbour; merchant ships on whose decks were un-naval but nonetheless efficient sandbag emplacements from which peered the snouts of machine guns.

Even in the evacuation, the Werwolf facility was leaving nothing to chance.

Andrea's overalls and identity card had belonged to Wulf Tietmeyer. No amount of oily thumbprints could obscure the fact that Tietmeyer, though roughly Andrea's size, had red hair and pale blue eyes. Furthermore, Andrea had no desire to end up on a Germany-bound merchant ship.

Muttering a curse for the benefit of his neighbours, he turned back into the crowd, forging his way through the press with shoulders the size and hardness of a bank safe, a dockyard matey who had left something behind and was on his way to fetch it.

As he reached the root of the quays one of the submarines emitted a black cloud of exhaust, and the morning filled with the blaring rattle of a cold diesel. Start engines meant that they would be sailing at any minute. He looked at his watch. In eighteen minutes, to be precise. And precise was what they would be.

He looked across the mouth of the harbour at the town of San Eusebio, glowing now in the pale dawn. The windows of its houses were smoke-blackened, empty as dead men's eyes, the campaniles of its two churches jagged as smashed teeth. But alongside the quays, in front of the blind warehouses lining the harbour, the fishing fleet was anchored two deep. And among them, on the outside near the front, were the tar-black hull and ill-furled red sails of the *Stella Maris*.

Four hundred yards away. A short swim in the Mediterranean. But the four-hundred-yard neck here had a roiling turbulence, with little strips of inexplicable ripples. The tide was going out, sucking at the base of the quay. It looked to Andrea as if there was a very large amount of water trying to get out of a very small exit. Andrea guessed that this might be a long swim indeed.

But Andrea had been brought up on the shores of the Aegean. Among his recent ancestors he numbered divers for sponges, and he himself had spent his childhood as much in as out of the water. Andrea swam like a fish –

A Mediterranean fish.

Slowly and deliberately, Andrea pulled a pencil and notebook from his overall pocket and walked to the seaward end of the outermost quay. Nobody paid him any attention as he passed the sentry at the foot of the gangway of the outermost U-boat. Why should they? He was a large inspector in blue overalls, frowning with his thick black eyebrows at the state of the quay. The Germans were a nation of inspectors. It was natural, in this little German world on the edge of Spain, that even in the final stages of an evacuation someone should be making notes on the condition of the quay.

At the end of the quay, iron rungs led down the granite. For the benefit of anyone watching, Andrea stuck his pencil behind his ear, pursed his lips and shook his head. Then he began to climb down the iron rungs.

As he sank below the level of the quay, he was out of sight of anyone except the sentries in the *fortaleza*, and he was hoping that with sixteen minutes to sailing, the sentries would have been withdrawn. From the bottom rung he let notebook and pencil whisk away on the current. He struggled out of his overalls, kicked off his boots, and removed the rest of his clothes. They hovered a moment in the eddy at the foot of the wall, then sailed off down the tide.

Naked, Andrea was brown and hairy as a bear. He touched the gold crucifix round his neck, and lowered himself into the green swirl at the foot of the rungs. He thought, it is freezing, this Atlantic.

Then he launched himself into the tide.

'*Ritter*,' said Mallory to the sentry at the foot of the gangway opposite the one up which Miller had disappeared.

The sentry was wearing leather trousers and a jersey coming unravelled at the hem. His face as he glanced at Mallory's identity card and handed it back was pale, with a greasy film of sweat. Scared, thought Mallory, as he walked up the gangplank. These may be secret weapons, but they are still U-boats, and U-boat crews do not live long. To drown in a steel box, inch by inch . . .

Mallory had tried that once. It was not something he ever wanted to try again.

But he was standing on the U-boat's grey steel deck, the worn enamel handles of the toolbox slippery in his hand, and there was a hatch forward, standing open. The torpedo room was forward. On a submarine this size, a grenade would do little damage. Unless, Miller had said, you used it as a fuse, a primer, stuck to the tons of Amatol or Torpex or whatever they used. Then you would get a result –

Mallory made himself walk towards the hatch. It would be easier to stay on deck, not go below, into that little steel space that might at any moment go under the water –

Easy or not, it had to be done.

The hatch was a double steel door in the deck. A steel ladder plunged into a yellow-lit gloom. At the bottom of the ladder a face looked up, sallow and bearded, blue bags under the eyes. A Petty Officer.

'What the hell do you want?' said the Petty Officer.

'Check toilets,' said Mallory, dumb as an ox.

'I don't know anything about any toilets,' said the Petty Officer. 'Go and see the Kapitän.'

'Where's the Kapitän?' Mallory could feel the minutes ticking.

'Conning tower. You'd better be quick.'

Mallory went back down the deck, and up the metal rungs on the side of the conning tower. He took a deep breath and let himself down into the tower itself.

The smell was oil and sweat, and something else. Peroxide. A man in a grubby white polo-neck jersey with an Iron Cross was arguing with another man. Both had pale faces and beards.

Mallory cleared his throat. 'Come to fix the toilet,' he said.

The man with the Iron Cross was wearing a Kapitän's cap. 'Now?' he said. 'I didn't know it was broken. Get off my boat.'

'Orders,' said Mallory. The morning was a disc of daylight seen through the hatchway.

'I'm Kapitän -'

'The Herr General was most insistent.'

'I shit on the Herr General,' said the Kapitän. 'Hell. Go and look at the toilet, then. But I warn you, we are sailing in ten minutes, and if you're still on board I'll put you out through a torpedo tube.'

Mallory said, stolidly, 'That will not be necessary.' But the Kapitän was back at his argument, with no time for dockyard mateys.

Engine at the back. Torpedoes at the front. Front it is.

Mallory hefted his toolbox, shinned down the ladder under the periscope and started along the corridor leading forward.

There was a crew messroom, racked torpedoes, bunks everywhere. The lights were yellow. There seemed to be scores of men, packed dense as sardines in a tin; but this was worse, because it was a tin in which the sardines had somehow suddenly come

221

alive. Mallory shoved his way through. There are no windows, said the voice in his mind. You are below the level of the water –

Shut up, he told himself. You are still alongside.

He walked under the open hatch. The Petty Officer glanced at him and glanced away. Ahead, the passage ran through an oval doorway and ended. On the other side of the bulkhead he saw a long chamber lined left and right with fat tubes. The torpedo room.

And on his right, a tiny compartment: a lavatory. Head.

He looked round. The Petty Officer was watching him. Mallory winked, went into the lavatory and closed the door. His hand was sweating on the handles of his toolbox. Count to five, he thought.

There was a new sound, a vibration. The engines had started. Somewhere, a klaxon began to moan. Now or never, thought Mallory.

He walked quickly into the corridor, scratching his head, and turned right into the torpedo room.

There were two men in there, securing torpedoes to the racks. They were like horizontal organ pipes, those torpedoes. Both the men were ratings.

'Shit,' said one of them. 'You'd better hurry.'

'Checking seals,' said Mallory. 'Couple of minutes. Which one of these things do you fire first?'

'Those,' said the rating, pointing. 'Now if you would be so good, go away and shut up and let us get on with getting ready to load those damn fish into those damn tubes.'

The torpedoes the rating had pointed at were the first rack, up by one of the ranks of oval doors that must lead into the tubes. Mallory wedged himself in behind the torpedoes, out of sight of the men. He found a stanchion on the steel wall of the submarine and looped the string lanyard on the grenade's handle over it. Then he unscrewed the grenade's cap, gently pulled out the porcelain button on the end of the string fuse, and tied it to the shaft of the torpedo's propeller.

First one.

He took out a spanner and crossed the compartment. The rating did not look up. He attached a second grenade to the port side lower torpedo, where the shadows were thickest. The third and fourth he attached to the next row up.

There were feet moving on steel somewhere above his head. The vibrations of the engine were louder now.

'That's okay,' said Mallory. 'Don't want sewage everywhere, do we?'

The ratings ignored him. He walked out of the torpedo compartment, down the corridor. The hatch was still open. He could smell the blessed air. He pushed past a couple of men, put his foot on the bottom rung of the ladder.

A hard hand took his arm above the elbow. A quiet voice said, 'If you're here to mend the toilets, what were you doing in the torpedo room?'

Mallory looked round.

The voice belonged to the bearded Petty Officer.

'Cast off!' roared a voice on deck.

Above his head, the hatch slammed shut.

Twenty yards away, Dusty Miller was in a different world. Miller was a trained demolitions man. He reckoned he had seven minutes. He had gone straight for the conning tower, checked out the Kapitän and the navigating officer bent over the charts. 'Come to look at the lavs,' he said.

The navigating officer gave him the not-interested look of a man ten minutes away from an important feat of underwater navigation. 'What lavs?'

'They just said the lavs.'

'You know where they are.'

Miller shrugged, feeling the weight of his toolbox, the hammer, the spanners, the four stick grenades in the bottom compartment. 'Yeah,' he said.

Mallory had gone forward, looking for the torpedoes. Miller went aft.

On most U-boats, the engine room consisted of a big diesel for surface running and to charge huge banks of lead-acid batteries, and an electric motor for underwater running. The Walter process was different. The diesel did all the work. When the U-boat was under water, the engine drew the oxygen for its combustion from disintegrated hydrogen peroxide, and vented the carbon dioxide it produced as a waste gas directly into the water, where it dissolved.

Miller went down the hatch in the control-room deck and crept along the low steel corridor. Men shoved past him. He took no notice. He wandered along, apparently tracing one of the parallel ranks of grey-painted pipes leading aft along the bulkhead.

And after not many steps, he was in the engine room.

It was as it should have been: the thick tubes coming from the fuel tanks, each with its stopcock: oils, water, hydrogen peroxide. There were men working in there, working hard, oiling, establishing settings on the banks of valve wheels. The big diesel was running with a clattering roar too loud to hear. Miller caught an oiler's eye, winked, nodded. The oiler nodded back. Nobody would be in a submarine's engine room at a time like this unless he had business there. And at a time like this, the business would certainly be legitimate.

So Miller stooped, apparently examining the pipes, and ran his professional eye over the maze of tubes and chambers.

And made his decision; or rather, confirmed the decision he had made already.

On the surface, the Walter engine was a naturally aspirated diesel. The changeover from air to peroxide was activated by a float switch on the conning tower. It was a simple device; when the water reached a certain level, the switch closed, opening the valve from the peroxide tank to the disintegrator. In Miller's view, the destruction of the valve would release a lot of inflammable stuff into a space full of nasty sparks.

There was a very real danger of explosions, thought Miller happily, opening his toolbox.

His fingers worked quickly. The float switch controlled a simple gate valve. Tape the grenade to the pipe. Tie the string fuse to one of the struts of the gate valve wheel. When the wheel turned, the string would pull out of the grenade. Five seconds later . . . well, thought Miller; ladies and gentlemen are requested to extinguish all smoking materials.

He arranged two more grenades, using the length of the string fuses to make for slightly greater delays, one on the water intake and one on the throttle linkage where it passed a dark corner.

Then he walked back, climbed into the conning tower, and said, 'All done.'

The navigating officer did not look up. 'Piss off,' he said.

'Oh, all right,' said Miller. He went up the ladder and into the chill, diesel-smelling dawn, and trotted down the gangplank and onto the quay.

He knew something was wrong as soon as his boots hit the stone. Two men were hauling the gangway of the boat opposite back onto the quay. Men were moving on the foredeck, waiting to haul in the lines when the stevedores let them go. Miller saw one of them bend and slam shut an open hatch. To left and right the quay was a desert of granite paving, dotted with a few figures in uniform, a few in overalls. Miller had worked with Mallory for long enough to recognise him, never mind what he was wearing.

None of the figures was Mallory.

So Mallory was still on the boat, and the boat was sailing.

On the boat opposite, a couple of heads showed on the conning tower. One of them wore the cap of a Kapitän.

'Oi!' yelled Miller, above the pop and rattle of the diesels. 'You've got my mate on board.'

The Kapitän looked round, frowning. The springs were off. They were down to one-and-one, a bow line and a stern line. They were sailing in two minutes. The Kapitän looked at the scarecrow figure on the dock, the chipped blue toolbox, the lanky arms and legs protruding from the too-short overalls. He shouted to one of the hands on the narrow deck.

The hand shrugged, scratching his head under his grey watch cap. He bent. He caught hold of the handles of the hatch, and pulled.

Mallory's whole body was covered in sweat. His mind did not seem to be working. Drowned in a steel room, he was thinking. No. Not that –

'What were you doing in the torpedo room?' said the Petty Officer.

'Pipes,' said Mallory. 'Checking pipes.'

'Like hell,' said the Petty Officer.

And at that moment, there fell from heaven a beam of pure

grey light that pierced the reeking yellow gloom of the submarine like the arrow of God.

The hatch was open.

Mallory knew that a miracle had happened. It was a miracle that would take away the death by drowning in a metal room, and let him die under the sky, where he did not mind dying in a just cause.

He also knew that the Petty Officer could not live.

Mallory looked up the hatch. There was a head up there. 'Now coming,' he shouted. The head vanished. His hand was in the small of his back, closing round the handle of his dagger in the sheath there. It came round his body low and hard, and thumped into the Petty Officer's chest, up and under the ribs. He kept the momentum going, shoved the man back onto a bunk, and pulled a blanket over him. Then he went back up the ladder.

The man on deck kicked the hatch shut. A stevedore had cast off the lines. Green water widened between the submarine and the quay. From the conning tower, a voice roared, 'Jump!'

Mallory looked round. He saw the Kapitän, a cold, vindictive face above the grey armour plate.

'Doesn't like dockyard people,' said the man on the bow line. 'Nor do I.' And he put up a seaboot, and shoved.

Mallory could have dodged, broken the man's leg, saved his dignity. But what he wanted now had nothing to do with dignity. It was to get off this submarine, quick.

He jumped.

He heard the toolbox clatter on the submarine's pressure hull. He saw the blue wink of it disappear into deep water.

It, and its three grenades.

Then the water was in his mouth and eyes, and he was swimming for the quay. He could hear the Kapitän laughing. He paid no attention.

He was thinking, five minutes to destroy the third U-boat.

How?

Andrea was swimming too. In fact, he was swimming for his life.

The waters of Greece were warm sapphires, blown by the meltemi certainly, but tideless, unmoving.

226

The waters of Vizcaya were different. The waters of Vizcaya were dark emeralds, cold as a cat's eye.

And they moved.

When Andrea had lowered his shrinking body into the water and let go of the iron rung, the eddy had taken him and spun him, so that the quays and the harbour whirled around his head. The cold had stolen his breath at first, so he trod water, and watched the harbour wheel a second time. Then he had fixed his eyes on the distant, ill-kempt masts of the *Stella Maris*, and started to swim.

On the face of it, things were fine. But he knew as soon as he entered the channel that this was all wrong.

He could breathe now. He was swimming, the great muscles of his shoulders knotting and bunching, driving his body through the cold salt water. He was swimming breaststroke. If they saw him, they would see only a head, a small head, that they would think was a seal. There had been anti-submarine nets off the end of the quays. But those nets were down now, folded away in the holds of the merchant ships, because the submarines were coming out.

So it was just a four-hundred yard swim to the *Stella Maris*. Ten minutes. Fine.

Except that it was not working out that way.

The tide was like a river, sweeping him out of the narrows and into the sea. The *Stella Maris'* masts were sliding away upstream, fast, terrifyingly fast.

This was new. And it was unpleasant, not because it was frightening, because nothing physical, not even death – especially not death – frightened Andrea. But Andrea's life was based on not letting people down, and allowing the things that had been planned to come to pass. He had perfect faith that Mallory and Miller would accomplish their part of the job.

He was beginning to have less faith that he could do the same.

In spite of the Benzedrine, he was growing tired. Even he, even Andrea, was growing tired. He knew his reserves of strength were finite. There was no point in trying to swim straight at his objective.

Brains, not brawn.

He turned until he was looking at the tall black bows of the merchant ships anchored in the harbour. He could hear the clank of their windlasses as they came up over their anchors, could see a couple of launches crawling across the glossy shield of the water. He began to swim, facing directly into the current and about ten degrees to the right.

For anyone else, it would have been instant exhaustion, suicide.

For Andrea, it was possible.

He swam with short, powerful strokes into the current, building a bow-wave of water on his nose. The quay where he had started had fallen away as he had been washed out to sea. But after five minutes of hard swimming, it had also fallen away to the left.

And the inner of the two merchant ships, which had been stern-on, was now showing its starboard side.

He did not let himself hope that he was making progress. He swam on doggedly, another two hundred strokes. He crossed a spine of white-tipped standing waves. A couple of waves smacked his face. He inhaled salt water, choked. He was really tired now. Now he had to look.

He looked.

The *Stella Maris* was a long way ahead, up-tide. But she was only some twenty degrees to the right.

He was getting across.

But his troubles were by no means over.

There was a bigger lift to the waves now, a regular roll. When he looked ninety degrees left and ninety degrees right, he saw not the quays of the town or the cliffs of the Cabo beneath the walls of the *fortaleza*. He saw open sea.

Andrea swam on. He was holding steady now. There was less tide out here. But he could feel in the screaming muscles of his legs and shoulders and the hammer of his heart that he was approaching the limit of his strength.

In Andrea's book, it was the mark of a man that he did not admit that there were limits.

Somewhere, Andrea found a reserve. With that reserve he started to move forwards. Progress heated his blood, and the heat of his blood helped progress. He found that he was moving up

228

the slack water off the beach on the San Eusebio side of the channel, and that the quays, with their double ranks of fishing boats end-on, were coming closer.

He trod water for a moment.

His feet touched bottom. He looked back the way he had come. Except for a strip of deep green in the middle of the passage, the water on either side of the channel was paling. It looked as if it dried out at low tide. Ahead, the water was also pale, darkening only where the channel swept in under the quay where the fishing fleet was moored.

It had been a big swim.

But if he had waited another five minutes, he could probably have walked most of it.

Another man might have laughed, or cried, or felt relief. As far as Andrea was concerned, none of that was necessary. An exhausting set of conditions had ceased to apply, and a less exhausting set now obtained. The objective remained: to get aboard the *Stella Maris* within the next – he glanced at his waterproof watch – four minutes.

He began to wade.

Hauptsturmführer von Kratow did not like Spain. Latins were a slovenly bunch, racially suspect and entirely lacking in culture. But von Kratow did realise that to an operation such as Project Werwolf, they had their uses. It was just, he mused, trotting up the stone stairs of the *fortaleza* to report to the Herr General, that there seemed to be something in the air. Organising an embarkation should not be difficult. But there was a spirit of . . . well, *mañana* . . . that made even SS order and system show a tendency to buckle.

Still, everything was in order now. The attack at the main gate seemed to have been a false alarm. The embarkation was almost complete. All that remained was to report to the General, who would be highly delighted. A bastard, the General, with his Turkish tobacco and what his troops reckoned was the limpest artificial wrist in the Reich. But an appreciative bastard, particularly if, like von Kratow, you were a cleancut Junker with a nice leg for a jackboot, and you did your work correctly. Von Kratow was pretty sure that three repaired submarines and a smooth embarkation would mean promotion.

He pushed open the elaborate door of the General's quarters, and sniffed for the Turkish tobacco.

There was no Turkish tobacco.

Von Kratow frowned.

For as long as he had been the General's ADC, there had been a cigarette smouldering between the General's artificial fingers. The only time he was not smoking was when he was asleep. He would not be asleep now, not with the evacuation nearly finished.

Von Kratow opened the door.

A buttery morning light was pouring through the part of the Gothic window not covered by the curtains. The tobacco smell hung stale in the air, and last night's fire had died to bitter ashes. Von Kratow walked across to the desk, and collected himself a handful of Turkish cigarettes from the box. The General would never notice. The Luftwaffe brought him new supplies weekly; God knew where they found them nowadays.

Von Kratow yawned and stretched. It had been a long night, in a long series of long nights. But now it was over.

Beyond the stone fretwork of the windows the harbour was a sheet of green glass lit by a heavy yellow sun glaring just above the mountains to the east. The merchant ships were up over their anchors, the launches heading back on what must be almost the last of their journeys to pick up the now diminished clods of men from the quay. Down in the repair facility, the Werwolf boats were emitting a blue mist of exhaust. The inshore boat had dropped her shore lines and seemed to be nosing towards the exit.

So that's it, thought von Kratow. Mission accomplished. Time to catch the boat. Time to make sure the Herr General caught the boat.

Von Kratow was a tidy-minded man. Before he went to knock on the bedroom door, he drew back the heavy brocade curtain that was half-obscuring the window.

That was when he found the General.

For perhaps ten seconds von Kratow stared stony-faced at the oyster silk underwear, the ivory-white skin of the face, the black flow of dried blood from the right ear. Then his hand went to the

230

cigarette box on the desk. He lit one of the General's cigarettes and thought, silk underclothes.

Then he put out a deliberate finger, and pressed the button behind the curtain.

The general alarm button.

Suddenly, the Cabo de la Calavera was full of bells.

Mallory crawled up the iron rungs on the granite wall, coughing water. The quays opened in front of his eyes: a sheet of granite paving and drying puddles, studded with cranes, riven by the three great crevasses of the submarine docks. The innermost submarine was moving. From behind him there came the clatter of diesels, and the churn of water blowing from ducted screws over rudders. That submarine – his submarine – was on the way out too.

The top of the conning tower of the last submarine was stationary. It stayed in his eye as he rested at the top of the ladder. He was tired now, Benzedrine or no Benzedrine, so tired that he could hardly drag himself up a set of rungs in the quay.

He saw a terrible thing.

He saw Dusty Miller on the conning tower of that submarine. Miller was arguing with a man in a cap, demanding admission, by the look of it. The man in the cap, the Kapitän, presumably, was telling him you are cluttering up the joint, and I am sailing now, so get off, before you get stuck.

Dusty Miller won. He vanished from view.

Quick, thought Mallory. *For God's sake, be quick.*

He looked at his watch. It was three minutes to five. Early, he thought. They're leaving early.

Too late.

Mallory began to crawl away from the submarine he had visited, the submarine with the dead Petty Officer in the head –

It was then he noticed that the harbour was full of bells.

The conning tower into which Miller had vanished began to slide along the quay.

Mallory could almost hear the orders: *in the event of problems, move out.*

So three minutes early, the U-boats were moving out.

And one of them had Miller on board.

Something snapped in Mallory. He clambered to his feet, exhaustion forgotten. He stumbled along the quay after that conning tower, yelling hoarsely with rage. But the conning tower slid away faster than he could chase it down the quay.

The three great U-boats gathered in the turning basin at the end of the quays, stemming the tide: huge grey metal whales the length of destroyers, solid as rocks with their squat, streamlined conning towers, white water churning from their propellers. Men scuttled on their decks, making the final preparations for sea. Their Kapitäns conferred, conning tower to conning tower, with the casualness of men who knew that a hundred metres of water made them untouchable.

Mallory looked over the edge of the quay, made frantic by the bells.

He saw a rowing boat.

It was a small, filthy rowing boat, a quarter full of water. But it held oars and rowlocks, and it was more or less afloat.

Mallory grabbed the painter that tied it to the bollard on the quay. He wound his ruined hands into that rope, climbed down it and cut it with his knife. The boat floated free. There was an idea in his mind, a crazy idea, born out of exhaustion. Go to that U-boat. Hammer on the hull. Tell them there had been a mistake. Dockyard matey inside. Needs taking off. Quick. Then they could go on, aboard the *Stella Maris*, and have at least some chance –

He pulled with the oars. The dinghy shot across the eddy at the end of the quay.

The tide caught it.

Four knots of tide.

Mallory could row at two knots, flat out.

The U-boats were gliding past at horrifying speed. Mallory turned, tried to get back.

Not a hope. The U-boats might as well have been in Berlin.

With a great sickness in his heart, Mallory began to crab across the channel towards the *Stella Maris*. Soon the air was full of whipping sounds, and little explosions, like fireworks. Someone was shooting at him. In fact a lot of people were shooting at him, from the merchant ships. Dully, he remembered the rings of sandbags on their hatch covers, the snouts of machine guns, other guns too. They would probably hit him.

Mallory found that he did not care. Something had gone wrong, he did not care what. They had lost Miller. A voice in his head, a voice like Jensen's, said: if Miller had to die, this was how he would have wanted to die.

Mallory's own voice answered: *rubbish*.

'Orders,' shouted Dusty Miller to the Kapitän of the last U-boat. 'From the General. I have to check the officer's head. You do not sail for five minutes.'

The Kapitän had a cropped bullet head and a broken nose, and a look of extreme exhaustion.

He said to the coxswain at his side, 'Take this man below. Make sure that he is on the quay when we sail. This is your responsibility.'

'Aye, aye,' said the coxswain. He was a small, pale man, and he did not look pleased to be sent off the conning tower. 'What is it you want?'

'Engine room head,' said Miller, rattling his toolbox.

'There isn't an engine room head.'

'I got my orders,' said Miller.

The coxswain said, 'I'll show you, then.' He started down the ladder, and headed towards the back end of the boat.

The conning tower hatch was a disc of daylight above the control room. As Miller started down the ladder, he thought he heard bells, and shouting. But he knew he had five minutes in hand. The bells must be meaningless. What was in the forefront of his mind was how he was going to get rid of this damned coxswain.

The central alleyway of the U-boat was familiar territory to Miller now: yellow lights, heat, sweaty faces. What was not familiar was the sound of the engine. It was still a huge, clattering roar. But now it was a roar that changed pitch, went on and up, held steady, and went up again.

The coxswain stopped. He looked at Miller. His lips moved. It was not possible to hear what he said over the racket of the diesel. But it was easy enough to read his lips.

Miller's heart thumped once, painfully, in his chest.

The words the coxswain's lips were framing were, 'We've sailed.'

For a second, Miller's face felt wooden with shock. Then he grinned. 'Well, then,' he said, though he knew the other man would not hear him. 'We've got a load of time.'

The coxswain arrived at the engine room. 'Look,' he said. 'No head.'

Miller grinned, his wide, starry-eyed idiot's grin. 'Oh, yeah,' he said.

The coxswain pointed back along the corridor towards the ladder. Miller could almost see the thoughts running through the man's mind: *this is not my fault, it's because we sailed early. All I have to do is get this fool back to the Kapitän. The Kapitän has forgotten him in the heat of the moment. I will be in the clear –*

Miller stared at the coxswain, still grinning, as the coxswain made pointing gestures back towards the ladder. Miller craved that ladder like a fiend craves dope. The coxswain came back to him and shoved him towards the ladder.

Miller hit him.

He hit him hard in the stomach. If it had been Andrea, the punch would have killed the man. But Miller was a demolition expert, not a bare-hands killer. The coxswain whooped and doubled up onto the deck. Miller looked round.

There were three men in the alleyway. They were all watching.

Miller stepped over the body on the deck, and walked smartly aft. The roar of the engines had steadied now. He walked through the water-tight door into the engine room. He slammed it, and dogged the handles quickly behind him. Ahead of him, hanging from a stanchion in the deckhead, was a chain hoist. Just like a mine, thought Miller, grabbing the chain. Miller had spent thousands of hours in mines, some of them very happy. As he wrapped the chain round the door handles, he felt right at home.

Someone was trying to undog the door now. When bare hands did not work, they started to hit the handles with what sounded like a sledge hammer. Bash away, thought Miller. We are talking good German chain here, and submarines are not built to resist the enemy within.

In fact, enemies within were virtually unknown on submarines.

Because when a submarine went down it went down, enemy within and all.

Miller told himself: it had to happen, one day.

It did not help.

He bent and opened the toolbox, and took out the two grenades.

Suddenly, he smelt tobacco smoke.

Round the end of the diesel block came a pale, oil-stained man in a singlet, with an undoubtedly illicit cigarette in his mouth. He glanced at Miller's face, the glance of a crew member who knows his shipmates and is baffled by the emergence of a new face from their midst. Then his eyes moved to Miller's hands.

Miller grinned at him, and put the grenades stealthily back in the box.

The man's eyes stayed glued to the grenades.

He went white as an oily rag. Then he picked up a wrench, dropped his cigarette, and came at Miller.

He was a short man, almost dwarfish, as wide as he was high. The coxswain had been out of shape because he only did whatever they did in the control room. This man was an engine room artificer, with big muscles under the white skin of his shoulders. He got both hands on his wrench, and he hefted it like a baseball bat, and he came down the aisle at Miller like an oil-stained Nibelung. Miller swung the toolbox at the man. It was an over-confident swing, inspired by too much Benzedrine and not enough judgement. It missed by a mile. The Nibelung smacked at the toolbox with his wrench. The toolbox flew out of Miller's hand, skidding down the gratings, bursting open as it slid. Tools and grenades spilled out. Miller caught a glimpse of the grenades, unarmed, useless, skittering into the tunnel where the propeller shaft ran. Then he threw himself to one side, and the wrench whacked into the steel bulkhead where his head had been.

Miller stood there, back to the door, panting, heart hammering. The yellow lights shone in the short man's sweat. His face was a flat mask of anger. Then Miller saw it flicker, and he knew why. There was a new note to the engine: a high-pitched whine. The deck was tilting underfoot, gently.

The whine was the disintegrator. The engine had switched from fuel-air to fuel-decomposed hydrogen peroxide.

235

The submarine was diving.

The squat man came at Miller again. Miller kicked him in the stomach. It was like kicking corrugated iron. The man came on regardless.

Away from the door, thought Miller. Can't move away from the door, or he'll take the chains off, and the rest of the crew will get in –

The spanner crashed against the metal. Miller skipped out of the way. Door or no door, he was no good with his head caved in.

Miller knew that he was losing.

But the squat man had forgotten the door even existed. He was a submarine engineer, and when people bring grenades into their engine rooms, submarine engineers lose the power of rational thought. He swung again.

Miller dodged clumsily. The wrench caught him on the shoulder, numbing his arm. He stumbled back against the engine, head between the clashing tappets, and rolled down to the grating.

He saw another wrench. Picked it up. Too heavy to swing. Better than nothing.

The Nibelung came at him again. Miller scuttled round the far side of the engine. Retreating, always retreating. This was a man who knew his patch, and what he was going to do was hound Miller into a corner, and kill him, and that would be that. A Werwolf on the loose, and all that work in vain.

It was the thought of the wasted effort that really upset Miller. Energy stormed through his veins. As the man came in again, he swung his wrench. The man jumped back. The heavy steel head whacked a pipe in the wall, just under the thread of a joint.

And suddenly the engine room smelt like a hairdresser's salon.

The Nibelung's face had changed, too. He was staring at that pipe that Miller had hit. And he did not look angry any more. He looked frightened out of his wits.

Miller felt the weight of the wrench in his hand. He knew he did not have many more swings left in him. One more.

The man still had half his mind on the pipe.

Miller swung the wrench at the pipe, then again, into the side of the man's head.

There was a solid *chunk* that Miller felt rather than heard. The man's eyes rolled back, and he went down like a bag of cement.

Dead, thought Miller. Dead.

Quick.

Peroxide was roaring out of the pipe, gurgling over the body of the engineer. As it hit the engineer's body, it foamed.

There was another catalyst that broke down hydrogen peroxide into hydrogen and oxygen. It was called peroxidase, and it was found in human blood.

Miller ran to the aft end of the engine room. There was a sort of cupboard next to the propeller shaft gland, a steel-doored locker that bore the words *Siebe-Gorman*.

The engine room was filling with free oxygen and hydrogen.

On the deck, the Nibelung's cigarette ceased to glow and began to burn with a hard, bright flame.

Quick, thought Miller.

It was all feeling very slow to Mallory, as if the world had started moving through a new kind of time, viscous and syrupy. He saw the flat green mirror of the water, the red and green tracers rising from the merchant ships, slow as little balloons, queuing up to accelerate round his head and kick the water to foam. Under the rocky brow of the Cabo de la Calavera he saw the U-boats moving, hovering, arranging themselves into line ahead. Miller was on the lead boat. Then came the other boat Miller had visited. Mallory's was last.

The rowing boat rocked in the little waves of a tide-rip. The sun was warm on his face. Something smashed into the transom of the rowing boat. He shielded his eyes from the splinters, felt the rip of flesh on his cheek, the run of liquid that must be blood. The rowing boat spun in an eddy. He saw the San Eusebio town quay, the fishing boats tied up alongside. The movement of the rowing boat in the eddy made the masts of the boats appear to be moving –

One set of masts was moving. The masts of the *Stella Maris*.

They were moving slowly, crawling against the spars of the other boats and the blank shutters of the quayside warehouses. They were accelerating, the black hull narrowing, the masts coming into line as whoever was at the wheel pointed the nose straight at Mallory. Coming to pick him up.

But not Miller.

The U-boats were moving out from the quays now, gliding slowly across the peaceful green satin of the water. The first was already in the channel, the green water rumpling over its deck, diving. Diving quickly, so as not to be seen leaving a neutral harbour. Diving with Miller on board.

Metal smashed into the rowing boat by Mallory's feet. Suddenly there was water where there had once been planking, water pouring in through three holes the size of fists. Mallory tried to stem the water with his foot, but his foot was too small, and suddenly the rowing boat was part of the harbour, and cold water was up around Mallory's neck.

An engine was thumping close at hand. The tar-black nose of the *Stella Maris* swept up, pushing a white moustache of foam. A head leaning over the bow said, '*Bonjour, mon Capitaine.*' The head of Andrea.

Andrea's hand came down. It grasped Mallory's wrist. Mallory felt himself plucked skyward, grabbed a wooden rail, and landed face down on the *Stella*'s filthy deck.

'Welcome aboard,' said Andrea. 'Where's Miller?'

A burst of machine-gun fire smacked into the *Stella*'s stern. Mallory pointed.

The lead U-boat was halfway down the channel. All that was showing was its conning tower.

Andrea's Byzantine eyes were without expression. Only the great stillness of the man gave a clue to his emotion. The *Stella Maris* turned, and headed down the channel. Mallory lurched aft and took the wheel from Jaime. He steered the *Stella* right up to the flank of the last U-boat. There were still heads on the U-boat's conning tower. One of the heads was yelling, a hand waving at this dirty little fishing boat to keep clear, keep out of the way. The fire from the merchant ships was slackening now, for fear of hitting the U-boat.

And down below, thought Mallory, down in the torpedo room the hands would be manoeuvring the hoists over to the first torpedo, opening the tube, loading up, ready for an enemy waiting out there in the Bay. The hoists would be lifting, stretching the string fuse of the grenade, scratching the primer, starting the five-second delay.

Mallory stood there in the cool morning breeze, watching the two conning towers ahead, one half-submerged, the other with its base awash. Sixty yards away, the water began to creep up the deck of the last U-boat. The heads were gone from the conning tower.

There was no explosion.

They have found the grenades, thought Mallory. How can you expect to destroy a U-boat with grenades and string? He wound the wheel to port, to keep the *Stella* in the narrow strip of turquoise separating the pale green of the shallows from the ink-blue of the deep-water channel. The U-boat's hull was under now.

It was getting away.

Mallory groped for a cigarette, put it in his mouth, and watched the channel.

The channel blew up in his face.

It blew up in a jet of searing white flame that went all the way up into the sky, taking with it millions of tons of water that climbed and climbed until it looked as if it would never stop climbing, a reverse waterfall that made a noise loud enough to make a thunderclap sound like the dropping of a pin on a Persian rug. A wall of water smashed into the *Stella Maris*, walloped her onto her beam ends and broke over her. When she lurched upright again, her mainmast was gone. But somehow her Bolander was still thumping away, and Andrea was up among the rigging with an axe, chopping at shrouds and stays, kicking the tangle overboard where it lay wallowing like a sea monster, mingling with the oil and mattresses and other less identifiable bits of flotsam emanating from the still-boiling patch of sand and water that had once been one-third of the Werwolf pack.

Must have been right down in the channel, thought Mallory. Otherwise it would have blown us up with it –

Further out to sea there was another rumble, followed by an eruption of bubbles on the surface. The bubbles were full of smoke. When they burst, they left a film of oil on the surface.

Hugues said, 'What was that?'

'Another U-boat,' said Mallory. The bubbles rose for thirty seconds: a lot of bubbles, big ones. No bodies. No mattresses. A machine of steel had become air and oil.

'*Bon Dieu*,' said Hugues, appalled.

Jaime said, 'The ships.' He was looking backwards, over his shoulder.

The merchant ships had their anchors up. Magnified and indistinct beyond the pall of smoke and spray still descending from the first U-boat, they looked huge. From the machine guns on their decks the tracers were rising again.

'*Merde*,' said Jaime.

The ships were faster than the *Stella Maris*. They would catch her up and sink her. At best, they would sink her. Well, Dusty, thought Mallory, with a new and surprising cheerfulness. We are all in this together. Andrea had pulled the Bren out of the hold, and was lying on the *Stella*'s afterdeck, taking aim at the lead merchant ship. Flame danced at the muzzle. A Bren against ships. Not fair, thought Mallory –

From the seaward there came a rumble that made the *Stella* shudder under Mallory's feet. When he looked round, he saw a white alp of water rise offshore. And he forgot about the merchant ships, forgot about everything. For that alp, collapsing as soon as it had risen, was a watery headstone for Dusty Miller.

Three out of three. One hundred per cent success.

But Dusty Miller was dead.

Bullets from the merchant ship lashed the air beside his head, and whacked into the *Stella*'s crapulous timbers. Mallory paid them no heed. He turned the fishing boat's nose for the open sea.

It was calm, that sea, its emerald smoothness marred only by patches of oil and debris. The old fishing boat laboured towards the northern horizon, reeking of hot metal from the engine room hatch, rolling heavily with the volume of water in her belly.

And on her heels, gaining ground, Uruguayan flags limp on their halyards, spitting a blizzard of tracer, came the merchantmen.

Hugues said, 'What now?'

Mallory grinned, a grin that had no humour in it. His eyes were shining with a brilliance that Hugues found completely horrible.

240

'We take cover,' said Mallory. 'They sink us, or catch us, or both.'

Bullets were slamming into the *Stella*'s deck. The air whined with splinters. 'She will fall apart,' said Hugues.

'Very probably,' said Mallory. They were out of the harbour now. The leading merchant ship was entering the narrows, spewing black oil-smoke from its funnel, heading steadily down the dark-blue water of the channel. Once it was through the channel, it would speed up. And that would be the end of the *Stella Maris*.

They did not bother to take cover. They watched the bow of the merchant ship: the high bow, with the moustache of water under its nose, heading busily along the channel. Above its nose was the bridge, the thin blue smoke of the machine guns on its wings, and the heads of men, pin-sized, watching. It would be that moustache of water that would be the last movement. The *Stella Maris* would rise on it just before the merchant ship's nose came down and rolled her under, crushed her into the cold green sea –

Suddenly, Mallory stopped breathing. Hugues was by his side, gripping his arm with fingers like steel bars.

For the moustache of white water at the stem of the merchant ship had disappeared. The steel knife-edge had risen in the water, and stopped.

The ship had run aground on the U-boat that had blown up in the channel five minutes previously.

As they watched, the tide caught the ship's stern, slewing it until the freighter was a great steel wall blocking the channel: the only channel out of the harbour.

For a moment, the gunfire stilled, and a huge sound rolled over that windless frying pan of water.

The sound of Andrea, laughing.

Then the machine guns opened up again.

This time they opened up with a new venom, bred of fury and impotence. The bullets lashed the sea to a white froth, and the fishing boat's hull shuddered under their impact. Mallory crouched inside the wheelhouse. Another five minutes, he thought. Then we are out of range. The noise was deafening. The air howled with flying metal. And mixed with it, another sound.

Hugues. Hugues, shouting. Hugues was standing on the deck,

241

yelling, pointing at something in the water. Something orange. Something that moved, raised an arm and waved, a feeble wave, but a wave nonetheless. Something that was a hand, holding a fuming orange smoke flare.

And when the orange smoke rolled clear of the face, the face, though coughing and distorted, was unmistakably the face of Dusty Miller.

Mallory spun the wheel. The *Stella* turned broadside onto the merchant ships' torrent of bullets. Hugues stood upright, insanely conspicuous, out of cover. Miller came floating down the side. 'Grab him!' yelled Mallory.

Hugues leaned over the side. As they passed Miller, he stuck his hand down, and Miller put his up, and the hands met and gripped. Now the *Stella* was towing Miller along, and Hugues' arm was the tow line. Hugues suddenly shuddered, and four dark blotches appeared on his vest. But by then Andrea was there, grasping Miller with his great hand. He gave one heave. And then they were all lying on the deck: Andrea, Hugues and Miller, Miller gasping like a gaffed salmon, leaking water.

Mallory turned the wheel away from the harbour entrance. The orange smoke faded astern. Soon they were out of range, and there were no more bullets.

Miller lit a cigarette. His face was grey and white, the bags under his eyes big enough to hold the equipment of a fair-sized expeditionary force. He said, 'Good morning. Do we have a drink?'

Mallory handed him the miraculously undamaged bottle of brandy from the riddled locker in the wheelhouse. 'How did you get out?' he said.

Miller raised the bottle. 'I would like to drink to the health of two Krauts,' he said. 'Mr Siebe and Mr Gorman. And the cutest little submarine escape apparatus known to science.' He drank deeply.

Andrea came aft. He said, 'Hugues needs to talk.'

Hugues was lying on the deck in a red pond. Mallory could hear his chest bubble as he breathed. Hugues said, 'I am sorry.' He could speak no more.

Andrea said, 'This man is a traitor.'

Mallory looked at the blue-white face, the suffocated eyes. He said, 'Why?'

Hugues eyes swivelled from Andrea to Mallory. Andrea said, 'To save Lisette, and his child. The Gestapo followed her to St-Jean. When they tried to pick her up with Hugues, he made a deal. They did not arrest us there, because it would have been more interesting for them to catch us in the act of sabotage. So when Hugues knew we were on the Cabo, he fed them information.'

Hugues shrugged. 'I did it for my child,' he said. Then blood came from his mouth, and he died.

Lisette was standing half-out of the hatch. She looked pale and tired, the shadows under her eyes dark and enormous. The eyes themselves had the thick lustre of tears.

'He was a man who had lost everything he loved,' she said. 'When he was in the Pyrenees the first time, he told me what had happened to his wife, his children. He was a lonely man. I can't described to you how lonely. He was a good man.' The tears were running now. 'A man of passion. For his country. For me. In war, these things can happen, and they are not so strange.'

'*Enfin*, he was a traitor,' said Jaime. Mallory looked at the dark, starved face, the heavy black moustache, the impenetrable eyes. Jaime shrugged, the shrug of a smuggler, of a man who would walk through mountains if he could not walk over them, of a man whose hand was against all other men. Nobody would ever know whether Jaime was fighting because of what he believed in, or because he wanted to survive. Probably, Jaime did not know himself.

Mallory looked at Andrea's face, dark and closed, and at Miller's haggard countenance, the oil and salt drying in his crewcut. Perhaps none of them knew why they did these things.

Perhaps, in the end, it was not important, as long as it was necessary to do these things, and these things got done. He clambered to his feet and put his arm around Lisette's shoulders.

She said, 'I did not love him. But he is the father of my child. And that is worth something, *hein*?'

It was not the sort of question Mallory knew how to answer.

EPILOGUE

Wednesday 1400

The *Stella Maris* was heading north on a broad navy-blue sea. Cabo de la Calavera had dropped below the southern horizon an hour ago. A radio message had been sent. Now there was nothing but the blue and cloudless dome of the sky, and dead ahead of the *Stella*, a tenuous black wisp no bigger than an eyelash stuck above the smooth curve of the world.

The eyelash became an eyebrow, then a heavy black plume. The base of the plume resolved itself into the Tribal class destroyer *Masai*, thundering over the low Atlantic swell at thirty-five knots, trailing an oily cloud of black smoke, her boiler pressures trembling on the edge of the red.

The Lieutenant-Commander who was her captain looked down at the filthy black fishing boat, stroked his beard, and hoped he was not going to get any of that rubbish on his nice paint. He walked down to the rail and said, 'Captain Mallory?'

The villain at the fishing boat's wheel said, 'That's right.'

There were two other villains on deck: red-eyed, sun-scorched, bleeding, unshaven. But the Lieutenant-Commander's eye had moved over the bullet-scarred decks and gunwales, and caught the glint of a lot of water through the open hatch of what was presumably the fish-hold. The Lieutenant-Commander said, 'I wonder if you would care for a spot of lunch?'

Mallory looked as if lunch was not a word he understood. He said, 'Could we have a stretcher party?'

'You've got wounded?'

'Not exactly wounded,' said Mallory.

The stretcher party trotted onto the *Stella*'s splintered decks. Mallory pointed them towards the bunkroom. A curious noise came into being, a high, keening wail. The Petty Officer in charge of the stretcher party looked nervously over his shoulder.

244

He had been on the Malta convoys, and he knew about Stukas.

Mallory shook his head.

'Five for lunch?' said the Lieutenant-Commander.

'Six,' said Mallory.

The Lieutenant-Commander frowned. 'I thought you lost someone.'

'You lose some,' said Miller. 'You win some.'

The stretcher came up on deck. Behind it was Jaime. Strapped to it was Lisette. And in her arms, wrapped in a red sickbay blanket, was a small bundle that wailed.

The Lieutenant-Commander gripped the rail. 'See what you mean,' he said.

'I was a little more pregnant than the Captain thought,' said Lisette. 'I hope I cause no trouble.'

'Quite the reverse,' said the Lieutenant-Commander.

They walked onto the destroyer's beautifully painted deck. A Lieutenant took them to the tiny but spotless wardroom, and poured them gigantic pink gins. 'I expect you chaps have had quite a party,' he said.

They stared at him, bleary-eyed, until he went as pink as his gin. A signalman trotted in, flimsy in hand. The Lieutenant read it. 'Captain Mallory,' he said. 'For you.'

Mallory's eyes were closed. 'Read it,' he said.

This was a horrid breach of etiquette. The Lieutenant said, 'But –'

'Read it.'

The Lieutenant squared his shoulders. 'Reads as follows,

CONGRATULATIONS SUCCESSFUL COMPLETION OF
STORM FORCE. TIMING PROVIDENTIAL. HAVE
ANOTHER LITTLE JOB FOR YOU. REPORT SOONEST.
JENSEN.'

Mallory looked at Andrea and Miller. Their eyes were bloodshot and horrified. So, presumably, were his.

He said: 'SIGNAL TO CAPTAIN JENSEN. MESSAGE NOT UNDERSTOOD. BAFFLED. STORM FORCE.' He held out his glass. 'Now before we all die of thirst, could we have a spot more gin?'

Where Eagles Dare
Alistair MacLean

'A real humdinger. The best MacLean yet.'   *Daily Mirror*

'There is a splendid audacity about *Where Eagles Dare* in which a handful of British agents invade an "impenetrable" Gestapo command post . . . MacLean offers a real dazzler of a thriller, with vivid action, fine set pieces of suspense, and a virtuoso display of startling plot twists.'

New York Times

'Alistair MacLean has done it again: produced another king-sized thriller of tremendous pace and excitement. The tension is almost unbearable at times, but you can't stop turning the pages in a feverish desire to know what happens next.'   *Liverpool Echo*

ISBN 0 00 615804 8

Hope
Len Deighton

The second novel in the superb new Bernard Samson trilogy, *Faith*, *Hope* and *Charity*

Bernard is trying hard to readjust his life in the face of questions about his wife Fiona, and her defection to the East. Is she the brilliant high-flyer that her Department seems to think she is? Or is she a spent force, a wife and mother unwilling or unable to face her domestic responsibilities? Bernard doesn't know but is determined to find out.

Bernard's boss Dicky is certainly not anxious to reveal what he knows, as he jostles for power with Fiona herself in London Central, and takes to the road with Bernard on a mysterious mission to Poland.

'As fresh and brisk as ever . . . a feast to be wallowed in'
Sunday Express

'It speaks volumes for Deighton's skill as a storyteller that, years after the Berlin Wall came down, he can still set the nerve-ends jangling with a thriller set in the Cold War . . . His sense of pace is extraordinary, as is his sense of mood'
Sunday Telegraph

ISBN 0 00 647899 9

Force 10 from Navarone
Alistair MacLean

The thrilling sequel to Alistair MacLean's tour de force
The Guns of Navarone.

Almost before the last echoes of the famous guns have
died away, the three Navarone heroes are parachuted into
war-torn Yugoslavia to rescue a division of Partisans. And
to fulfil a secret mission, so deadly that it must be hidden
from their own allies . . .

'Compulsively exciting'
Daily Telegraph

'Terrific dam-busting climax'
Evening Standard

'Cliff-hanging suspense'
Sunday Telegraph

ISBN 0 00 616433 1

HMS Ulysses
Alistair MacLean

'A brilliant, overwhelming piece of descriptive writing'
Observer

This is one of the great war novels of our century and one of the finest achievements of Alistair MacLean's best-selling career. It is the story of Convoy FR77 to Murmansk – a voyage that pushes men to the limits of human endurance, crippled by enemy atack and the bitter cold of the Arctic.

'A story of exceptional courage which grips the imagination'
Daily Telegraph

'It deserves an honourable place among twentieth-century war books'
Daily Mail

'*HMS Ulysses* is in the same class as *The Cruel Sea*'
Evening Standard

ISBN 0 00 613512 9